In the Court

of the

Yellow King

In the Court of the Yellow King

All stories copyright their respective authors.

ISBN: 978-4-902075-69-4

Celaeno Press
#403 Tenjin 3-9-10, Chuo-ku, Fukuoka 810-0001 JAPAN
www.celaenopress.com

In the Court of the Yellow King

Edited by
Glynn Owen Barrass

Celaeno Press
2014

This book is dedicated to

C. J. Henderson

who left us before he could see his story in print.

Cassilda 1

Eric York

Contents

Cassilda's Song

Along the shore the cloud waves break,
The twin suns sink behind the lake,
The shadows lengthen
       In Carcosa.

Strange is the night where black stars rise,
And strange moons circle through the skies,
But stranger still is
       Lost Carcosa.

Songs that the Hyades shall sing,
Where flap the tatters of the King,
Must die unheard in
       Dim Carcosa.

Song of my soul, my voice is dead,
Die thou, unsung, as tears unshed
Shall dry and die in
       Lost Carcosa.

— *The King in Yellow*, Act 1, Scene 2

Introduction

It started with a play, a play with the power to warp reality and the minds of those who dared read it. There was a mysterious stranger – *Tell me, have you seen The Yellow Sign?* – a Phantom of Truth wearing a pallid mask of lies, and a king, The King, dressed in a robe of yellow tatters.

These characters appear in the banned play The King in Yellow, set within a palace in the city of Carcosa, on the shores of Lake Hali. With black stars overhead, where "shadows of men's thoughts lengthen in the afternoon" Carcosa is lit by twin suns that sink into Lake Hali only to rise again the next day. Heaven protect those that have fallen under the thrall of The King, those that have seen the Yellow Sign, seen beneath the alien god's scalloped tatters, and know the secret festering behind the Pallid Mask.

The authors within this book know the secret, have beheld The Yellow Sign, and from their creative madness have spun eighteen tales written in tribute to their Yellow King.

Some of weird fictions favourite sons and daughters have put madness to paper within these pages: W. H. Pugmire, Christine Morgan, Edward Morris, Stephen Mark Rainey, Jeffrey Thomas, Lucy A. Snyder, Tim Curran, Greg Stolze, William Meikle, Brian M. Sammons, Gary McMahon, Laurel Halbany, Robert M. Price, Pete Rawlik, Cody Goodfellow, T.E. Grau and the late and very much missed C.J. Henderson, whom this tome is dedicated to.

Their stories take place in the past, present and future, across space and time and within dimensions terrible to behold. Here you will read stories of CIA deals with otherworldly creatures, a cult deprogrammer with a deadly secret, Viking marauders, the secret history of Elvis Presley, the psychological terrors of haunted minds, and more.

The King in Yellow Mythos (or Carcosa Mythos, as it is sometimes called) began in 1895 with a collection of ten short stories by author Robert W. Chambers, and was published under the title *The King in Yellow*. It featured amongst other tales four interconnected stories: 'The Yellow Sign', 'The Repairer of Reputations', 'The Mask' and 'In The Court of The Dragon.'

The tales are linked together by three main plot devices:

A mysterious and cursed play in book form, banned since its release, called *The King in Yellow.*

A supernatural entity mentioned in the play also called 'The King in Yellow.'

A mysterious symbol called 'The Yellow Sign' which is connected with the play and the King in Yellow.

Within the fiction, those that read the play often end up insane or possessed by evil. Many suffer their minds being blasted by the horrible tale the play reveals or are haunted and hunted to death by the play's monstrous avatars. Those that find The Yellow Sign suffer just as terribly as those that read the play.

Over the decades since Chambers collection first appeared, many other authors have written stories featuring his creations, adding to the rich canon of King in Yellow tales. This includes author H.P. Lovecraft, a name all fans of weird fiction will be aware of. Here, for your reading pleasure, is a collection we humbly add to the canon of the Mythos.

Welcome to your personal apocalypse, in The Court of the Yellow King.

Glynn Owen Barrass, August 2014

Cassilda 2

Eric York

THESE HARPIES OF CARCOSA

W. H. PUGMIRE

smiled at the canvas on the wall, and felt the shadow of its artist at my left. "It's interesting, isn't it?" I told the fellow without turning to him, not wanting to take my eyes from his painting. "I've never known buildings to look so . . . tattered. The city itself oozes of self-extinction, although how a city could commit suicide is a perplexing puzzle. There is not a trace of life, except for the two sirens in the sky; and yet they look so fantastic that one guesses that they may be mere figments of twisted dreaming. Look how they hang there in the air, horribly illuminated by the lifeless light of the twin porphyry moons, those globes of ghastly reddish-purple rock. Finally, our eyes take in the figure in its yellow robe, with its pallid artificial face and arms outstretched. I cannot comprehend why his hands should be so crimson."

I turned my head slightly and looked at the artist; and although his eyes were fixed onto his creation, I knew that he listened to my language. "Now," I continued, "there is one minute glimmer of natural light, and yet it emanates from an artificial relic. Do you see it, there, in the corner of the canvas, like something dropped onto the road, forgotten and forsaken? Yes, the brass crown with its synthetic jewels. One feels that it sits in proxy for something more authentic. And that long knife sitting beside it looks so nasty, doesn't it, like some implement designed exclusively for mayhem? The entire thing makes one shiver and wish for movement, for some shifting of starlight or some song of wind. But those obsidian stars in the painted sky do not crawl, of that I am certain; and the air of that deserted city, one knows, is dead and still. And yet – and yet, how *captivating* it seems, this painted image, how it tugs at the brain and makes one wonder how it would feel to weep beneath those black stars, to inhale the lifeless air. However did the artist come up with such an image, one wonders?"

"It's from a play," my companion finally spoke.

"Indeed? And where would one find this play?"

He did not hesitate in his reply, and yet he spoke as one who had lost his way in reality. "I read it in a dream. I read it aloud, and the dream took on solidity. I could hear the waves of the lake breaking on the shore, and when the wind arose I could hear the flapping of the tatters of the King, that flapping that should never be sounded. They had such a strange rhythm, and I tried to sing in accompaniment; but my mouth was dry and my voice was dead, like the lost city that festered all around me. God, the *hard* light of those twin moons, burning their essence onto my eyes. And when I finally awakened, I could still feel that acidic impression on my eyes; and the world looks weird, and its inhabitants look like puppets." He then turned to me, smiled and chuckled. "Sounds completely kookoo, I confess."

I shrugged and returned my attention to his creation. "The fantastic artist sees the world in singular ways, divorced as he is from the dull world of dreary reality. How far more creative and captivating, to live within a dream."

He turned his gaze again toward the painting. "I really *would* prefer to live there, godless region though it may be. I wouldn't have to pretend all the time. So, you like this?" He motioned to the canvas.

"Oh, yes," I assured him, "for I long to live there myself." Bowing to him, I walked to the door and exited the gallery. The sun was beginning to set, and the sky was a gorgeous bouquet of color. I stood there and admired the mixture of gold and mauve and amber, and I felt his shadow blend into my own.

"Are you an artist?" he asked.

"I exist within a realm of Art," was my esoteric response. We walked away from the city, toward the hill that rose before us. It was early spring, and the trees that lined the lane were sweet of fragrance and delicate upon the eye. We had almost reached the apex of the hill when we encountered the murdered thing. The artist knelt before the feline corpse and studied it for a little while as the sun continued sinking; and then he removed the long knife from the cadaver and wiped its blade on a patch of clean grass. How deftly he handled the implement. Rising, he held the knife with hands that were clasped together as if in prayer.

We stood atop the hill and watched the death of day. He shut his eyes for a moment, and then he flinched as his body began to tilt. Sheepishly, he smiled. "Sorry. I'm feeling a bit faint."

"When was your last meal? Your face looks haggard with hunger."

He shrugged. "I'm an artist."

Reaching into my pocket, I took out a folded piece of paper. "I don't have any money on hand, but perhaps this will aid you." Putting the knife under his arm, he took the paper and unfolded it. I do not think he understood the Yellow Sign traced onto the paper. Folding it again, he placed it in his bosom. The moon rose within the darkening sky, and we noticed the distant object that reflected the lunar light. "Ah," I sighed, "it's your brass crown. How golden it looks in this unearthly light." We walked to it, and he bent to pick it up. "Yes," I continued, nodding, "it is quite golden, and its diamonds are authentic. Will you don it, the golden diadem?"

How near the white moon seemed to the hill on which we stood. Its dull light shimmered on the crown as he lifted it above him and then placed it on his head. The leaves in one nearest tree began to rustle in the rising wind, and the branches of that tree began to sway. I could not help but warble.

> *"Atop the hill he makes his stand,*
> *In wind that sings a saraband,*
> *And we uncover*
> *Lost Carcosa.*

"There are no stars on this strange night,
Just one strange moon that sheds its light
Upon our dream of
        Lost Carcosa.

"See how the moon divides its sphere
Into twin globes that mock and leer
Above the streets of
        Lost Carcosa.

"Ah, double globes, grotesque, divine,
Evoke the ageless Yellow Sign,
Return of hearts to
        Lost Carcosa."

I moved in little steps to the music of the wind and clapped my hands as he removed the long knife from under his arm and held it before him. Reaching into my bosom, I removed what was folded there and held it before him, winking. He watched as I unfolded the pallid mask and fastened it to my face. I think he shuddered just a little as the moon began to darken and divide. I watched the division of those spheres and listened to the sound of their wings unfolding. He turned at last to face them.

"They come to adore you, these sirens of suicide. They come to take ye home. You hold the key. Will you plunge it into place?"

I danced toward him and hummed a little song, unable to contain my joy. His length of hair moved in the wind aroused by dæmonic wings, and his mouth began to hum in accompaniment to my noise. Lowering his eyelids, he raised the knife and thrust it into his throat. Shouting in ecstasy, I moved to him and caught his flow of blood with greedy hands. Somehow, he refused to fall. I stretched out my arms and offered my hands to the creatures of nightmare, and laughed as they floated to me and kissed my palms. Their attention was then caught by the wobbling of his body. Licking their moistened mouths, they flocked to him and caught him by each arm. Bending, I picked up the fallen knife and raised it to their blurring forms, as they blended again into one solid sphere.

The Viking in Yellow

Christine Morgan

ulls cried faint and unseen through a heavy morning mist that cast all the world in damp and dripping grey. Distant waves rushed foaming upon the pebbled shore, filling the cool air with scents of salt and brine. Here, where the river widened to meet the sea, the waters mixed in eddying whorls. Ripples lapped the muddy banks. Splashes sounded where fish leaped, or struggled in the nets and traps.

Wigleof led the way from one spot to the next. His little sons followed, lugging the baskets that would soon be filled with this day's rich catch. They whispered to each other, joking, teasing. They were good boys and dutiful, twins, sturdily built, curly-haired like their mother. He loved them well.

At their home, a small thatch-roofed hut walled in wattle and daub, Wigleof's sweet-natured wife Aelda would be hard at work, helped by their daughters and tending the baby. Perhaps later, she'd walk to the village by the abbey, to trade smoked fish for milk, eggs and honey.

Or she might send Aeldwyn, their eldest, who greatly admired the nuns – Sister Gehilde most of all – and spoke of joining their order. Wigleof had no objections to this, though he held a private measure of doubt for her reasons. If Aeldwyn thought the life of a nun was nothing but restful prayer, candle-making, clean robes of soft wool and hymn-singing, he suspected she might be in for a surprise.

He chuckled to himself as he hauled up the first wicker-woven fish traps. They were well-full with sleek silver-scaled bodies that flapped and flailed, gulping. The boys chattered eagerly as they opened and loaded the baskets.

Then they hushed, frowning.

"Father," said Leofric, his tone unusually subdued, "what happened to this one?"

Wigleof looked at what the boy held in his small hands. The fish did not flail, flap or gulp. "That one's dead," he said.

"But what happened to it?" Leofwald asked, his tone also subdued.

Expecting to find nothing out of the ordinary, Wigleof took the fish, and frowned himself. An odd oiliness sheened its skin, and its flesh felt strangely warm. He had never pulled a warm fish from the river, or from the sea. Its eyes bulged, yellow-white and murky, rather than shiny black. It might have already been partially stewed.

Upon a closer-yet inspection, he found that its fins and tail were tipped with fine barbs curved like cat's claws, and in its mouth were not teeth but stringy tendrils. Something about it struck him as altogether loathsome, unnatural, and vile.

Both boys gazed at him, solemn, waiting for him – their trusted father – to have all the answers. He found himself speechless. His mind was torn, half of it wanting to hurl the fish as far away as he could, the other half thinking to take it to the village as a curiosity.

It twitched in his grasp. He dropped it with a stifled cry of revulsion. Leofwald bent as if to reach for it and Wigleof drew him back. The three of them watched as the fish writhed and clenched.

"You said it was dead," Leofric said.

"I thought that it was."

"It's trying to burrow into the mud," said Leofwald.

"Father, I don't like it."

"No. Nor do I."

The frightened tremors in their voices decided him. Wigleof seized a nearby branch, snapping it off so that the end came to a rough point. He drove this down into the fish, puncturing it through the gills, nailing its body to the river bank. Thin blood oozed out, almost more yellowish than red. The fish thrashed a bit more, then fell still.

Silence held.

They watched it warily.

It did not move again.

Silence yet held, a silence that seeped into Wigleof's consciousness. The gulls, which had been shrieking their cries, had fallen mute. He could not hear the steady rush of the surf, a noise as constant and familiar to him as his own breathing. The moisture, which had been collecting on the leaves, making them glisten, dripping off in a soft wet patter, now made no sound. Nor did the water lapping along the shore, although he saw its regular ripples.

Each of his boys held him by an arm. He felt their touches, felt their trembling, felt them press close against his legs. They looked up at him with identical pleading expressions, but did not speak. Perhaps could not speak, just as he was unable to find his own voice to reassure them.

A stirring in the heavy, silent grey gloom caught his eye. Out on the river, a shadow appeared, mist-blurred and indistinct, then coalescing into a shape . . . a long, low, narrow shape that brought dread to his heart . . . a shape with graceful curves rising at prow and at stern, curves topped with carven beast's heads . . . a shape, a ship . . . a ship with a single mast, from which belled a striped sail of yellow and white . . . a ship with many slim oars jutting out to each side . . . oars dipping and stroking in unison . . . the oar-blades slicing without splashing . . . the hull gliding in utter silence, water parting ahead of it and sluicing together in pale roils in its wake. . . .

Terror welled up within him.

He should have fled already, run for the village to warn them, run for his house, for his wife and daughters, to take what valuables they could and seek refuge, seek safety hiding in the woods and the hills.

A Viking ship, a longship, a ship of pagans and killers from the savage north! A raid! Fire and plunder, murder and rape!

He should have fled already.

Yet he was unable to so much as move. The boys clung to him, quaking.

The oars rose and fell, rose and fell. Upon its oar-benches sat men in mail-coats, men in leathers and furs. Their faces were pale, their hair fair and stirred by the same wind that filled the striped sail, though no wind rustled the leaves on the shore and no wind tugged at Wigleof's own hair or clothing.

A row of shields hung along the ship's side. Round shields of lime-wood, some with rims and bosses of iron. Shields painted . . . painted not with horses or ravens, dragons or wolves . . . painted with . . . symbols? letters?

Wigleof of course could not read, but he had seen some writings. And if these were letters, they were like none he had ever seen. They were . . .

They were hideous, those painted symbols, those yellow signs. Hideous and horrible. Loathsome to the eye, to the mind, in much the same way as the strange fish had been. Unnatural. Vile.

The ship glided on. The oarsmen never turned from their labor. If they noticed the fisherman and his sons on the river's bank with their fish-traps and baskets, they gave no indication.

At the stern, upon the steering-platform, stood a tall figure, wrapped in a long and tattered cloak of yellow leather trimmed with the jaundiced-looking fur of a far-northern bear. He wore a gilded helm with a lank yellow horse-tail for a plume, the coarse strands blowing about his shoulders in that same unfelt wind. His helm's visor was made from ivory or bone, its aspect pallid and inhuman.

He alone among the men turned his head as the ship passed by. His gaze sought and held the three of them, there on the shore. Through his visor, his eyes seemed to blaze as black as the stars.

. . . as black . . . as the stars?

How could that be? That could not be. That made no sense. No sense at all.

Rising and falling, the oars cut the water. The striped sail swelled full from the mast. The yellow-cloaked Viking kept a thin-fingered hand curled to the steering-oar. He tilted his helmed head ever-so-slightly in wry acknowledgment, then faced forward again, faced the carved prow, faced upriver in the direction of the unsuspecting village and abbey beyond.

Skeins of mist whirled and wafted about the longship's stern. It became shape again, shape and shadow. Then it was no more to be seen.

Wigleof blinked, as if one emerging from a dream. He glanced at the baskets and fish-traps, and saw that every last fish – even those not yet pulled to land – lay or floated lifeless.

Somewhere, very faint and very far, a lone gull cried a dirge. Rain began to patter on the leaves, in the mud.

The boys looked at their father. Both had soaked their breeches. Becoming aware of the clammy wetness at his crotch and thighs, Wigleof realized he had done the same.

The village. The abbey.

His house. Aelda and the girls, and the baby.

Raid, rape and plunder. Fire and murder and blood.

Those shields, painted with those yellow signs.

He crouched and put an arm around each of his sons. He hugged them tight to his sides, picked them up, held them to him. They twined their little arms around his neck, and buried their faces against his shoulders.

Neither of them struggled as he carried them into the river, wading deeper to the dark channel where a strong current swept toward the sea. Nor did they make a sound, even as the cold water closed over their heads.

The blinded monk had passed another bad night. His urgent wordless gurgles grew louder, into raving grunts and groans. Though his hands were swaddled in soft wool wrappings, he tugged at them, pulled at them with his teeth, until Sister Gehilde was forced to restrain his wrists with strong bonds.

At last, she'd been able to persuade him to drink a sleeping-draught, though the sleep to which he finally succumbed was shallow, and fitful. His head tossed. Low, guttural mumbles issued from his sore-scabbed lips.

Only when the sky began to lighten and the fog gave way to rain did the monk sink into a true slumber. Gehilde, her own weariness weighing upon her, drew a blanket to his shoulders. The bandage about his face had come askew, and with a murmured prayer she adjusted the cloth over the weeping wounds where once were eyes.

She stretched. She sighed. She rubbed her brow, and temples. For a moment, the thought of her narrow bed beckoned, tempting her with its promise. But day had dawned, if damp and dreary. The morning business of Marymeade Abbey must be done.

It had been built about the remains of a stone fort of the old Romans, moss-grown ruins, tumbled walls and archways, a few intact inner chambers with floors of tiled mosaic. From a hilltop, it overlooked the winding ribbon of the river valley. Behind it, beehive-dotted flower meadows and orchards sloped away toward the green farms and grazing lands around the village.

The nuns kept the bees, collecting combs and honey, making candles and sticks of colored sealing-wax. These were their main source of livelihood in addition to what they received from the church. They also brewed fruit-wine to sell and trade.

At any given time, some three dozen women called it home. Not all were sworn to holy vows; some were lay-sisters, widows or forsaken wives. Their father-monastery was St. Neot's of the Stave and Crook, located further inland and upriver, some days' ride away at Shepsbury. Twice monthly, or more often during holidays, priests would come from St. Neot's to lead services, and supervise the running of the abbey.

And, when one of their monks might fall injured or ill, Marymeade was where they were sent to be tended as they recovered.

Monks such as Brother Oston, this poor and damaged soul. And Brother Camden, to whose room Gehilde now went. She found her sister there – Gamyl, her sister by birth as well as in their holy order. Gamyl was the younger, and of slighter frame. Otherwise they much resembled one another, with fine features, fawn-brown hair beneath head-coverings of white linen, and eyes the blue of ripe bilberries.

"How does he fare?" Gehilde asked.

Gamyl glanced up from where she sat upon a stool at the monk's bedside. "He woke for a while, spoke for a while," she said. "But he still does not know me, or himself, where he came from or where he is."

Brother Camden, though gone to grey, had been a hale and hearty, vibrant man … jovial in his humor, stalwart in his faith. Now he lay stricken, the entire right side of his body gone feeble and frail. The right half of his face hung slack, those corners of eye and mouth drooping. Age seemed to have draped him in a sudden cloak of additional years. If not for the slow swelling of his chest with each breath, he might have been a corpse awaiting the shroud.

"He inquired again after someone called Silvia," Gamyl went on, "then wept a bit, bade me be sure to remember to feed the cat, and …" She trailed off with an expressive, hopeless gesture at the monk.

"Did he take any broth or gruel?"

"Not much, no."

They watched over him together a moment, each speculating on who this Silvia might be. Mother? Sister? Lost sweetheart from Brother Camden's youth, before taking his vows?

Then Gamyl spoke. "How fares Brother Oston? I heard him through the night."

The weariness settling onto her again, Gehilde nodded. "Worse than ever. I had to bind down his wrists for fear he'd do himself more harm."

"What could have caused—?"

"It is not for us to wonder," Gehilde interrupted sharply.

"But after Brother Rubert, sister, surely you must—"

"I must not, I do not, and neither shall you."

They crossed themselves at the mention of the unfortunate monk's name. He had come to their care from St. Neot's greatly troubled, greatly distraught. After a time, he'd begun to regain both his senses and spirits . . . then went missing and was found in the orchard, a length of rope 'round his neck.

As she and Gamyl shared this conversation, Gehilde remained attentive to the quiet and orderly bustle of Marymeade's morning routine. Now it was disrupted in a flurry of commotion. Voices rose in anxious queries. Footsteps slapped quick in the halls. Robes swished and rustled.

"Sister Gehilde!" That was Magrin, not a nun but a short and stocky widow who served as a kind of gruff but well-meaning mother-bear nursemaid to them all.

Gehilde hastened from the room, Gamyl close behind her. In the abbey's main chamber, which they used as their common space for dining and sitting, the tables had not yet been set for the fast-breaking. Nuns and lay-sisters crowded in, wide-eyed, looking alarmed and frightened.

And with good reason.

Vikings.

Vikings, pagan sea-raiders, attacking the village below.

Through the fog and rain, they could see nothing of it. But they heard the shouts and screams, and the brief clash of battle.

Aeldwyn, the fisherman's daughter, had brought the grim news when she fled her family's house down by the shore.

"Mother told me to run, to take Wigla and the baby and get far away," the girl said, gasping for breath. "She went to look for Father and the boys."

The baby, red with indignation, fussed and squalled in a bundle slung across Aeldwyn's back. Little Wigla, a pretty child with long curls and freckles, began to sob.

Everyone looked then to Gehilde, their abbess. Weary though she was, she cast it aside at once. She barked swift instructions to Sister Udela, bidding her fetch the treasures of their humble church – a silver crucifix, an ivory cup set with garnets that had been a gift from Alfred of Wessex, the bronze-inlaid reliquary containing a clump of straw from the manger in which Christ had slept, and their holy books – and for the others to gather only their most prized possessions.

"Meet by the well-stone," she told them. "There is a tunnel there, through the old Roman bath. It leads to the hut in the orchard. Magrin, you know the way."

The stout widow nodded.

"Go, then, and hurry! Aeldwyn, you and the children go with them."

"Our mother—"

"Would want you to be safe. Go with Magrin."

The rest scurried to obey. Their lives of humble piety and simplicity here meant that they had little in the way of belongings. It would not take them long.

"What about you?" Gamyl asked.

Gehilde shook her head. "Marymeade is in my charge. The monks are in my care, and they are in no fit state to be moved. I will plead for them."

"The Vikings will surely kill them where they lay!" Gamyl protested.

Remembering Brother Rubert, who had damned himself by taking his own life, Gehilde softly said, "If that is God's will, then so be it and let it be a mercy."

Gamyl raised her chin in a manner Gehilde knew all too well from their girlhood. "I am staying with you," she declared.

There would be no arguing. Gehilde smiled and squeezed her hand.

Soon, the others had gone. The abbey was empty but for the four of them: the two ailing monks and the two sisters.

No more sounds of violence reached their ears from the direction of the village. They could make out a dull glow that might have been the smoldering fires of thatch-roofed houses, but nothing else.

Out of the grey fog and rain, the Vikings appeared. They came in a line, round shields held before them as if they expected to be met by armed men.

A wretched, despairing moan slid from Gamyl's lips. She covered her mouth, then murmured through her fingers. "Gehilde ... their shields ... do you see? ..."

"I see," said Gehilde, touching the rosewood cross she wore on a cord around her neck and sending a silent prayer to the blessed Virgin.

"They are the same that Brother Oston would—" Gamyl could not go on.

Brother Oston, however, had lacked yellow paint. Or indeed any paint or ink with which to inscribe the hellish symbols. It had not stopped him. Nor had the absence of his sight, just as the tearing out of his eyes had not stopped him from seeing the marks ... the words. With gruel, or blood, or excrement, he'd etch them upon the walls. When prevented from doing that, he'd claw them into his own skin, gouging wounds and scars.

"Do not look," Gehilde, shuddering, told her sister. "Do not look at their shields. Do not look at them."

The Vikings came closer, came to the abbey's very door. There, they stood and waited. Their faces were corpselike. Their eyes were empty, and dead.

Another emerged from the mists. This one did not wait at the door but crossed its threshold undaunted. He was tall, with a cloak of tattered yellow leather sweeping from his shoulders and a yellow horse-tail as the plume of his helm. The contours of a visor carved from ivory obscured his features with a pallid mask, but for glittering eyes like dark jewels, or shining black stars.

"You have three monks here," he said, in a voice that rasped, the voice of a dry desert wind. "I want them."

"We have only two," said Gehilde, straightening her spine. "And you may not have them."

"Two?"

"The third hanged himself."

"Pfah. He was weak."

"The others are ill," she said. "Ill unto death."

"They have done you no harm." Gamyl stepped up beside her, chin again defiantly raised. "And harming them will do you no good, whatever your evil intention."

"Leave them in peace," Gehilde said. "Leave this place in peace. This is a house of God, and you are not welcome here."

The man laughed, and it was the scrape of a spade upon stone, the grind of bones in a grave. "They have looked upon that which should not have been seen. It is for their own sakes, and yours, that you stand aside."

"Looked upon something?" echoed Gamyl. "Are you saying that's what brought this misfortune on them? That's what left Brother Camden brain-stricken, what drove Brother Oston to his state, what made Brother Rubert take his own life?"

"As I said, he was weak. They are all weak. Cowardly, and mad."

Gehilde shook with anger. "You come here, nameless and face-hidden, and call them weak? Call them cowards? For shame! Take off your visor, then! Show yourself unmasked, if you have such strength and courage!"

"My visor?" He removed his helm with its horse-tail plume and met her gaze with his blazing black eyes. "As you see, I wear none."

Or perhaps it was not anger that shook her. Perhaps it was terror.

"No visor ..." said Gamyl in a high, fainting whimper. Tears spilled down her cheeks. She clutched at Gehilde's sleeve. "Sister ... he wears no visor ..."

They put their arms around each other, held tight in a trembling embrace, as the tall man in the cloak of tattered yellow slowly advanced.

Gehilde kissed Gamyl's brow, then leaned her own against it.

"Pray, sister," she whispered. "Let us shut our eyes, and pray."

He stood atop a rise as the day waned, as the sun sank like a fiery bauble in the west. The rains of previous days had passed, leaving clear the skies now darkening to woad, indigo and violet. The first few stars – white, and sharp – glinted in the gloaming.

Before him was a scene that, upon first glance, looked both peaceful and pastoral. Sheep grazed across the hillsides. Geese waddled, honking, to and from ponds where a few swans sailed with necks arched regal. Smaller birds darted from the bushes and whirled above the trees. The town spread in amiable clusters in front of the monastery's gate, the tanneries set further off.

Sheep, yes, sheep, a great many of them ... the wool and mutton secondary to the main industry here, which was the making of fine vellum from the sheepskins. The monks had endless need of vellum. And for goose-feather quills and pots of ink in many colors, for blotting dust, for sealing wax. They needed leather for book-binding, gilt with which to emboss and stamp.

The monks. Yes, the monks. The monks of St. Neot's of the Stave and Crook.

The monks who busied themselves long hours, bent squinting by candle-light or the little flicker of tallow-oil lamps. Reading. Writing. Copying. Transcribing and translating. Adorning their calligraphy with glorious illumination and illustration.

Somehow, and to their sorrow, they had come by a tome of dire potency and power. Had the thief who'd stolen it sold it to them, unmindful of what it contained? Did they think to learn from it? To add its lore to the writings of their kings and saints?

Whatever their reasoning, they now paid the price.

Witness the monks who'd read from those pages. Who'd sought to make copies of the manuscript, perhaps to send to all their churches, add to their libraries.

Witness the one called Brother Oston, who had torn his own eyes from their wet sockets to spare himself having to see another word, only to find to his horror that he could not unsee them even then! How, in his madness, he'd shouted them, reciting passages until his fellow monks could bear hearing it no longer! They wrenched wide his jaws and severed his tongue at the root. But even then, blinded and dumb, he'd written the words, drawn the symbols and the signs.

Witness Brothers Camden and Rubert, one left shattered of mind and body, the other driven to the worst of sins.

And now, witness this scene . . . so pastoral and peaceful . . .

Upon first glance.

Further glances showed that all was not as it seemed or should have been.

The sheep roamed the hills unshepherded, at an evening hour when they belonged safely sheltered in their sheep-byres. The honking geese likewise went untended, nary a goose-girl to be seen.

In the town, light shone in but few windows, and smoke curled from fewer chimney-holes. No peasants trudged home from the fields, or from the woods with faggots bundled on their backs.

The monastery's belfry, a square structure of tarred timber and hewn logs, was silent. Its bell had not tolled for vespers. No robed and tonsured figures moved about within St. Neot's walls.

The tall man who stood upon the rise, the tall man in his tattered cloak of yellow and helm with horse-tail plume, nodded with grim satisfaction. He raised one pale, thin-fingered hand and gestured his warriors to follow.

They moved wraithlike through the town. Only frightened, snarling dogs opposed them, readily dispatched with a spear-thrust or swung axe-blade. The smith's forge held just a bed of ashes. The bread-ovens were dark and cold. Rats capered in the granaries.

Here and there were indications of looting and swift departure. Several of the buildings sat abandoned, empty and forlorn. Those that still seemed to harbor life did so with a furtive doom and resignation, as if the people within huddled behind barricaded doors, gripping useless weapons while they waited for the end.

Once, a haggard, naked crone spat curses from a doorway, then plunged a knife into her scrawny belly and ripped it sideways so that her entrails bulged out, glistening. They passed her by, and left her where she fell.

The gates of St. Neot's were open.

Crow-picked corpses littered the outer yard.

Fly-crawling corpses littered the inner halls and chambers.

Some, like Brother Rubert, had hanged themselves. Some had taken their own lives in other ways – veins cut so that the blood pooled thick, or with cups from which poison had been drunk still clutched in death-rigid hands.

Others had turned their violence outward. In the dormitories, several monks lay suffocated in their beds. One had been stuffed headfirst into the kitchen hearth, held there as he roasted. Another had been crucified and emasculated. There were bludgeonings and stabbings, drownings and strangulations.

A few yet lived, if such could be said to be living. They crawled, mad and cackling, mutilated. They rocked back and forth, slamming their heads into stone walls. They wept. They laughed. They wallowed in their filth, eating of it.

"Finish them," said the man in the tattered yellow cloak.

His warriors obliged.

It was no battle, merely butchery.

As they saw to their deadly business, he saw to his own.

He went from one room to the next until he came to the library with its long lines of desks. Ink pots had been spilled. Books were scattered. Most of the candles had burned down or gone out; one had tipped and it was a wonder that a fire hadn't started.

A sole dead monk sprawled on his back, eyes and mouth agape in final shocked surprise. An *aestel*, meant for following a reader's place, had been put to different purpose ... the slender wooden rod of its pointer had been driven into the monk's throat, the enamel and crystal handle jutting like a strange ornament.

And here ... here were sheets of vellum, manuscript pages, copies and translations half-finished. He collected them, studying each, tossing aside those of no interest to him and keeping the rest.

He noted the beautiful work, the lavish illuminations of rich and brilliant color. He noted the cunning illustrations done along the margins – a crown of diamonds and gold, a corpse-cart pulled by dark horses, a pure white lily with a beam as of sunlight shining from its heart, black stars blazing in a dome of sky, a disheveled cat with a slim pink ribbon serving as collar, the towers of a city rising behind tormented moons.

Gathering them into a pile, he rolled the pages together, tying them with a length of yellow cord. This thick scroll, he tucked through his belt, and drew his cloak to conceal it.

Next he searched among the scattered books, indifferent to bibles and scriptures, gospels and homilies, the writings of the saints and disciples. At last, partly hidden by the dead monk's outflung arm, he found a slim volume bound in leather more ancient and tattered than that of his cloak.

His long, pale, thin fingers folded around it. He picked it up, turned it over. There on the front, stamped in gold, faded and worn, was a familiar sign ... the same sign his men bore on their shields. He traced it with the pad of his thumb, dry skin hissing against skin even drier.

Summoned, his warriors returned, weapons dripping. They brought no other plunder, had not looted the monastery of its silver, just as they had not ransacked the village or town.

He thought briefly of the women, the two sisters, the nuns. So brave … strong and willful … the elder of the pair most of all. Perhaps he should not have spared them and left them to their abbey. Perhaps he should have brought them along.

They might have made fine queens.

But, no.

He had what he'd come for.

Soon the shields hung again along the ship's sides. Soon the oarsmen took up their oars and the striped sail belled in the wind. The carved beast's head at the prow faced away from the land, the one at the stern watching the shore recede.

A gradual, sighing mist engulfed them as they lost sight of the rocky coast, as the ship leaped and crashed in the waves over the cold grey sea.

Then the mist changed, changed and warmed, became steam. The water flattened, smooth as glass, burnished as a mirror.

Overhead, blazing black, shone the stars. The hot, fuming lake stretched out vast on all sides. Fish flickered in the depths, the barb-finned and hair-mouthed fish of Hali.

And the longship sailed on, toward the far horizon, where the towers and spires of a great city rose behind tormented moons.

Who Killed the King of Rock and Roll?

Edward Morris

aturday night again. Hello, everybody. How y'all? Good old Erin Brew, formula ten-oh-two, northern Ohio's largest-selling beer, makes it possible for us to be with you a whole extra half hour on Saturday nights. Pop the cap as we stumble together down our musical Memory Lane. 'The Big Beat in American Music' was here a hundred years ago – it will be here a thousand years after we are all gone. So! LET'S ROCK AND ROLL! All ready to rock? Atta boy. We're gonna have a ball.

This is Alan Freed with you tonight, the Moondog, the King of the Rock & Rollers, with a hearty welcome to all our thousands of friends in northern Ohio, Ontario, Canada, western New York, western Pennsylvania, *aaaand* West Virgin-eye-ay. Along about eleven-thirty, we'll be joining the Moondog Network.

Enjoy Erin brew, ten-oh-two, and the Moondog Show. And don't sneer at crazy people. Their madness lasts longer than ours. That's the only difference. There is only Christ to cry to now, and none to repair my reputation. Please arrange your dials of Judgment in a fulminating order to receive the Yellow Sign. . . .

(I couldn't be dreaming. I've never slept this deeply behind these damn drugs. Sometimes, I do sleep, though. Just not now. . . .)

Tonight we are actually broadcasting live on whatever decimal fraction of the FM dial. I just learned yesterday that this control booth was here. That there was a baby transmitter. Here. That there was even a Here here, back back back in the back of the first floor of the hospital where they sent me to dry out from that yellow river where I almost drowned.

I don't know if I'm drying out. I sleep all the time, and no matter how much they dope me I can't relax. There are dreams. Dreams. And sleepwalks. Like the one where I woke up here. Playing with switches and trying to get a level.

I don't know why this transmitter is in this room of this hospital, or what the breakers in this section were doing *all the way on*. Some of the desks and keyplates and such are stamped CIVIL DEFENSE, with one puzzling lead plate on the panel hiding this very microphone, IMPERIAL DYNASTY OF AMERICA.

It's quiet here. They don't know I jimmied the other entrance, the one through the broom-closet in the hall. This room is soundproof, and the Moondog can yell as loud as he wants. When I can get out of bed. Sometimes, I just scream.

Ah, you wouldn't believe me if I told you all about this place. About what a beast that big nurse, the redhead with the bullet-bras, can be to the long-timers. She's not on my floor, but she kind of thinks she's security chief for the whole building. No matter how long it's been since I even thought about a woman, I'd hate for her to catch me in a half-nelson during this broadcast. All you cats and kittens can understand, that is just too much dead air for the Moondog. Too much.

They're not all like her. Most of the nurses on my floor are good people who know how to pity a man who can bear no more. Cathy, the RN who works the graveyard shift up on my floor most nights, she always tells me that the human soul never really has anything to fear. That I always exist and nothing can harm me and anything else is just driving myself nuts. When she's there, I listen. Graveyard gets long.

So do the days. What gets me through my days, or most of them . . . Well, it's the fans who kept me rockin' and boppin' and not stoppin', back then, for them, until the gods all went home and the clocks melted down. The memories of playing myself in three movies about what all we were doing. The crowds in New York, and everywhere. The roaring seas of people I conducted like an orchestra, the conductor himself turning back and forth between performer and audience and down left right up and a one and a two and a. . . .

In Johnstown, I learned elocution on the street corner trying to talk faster than any girl in my class I could chat up. At WJAC-Johnstown-Altoona, then on my Ohio Tour ending in Cleveland, I raised the pennon of my own gold star under the goldhorn shadow of Jazz, until to the streets of Manhattan I wandered away, to my tattered cloak and beer-can crown as the King of the Rock & Rollers. Thousands of my subjects conscripted new listeners to WJW and then WINS-New York, and taped the shows themselves. At home. Nobody ever taped my shows but the occasional station-manager.

My shows. Because it was me.

Never in word or deed or thought had I betrayed my sorrow, even to myself. The mask of self-deception was no longer a mask for me, it was a part of me. Night lifted it, laying bare the stifled truth below; but there was no one to see except myself, and when the day broke the mask fell back again of its own accord.

What tied my days together was obligation. My obligation, as Hank Williams put it to me years before, to post and blaze the trail. Sometimes, I was obliged to protect the music, sometimes support it, and toward the end it was through a great crisis. Whatever it seemed to be for the time, its weight rested only on me, and I was never so ill or so weak that I did not respond with my whole soul.

Not even now.

Not even now. I'm tired. I've broken again. I've broken and done this thing. They'll just look at me funny. No one punishes my sort much here, not the way they punish the real nuts. But my sort aren't usually up causing this much trouble.

Except I cry, you dig? I cry so hard in the night with no voice. The bitter wretchedness of the whole elaborate construction of tinsel and mud that's all any man's misspent life ever is, that all comes back with an icepick headache of shame and disgrace.

They will be very curious to know the tragedy – they of the outside world who write books and print millions of newspapers. They may send their creatures into wrecked homes and death-smitten firesides, and their newspapers will batten on blood and tears, but with me their spies must halt before the confessional.

But the shame calls forth the memory of honor, and the tears likewise of sacrifice, and my tachycardiac old ticker still telegraphs the story for all the cats and kittens not yet even born. For Rock & ROLL.

For a minute or two now, until they pinion me and whack me up with something subcutaneously, I have a voice and it's alive. I cast my lot with the wild Indian who swallows the sun in the sacred mushroom and rises in the dark morning of the eighth day with a song. A big beat and a song. I can feel my voice going out on the air now. On the ether. I can.

I can. Someone is listening. Story time with Uncle Moondog, tonight. Gonna tell you how one day a King was born in Tupelo, a King I sat before and heard him sing something few others would hear. And some of the rest. The parts I have the strength to croak.

The Moondog wants to tell you what the King In Yellow sang. About Carcosa Radio and the Big Beat. Have a seat. Turn your radio up. Is there still radio? Are there still all the hits all the time?

Time. There is this microphone. Whatever those pills are is some heavy shit, and not in that Times Square kind of way. The microphone's the thing, whereon I'll tell my audience with the King.

The parts of the King Of Rock & Roll that came from somewhere else. The parts that didn't fit the rest of him. The larva inside him, the spy that took control of the flesh. The real King, killed and cut up and reborn like ten, like a tapeworm that squishes in your hand, and all the parts not left to regrow are eaten and shit out and eaten again, forever.

Before Elvis Aron Presley, there was *nobody* white like that, no one the networks would let me run on prime time, anyway. Bill Haley was the rock-and-roll Frankie Sinatra, a dinosaur with feathers, like my old band in Johnstown that we called the Sultans. Heh. The Sultans of Swing.

WHO KILLED THE KING OF ROCK AND ROLL?

What an antique time. I suppose I helped kill it, me and guys like Carl Perkins and Buck Owens and Jerry Lee Lewis. . . . Oh, brother. What Prometheus did we let loose, kids? The Beast touched down in Tupelo.

I don't like talking about the first time I met him. The second time, that was just for the press. Or they thought it was. Public Relations, you understand. No, I did my own research, when I thought I was on top of things. Hell, I went to *Jamaica*, to hear this new kind of music the Calypso orchestras were playing when the tourists weren't around, this Ska stuff that a half-Chinese bandleader named Byron Lee was trying to figure out a way to bring to the mainland. There was so much I didn't get to do. Is. So much.

So much. I'm transfixed with rage and despair, seeing a man's life and every hope and ambition prostrate, bleeding and infuriated. The thing which is to come has escaped His primary vessel, or will, and already seized throne and empire. Woe to any who try to countenance the King when He opens his tattered mantle!

The first time we met, it was at his old home place. I was supposed to write it down, or keep notes. The memories are a vast black gully-buster stormfront rolling yonder, a mighty river of clouds that, when beheld in approach are actually a lake. A hole in the sky.

The lake of Hali, which hides the city of Carcosa. Far out in the lake, distant thunder rumbles like the belly of the Beast that cometh down between worlds, down in the Big Blow, the big Delta Hurricane of 1936, to a shotgun shack with a leaky tin roof and no crib for a bed, slouching toward Carcosa to be bound, where hens don't lay nor roosters crow, where owls hoot at noon and children write HELP backwards in the frost on windows no one ever sees. Listen to the beating of your blood. Daub it over your own transom. Listen to the rain of maggots. Frogs. The King walks upon Nashville and New York. . . .

Came I then to Tupelo, and the kaleidoscope sun. And the heat. And the chiggers beneath the skin. The hot rocks of the road barefoot coals. Came I then to Tupelo to eat with a fiend, and watch the Book of

Revelation born in a borrowed bed.

Came I then to Tupelo. I had a whole new cross to bear later, but I had to visit the birthplace first. No more than an hour's drive from Memphis, that two-room shack where his twin was born dead, where his Mama brought him that hardware-store guitar. I had to look. I had to see.

I got good and loaded on the way there, at some juke-joint in their little strip of a downtown where a spade cat poured me "good whiskey" when I asked for it by name and tip, and two other spade cats (one with a hollow-body guitar, and one walking an upright bass) were there on the little stage playing dirty blues and owning the whole block with lost chords, with howls and moans and waking sagas. Singing for their supper.

I left the rental car downtown. I knew better. And no glen-plaid Brooks Brothers suit for the Moondog, either. The clothes I wore that day came from L.L. Bean, and the sneakers P.F. Flyers that looked so age-inappropriate on me when I got them on that I made a note to go pick up four more pairs when I got back to the Big Apple.

I got down and walked as far as I could. After a while, I stripped to an undershirt and only smoked where there was shade. After a while, I realized there were no more cotton plants in the fields around, nor sorghum nor anything but rocks, rocks, rocks and bones for a half a mile. The dirt was powdery gray, and not a flower or blade of grass to the sky.

I had to see the shack, and couldn't have held back if my own life had been the prize. The little flat-roofed white crackerbox. The sharecropper's shed, only Vernon didn't even have his shit together enough to sharecrop.

Even from the sandhill two miles out, I could feel someone watching me from the yard like they knew who I was, what I brought, the other thing I'd come to see. Someone who maybe didn't want to be rude to Yet Another Feller From The City.

She was barefoot. Her feet were caked with gray mud and red clay, but even that was fetching, where the pale shell-pink creatures (callused into hooves by going barefoot half the year) swung from way up the trunk of the big mimosa tree in the front yard and out onto the thickest branch, looking off into the distance. At me. Or so it seemed.

Her lovely head of black, wavy hair was crowned with a headdress that looked like it came from some fabulous other race out of *Weird Tales*. She wore a homespun dress edged with silver. From that far away, I could hear her singing some bloodthirsty old Scotch-Irish ballad like 'Down In The Willow Garden," you could tell by key and meter, but that wasn't quite it.

Not quite it at all. When I passed her on the road, the girl in the tree shouted something in a language I didn't understand.

I stopped, shading my eyes and trying to make out her face. A gold chain with a cross on it hung between her pale, freckled breasts. Every yellow ray of sun seemed to follow her hand, tipping her azure-veined white arms with gold wings and tingeing her hair with rose, as if from some faint warm light within her skull.

"Say again, little lady? I don't speak that lingo. *Je suis Americain*. I'm a disk jockey with the ABC Radio Network in New Y—"

"I shall not tell you. It is a secret," she called back in a honeyed drawl that didn't sound French any more, and maybe a little older than I guessed. On both cheeks a pink spot was burning, and her eyes were very bright. "Our hunting-falcon arrives. Now we got to starve you. Then you learn to hunt."

Those words should have been creepy. Instead, they filled me with a kind of breathless expectancy that began wearing me out almost imme-diately. Hell, friend, I wasn't even sure why I ran until I stopped running.

And when my jets cooled and those crazy kid sneaks quit laying rubber, I looked up and then I had to go to Memphis.

After that, I'm afraid everything got a little weird.

In the Court of the Yellow King

The sun hung, a purple globe, above the misty Blue Ridge. Nothing at the bungalow in Memphis looked fully unpacked. It was a queer chaos of odds and ends, hung with threadbare tapestries. An old six-string guitar in good repair stood by the window, looking strangely like an instrument of torture in a medieval gallery.

I knew that the time had come, with no escape, to sound out the troubadour who could bring blues music all the way to white radio. His eyes burned like black stars, and the shadows of my thoughts melted like twin suns into that accursed lake. I knew that the time had come. The world now trembled before him.

"Come in, Mister Freed, come in." The voice had an odd ringing quality to it. The batwinged cherub of juvenile delinquents everywhere (to hear some of those idiots in Congress tell it already behind closed doors) was chunky, but it was merely puppy-fat and shirttail-poor work muscle, with raw bones behind that.

His face looked like a pallid mask, as pale as his short-sleeved undershirt and hair were black, his eyes the expert drillbits of dexedrine holding something behind them, framing something in place. Something with two layers, Past and Distant Past. Something else behind those. I wondered what ailed him.

"Welcome. You, uhh, kinda came when we was cleanin' up," the joke had been shared on the telephone already, "But . . . Yeah, yeah, this'll be good to do. I think we'll be talking a long time."

When the King shook my hand, his grip felt like iron. He showed no signs of haste, nor of fatigue, nor of any human feeling. There began to dawn in me a sense of responsibility for something long forgotten. "I've already been gone so long, the wife's making jokes that I got taken by aliens in a flying saucer," I joked. "So what the hell?"

His eyes got strange again. "Oh, those kind weren't never from Space," he said out of nowhere. "It's way more complicated. They come from outside. Between. Anyway. Come on in. Make yourself a drink."

My shudder reached a long way back, as though it had been dormant for years and now rose to confront me. I knew that meeting him brought him nearer to the accomplishment of his purpose and my fate. "This is all Fate," Elvis read my thoughts with startling alacrity, "For a purpose. Because my brother Jesse got taken too soon. I swear to God, no one knows how lonely I get without him. And how empty I really feel. Except in the tunes, baby. Except in song."

He led me into the living-room, still talking, and showed me where a bottle of Kentucky bourbon was kept, and a big Ball jar of something called 'branch-water' in the cupboard that I took to be springwater. Fine. Ice, too, and I found that in the icebox, like anybody.

I didn't notice Elvis taking a drink. But watching this boy-king, this Tutankhamun, pace around from living-room to kitchen with that twinkle in his big brown eyes, I realized that I was seeing the phantom future of Music itself. Women would melt for this. (Some men, too, especially in the Village.)

But when Elvis looked at me again, I felt sick. "You know your public. Which are also mine. You're kinda like a . . ." He snapped his fingers. "Like a lightning-rod for music. Like a prophet, Mr. F-"

I waved a dismissive hand. "The King calls me Prophet, the King can g'wan call me Alan."

His upper lip curled, and the smile touched his eyes. Briefly, I saw the dumb kid with a spark behind all this. The dumb kid that had waved a six-stringed wand and opened a door to a world bigger than he could survive and stay sane. "You got your finger on their wants, Alan. I look beyond their wants and I can see their needs."

I smiled back, somewhat indulgently. "Well, I do fear to tread where you rush in."

At that, Elvis Presley sang the entire first verse of "I Can't Help Falling In Love With You" until we were both snapping our fingers. But this time the shared smile never went above his lips. His eyes stayed the same.

"Now, I know there's a lot you probably want to know," the King told me. "And we'll kinda start in the middle and work at both ends, but . . ." Something happened to his eyes. Something I didn't like.

"First, I want you to meet my Mama."

Welcome to our home, Mr. Freed. Pay no mind to all these danged old cats. Won't you sit down?

Baby . . . I mean Elvis, my dear son, he says this won't be home much longer. Neither will the old place, the one those newsmen always talk about. The one that still feels like home to me. This one's much nicer, and to hear my boy talk there'll be something I can't even imagine.

Oh, you were there? At the old place? Just walked on by, you say? That's nice. You're the disk jockey, yes. I listen to your programs. You seem all right.

So you saw the old place. Hope you got a photo. Baby's having some men come in and bulldoze the old place, then seed the ground with salt, just like back in the Biblical times. We're Assembly of God here, probably donate the plot to the church right up the road.

Vernon built that little wooden icebox of a thing the year before the big hurricane hit, the Big Blow. No running water, no indoor plumbing. Elvis says he's going to build me . . . us . . . a new house. I told you that. You seen the Caddy parked out in the shed, I'm sure. Not that we know what to do with it besides a coat of Simonize and taking it to church on Sunday.

I say 'we.' Maybe like Queen Victoria meant it, the royal 'we.' I won't let Vernon drive it. He'd have the paint all scratched-up using it to go on scrap runs or haul lumber wherever to put someone's new porch on for them for a tenth of what it's worth so he can go drink that weekend. I'm past caring about any of that, now.

No, I am. I see the look on your face. Vernon did his part already, so be damned to him. I forget if he's in jail this month or not. Haven't seen him around. Even a layabout with broken shoulders can still use his pecker. He did. I wear the pants here.

Well, there must be a lot you want to know. Baby only recorded his first two songs three years ago. They were for me, Gospel songs for my birthday, and he paid Sam Phillips for the studio time out of the wages he got driving that delivery-truck fulla light bulbs.

My boy is the Prince. He will be King, one day. My family will reclaim their birthright, as of old. Papa's line only got Ellis-Islanded to Smith, but that family Bible that baby – Elvis – won't let no one touch still says Castaigne, from Papa's granny.

Oh, I see you glancing at that bookshelf. Yes, yes, most of those histories are incomplete, but that one's not. It's two centuries old, and . . .

Oh, no, not the one you're thinking of, the one that art-school student turned his back on in midstream to go pluck the lower-hanging fruit, then went back and tried to . . . No, he *dreamed* about Americanizing this version.

A poet wrote this version in jail, back in the Old Country. A thief named Villòn, in 1456. Not our kin, he just knew us. This is the true KING IN YELLOW. Every emperor who ever lived had no kind of ambition compared to the King, who doesn't rest until He speaks even to the dreams of the unborn.

Emperors have served Him, and we serve His mandate between God and Man in this house too. It . . .

Oh, are you sure you want to just pick that old folio right on up and start reading? Well. Then let me fix that drink, Mr. Freed. It looks broken. Ha-ha. You opened right to page one. *"When from Carcosa, the Hyades, Hastur, and Aldebaran . . ."*

Here you are. Oh, something's fallen out of the folio. Have you found the Yellow Sign?

In the Court of the Yellow King

(Alan Freed turned the ebon brooch over in his hand, and it was a Port Authority subway-token, stamped with a single word, PAYOLA. When he turned it over again, he gasped.)

See, there, it looks a bit like a scorpion, or a hog's pecker. Then in the center, the Eye. Have you ever read the Chambers version? Both are books of great truths. Here, I'll take that brooch from you now. It was Grandmother's. What . . . Oh, you're looking at who's on the mantel. You're . . . curious.

Well, you know.

Baby Jesse was stillborn. Now he can always be with us. It . . . Why, I can hear a good Catholic boy like you *thinking* it, Mr. Freed. Those eyes were closed *before* Old Lady Two-Head put Jesse in that there jar. He is *not* looking at you. Ahem. In my own home, men think these things. No respect for the dead.

There's someone up the front walk. That'll be time for—

Oh, I see you weren't introduced. This is my sister's foundling. El-vis calls her 'Scylla, from when they were babies, but her proper name's Cassilda. Cassilda Presley.

Oh, you have met? *Tree*-climbing. Mr. Freed. You're old enough to be her—

I see. My apologies for doubting a married man's intentions. I'm sure your gallantry is quite old-fashioned enough for our tastes, when we get to know you. We won't be cruel.

Cassilda, you did not never have a dream about Mr. Freed coming here! Now whup on out to that side yard and cut some flowers for the table before we sit down to supper.

Kids can be so rude. Now, where was I? Oh, sure. Well, Elvis told you just a little while ago that we're kind of . . . remolding him. Rework-ing the way we do things, with . . . this. Bob Neal, his manager, well, you probably heard. He got Elvis a . . . like an advisor, or an attaché.

Bob met this military fella, a reservist from the Louisiana State Militia, used to bark in the gilly, claims to have served a special branch called the Imperial Dynasty of America. Colonel Tom Parker, the Repairer of Reputations. Keeps Elvis whipped into line. The way all boys should be. Under the Dragon's wing. All boys got the Devil in them. Mine the most of all.

Most of all. Colonel Parker says that my boy is an investment more valuable than gold, or diamonds, or workers, or any human capital. He says they can make Elvis a household name, a brand name. I don't quite understand how all that would work, but the money. The money.

Only the Colonel has a contract with my boy now, and as far as I'm concerned, Tom is family. He got that song "Heartbreak Hotel" all the way to you, sir, and that's mostly why you're here, I guess. Elvis has a new one for you very shortly, as soon as my boy gets all the way in . . . character, and no commercial breaks, either. Won't ever hear this one on Ed Sullivan, or out there in Hollywood where they'll want him to be in those filthy pictures, instead of the ones we want to make.

What? Were we starting one? Oh, that old film can on yon shelf. It's only fifteen minutes of film. Yes, directed by *that* Edward D. Wood, Jr. Sacrilege that he even wrote THE KING IN YELLOW on that film can in grease-pencil. We don't speak that morphadite's name in this house. That is one movie that I will never allow Elvis to make, no matter what the Colonel or that horrible Peter Lorre person ever tell me on the telephone. But Elvis says we keep that reel, so we keep it. At the new place, I expect it will go in the safe.

If my boy starts letting the fame corrupt his ability to . . . well, to channel, to be the voice of the King, the Colonel says a two-year hitch in the Army will clear that right up, like it did for him. (Always want to ask him which army, but it's none of my affair.) Not only that, it will space out record-releases. There will be time.

There will be time, for these new things. These subliminal messages the psychoanalysts back on your side of the hills are on about, and the back-masking, the multi-track recording, the stereophonic effects to let millions of people receive the Yellow Sign, as it was in Aegyptos, the school of Greece, and is now at the dawn of . . . this.

Do you want to see what the King of Rock and Roll is capable of, when he comes through in my boy as votary? It will secure the happiness of the whole world! Look. He comes. Now you see why I arranged the candles the way I did.

He comes, the way we perform when we have church at home. Behold, the diadem of the Castaigne upon his fevered brow. Behold, his silken vestments. Yes, that's the same letter on Grand-mamma's brooch, Mr. Freed. It means 'CROCUS REX'.

What?

Well, what do you mean, 'mask?' Elvis ain't wearing one. That's just . . . you see, the crown, and then . . . Oh, hush. Cassilda, I hear you creeping. You sit and hush, too, and none of your jill-flirting. The Colonel will put a stop to you two again. It's not Biblical.

Now hush, and listen.

Incredibly, the girl began to hum. "Not upon us, King," she breathed, in a Marilyn Monroe impersonation that raised both my gorge and the hair on the back of my neck simultaneously. "Oh, not upon *us*. . . ."

"This is one they don't get on the airwaves. 'Cassilda's Song' . . ."

A gospel organ seemed to break a low G-chord somewhere. A dazzling goldenrod-colored light filled the living-room, shadowing Elvis in my eyes. He played a four-chord run to tune, to test the edge of the first crooning breath that held something I seemed to have heard before, something indefinable, like the theme of an Arthurian lay, or some quaint verse I'd seen in an old manuscript.

> *"Be of good cheer, the sullen month will die,*
> *And a young moon requite us by and by,*
> *Look how the old one, meagre, bent, and wan,*
> *With age and Fast, is fainting from the sky. . . ."*

WHO KILLED THE KING OF ROCK AND ROLL?

The knot in my own disk-jockey throat sounded like a pine knot booming in a fireplace when I tried to swallow it.

> *"Crimson nor yellow roses nor*
> *The savour of the mounting sea*
> *Are worth the perfume I adore*
> *That clings to thee.*
>
> *The languid-headed lilies tire,*
> *The changeless waters weary me. . . ."*

Cassilda was singing harmony, in a breathy whisper that sounded like Sarah Carter. Maiden and Crone faded from their respective love-seats, and even the spackled ceiling fell away. I raised my seared eyes and saw black stars hanging in a soup of hurricane sky, and the wet winds from the lake of Halì dampened down my very breath, every other voice but His, singing to three moons over a lost city called Carcosa.

> *"I ache with passion's ire*
> *For thine and thee.*
> *There are but these things in the world—*
> *Thy mouth of fire,*
> *Thy breasts, thy hands, thy hair upcurled*
> *And my desire."*

The King's voice, and Cassilda's, rose and fell through that starblind terror, and when He looked up at me through all that light His face squirmed and chewed with only spots for eyes, and barbs for a mouth, sick warm pulsing flesh that glowed, and seized all, and turned it to frozen Midas gold. The air grew dank with black frost, painful in my lungs, wearying and saddening.

> *"Along the shore the cloud waves break,*
> *The twin suns sink beneath the Lake,*
> *The shadows lengthen*
> *In . . . Car-cosa. . . ."*

How the King's face gleamed in the darkness, drawing swiftly nearer! It bore down on me from the fathomless shadows in His eyes. Part of me, the part that was starting to fall apart back then anyway, had recognized Him almost from the first. In the labyrinth of sounds now issuing from that human instrument, there was the call of a predator tearing His way back to our world through something thicker and worse than Time.

> *"Strange is the night . . . where black stars rise,*
> *And strange moons circle through the skies*
> *But stranger . . . ssstill is . . .*
> *Lllllost . . .*
> *Car-cosa. . . ."*

Cassilda popped to her bell-ankled little bare feet and hurled a vase at the troubadour, which exploded in midair before it even got close. "YOU HAVE CLAIMED ANOTHER!" she screamed. "THE DEMON THAT WILL EAT YOUR LIFE!!"

When Cassilda Presley ran from the room, weeping, my first sensation was like that of a very young child badly hurt, when it catches its breath before crying out. I had never doubted what He had come to do; and now I knew that while my body sat safe in the cheerful little living-room, the thing inside Elvis Presley had been hunting my soul.

No bolts, no locks, could keep that creature out. He never turned, but there was the same deadly malignity in his white profile that there had been in his eyes. His yellow Goya eyes, with the black diamond pupils, like a cat or an owl, or a monster that had learned to cut its own toenails. . . .

> *"Songs that the Hyades shall sing,*
> *Where flap the tatters of the King,*
> *Mmmmust die . . . unheard . . .*
> *in Dim . . .*
> *Car-cosa. . . ."*

At some point, Grendel's Mother had left the room. Behind those black diamonds that held me now as sole captive audience, I saw the chill lake of Hali, thin and blank, with no fish or ripple of wind to break its meniscus that reflected the towers of Carcosa rising behind the triple moons in a chiaroscuro old Hokusai himself couldn't paint. Gray serpents slithered just beneath those depths, and hawks wheeled down to catch the squiggling meat, forming the same figure as the brooch. Like a crooked cross. Or, for that matter, a hog's pecker.

> *"Song of my soul . . . mmmmy voice is dead;*
> *Die thou, unsung, as tears unshed*
> *Shall dry . . .*
> *and die*
> *iiiiin . . . Llllost . . . Car-cosa. . . ."*

CLAP.
CLAP.
CLAP.

The colorless tarns of the King's kaleidoscopic eyes sought mine,

"The fans may turn on you," I suggested.

"I don't think so," Elvis murmured thoughtfully, "I got the mojo, baby. And when that don't work, well . . ." His eyes turned to coffin-worm eyespots in my unblinking, swimming gaze. "Well, I invite them to have a little chat with me. A concert from the King . . ."

Time froze, and sped up in part, and the end of things drew frightfully near Showtime. Everything that happened after that is hard to put into perspective, being the vomited human ambergris of this Moby Dick nation whose architecture eats itself continuously and shits out the craving for Decency that sweeps away old horrors in favor of more lasting ones. New vessels to set before the King.

J. Edgar seized the two hundred seven-inch 45's of "Cassilda's

Song" I managed to press from the little recording-gadget in my shoe-heel that my assistant let me borrow before I even left. It got played on a few Negro blues stations here and there on various continents, in the neon backwaters of Hip in various cities, barred out here, confiscated there . . . but not denounced by Press and pulpit, or censured, even by the most advanced of paranoiacs.

Because they couldn't. No definite principles had been violated in the first Elvis Presley bootleg record ever, no doctrine promulgated, no convictions outraged. It could not be judged in any court except the United Nation of Art. Yet, they knew. They knew that playing it often enough would make Elvis lose some of his mojo.

So they buried it, and found some other ways to kill me. But I wonder when they will send their scion to finish me off.

Every night in this hospital, I hear Him creeping like Cassilda in the hall. I dream the bolts of my door rotting at His touch, and His fingers no longer Presley's, but someone swollen and bloated and dead. But my end will be worse than that.

It's over. He's spoken one more time, and I already knew. My end was always the same, a bridge which no one passes.

Even now, I hope someone still has one of those 45's. I hope it got played enough. Or that some hip kid with a huge record collection still plays one of them, once in a while, late at night when the stars turn black and the sky looks like the sea. I hope she leans in close to the console, and turns that Volume up.

So we can send Him home again, someday. Or try. Come on. Dance with the Moondog, here.

Yes, those sounds are drums, and behind them something like a receding surf. Shutters going up. Those are cymbals, and soft Bop brushes. A new broom sweeps clean. In the middle of the horn section will fall the first shell.

The cops still don't want you to have a good time, kids. But we're going to have a party, so we gotta post a guard outside. Come on, everybody. You all know how these questions are settled.

It'll be a riot.

SACRED TO THE MEMORY OF ALAN FREED & JOEL LANE

Masque of the Queen

Stephen Mark Rainey

She should have made her way to Hollywood five years ago, back when she had enough money to travel farther than between Upper and Midtown Manhattan. She would wager that, by now, she could have at least snagged a part in some sitcom or second-rate motion picture — something that would have gotten her name out farther than the next block off Broadway. Finances were tighter than ever, and though she had no problem lining up auditions, landing a role that paid for something more than a few drinks was tougher now than the day she had spoken her first line on the stage at the Fugazi Playhouse, now closed. She sure as hell couldn't afford to move to a new place, even in a worse neighborhood. By any standard, her cozy apartment in Manhattan Valley was a bargain, though uncomfortably far from the law office where she temped as receptionist, not to mention the theater district.

Tonight, as usual, the bus was jammed with bodies, but she had managed to grab a seat near the back. To get it, she'd had to physically remove a large shopping bag owned by an older Hispanic woman who had strategically placed it to discourage potential seatmates. On a crowded bus, Kathryn Stefano refused to tolerate such discourtesy, and now the woman, her bag tucked under her seat, sat peering out the window radiating hot, silent hatred.

Kathryn had felt so good about the last audition. They seemed to love her, but her phone had been silent for two weeks, and they had promised an answer within a few days. Bryon Florey, her ersatz agent, had pestered the director enough, perhaps beyond his tolerance level, clearly to no avail. The damned thing would have paid well, too.

She was 28, and her time for grabbing choice roles was rapidly slip-slipping away.

In the Court of the Yellow King

She had never heard of the play before. *The King in Yellow*, a two-act exercise in surrealism, produced by an unfamiliar company — Mythosphere, it was called — though she knew of the director, one Vernard Broach, who had gained notoriety two decades earlier by helming a production of *Jesus Christ, Superstar* that took a page from the Gospel of Phillip, in which Jesus and Mary Magdalene were engaged in an amorous relationship, portrayed quite graphically on the stage. For *The King in Yellow*, Kathryn had read for the part of Cassilda, the queen of a mythical city called Hastur, somewhere on or off the earth, she had no idea. She had not read the entire play, but it supposedly ended on a tragic note, and she'd always had an affinity for tragedies.

At 109th, she disembarked, her seatmate bidding her rude farewell by way of a low "*Reina puta,*" and had walked most of the block to her building when she felt her jacket pocket vibrating. It was Bryon on the phone.

"You got Cassilda," came his excited voice. "She's all yours."

"Well, thank *you!*"

"Rehearsals start this Friday night."

"Seriously?"

"The schedule's going to be intense. Hope you're up for it. Can you get to their office tomorrow afternoon and get the paperwork done?"

"I guess I can take a long lunch."

"Do it. I have a good feeling about this one."

"So do I. I think."

"You impress Broach, things are going to start falling into place. See if they don't."

"I'll hold you to that."

"You'd better."

She signed off just as she reached the front door of her building, an ancient, nine-story monstrosity that took up half the block between Amsterdam and Broadway. Her apartment was on the top floor, a single-bedroom cubbyhole she shared with her roommate, Yumiko, whom she actually saw about twice a month. She found herself hoping Yumiko would be there now. At first she thought it was because she was excited about sharing her good news, but as the elevator took her up to the dim, deathly silent hallway, she realized she was not excited but nervous. More than that — unsettled, apprehensive. Not the little butterflies that came before stepping on stage but the cold anxiety she might feel if a stranger were to fall in behind her and rapidly close the distance.

Unfortunately, she discovered as she opened the door and entered darkness, the place was deserted, except for Koki, Yumiko's cat, who occupied his traditional spot on the windowsill. The gray and white tabby gave her a brief, unconcerned glance and returned to peering at the alley outside. For a moment, the view out the window seemed somehow *off*, and she realized there was an odd reflection in the glass: some kind of swirly pattern in bright, yellow-gold, as if cast by an illuminated sign at the entrance to the alley, though she knew no such sign existed. The reflection lasted only a few seconds and then vanished, as if whatever was producing it had dissolved.

That was strange, she thought, but hardly worth dwelling on. Koki was displaying no interest in anything, indoors or out, and if the Feline Early Warning System didn't go off, all was right with the world. More or less.

Damned peculiar: the script the office manager had given her was incomplete. A number of random pages had been excised, including the final scene. Still, from it, she pieced together as much of the story as possible.

The play opened with Queen Cassilda — many thousands, perhaps millions of years old — gazing on the vast Lake of Hali from her palace in the far-off city of Hastur. For eons, Hastur had been at war with its sister city, Alar, and the endless siege had made Cassilda into an embittered, apathetic, largely impotent monarch. She occasionally entertained the idea of passing her rule to one of her two sons, Uoht or Thale, she cared not which. Both princes desired to marry their sister, Camilla, and Cassilda finally decided that whichever son won her daughter's hand would ascend to the throne and take the name "Aldones" — the name of every king that had ever ruled in Hastur. Then Cassilda would give to Camilla the royal diadem, which had been worn by Hastur's queen since the beginning of time. Camilla, however, dreaded such a transfer, for legend told that the recipient of the diadem might also receive the Yellow Sign — a harbinger of death, or worse — from the mysterious King in Yellow: a nightmarish, inhuman being that resided in the fabled, spectral city of Carcosa, which existed somewhere beyond the Lake of Hali.

One day, a stranger wearing a pallid mask appeared in Hastur. To Cassilda's horror, he also bore on his garment a representation of the Yellow Sign, a bizarre pattern rendered "in no human script." The queen's high priest, Naotalba, declared the stranger the embodiment of the Phantom of Truth, an agent of the King in Yellow. The stranger, however, explained that he was an ally of Hastur, who could wear the Yellow Sign with impunity because the pallid mask concealed his identity even from the all-powerful King. His purpose, he claimed, was to end the stalemate with Alar, for any kingdom that could bear the Yellow Sign as its standard would be invincible. To make this possible, he suggested Cassilda put on a "masque," wherein the attendees themselves would wear pallid masks in the presence of the Yellow Sign. At the appointed hour, they would unmask and find that the Yellow Sign no longer held power over them.

Despite suspecting treachery, Cassilda believed the gamble worthwhile, for no matter its outcome, the conflict with Alar would end. Act 2 opened with the masked ball in progress, with Cassilda and all members of her court wearing pallid masks. At the sound of a gong, all removed their masks — all except the stranger, who then revealed that he wore no mask at all. He had deceived them so that Alar, not Hastur, might emerge victorious from the endless war.

Suddenly, with a cry of "Yhtill!" — a word meaning "stranger" — the King in Yellow appeared. Taller than two men, garbed in flowing, tattered, golden robes, the King struck down the faceless stranger, proclaiming himself a living god who was not to be mocked. He told Cassilda that Hastur *would* prevail over Alar, but with a heavy price: from that moment on, every inhabitant of Hastur, including Cassilda, would wear a pallid mask.

Cassilda, regaining her regal manner for the first time in eons, approached the King and boldly refused to accept his terms.

And there the script ended.

There was clearly more to the final scene. Whoever had collated this copy, Kathryn decided, was anything but thorough at his or her job.

Something in the script had seized Kathryn's attention and, for reasons she couldn't fathom, sent her mind reeling, as if gripped by vertigo. She flipped back through the pages until she found the passage.

"The city of Carcosa had four singularities. The first was that it appeared overnight. The second was that it was impossible to distinguish whether the city sat upon the waters of the Lake of Hali or on the invisible shore beyond. The third was that when the moon rose, the city's spires appeared *behind* rather than in front of it. And the fourth was that as soon as one looked upon the city, one knew its name was Carcosa."

Something about that name, *Carcosa*. She felt a strange, tingling excitement, as if she had discovered something indecent or forbidden — the way she had felt when she bought her first vibrator all those years ago. She had taken it home feeling dirty, giddy, almost breathless with anticipation. *How could she possibly feel this way now?*

That night, she dreamed of a soft, reed-thin voice saying, "The truth *is* but a phantom — a ghost that can be used or murdered at whim. Have you found the Yellow Sign?"

The first read-through with the full cast in the rehearsal room of the Frontiere Theatre:

Upon her request for a complete copy of the script, the production manager, Earl Blohm — a bearded, long-haired young man who dressed as if he had fallen out of the early 1970s — told her it was all she would get. "You'll find out the ending when everyone else does," he said. "It never ends the same way twice."

"I didn't think this play had been produced before."

"Oh, it's very old. It's just that no one alive has ever seen it."

Strange, *strange* man, Kathryn thought. In fact, the whole ensemble struck her as peculiar. Usually, when cast members gathered for the first time, a certain excitement ran through them like a humming electric current, but here, a somber, almost funereal atmosphere pervaded the chamber. Director Vernard Broach, a portly, swarthy man with dyed black, slicked-back hair and a pencil-thin mustache, spoke so softly she could barely make out his instructions.

"The audience is *there*," he said, pointing to the farthest wall of the long, deeply shadowed rehearsal room. "We do not concern ourselves with them. You are in the city of Hastur on the Lake of Hali." He gave the group his most theatrical scowl, pointed to the opposite corner of the room, and said, "The King in Yellow lives *there*. We do not look there, we do not speak of there, we do not go there. Now, look at your scripts, look at them. We have Queen Cassilda and her daughter, Camilla. Who is Camilla, where are you?"

"Here." An attractive young black woman raised her hand and then pointed to herself. "Jayda Rivera."

"That doesn't matter," Broach said. "Read, will you?"

Jayda Rivera gave him a questioning look, and Broach replied by staring at her with impatient eyes and stamping one foot.

Jayda glanced at Kathryn and drew a steadying breath. "Forgive my bluntness, my queen, but you have been looking for Carcosa. Again.'"

"'The Hyades have not yet risen, thus Carcosa may not appear. I am simply watching the Lake of Hali swallowing the suns. Again.'" Kathryn's gaze at Jayda was haughty, but her voice carried a wistful note. She felt Broach's eyes warm with approval.

"'If only the lake would swallow our enemy,'" Jayda said, her voice gaining assurance as she began to immerse herself in her part. "'But, Mother, does it not lie within your power to destroy Alar?'"

"'It does not, and you know this.'" She drew herself up and in a commanding voice said, "'Listen well, daughter. Do not mock me, for I still have power in Hastur, and I would as soon you never live to succeed me.'"

Jayda's eyes widened in pure, authentic fear. "'I do not mock, my queen. You withhold powerful secrets. I desire only to learn.'"

"'I should first share them with agents of Alar.'"

The ensuing silence felt so deep that Kathryn swallowed hard to make sure she could still hear. From the direction that Broach had indicated lay the purview of the King in Yellow, a movement caught her eye. *Do not look there.*

She looked. Just for a second.

A tiny figure, standing in the shadows, barely visible. *A child.*

A sudden rhythmic clattering drew her attention back to director Broach. The stout man was doing a weird little two-step dance to himself, a blissful grin broadening his already broad face. The sounds of his feet tapping on the floor were soon joined in syncopated rhythm by another set of echoing, *tap-tapping* footsteps.

In the room's far shadows, the child was dancing as well.

Three weeks later: lunch at Brodjian's Café with Jayda, who, it turned out, worked by day in a nearby office.

"I don't like those damned masks," Jayda said, giving her chicken salad wrap a suspicious glance. "They're creepy and uncomfortable."

"Creepier on some than others."

Jayda smiled and nodded, then looked back at her lunch. "I asked for no walnuts. Screw it, they won't kill me. You think this play has a chance of taking off?"

Kathryn's turkey and brie croissant must have sat on the counter overnight. It was not thrilling. She shrugged. "It's the weirdest thing I've ever been in. I tell you, if I were in the audience, I don't know I'd sit through it — at least as much of it as we can perform."

"Please! What *are* we going to do at the end? Stand there like dummies as the curtain falls? And who's that little girl? One of the cast members' who can't find a babysitter?"

"Little girl?" For a second, she drew a blank. "Oh, wait. I thought it was a little boy."

"Pretty sure it's a girl."

"Okay." Boy or girl, the kid was a mystery. Always lurking in the shadows, never quite revealing his or her face. Six or seven years old at most. She had never heard the child speak, yet he — she was *sure* it was a boy — sometimes mimicked the actions of the players during rehearsal. She didn't think the kid was Broach's; he was reputedly as gay as they came and had been an old bachelor since before Moses' day.

"We still don't even know who that is playing the King."

"Nope. Could be anyone, since we never see his face."

"The orchestra's on tonight. You ready?"

Kathryn nodded. The play featured a single musical number, "The Song of Cassilda," in the second scene of Act 1. Till now, she had simply sung it *a cappella* from the sheet music, which, most curiously, Broach had transcribed by hand. This evening, the prior production having finally cleared out, the theater proper would be open for rehearsal, and she would sing with orchestral accompaniment. She had a fair mezzo-soprano voice, best suited to singing in a chorus, but in college she had held her own as Lady Macbeth in their production of Verdi's *Macbeth*, and more recently as Luisa in a revival of *The Fantasticks*. She had no doubt she could nail the song, yet for some reason she was on edge about it.

Like about so many things in this play.

"What are you doing?"

Jayda was looking at her, one eyebrow raised. Kathryn realized one finger was tracing a pattern on the table and had twisted a portion of the tablecloth into a knotted mass. She'd had no idea she was doing it.

A chilly worm slid down the back of her neck. "I'm done," she said, pushing away her half-eaten croissant. "Not hungry. And I gotta get back to work."

"You really are nervous."

"Something about being poor as dirt, I guess. I need this play to fly, and I'm not sure it's going to."

"If it doesn't, it won't be on your account."

"Well, thanks for that."

They settled their bills and headed out of the café into the afternoon sunshine. Lunchtime pedestrians and traffic choked West 47th Street, the usual barely controlled chaos. For the moment, the aroma of cooking meat from a dozen nearby eateries overwhelmed the exhaust fumes, just barely.

"Till tonight, then," Kathryn said. She gave the younger woman a little wink. "If you see crowds of people running away, it's because I'm practicing my song in the streets."

"Now, that I believe."

"Oh, and Jayda?"

"Hmm?"

"It's a little boy."

Jayda returned an exaggerated sneer. "Yes, Mother."

In the Court of the Yellow King

Dark, *dark* theater.

The cavernous space beyond the stage might as well be outer space, Kathryn thought, the only illumination out there the murky red glow from a pair of exit signs over the far doors, like ancient, dying suns floating in the void. The Frontiere, once a posh venue for first-run shows, had decayed as old buildings will decay over the course of a century, and nowadays audiences rarely filled more than half the seats, even for its biggest shows. Still, its acoustics were phenomenal, the ceiling rising to dizzying heights, the spacious stage framed by columns and faux-Greek sculptures.

The cast had assembled within a warm island of light on the otherwise barren stage, and director Broach was in a corner conversing with Joseph Morheim, the orchestra conductor. Down in the pit, the musicians were tuning their instruments, producing a stream of background noise that alternated between soothing and jarring. This felt *almost* like a normal production, Kathryn thought, which in itself seemed bizarre, since little about *The King in Yellow* had so far been "normal." She had no understudy; no one did. At their read-throughs, the director stopped them at varying points before the non-existent ending. It wasn't only her script that was incomplete. Broach — or perhaps the anonymous playwright — had excised those portions of the play, the director's explanation being that "Spontaneity, my children, will have its day, and your reactions will be as authentic as the audiences'." Three actors — none, thankfully, in major roles — had dropped out after only a few rehearsals, claiming the play was causing them "psychological distress." While Kathryn and Jayda Rivera had hit it off from the start, the actors who played Cassilda's sons, Uoht and Thale, never associated with the rest of the cast. The former, a handsome, chisel-faced youngster named Les Perrin, always appeared sullen and withdrawn, his every free moment spent with his face stuck to his iPhone. The latter was a chunky, bearded gentleman named Kenton Peach who had starred in several noteworthy shows, including *I'm Not Rappaport* and *The Odd*

Couple; ironically, he was old enough to be Kathryn's father. He seemed polite enough but frequently faded into the shadows as if performing a soliloquy for no one.

Labeling Broach an 'eccentric' was like saying Jenna Jameson was a little audacious. The director's moods swung between exuberance and depression, sometimes within minutes of each other. At least he seemed taken with Kathryn's portrayal of the moody Cassilda. "You give her life," he told her, "which is more than she ever knew before."

To date, the "Yellow Sign" had been represented by an "X" rendered in yellow paint. Why, she wondered, did that bother her so? Not to mention the fact the King in Yellow himself was played by some anonymous actor, whose identity only Broach knew.

Kathryn's roommate, Yumiko, after one read-through, refused to practice with her any further. "This play is not happy for me," she had said. "It feels bad."

Two weeks remained before the opening. Broach had promised the sets would be "phenomenal," and the stage crew had their work cut out for them. Until then, there would be rehearsals every night, but they still had no inkling of how the play would actually end.

However, as Kathryn had hoped, the first stage rehearsal felt different. *Good* different. Even without the sets in place, the theater aura bolstered her confidence, and as Cassilda slipped inside her, the two of them breathing together as one, the orchestra sent up swirling, mystical strains from woodwinds and strings, weaving an otherworldly atmosphere that was at once dark and lovely. As Scene 2 of Act 1 — Cassilda's song — loomed nearer, the music became more intense, the brooding bass deeper and more ominous, the ethereal flutes more melodic.

The introduction to the song began. Weird and wistful, the instruments assumed the quality of human voices, humming and warbling in an eerie melody that gave Kathryn a chill.

She needed no cue to begin.

> *"Along the shore the cloud waves break,*
> *The twin suns sink beneath the lake,*
> *The shadows lengthen*
>   *In Carcosa."*

Her voice was not hers. *Alien*, it seemed, more assured and more beautiful than any her vocal cords could produce. She felt herself diminishing. All she could perceive — all that was left of her — was her voice.

> *"Strange is the night where black stars rise,*
> *And strange moons circle through the skies*
> *But stranger still is*
>   *Lost Carcosa."*

> *"Songs that the Hyades shall sing,*
> *Where flap the tatters of the King,*
> *Must die unheard in*
>   *Dim Carcosa."*

Her heart swelled, and her feet seemed to leave the floor, her body as light as a dust mote, her emotions overflowing, spilling into all those within her presence.

> *"Song of my soul, my voice is dead;*
> *Die thou, unsung, as tears unshed*
> *Shall dry and die in*
>   *Lost Carcosa."*

The last syllable echoed away into pure, empty silence. She had no breath left in her lungs.

Camilla — no, *Jayda* — stood nearby, her eyes bright jewels, tears glistening on her cheeks. Kenton Peach lifted an arm and propped himself on Les Perrin's shoulder, as if to keep from toppling. Somewhere beyond the island of light, a soft female voice breathed, "Oh, my."

At the edge of darkness, stage left, Vernard Broach stood with his hands folded together as if in prayer, knees slightly bent, face to the heavens, eyes closed. After a moment, he began to shiver as if clutched by bone-numbing cold. Then he was not shivering but *vibrating*, his entire body quivering in a way no human body could or should move.

Behind Broach, a shadow stirred, and the reed-thin voice Kathryn had heard in her dream sang out: "Aldebaran."

Sometime in the night, she woke to an odd flapping noise, unlike anything she had ever heard in her apartment. She rose and peeked into the darkened living room. Yumiko was not on the pullout sofa bed, and she didn't see Koki anywhere. The heavy flapping came again, and she now determined it originated outside her window, which overlooked the narrow alley. She drew up the venetian blinds and then staggered backward with the realization that she was not awake but dreaming.

Where the opposite brick wall should have been there was vast, dizzying space: a midnight blue sky lit by alien stars over an endless body of inky water. High above and to the right, a huge, blood-red star lit the night sky, and she knew *this* was Aldebaran, the sun that blazed above the city of Alar. Around it, a cluster of stars — the Hyades — glittered like the jewels adorning Cassilda's diadem. And now, slowly, the rim of the silver moon breached the farthest edge of the Lake of Hali and rose until it resembled a cyclopean eye, its gaze burning through her body straight to her hammering heart.

Then, on the horizon: an impossible array of gleaming, dizzying spires that wavered like ghostly tendrils before taking solid form *behind* the bright, full moon.

Carcosa.

Moments later, it came: the thin, childlike dream voice she had heard before; distant, barely comprehensible.

"Doggy!"

No. The word only sounded like "doggy." That wasn't what it had really said.

"Joggy!"

It was still too far away, too difficult to understand. The flapping sound came again, and now, in front of those distant, luminous spires, a silhouette appeared in the sky, its contours vague, imprecise. It was coming toward her, trailing black smoke, as if it were on fire.

"Bloggy!"

A little clearer now, the reedy voice sounded excited. The shape in the sky was no clearer to her eye than the voice was to her ear. It seemed ghostly in its way, surrounded by an aura of indeterminate color. Was this what it was like to be color blind? It was neither gray, nor silver, nor white, nor violet. But it *was* color.

"Byakhee!"

Now the thing was rushing toward her, and she could see its eyes, burning with that indefinable, radiant gleam. She backed away from the window, knowing the thing was aware of her, had *targeted* her.

Then a hand touched the small of her back. She spun around and looked down. Standing before her was the child she had seen at rehearsals. Even now, she couldn't tell whether it was a boy or a girl. Curly dark hair hung low over big blue eyes, its short, slightly pudgy frame garbed in a pale blue robe, a tiny replica of Cassilda's jeweled diadem adorning its oversize head. Those eyes were too mature to belong to a child.

The tiny, cherubic mouth spread into an overly huge grin, revealing two rows of polished, very large, very adult teeth.

"Grandmother!" it said.

"I want out of this," she said, and from the long silence, she didn't know whether Bryon had even been listening to her. "I can't do this play."

The low voice that finally replied was disbelieving. "You signed a contract."

"Screw the contract."

"You do *not* back out on Vernard Broach. Are you fucking serious?"

"There's something wrong with him. He's not *right*."

"What's he done? Tried to rape you or something?"

"No, of course not. But I can't eat anymore. I can't sleep — not without these nightmares. I see things that can't be real. Bryon, no play is worth my health." Then she whispered, "Or my mind."

"You break this contract, you'll be temping and waiting tables till that drama mask tattoo on your ass is sagging to your knees. Are you that damned stupid?"

"This is not negotiable. Call. Him."

"You're not my client anymore. I'm done with you. You tell Broach yourself."

Bryon Florey hung up on her.

Her eyes were swollen from crying, and her throat felt as if she had swallowed razor blades. She'd had to call in sick at the temp agency, and they were hardly any happier with her than Bryon was. For that brief moment, when she had sung Cassilda's song on stage, there seemed a chance that everything might yet turn out as she had hoped. But then came the aftermath, so repulsive, so full of unendurable *dread*.

She had barely put her phone down on the nightstand when it began to vibrate. It was not a number she recognized. "Hello?"

Director Vernard Broach's voice. "I know you wish to leave the play."

"How did you—?"

"If you stay, I promise something wonderful will happen. Kathryn, you are our shining star."

"Mr. Broach, this is taking too much out of me. I feel awful, physically and mentally. I just can't do this."

"I will double your pay. No. Triple it. Kathryn, you *are* Cassilda.

Trust me when I say that, after the first performance, things will be very different."

"I don't know what that means."

"I've treated you well, have I not?"

She had to concede that, personally, Broach had shown her only respect. What if she *were* to face her fears and finish out this play? All kinds of new doors would open to her. And this bullshit would be behind her.

"When you wake up in the morning, the money will be in your account. And you will have a new agent. A real agent."

"Mr. Broach, I—"

"Kathryn. Please?"

"All right. All right. I'll sleep on it and call you in the morning. I promise."

There was a long silence. "I trust you, my good friend Kathryn. Now I ask you to trust me. Tomorrow morning, call me and say you will stay. I will honor my word to you."

"I'll call."

"Until then, Kathryn."

Opening night:

Upon her arrival, her first reaction had been to the brilliant sets. Everything looked as it had during the final dress rehearsal, but nothing *felt* like it. The balconies of the palace rose almost to the ceiling, and — more disturbing to her — the backdrop of the Lake of Hali uncannily resembled her vision from that night. The lavish interior sets were modular and could be moved by stagehands to their designated marks almost instantaneously. She had seen all these during their construction, but now she felt as if she were viewing for the first time a realm that actually existed.

Vernard Broach had been true to his word. By any standard she could measure, she was now a wealthy woman, about to sign a contract with a brand new, very reputable agent.

The *King in Yellow* opened with an overture: a haunting, wistful composition built on the melody of "Song of Cassilda," but that ended on a series of harsh, dissonant notes that set her teeth on edge. As she took her place on the palace balcony, she felt a moment of vertigo, and just for an instant, an image of that black, smoking silhouette with burning eyes flashed in her mind's eye.

There was a rumble as the curtains separated and spread wide, and then the spotlights were on her, and beyond those lights, there was nothing — only a gaping abyss, blacker than the sky over the city of Alar. Behind her, Jayda spoke her lines, and the play commenced. Uoht and Thale argued over which of them would take their sister's hand in marriage. Cassilda turned thoughtful as she decided that one of the brothers would succeed her and that Camilla would inherit the royal diadem.

Something seemed wrong. The space beyond the stage was too silent, too still. She felt as if she were trapped within a sealed sphere of light, barely able to breathe. But it was when she was supposed to describe to Camilla the four singularities of Carcosa that she received her first shock.

It wasn't Jayda who knelt before her to listen. It was the child.

"Grandmother!" it said. "Tell me of Carcosa."

Deaf and blind, existing somewhere apart from herself, her body continued to play her part, speaking the lines she was meant to speak. When awareness returned to her, the music told her it was almost time to begin her song. For a moment, the spotlights were turned away from her, and she chanced a look out at the darkened chamber.

It was empty. No living soul occupied a single seat.

She stepped in front of Brad Silva, who played Naotalba, the priest, her disbelieving eyes sweeping the empty space. "There's no one there. There's no one out there!"

She felt something tugging at her long, crimson skirt, and she looked down to see the child's huge blue eyes peering up at her.

"There is an audience, Grandmother. But sensible souls in Hastur hide their faces."

Inside, she began to scream. She tried to leave the stage. She pleaded, cajoled, threatened Cassilda, but the character refused her, and Kathryn played on.

The masked figure — the Phantom of Truth, played by a young man named Zack Cheauvront — appeared before her, and for the first time, she saw it. Not a crude, painted "X" but a blazing, yellow-gold sigil, simultaneously adorning the character's robe while floating in some dimension in front of it. She could not have found words to describe the Yellow Sign, for it was rendered by no human hand.

The masked stranger was full head taller than Zack Cheauvront.

Kathryn sang "The Song of Cassilda." And the empty, soulless auditorium erupted with thunderous applause.

This was all in her mind.

She agreed to the stranger's proposal, and the curtain came down on Act 1. She fell to her knees, sobbing, barely aware of tiny hands pulling the pallid mask down over her head.

The child took the stage and spoke to the emptiness.

"'Your chance to escape has passed. Bound to us, at last.
No harm can come to you in fantasy, and this is not reality.
No sensibilities offended, no immorality decried.
But 'tis now too late, for your sin is complete.
You have crossed the threshold and the door is barred.
Lament what you will, but here you abide;
Sit and listen, for you are ours forever,
And until the end of time, we are also yours.'"

The gong sounded.

Zack Cheauvront — it *had* to be Zack — as the Phantom of Truth stood before her, pointing to her face. She was supposed to remove her mask, but as long as she wore it, she couldn't be seen. She did *not* want to be seen.

But she tore the mask from her face and regarded the horrid Yellow Sign on the stranger's robe. She heard Camilla say, "You, sir, should unmask."

"Indeed?"

That was not Zack's voice.

"It is time. We have laid aside our disguises. All but you."

"But I wear no mask."

"No mask!" Camilla's eyes turned to Cassilda's, bright and bulging with horror.

"*'Yhtill! Yhtill! Yhtill!'*"

The King in Yellow appeared before her and, with a glance, struck down the masked stranger. The monstrous figure floated above the stage: a giant garbed in tattered, brilliant yellow robes, its face covered by a golden mask that revealed only its eyes — eyes so black they glowed. One hand rose to point at her, and the King's voice boomed across space: "Have you found the Yellow Sign?"

It was not the costume from their rehearsals.

It was not the same man.

It was not a man at all.

The King pronounced Hastur's fate. Declared its victory over Alar. Condemned every man, woman, and child in the city to wear a pallid mask for the rest of eternity.

Cassilda felt another soul inside her, one struggling to escape, protesting these events that never began and never ended. At last, it was time for her to rule in Hastur, to no longer revel in the ennui of perpetual siege. She stepped forward and gazed into those blazing sockets in the golden mask. "No," she said, her voice firm and strong. "This will not do."

That was where the script ended.

Kathryn stood under the hot stage lights, glaring at the thing floating before her. It seemed diminished somehow, as if wilted by her refusal. She heard rustling and other little sounds in the darkness, and her attention shifted to the great, empty hall beyond the orchestra pit.

The theater was filled to capacity. Not a seat remained empty. As she stared, the applause began, at first sparse, then rising to a consuming thunder. People rose to their feet and began to shout. When she looked back toward the King, he was gone. Only the unmasked people of Hastur — these actors — surrounded her, radiating approval.

Her children — Jayda Rivera, Les Perrin, and Kenton Peach — came to her, smiling, and the two men took her arms, evidently to escort her offstage. But no; at the far end, on a dais, there was a throne. The original throne of Hastur, first occupied by King Aldones, before the beginning of time. *Not one of Broach's sets.* They led her to the throne and knelt as she ascended the dais and took her rightful place.

The child appeared and stood before her, its big blue eyes gazing at her, inquisitive, appraising. The eyes turned cold and black, mimicking those of the King in Yellow. Kathryn heard a series of metallic *snaps*, and a second later realized that manacles had closed around her wrists and ankles, binding her in the throne.

"What is this?"

She heard a clatter behind her and smelled something thick and pungent. From the shadows offstage, actors were carrying bundles of wood and piling them on the dais beneath and around the throne.

My god, they were going to burn her.

"No," she whispered to the child. "What are you doing? Why?"

The small creature laid one finger beside its nose and said, "Grandmother. Did you think to be human still?"

Jayda appeared, carrying a lit torch, her eyes reflecting the flames until they burned pure gold. From the painted stage backdrop, Kathryn detected movement, and — as in her dream — saw a smoking silhouette with glowing eyes drifting through an endless, star-filled sky.

"When all is done, Byakhee will feed," Jayda said.

The child pointed to a blood red star above the Lake of Hali. "Adebaran."

She could see Carcosa behind the rising moon, and as Jayda dropped the torch and flames began to rise around her, catching her skirt and enveloping her sleeves, she saw the distant spires glowing gold.

Before her screams became the only existing sound, she heard the child addressing the audience.

"This ends the story of *The King in Yellow*, a tragedy told in fire and verse."

The child danced its way off stage, while Kathryn and Carcosa burned together.

She awoke to a pair of blurry figures leaning over her and discovered she could not move. Something covered her face, something with slits for her eyes that barely permitted her to see out.

"Stay still. We just want to help you," a young male voice said.

Paramedics.

"We need to try to get that off her face."

"What is it?"

"Looks like some kind of mask."

"No!" she cried, her voice muffled. "Don't take it off."

"What did she do?" another voice asked.

"She burned herself."

"Oh, my god."

"It's bonded to her skin," the second voice said. "We can't remove it here."

"Look at that pattern on her chest. Why is it *yellow*?"

"Who knows? Let's get her in the ambulance."

Kathryn closed her eyes. She felt no pain, felt *nothing*. As long as she wore the mask, she would never have to face the King again.

"How bad is it?" the first voice said.

"Bad. No one will ever recognize her."

Ever.

And so, at last, Kathryn and Cassilda were free.

Grand Theft Hovercar

Jeffrey Thomas

He loved the freedom most of all, a sense of liberation he couldn't equate with anything in his life prior to the game. The game had an elaborate plotline that was admirably constructed, giving one the feel of an interactive movie or novel, introducing an array of fascinating comrades and enemies, sending the player on a seemingly endless string of exciting and challenging mini missions. And yet, in navigating around the virtual facsimile of the city of Punktown – in any variety of vehicles or on foot – Giff had discovered that he actually preferred random and directionless exploration to the confines of the plot, however sprawling that storyline was. He had strayed from his latest mini-mission several weeks ago, and hadn't returned to the storyline's path since. He wondered now if he ever would.

Giff had been introduced to the game *Grand Theft Hovercar* by Donny, a much younger coworker in the same department at Fukuda Bioforms. The two men, both of them born here on the planet Oasis as the descendants of colonists from Earth, worked in the "love organs" division, managing and shipping out inventory. Love organs were bioengineered pets that functioned as living sex toys, all but mindless and hence always willing to accommodate their owners. There were numerous varieties: some like a phallus, others with openings like a vagina or anus, others with a phallus on one end and orifice on the other, and in every skin tone from Kalian gray to Sinanese blue. Love organs could go a long time without being injected with sustenance, but not indefinitely, so Giff and Donny and the other worker in their area, Beau, had to be sure the inventory shipped out promptly. No customer wanted to open a cheerily colorful plastic box to find a rotting love organ inside.

When he had first started at Fukuda Bioforms Giff had thought the work might be fun, because of the whimsical products he dealt with, but like all the jobs he had worked at over nearly four decades it had proved tedious, dispiriting, and financially inadequate.

The day Donny first told him about *Grand Theft Hovercar*, they had been busy in the early morning preparing several pallets for the robot lift to bring down to the shipping dock. The men had stacked the boxes – filled with patiently inert love organs – on the pallets themselves, rather than have the robot palletize them, more out of boredom than anything else. But later there was a long lull in filling new orders and investigating late orders, all the inventory reconciled for the time being, and so they had stood around talking while Beau slipped away early to the company gym.

"I've played a few games set in a VR Punktown before," Giff told the enthusiastic young man, who had just related how caught up he was in this new game. "VR Miniosis and some Earth cities, too. Of course, that's over ten years ago."

"Oh come on, ten years ago . . . you should see *this* game! Like, you can pick up a candy wrapper off the ground . . . smooth it out and read the small print. You can *feel* the wrinkles in the plastic. You can *smell* the chocolate that was inside."

"So," Giff lowered his voice, smiling, lest any female coworkers nearby should overhear them, "the prosties . . . pretty real, huh?"

"Realer than real! But not just AI prosties; you can have sex with the avatars of other players, and man . . ." Donny trailed off, grinning, his eyes gleaming feverishly. "But I'll get to that, I'll get to that. I want to tell you about the *world*, how *huge* it is. Bigger than any VR Punktown before. I mean, not only does it have every single location in Punktown right down to the most obscure utility chute in Subtown . . . the game lets players map their own apartments and add them to the game, so anyone can go inside. If the person doesn't want to let you into their apartment, though, maybe you can find a way to break inside. I added my apartment, but I don't live there; I hacked my way into a beautiful apartment in Beaumonde Square, when the owner was out, and I changed the code on his door so he can't get back inside." Donny laughed wildly. "And there are thousands and thousands of players in Punktown, so the places you can go . . . it's like infinite in possibilities."

Giff was very intrigued by that line. Infinite in possibilities. A sense of infinite possibilities would be a refreshing thing to experience, wouldn't it? An intoxicating thing.

That night, in his own little cell-like apartment where he lived alone except for a love organ he had smuggled home from work a few months back, he pasted ultranet interface disks to his temples, connected with the site that produced *Grand Theft Hovercar*, and paid for a connection to the game.

He connected every evening as soon as he'd had a bite to eat. Sometimes he skipped eating, in his anxiousness to get inside the virtual replica of the city nicknamed Punktown that he lived in. He'd eat something in the game, in some restaurant he couldn't afford out here. His body would be tricked into feeling fulfilled. Later, before he went to bed for a few hours before another stultifying day at work, he'd throw together a quick snack of junk food.

He liked to wander in a different section of the city each night. One night he might explore the neighborhood he'd grown up in. Staring up at his old apartment building from the sidewalk, he'd almost expect to see younger versions of his mother or father come to the windows and look down at him in turn. He tried to revisit their old flat but found that it hadn't been mapped and added to the game, though he could stand in the hallway right outside the door.

His father was dead, now, and his mother lived in a retirement community. He had no desire to go to its virtual equivalent. It was depressing enough in reality.

Another night he might venture into a section of the city he would never dare visit in real life, such as Warehouse Way with all its derelict factories and warehouses. In such a place, he would be attacked by AI muggers and mutants but also the avatars of other players, and he had acquired virtual weapons with which to defend himself.

Some hardcore players chose a game mode so immersive that they could even experience the sensation of physical pain in such altercations – though *Grand Theft Hovercar* set a limit on how much pain could be had in this way. Giff's heart always beat madly and adrenaline flushed through him during any such violent encounter; in the back of his mind lurked the knowledge that occasionally people did die in reality from experiencing death in the ultranet – though only by suffering heart failure or an aneurysm, not via imaginary gunfire or illusory car crashes. He himself chose a setting that permitted him to feel only practical and pleasurable physical sensations. He didn't care for pain.

Punktown was so vast a city that, though he had lived there fifty-odd years, there were parts of it he had never seen before the game. He might ride a hovertrain on its repulsor rails or a shunt on its overhead cable to some remote area to explore, but more likely he would steal a hovercar, riding low to the ground, or fly high above the streets in a helicar, speeding crazily between the city's monolithic towers on a network of unseen navigation beams while other vehicles honked at him in alarm.

In real life he'd never owned a helicar. Tonight he had stolen a classic Icarus, aqua with chrome trim and big dual fans. But he kept sideswiping other helicars recklessly and scraping along the flanks of buildings, until he finally brought the poor thing down – dented and trailing smoke – on a rooftop landing pad and abandoned it there. Taking the elevator, he descended to street level to continue his meandering, aimless questing on foot.

He would stop to say hello to other people on the sidewalk; humans like himself, or other races who had also colonized Punktown, many far from human. From such brief interactions it was impossible to tell which were AI and which were players like himself. These people might greet him with surprising exuberance and warm smiles, such as one might not so readily encounter on the actual streets of Punktown, surprising Giff and making him feel oddly grateful (though these were probably the AI). He was always ready for the person who spoke rudely, though. That was why he said hello to so many strangers . . . to flush out such people, and react to them. It was a way to vent frustration after his long day at work.

When he emerged from the building he'd landed the helicar on, he saw a tall and attractive young woman with spiky black hair and glowing blue lipstick strutting past on the sidewalk in click-clacking high heels. In real life he would be too self-conscious of his age and shabby appearance to approach her, but he had designed his game avatar to resemble Marcel Valentin, a popular actor who often played gangsters. Thus, he strode after her and said in Marcel's tough guy voice, "Hey, sweetness, where you off to in such a hurry?"

The woman stopped and turned to face him, pillow-like blue lips bunched distastefully. "*Ooh* . . . Marcel Valentin. How original." Then she twirled away to continue click-clacking along the sidewalk. "Blast off, you sorry wanker."

Giff figured her for a player, not AI. It was hard to synthesize such pure contempt. Into his hand popped a combat knife, and he skipped after the strutting woman to punch the blade once, all the way, into her lower back.

She fell forward onto the sidewalk, crying out shrilly, "Hey!"

Giff bolted, glancing back only once to see that she had rolled onto her side in pooling blood and was lifting her arm to call for the forcers on her tacky gem-encrusted wrist comp. Other pedestrians were reporting the attack on their wrist comps, too. If the avatar didn't first die from her wound, she'd be taken to a hospital to be healed. If she did die before help came, the player would be signed out of the game and would have to log in again. Ha!

He ducked into an alley, found its far end blocked by a chain link fence. He scrambled up and over it, dropped to the other side in a lot that had once been occupied by a tenement building, since torn down and replaced with heaps of junk and trash as if the structure had exploded into this chaotic rubble. He ducked down close to the stripped and burnt shell of a hovercar, near the center of the lot, and waited as he heard sirens approach. He huddled so close to the car's husk he could smell its scorched surface. Eventually, a black helicar floated by above, sweeping its spotlights below, probably sweeping invisible scanner beams as well, but they did it half-heartedly because most of the forcers in the game were AI, and even in real life forcers would be lackadaisical due to the sheer volume of crime in Punktown.

The black helicar drifted away soon enough, and Giff emerged from cover, continuing to the other side of the empty lot and entering another narrow alleyway, so as to make his way onto a major street again.

There was a pale yellow glow in this tight alley, radiating onto one wall from the wall opposite, almost like light from a curtained window, but there was no window in the alley. As he drew nearer, Giff saw it was graffiti, which was by no means remarkable in Punktown, sprayed in luminous yellow paint. Some type of glyph, which he assumed must be the identifying symbol for a gang . . . from the looks of it, a gang of beings from one of the other planets or dimensions who had made this gigantic metropolis their home.

Yet as common as graffiti was, Giff still found himself stopping to gaze at the symbol, as if its crooked ends had snagged his eyes like fishhooks. It was as he was staring at the glyph that a voice came to him from a heap of trash bags piled against the wall directly below the symbol.

The voice, sounding like something between croak and regurgitation, said, "You've found the Yellow Sign."

Startled, Giff looked down to see those weren't a jumble of trash bags, after all, but a bulky figure slumped against the wall, no doubt a homeless person or mutant addled by drugs or drink. A head covered in a floppy wide-brimmed hat lifted, and Giff saw a puffy white face beneath it. He had seen many a grotesque mutant in Punktown, so he didn't know why this bloated bleached face should unnerve him so, but he immediately turned away from it and plunged out of the alley onto the street, like a drowning man bursting up into the air.

He resented the fear and disgust the figure had inspired in him, and was tempted to produce his handgun and return to the alley to pump the mutant full of virtual bullets, but a glance back at the shadowed corridor dissuaded him. In the fungal luminescence of the glyph, the mutant was an amorphous black mound with a pale white circle floating at the top, which turned toward him. The face's unseen eyes on him felt like a slimy caress on naked skin.

Giff swiftly moved off down the sidewalk to pursue other adventures.

"I've met this girl," Donny whispered to Giff at work, when Beau had gone into a neighboring department to chitchat with a friend there. Beau, closer to Giff's age, was a little straight-laced – though even he had started taking interest in listening to Donny rhapsodizing about *Grand Theft Hovercar*. "I really like her, man."

"You mean . . . in the game?" Donny had been married for less than a year.

"Yeah yeah, in the game. She's beautiful, *gorgeous*, with this pristine white skin like . . . like *snow*. She's like a statue come to life, Giff. She's a Carcosan."

"A what?"

"From Carcosa – it's a planet."

"Yeah? I've never heard of any Carcosa or Carcosans."

"Hey, there are new races popping up in Punktown all the time.

Anyway, I've taken her to my nice new Beaumonde Square apartment a few times, and . . . ohhh man." Donny wagged his head, grinning, but then his grin lost its foothold. "I'm sorry now I got married to Tessy so fast. I'm still young, y'know? She doesn't seem too happy, either. Lately I've even been thinking . . . maybe we should just get divorced."

"Whoa, Donny," Giff said. He'd had a wife once. Many times he'd regretted their divorce, though in his case it hadn't been his decision. "Hold on, now. There's no reason to throw away your real life relationship to pursue a virtual relationship. Can't you just keep doing that on the side?"

"Yeah, but you don't understand . . . Tessy's always complaining about the time I spend in *GTH*. It's getting hard to enjoy it like I should."

"Well, maybe you are playing it too much, from the sound of it."

"And you're not?"

Giff ignored that comment. "This Carcosan girl . . . is she an AI, or a player?"

"I don't know," Donny said. After a thoughtful pause he added, "I guess I don't care."

The next day Beau announced that he had taken the plunge and bought himself a connection to the *Grand Theft Hovercar* universe, too. Giff only smiled, but Donny whooped and clapped him on the shoulder. "Join the club, Beau! Now you can come to work with only three or four hours sleep, too, and a headache from listening to your wife bitch your ears bloody."

At Donny's insistence, Beau finally shyly described the avatar he had customized: a much younger man bulging with muscles. "I didn't make him *too* huge, though," Beau explained, "because I want to take him to the gym, in there, and bulk him up gradually."

"Sounds fun!" Donny said. Then he bugged his eyes. "Hey! Guys!

The three of us should meet up in *GTH* sometime, right? And go for some beers?"

Giff agreed, though he thought it was funny that the three of them had never done that in real life.

Giff stayed up too late playing the game, allowing himself only a forty-five minute nap before he was up again and showering for work. He'd thought maybe the nap, and an energy capsule washed down with black coffee, might be enough to help him slog through the day, but slouching in the shower he decided to call in sick. He sent a message to his manager, Pierre. Rather than return to bed, though, after he finished his coffee he sat down in front of his computer again, reaffixed the ultranet interface disks to the sides of his head, and delved back into the replica of Punktown.

Today he decided to revisit the neighborhood he had been living in twenty years ago, when he was still married. He visited it often enough in the real world, so he was very familiar with it, but he was curious to see how the facsimile compared. It was a fairly well-to-do area, too (he'd had a somewhat better job back then, and his wife had also been doing well), so he could also rob some local pedestrians for decent money with which to buy more ammunition for his guns.

He was also saving virtual money in case he wanted to put down rent on a nice apartment. He hadn't mapped his real-life apartment. He didn't want people getting inside it – strangers, or potentially nosy acquaintances like Donny – and seeing how tiny, dirty, and cluttered it was, maybe going through his personal belongings and discovering his love organ inching along the floor like a caterpillar.

From his last saved point, he rode toward his destination in a powerful Warper hovercar, but in speeding along maniacally he smashed it up against other cars until its belly began to scrape the pavement as it floated along. He abandoned it, carjacked a fluorescent orange Razer hovercar instead, and rode the rest of the way in that. When he arrived, he left the once-beautiful Razer, dented and scratched, by the curb.

He walked along the sidewalk, saying hello to passersby, waiting to see if someone would prompt him to attack them and take their money (perhaps leading ultimately to a massive standoff with forcers, which was always good fun, though it always resulted with his death and having to sign back into the game). He was restless for a woman, too. This wasn't the best location to find a prosty, but prosties were everywhere in Punktown.

He wondered if his ex-wife ever played this game, and if so, if she too would be nostalgically drawn back to this area. Would he even recognize her if he passed her on the street? What younger actress or singing star might she choose as an avatar? Knowing her tastes in films and music, that might be the only way to spot her. He hadn't seen her in the flesh for over a decade.

Up ahead, as he walked on, Giff spotted a holographic sign floating in the air in front of a building's brick face. The sign, in glowing yellow letters, read *Imperial Dynasty*. He slowed his pace, his brow rumpled. Strange; he didn't recall any such establishment from this neighborhood he knew so well. It could have sprung up only very recently, though: the map of *Grand Theft Hovercar* was kept up-to-date on a real-time basis.

He stopped in front of the establishment, which had a large window facing onto the sidewalk. With a name like *Imperial Dynasty*, he figured it might be a Chinese restaurant. He peered through the window.

The room beyond was full of tables, at which people were sitting, but no lights appeared to be on . . . so that only the people at the tables closest to the window could be seen somewhat clearly. For all he could tell from out here, the room full of figures seated at little circular tables might stretch back for miles . . . to infinity. Everyone's clothing was either darkened by the gloom or black, and every white face was turned to stare back at Giff through the window. Otherwise, the figures were immobile. Might they be mannequins in some kind of shop display, and not restaurant customers?

All those pallid faces, though vague, put Giff in mind of that derelict mutant who had spoken to him in the alley. A shudder buzzed through him, and he spun away from the window so abruptly that he almost collided with a woman who was walking briskly along the sidewalk.

Giff watched her walk away from him. She wore a silk dress that snugly encased her slender body, black with a gold pattern of what he took to be stylized flowers, though they might have been something else. Because it reminded him of a high-collared Chinese dress, and because her short bobbed hair was so very black, and even because he had thought he was standing in front of a Chinese restaurant, he had the impression the woman might be of Asian descent . . . though he couldn't see her face. The way her body moved in her tight silk dress caused him to start walking after her instantly, the darkened room of motionless figures sliding from his mind.

She was sexy, no question, but he had the sense she wasn't a prosty. There was an elegance about her, almost like something regal that he couldn't put his finger on. He hastened his step but somehow couldn't quite catch up to see her face. It didn't seem appropriate to call out to her in Marcel Valentin's voice, "Hey sweetness," but he wanted to catch her attention, so instead he said politely, "Excuse me, miss?" Anything to get her to stop, turn, show him her face. It must be as beautifully, snowy white as her slim arms and legs.

"I'm sorry, I have to hurry," the woman said without slowing or looking around at him. "I'm going to see the play."

"The play?" Giff still couldn't catch up with her strides, although she was petite so her legs weren't long, and he was all but jogging by now.

"You should see it, too," she said.

"Uh . . . where is it?" he asked, just to keep her talking with him.

"It's all over the city," she called back to him, as she turned the corner of the street.

The pedestrian traffic grew thick at the corner, where people were waiting for the lights to change at the crosswalk, and Giff hit a tangle of bodies. "Out of my way," he snarled, this time in the manner of Marcel Valentin, shoving his way through them, but when he rounded the corner he found the woman in the black dress with gold designs had disappeared.

"Well, look who decided to visit us today," Beau remarked when Giff walked into their department the next day, twenty minutes late.

Giff grunted, not in the mood. He'd only had two hours of sleep and was all out of energy capsules.

"Whatever you had yesterday must be catching," Beau went on. "Now Donny's out sick today."

"Oh, really?" Giff said.

"Yeah. But I think I know what you two are really suffering: an overdose of *Grand Theft Hovercar.*"

Giff grunted again.

Beau continued, "I'm sorry I spent all that money on it, myself – I think I'm going to stop, and maybe let my son take over my account."

Giff had been surprised that Beau had tried the game out in the first place. "Is your wife complaining about the time you spend on it?"

"Not really . . . I don't spend too much time on it . . . it's just that it's too weird for me."

"Weird?"

"Well, the last time I played this guy came running into the gym from the street, and started fighting with everyone, screaming and acting crazy. One of the other players had to kill him with a hand weight. The guy had no eyes, like someone tore them out . . . or maybe he did it to himself. He kept asking us if we saw the sign, or something like that. If we'd found the sign yet."

"You act like you haven't lived in Punktown your whole life."

"Exactly. I think I'd prefer a game that got me away from all the scary stuff in this city," Beau said.

Now, night after night, Giff found himself obsessed with finding that beautiful woman in the black and gold dress again. The impulse was so strong, and seemed so beyond his control, that he wondered if it was all part of the game's central storyline, trying to pull him back in.

He repeatedly checked the area where he'd first seen her, but couldn't find her again. He noticed that the hovering holographic sign reading *Imperial Dynasty* had vanished, and the room beyond the window was entirely swallowed in blackness, the people and even the tables he had seen previously now apparently all gone.

Yet one night as he was prowling in his search for the woman in the silk dress, as his stolen car crossed a high, elevated bridge he happened to look down at the street below and spotted the luminous yellow letters that spelled out *Imperial Dynasty*, hovering in front of another building with a large dark window out front. Was it a chain of restaurants, then, or the same business . . . hopping from one location to another around the city? As restless, perhaps, as he was.

He always entered Fukuda Bioforms through one of the Employees Only side doors, but today when he'd parked his brand new fluorescent pink Razer and walked to the entrance, he realized he didn't have his company ID card on him. He asked the door scanner to read his face and voice, but it didn't respond. Probably a glitch. Frustrated, he decided to try the building's main entrance instead. It was a large structure, so as he turned away he was prepared for a bit of a walk, but he had only taken a few steps when a series of loud cracks caused him to flinch to a stop.

He looked toward the parking lot, and saw a figure walking between the vehicles, carrying a bulky assault engine – the kind of military weapon that could fire solid projectiles, beams, shotgun pellets, even mini rockets from its various muzzles. He knew this, because he often used one himself in *GTH*, usually when fighting forcers or street gangs. This person had set the gun to single-action fire, solid bullets, and was pumping rounds into the parked vehicles as he maneuvered between them. Windshields erupted into crystalline sprays, black holes popping open in the vehicles' hoods and flanks. Giff realized the man was laughing wildly as he fired.

The man turned his head and noticed that Giff was rooted in place, staring in stunned disbelief. That was when Giff recognized it was Donny.

"Hey, Giff!" Donny called to him. "Have you found the Yellow Sign yet? It changes the whole game, man . . . it changes *everything!*"

Giff held up his hands as Donny started walking toward him. He wanted to whirl away and make a run for it, but was afraid to set the younger man off. "Come on, Donny . . . easy, guy."

"I'm glad you're here, Giff." Donny kept coming. "You understand! You're addicted, too." Grinning, he turned the big gun around in his hands. "Hey, watch this, man . . . the sign wants to get inside us . . . you got to let it in!"

He stopped about ten feet from Giff, raised the assault rifle so that one of its muzzles pressed against his own forehead, and pulled one of its multiple triggers.

Giff jolted to consciousness.

He was slumped back on the love seat that could be folded out into his bed. The stink of excrement greeted him, and he realized his pajama pants were soiled, and thoroughly soaked with urine. So was the cushion he was seated on. "Oh God," he groaned, and in speaking discovered that his throat was as dry as a tube of cement. He stripped off his pajamas, dropped them into the trash zapper, and before stepping into the shower leaned over the sink to cup handfuls of water into his mouth. When at last he straightened, in the mirror he saw the ultranet interface disks stuck to his temples. He peeled them off.

No wonder he couldn't get into Fukuda Bioforms, he thought. For security purposes, of course the company wouldn't allow its interior to be mapped for *Grand Theft Hovercar*. Or had that been reality, after all, and he was now immersed in the game? No . . . no . . . this reflected face was his, not Marcel Valentin's. That was the only real way he could tell.

He showered, then emerged to stare at his love seat in disgust. Cleaning it would be a headache, but he couldn't afford replacing it right now.

Time. He glanced at a clock and groaned again; he was over an hour late to work. He was afraid to talk to his manager, Pierre, so he decided to call Beau and Donny to tell them he'd be in late. But his head pounded so much from the hunger that yowled in his belly, he knew it was better to just tell them he wouldn't be in today.

Before calling his friends on his computer's vidscreen, he went to put on a fresh t-shirt and sweatpants, and that was when he spotted his love organ curled on the worn carpet beside his bureau. It had blackened and shriveled in death, its taint of decomposition masked by the stench of his own waste.

He dumped the starved love organ into the trash zapper, too, then called his department at work.

Beau came on the screen, and immediately blurted, "God, Giff, you really had me worried! Where have you been?"

Only an hour late and Beau was this worked up? Trying not to sound irritated, Giff told him, "I feel horrible, Beau . . . can you tell Pierre I need the day off?"

"*Again?* Giff, I don't know if you're going to have a job left when you get back."

"What do you mean, 'again'?"

"This will be the fourth day in a row you've been out. Don't you know that? Are you on drugs or something, Giff? Do you even know about Donny? I was beginning to think the same thing happened with you. Pierre has been calling you and calling you . . . we were getting ready to come out there and look in on you."

"*Three days?*" Giff croaked in his still parched voice. Then his befuddled brain backed up a few steps. "Wait . . . what happened to Donny?"

"Oh God, you don't know. Oh God, Giff . . ."

"Tell me," Giff said. Though he did know, in fact. Had seen it, in fact.

"Donny shot himself yesterday. At home. He shot his poor wife Tessy first, and then he shot himself. He left some crazy note painted on the wall of his living room, I guess."

"Something about a . . . Yellow Sign?"

"I don't know, Giff; the forcers haven't released that to the public. Why, did he say anything to you about what was going on in his head?"

What was going *into* his head, Giff thought. "No," he replied.

"You know what I think was wrong with him? And what's wrong with you, too? It's that blasting game. I played it. . . .I know how crazy it is. Why do you think they announced they're shutting it down?"

"Shutting it . . . down?"

"You really have been out of it, huh? Yes, Giff. Go look at the news on the net. I think that game poisoned Donny, and it's poisoning you, and—"

Giff ended the call abruptly, and navigated to a popular news site on the standard net. He did a search on *Grand Theft Hovercar*, and right away came up with a press release from the company that had created the VR game. It was as Beau had said: effective immediately, the game was going to be made unavailable due to a virus that had somehow been introduced into it. Intentional sabotage was suspected, but was still unproven. The virus, which had not yet been pinned down, had created "unfortunate irregularities and distortions in game play."

"No," Giff said aloud as he read this announcement. He was distressed almost to the point of desperation. Shut down *Grand Theft Hovercar*? It was like hearing his own death sentence pronounced. At the very least, like hearing himself sentenced to live the rest of his life locked in a tiny cell, all his freedom forever denied.

He retrieved his interface disks from the corner of the bathroom sink, pasted them back on his temples, returned to his computer and tried logging on to the game.

He was successful.

Grand Theft Hovercar had other ideas about being shut down.

He was spawned in the game standing on a fire escape platform, three floors up from street level, at about twilight. He recognized the neighborhood: it was the mutant slum dubbed Tin Town, which was always a good place to go in the game if you wanted to end up fighting for your avatar's pseudo life.

He wasn't alone on the fire escape. Beside him, even more out of place in this neighborhood than himself, the woman in the gold-patterned black silk dress leaned against the railing looking down at a vacant lot directly below. His heart sitting up like an eager dog, Giff moved to the railing alongside her, but a curved wing of her glossy bobbed hair shielded the side of her face from his view.

She pointed below. She said, "The play has already started."

Though he hated to take his eyes off her, Giff followed her graceful gesture.

It didn't look like a play to him; more like some kind of ritualistic dance. A dozen mutants cavorted below, in a circle, as if drunk or insane or both. Their afflictions varied wildly. One had eight or more stick-like, crooked limbs hanging out of its torso, thrashing as if to some unheard music. Another's head looked composed of a bunch of giant, flesh-colored grapes. The blighted beings shared only two things in common. All twelve of them were naked, and all of them bore on their forehead (or what approximated a forehead) an identical glyph, the symbol Giff had seen painted in the alley, glowing yellow against their skin like a holograph. Glowing like a fiery brand.

The woman turned toward Giff directly, at last. As he had imagined it, her face was perfection, her white skin flawless as porcelain, though her eyes were not Asian as he had expected. Rather, they were two empty black apertures such as the eyeholes in a mask, with infinity behind them. Giff was flooded full with devotion. What greater freedom was there than infinity?

"We need one more player," she said to him.

She placed a fingertip against his forehead, and traced a figure there. Though Giff couldn't see it, he felt the yellow heat radiating from his skin.

Wearing a hard bright grin, like a knife blade laid across his face, Giff began descending the metal steps of the fire escape, peeling off his clothing as he went.

THE GIRL WITH THE STAR-STAINED SOUL

Lucy A. Snyder

This is the second adventure for young Penny Farrell. In "The Abomination of Fensmere" (a tale that appears in Hazardous Press' *Shadows Over Main Street*) her dead mother's relatives lured her down south to serve as a virgin sacrifice in a ritual to summon the Elder Ones. She escaped her brush with Yog-Sothoth with her mind (mostly) intact, but now she must face a whole new horror here in *The Court of the Yellow King.* . . .

azed, Penny stumbled through the gray ash and blasted debris. Charred human fat stained the fractured rocks of the old stone church. Blackened bones jumbled with the splintered charcoal of the pine roof beams. Most all the men of Fensmere, Mississippi lay dead around her, and many of its womenfolk, too. She spied a bit of wrought iron candelabra here, a burned scrap of a Klansman's hood there.

She looked up at the broken wall where the skylight had been, and the Reverend Houghton's order reverberated in her mind: *"Brothers, place her beneath the stars!"*

The girl shuddered and hugged herself as she remembered the cold touch of the old gods probing her mind, examining the Earth through her memory and dismissing her world as unripe fruit. But their thronging dark minions had clamored to devour the planet, and Penny had seen through the old gods' eyes what terrible, craven, worthless creatures humankind was, and the darkest power of the cosmos had flowed into her, and she could have opened the doorway to let the minions in to end it all.

And for a moment, she'd considered it. It's what the Reverend – her own grandfather – had brought her here to do. Exactly a month after

Penny's mother's death, the Reverend's sister brought her to the family mansion for the summer under the guise of a family reunion. Instead, the Haughtons wrenched her mind open with the mad Arab's book, drugged her and kept her penned like a sacrificial calf until the night that the stars were right.

And she'd almost done it. She'd almost opened the door and let in creatures that would almost certainly end humanity. In those moments, she'd been the most powerful person on the planet, a living goddess, and yet still nothing more than a child trying to decide whether to open the latch for the stranger on her parents' porch.

Instead, she'd chosen to use the cosmic power surging through her to turn her body into a momentary sun. And with the coldest blood, she blasted the Invisible Empire cultists gathered around her to ashes.

Penny couldn't stop shivering. Her own mind had been overlaid with a new dark consciousness, a terrible inhuman logic. Was she a puppet now? A servant of one of the old gods that had briefly gazed upon her as a man might gaze upon a mote of dust? No, she finally decided. Her mind had been left to its own devices. But the cosmic fires had forged her soul into something new, and she was a stranger to herself.

And in that moment of realization, two things occurred to her simultaneously.

The first was that the Haughtons had almost certainly engineered her mother's fatal automobile crash. It could be no accident that the one adult in her life who'd kept her safe had been removed right when Penny was old enough for the ritual. They had the money and resources to make it happen, and it had been done. Her cold new overmind shone a light on her past, and Penny realized they'd probably arranged to have her father murdered, too.

The second thing Penny realized was that, had her nuclear physicist father lived, and had her mother not remarried a Christian man when Penny was just a toddler, she might be having her bat mitzvah this summer instead. Her parents would have thrown her a big party with cake and Peach Melba and all the friends Penny didn't have in her current life would have come to celebrate her becoming a daughter of the commandment under Jewish tradition. And her father would have given thanks that he could no longer be punished for her sins.

"I'm responsible now," she said to the dead who lay scattered around her, and she threw back her head and laughed, spinning in circles with her arms outstretched in the cold moonlight. "I'm responsible for everything!"

She spun and laughed and laughed and spun amongst the dust and bones and soon she was wailing, weeping to the stars that hung deaf and mute and harsh.

"Miss Penny!" a woman exclaimed.

The girl stopped spinning, blinking in bright headlights, and wiped at the muddy tracks her tears had made in the ashes on her cheeks.

"Who's there?" she called back.

Three figures stepped out of an old Hudson sedan, and when they came into the light she recognized Georgia and her daughter Bessie, both servants at the Haughton's mansion. The third was a strong-looking man a few years younger than Georgia, and they looked enough alike in face and build that Penny guessed they were kin. Penny knew Georgia and Bessie couldn't afford a car, so she guessed the truck belonged to him.

"Who are you?" she asked him.

"Name's Jay. I'm . . . I'm Georgia's brother." He was staring at his battered work boots, clearly averting his gaze. It was only then that Penny realized that her dress had been burned off in the blast.

The Klan would lynch any negroes found in Fensmere after dark, so Georgia and her family had taken a terrible risk coming to the old stone church . . . unless they'd been pretty sure the Klansmen were all dead. Penny guessed that blowing up the church made a bit of noise.

"Miss Penny, oh my goodness, where are your clothes?" Georgia fussed. "Bessie, go get the blanket!"

"Yes'm."

"But naked's better than dead, isn't that right?" Penny asked, fixing Georgia in a pointed stare, remembering the cups of drugged tea that Bessie had slipped through the food slot during her imprisonment in the mansion. "You knew damned well they meant for me to die here. And you didn't do anything to stop them."

"Miss Penny, I know you're angry." Georgia's voice shook. "But understand, we did as much as we could. Morinda can't be bothered to do nothin' on her own – she had me brew up the tea and I changed the recipe so your mind would be able to stand everything they put you through. I know we still put you in harm's way . . . but if we'd done more they'd have found out and lynched me and Bessie and probably burned a few houses in Bucktown as a warning."

"Changed it?" Penny replied, remembering the medicinal bitterness of the tea.

Bessie padded up with an old cotton blanket. Penny took it and wrapped it around herself.

"How did you know to change it?" Penny asked.

"This ain't the first time the Haughtons did this. They tried it with your momma back when she was just a few years older than you. A hoodoo woman from New Orleans come up to warn us what they planned to do, and she showed me what herbs to switch in and out. Your momma was able to hold off the star-devils when they put her on the cross, and we reckoned that if we made the tea right and said our prayers, you'd do the same."

The old theatre downtown, Penny thought. *So* that's *how it burned down.*

"Is the Reverend dead?" Georgia asked, looking anxious. "We need to know. If that evil old buzzard survived –"

"My grandfather is dead. Aunt Morinda, too," Penny replied. "Come see."

She led them over to a blasted corpse that still wore purple silk tatters of a Grand Dragon's robes. The fractured remains of a black, crablike creature still nested in his hipbones. Just as dead as the Reverend.

"Oh Jesus, what's that?" Bessie breathed, and her uncle muttered a prayer under his breath.

Georgia inhaled sharply but didn't react in terror like the other two; Penny figured that the older woman had either seen the abomination, or had guessed that it existed.

"It controlled him like a puppeteer," Penny said. "But I think he was perfectly willing to be used by it."

She turned to Georgia. "You said my mother wouldn't open a portal to the stars?"

Georgia shook her head. "She shut 'em down like you did. Only she just set a fire, and most everyone escaped."

"Then where did this thing come from?" Penny asked.

"I reckon he didn't have it before he went on that expedition in Arabia and came back with all those relics, like that evil book they left for you to find," Georgia replied.

"We better check the house," Penny replied, staring down at the broken black shell and curled arachnoid legs. "The thing about spiders and cockroaches is that if you see one, there's almost always another one somewhere."

Georgia nodded. "I recollect the movers brought in a lot of big crates, and they took them down to the basement. Morinda forbade me from going down there. I didn't want a caning so I never disobeyed her, but I know where she hides the key."

Early the next morning, Georgia let the four of them into the musty old mansion. Penny wore a clean shift and pair of Mary Janes she'd borrowed from Bessie. Jay carried a burlap sack laden with pry bars, rope, matches, candles, and a couple of flashlights.

"The Sherriff and his deputies were all Klan," she said as she shut the heavy oak doors behind them. "So I reckon they died at the church along with everything else. Everybody in Bucktown knows to sit tight. But some of the Fensmere womenfolk got left at home with their kids; sooner or later the state police will come 'round here asking questions. So we best find what we gonna find before then."

Nobody, it seemed, wanted to go to the cellar right away. So they went up to the Reverend's rooms on the third floor and searched every closet, drawer, and wardrobe. They found nothing out of the ordinary but some strange and oddly cold figurines carved from black stone. Every time Penny touched one, her mind flashed back on some horror she'd glimpsed among the stars.

"I think we have to go to the basement," Penny said, trying to work the feeling back into her numbed fingers.

Once they descended the long, curving staircase, they found themselves in a hidden warehouse beneath the mansion. Old-fashioned gas-lights guttered in sconces on the walls. Penny surveyed the boxes and old furniture with dismay; almost any number of creatures could be hiding down here.

But she realized that the hairs were standing up on the backs of her arms, and she could feel a low humming vibration from somewhere further into the basement. Penny led the others toward the faint sound, and they found an ancient Middle Eastern temple built from blocks and columns of black basalt crouched on the concrete floor. It was maybe fifteen feet tall, the peak of the terraced roof nearly flush with the basement ceiling, and probably twenty feet wide along each side.

The only thing upon it that was not a flat, oppressive black was a single bronze door at the top of a short flight of steps. Upon the gleaming metal was some strange symbol wrought from shining gold. When she gazed upon it, Penny shivered as she had amongst the dead cultists at the old stone church, and she guessed that whatever language it was written in was not one humans could comprehend.

"This thing gives me the heebie-jeebies," Jay said as they carefully circled the temple.

"They must have brought it in pieces and put it back together down here," Georgia said. "I don't see but the one door in or out."

"I'll go in," Penny said, responding to the others' unspoken question.

She might find nothing but darkness and dust inside the temple, but she might also find something that might utterly destroy her. In the back of her mind, she knew she hadn't yet come to grips with having slaughtered most of the town. They'd surely had it coming, but it was all still a sin on a massive scale, wasn't it? Even knowing the gods in the universe cared nothing at all for the human race wasn't enough to take the sting of guilt from what she'd done. Because if there was no gentle afterlife to hope for, then that meant the life here on Earth was the most precious thing of all. If her mind ever fully felt the gravity of the lives she'd snuffed out and the orphans she'd created, she wasn't sure that she'd care to go on living.

So, she would leave her fate to the black temple. She'd fight for her life, but if she wasn't strong enough to fend off whatever lurked inside, she'd take death as her due.

"Just . . . don't leave me down here, okay?" Penny added. "Wait for me to come back."

They nodded and gave her a flashlight and a crowbar. She walked up the steps, took a deep breath, and pulled open the heavy metal door. Her flashlight illuminated nothing but unadorned black walls inside the temple, but then something gold shone bright in the beam: another of the strange symbols, this one on the far wall.

Penny stepped inside, gripping the crowbar in case something came flying out at her from the darkness.

The floor beneath her gave way. She shrieked as she tumbled down a stone chute, first in darkness, and then in a blue, indistinct twilight –

– she fell onto her hands and knees on a hillside. Instead of grass, she'd landed on a thick mat of gray lichens.

"Clumsy!" her mother exclaimed.

Penny looked up into the strange woman's face and felt herself smile in recognition. "Sorry, Mama!"

Her mother helped her to her feet and they dusted the gray flecks of lichen off her clothes. These hands were not hers, nor the body. Inside this strange new self, Penny reeled. Everything was weird; the air had an unhealthy fungous taint to it, and in the sky – the sky! – there hung a trio of strange, misshapen moons, and opposite the setting sun three black stars rose, their bright coronas gleaming through the streaked clouds.

"Come, Cupra, we better hurry," her mother said. "Your father will be home soon."

The girl took the strange mother's hand and stepped back onto the rocky path toward home. Her old life as Penny and the horrors of Fensmere were rapidly fading away in her mind as if it had all been naught but a daydream; *this* is where she belonged, here in Carcosa with her loving mother and father. She remembered her childhood upon the moors and playing along the shore of the cloudy sea, of going out with her mother to pick herbs and fungus for food and dyeing cloth. Their baskets were full of the most precious mushrooms that produced the royal yellow dye, the colors of the mysterious King and his court, and woe would befall them should any of the nobles be displeased with their craft.

Cupra had heard tales of the King; the whole of Carcosa feared him. She'd seen his minions at the market in town and they were gaunt men and women with faraway stares, quick to anger and quicker to kill. Her parents told her that they were gentle as the spring wind compared to the King himself, and none could so much as look upon the King and maintain their sanity. Cupra had nightmares of the King sometimes, but when she was awake, a tiny part of her thought it must be very exciting to be one of the few who had seen him and lived to tell the tale.

It was nearly dark when she and her mother reached their hut upon the moors. Cupra got to work sorting the lichens and mushrooms onto their drying tables behind the fireplace, and her mother started chopping root vegetables for a stew.

The door banged open. "Ho! Where's my girl?"

"Papa!" Cupra sprang up from her workbench and ran to embrace her father. He caught her in a mighty bear hug, lifted her off her feet and swung her around as if she were a small child. His great red beard tickled her forehead.

The tiny part of her that was still Penny basked in the love like a seedling feeling sunlight for the first time. There in the cozy hut with the lovely smells of her mother's cooking, wrapped in the strong warmth of her father's arms, she was the happiest she had ever been in her life. In that perfect moment, it was as if a door inside her soul had been opened, a door that led to the best possible person she could be. She felt a joy as pure as gold and heady as whiskey.

But then she felt a chill, and there came a slow, thunderous knock at the door.

Her father set her down and quietly shooed her over to her mother's side.

"Who's there?" he called, gripping his hatchet.

The door blew open on a gust of icy air, and there stood the King in his scalloped tatters. A pallid mask obscured his features.

"It is I," the dread King replied in a voice that made Cupra want to tear her ears from her skull. "I have come for new fabric."

"It . . . it's not ready yet, my liege," her mother said, her voice trembling.

"That is . . . unfortunate." The King made the barest motion of his hand, and her mother's and father's heads split right down their middles as if they'd been cleaved with invisible mattocks. They fell where they stood, their dark blood spilling across the tidy floorboards.

Cupra wanted to scream, wanted to run, but she found herself rooted to the spot, unable to utter anything but a faint strangled noise.

The King moved toward her, so smoothly it seemed he floated like a ghost. "It's a dangerous thing to fall into the path of a living god, but then you'd know that, wouldn't you, little changeling? Little dimension-hopper. Little murderess."

"Why?" she managed to gasp, staring down at the bodies of her parents.

"Your Lord works in mysterious ways." He took off the pallid mask, and she recoiled from the monstrosity she saw beneath it. But the worst was his eyes: they were the same terrifying black as the dark stars she'd seen upon the horizon.

He leaned down and gave her a kiss, and suddenly that dreadful darkness was flowing into her mouth, down her throat, filling her very core, and she knew this was a living curse.

She stumbled back, retched, but the darkness would not leave her, and when she looked up again, the King was gone, and she was alone with her slaughtered parents.

Her world destroyed, Cupra fled. Where could she go? Her mother's sister lived in Carcosa City. Perhaps she would take mercy on her. The girl ran two miles to the city of tall towers, but the guards at the wall barred her entrance.

"You bear the curse of the King, and you may not enter," the first guard told her, solid and immoveable as a stone in his gray uniform.

"But he killed my parents; where can I go?" she pleaded.

"Go find someone who could love the likes of you," the second guard said. "But that is surely not here."

Despondent, Cupra turned away from the city gate, but a beggar in grimy rags called out, "Hoy, girl!"

Cupra approached the beggar. "Yes?"

"Lost your parents, did you?" His tone was sympathetic.

Cupra nodded, heartbroken.

"Go to the kingdom of the South. The King and Queen there are known to love all who enter their realm."

And so Cupra walked for days and weeks, living off what edible lichens she could find, drinking what dew she could collect in leaf-funnels overnight. The darkness inside her was as heavy as a mountain; she felt she was always a moment away from tears, but as time wore on it became harder and harder to cry. Sometimes, she'd come to a town and try to find a doorway to sleep in or a scrap of discarded bread, but a guard would always find her and chase her outside the city limits.

She was but skin and bones when she reached the border of the Southern kingdom. As she crested the hill outside the kingdom's gates, her eyes widened as she beheld the line of ragged people on the red carpet that stretched across the barren valley below her, all waiting to be admitted to the green meadows and fruit-heavy orchards beyond the gates.

Cupra climbed down the hill and took a spot at the back of the line, half expecting the people around her to start pointing at her and shout her away back into the wilderness, but nobody did. The others were just as thin and ragged as she, just as travel-weary, just as desperate. They couldn't see past their own miseries long enough to realize that she'd been cursed.

The line moved forward, but it soon seemed people were just pressing up against the front gates rather than moving through. The crush of bodies made her nervous, made her think about abandoning the line entirely, but she heard beastly howling and realized that someone had released huge dire wolves that were pacing just beyond the red carpet, eyeing the people hungrily. Each monstrous canid wore a red, brass-spiked collar decorated with the royal crest of the Southern kingdom.

"Prospective citizens!" called a woman, her voice floating like music over the crowd.

Cupra looked up, and her breath caught in her throat. Atop the kingdom gates stood a man and a woman dressed in silver and silken sky blue robes, and they were both the most beautiful people she had ever seen. In that moment, Cupra had hope that if she could just be in the same room as the King and Queen of the South, she might find her happiness again, and the curse of the King in Yellow might be lifted.

"We are honored that so many of you wish to join our kingdom," the handsome king said.

"We are a kingdom of love, and once you step through our gates, you shall need nothing else!" the beautiful queen declared. "You will never be hungry or thirsty again, because you shall not need food in our land, only our love."

"Therefore, to prepare yourself, we ask only that you remove that which you shall not need."

Two soldiers carrying large leather sacks began traveling down the line handing something out to each person in the line. Cupra wondered what it could be until a soldier pressed the handle of a very sharp knife into her hand. She stared down at the shining blade, wondering dumbly what she was supposed to do with it.

"Do you love us?" asked the queen.

"We love you!" cried the crowd.

"Do you want our love?" asked the king.

"Yes!" the starving people moaned.

"Then hollow yourselves," the queen ordered. "Be rid of your distasteful entrails. Hollow yourselves, and we shall fill you with our love."

A man near the front of the line screamed.

Another cried out, "Ah, it hurts, my queen!"

"If your love for us is true, you will be strong, and you will survive! Only those whose love is false and weak shall fall and be fed to the wolves."

Shrieks and wails rose all around Cupra as the desperate people began to hollow themselves in hopes of gaining the love of the beautiful king and queen. The darkness inside her ached like molten lead as she stared down at the knife blade. All around her, people fell to the rocky ground outside the red carpet – now, finally, she knew why it was red – and she could hear the snarling and rending of bone and flesh as the dire wolves put those who hadn't quite managed to hollow themselves out of their misery.

"Girl."

She looked up, and a blue uniformed soldier upon a dappled gray warhorse loomed above her. He pointed his crossbow at her. "Don't you feel the love?"

"Yes," she replied. "I do feel it."

Cupra plunged the blade into her belly, and the darkness spewed forth from her wound, the darkness of a million poisoned stars, and it flooded the whole landscape, sweeping away the soldiers and wolves and miserable people. The gorgeous king and queen screamed and tried for higher ground but there was none to be found, and they, too, were swept away in the black ocean.

Finally, the darkness receded, and Cupra stood alone in the wasteland, mutely clutching her wound.

Alone but for the King in Yellow at her side.

"Well done, my child," he said. "Carcosa has but one King, and I shall stand for no others."

He paused. "Tell me, child. You came here as your last hope, and you found nothing but death. Is your spirit broken? Have you lost all faith?"

"Yes," she whispered.

"Good," he replied. "Then I have one last task for you. I've been to that planet of yours, and I think I'd like it best if the only sounds were the wind in the dead trees and the waves crashing upon empty shores."

He gave her a shove. The ground opened beneath her and she tumbled into a great dark chasm –

– Penny landed hard on her back inside the temple, trying to pull the crablike creature off her face.

Just relax and open your mouth, it whispered inside her mind. *Be a good girl and it'll all be over soon.*

Keeping her mouth clamped shut, Penny struggled to the bronze door and kicked it open.

"Oh, sweet Jesus!" she heard Jay exclaim.

"Don't just stand there; help her!" Georgia shot back.

The others finally pried the creature off her, and they beat it to death on the concrete with crowbars and baseball bats while Penny coughed and gasped for breath.

"Miss Penny, are you all right?" Georgia asked after it was clear the creature was dead.

She nodded, rubbing her throat.

"What do you reckon you want to do now?" Bessie asked.

"We can't ever let anyone go in there ever again." Penny nodded toward the basalt temple.

"Should we get some bars to put across the door?" Georgia asked.

"We should burn it," Penny told the women who had labored in the mansion for years in near slavery. "Burn down the whole place to the ground and if it leaves a hole we fill it with concrete."

"Why, bless your heart. I believe that'd be my pleasure to do that very thing."

THE PENUMBRA
OF EXQUISITE FOULNESS

TIM CURRAN

Camilla: Oh please, please don't unwrap it! I can't bear it!

Cassilda: (Setting the wriggling bundle before them.) We must. He wants us to see.

Camilla: I won't look. I refuse.

Cassilda: It squirms like an infant, but how soft it is— like a worm.

Camilla: Its lips move . . . but it makes no sound. Why doesn't it make a sound?

Cassilda: (Giggling now.) It cannot. Its mouth is filled with flies.

The King in Yellow, Act I, Scene 4.

In chaos, I found purpose. In bedlam, there was purity of vision. That is the skin of my story. And the blood and meat of my little tale is that you can only hide from insanity *within* the cloak of insanity. This will make precious little sense to those of you who've never opened the book—blessed are the meek and ignorant—but to those of you who have (and you are many, aren't you?) it will make all the sense in this world . . . and out of it.

Now let me confess, let me expose the yellowed bones of my tale. Once the idea occurred to me, I had no choice but to see it through and do those things that were demanded of me. Let's call it a cold, blind compulsion. That will sit easier with most. A mental derangement, an insanity, a stark mania. With that in mind, listen: on a perfectly ordinary Tuesday morning, I gave baby Marcus a bath. I sudsed him up and rinsed him thoroughly because a clean baby, so soft and pink and fine-smelling, was a happy baby. As he gooed and gurgled, the madness pierced me like hot needles. I tried to shake it from my head and I tried to shiver it from my body. But I couldn't get rid of it anymore than I could shed my own skin. So, I leaned there against the tub, a sweat that was foul-smelling and cool running from my pores.

It was communion. Something—I dare not say what—had made me part of it. I had been named, chosen. And in my head, a voice, a very soft and smooth voice said to me, *The King comes now. He comes for what is his and you are made ready.*

In my head, a fathomless darkness sucked my mind into nether regions and I saw black stars hanging over a gutted landscape. My hands were no longer my own but instruments of something malevolent that crowded the thoughts from my brain. They—the hands, looking jaundiced and almost *scaly* in the weak bathroom fluorescents—seized Marcus by the throat and held him beneath the sudsy water until he stopped moving, until his cherubic face was erased and replaced with that of a bluing corpse-child, lips blackening and pink skin mottled, eyes like staring black holes looking straight into the vortex of my soul.

Once the act was complete, I sat there, tears running down my face.

Sobbing and whimpering, I studied the hands that had just murdered my darling little boy. I studied them in detail, knowing they were not my hands but those of another, one that did not belong but crept in silent, silken moonlight. Baby Marcus sank like a rock. That is crude, but perfectly descriptive. He would resurface, I knew, when the time was right. And in my horror, I could almost envision that moment: his puckered face breaking the tepid, bubbly water like lips parting, his voice cutting deep into my brain like a scalpel.

The hot needles burning deeper, fed by the kindling of unspeakable guilt, I opened my wrists with a razor, staring at the corpse of my baby drifting like a swollen dead cod at the bottom of the tub. As blood bubbled from my gashed arteries in scarlet rivulets and freshets, I dipped a skeletal white digit into the ragged, spurting inkwell of my left wrist until it was dyed a brilliant red. The vibrancy of my glistening fingertip fascinated me. Without further ado, while the ink of life was still wet and running, I sketched out the form of a simple stick man on the white tile wall of the bathroom in slashes of crimson. It wasn't until I had drawn in the ruby blobs of its eyes and the tattered mantle blowing out from it that I began to scream. For it was then that my stick figure became something much more and I saw it move as it has moved in my nightmares ever since.

As I slowly came out of it, there was panic. Night-winged panic that filled my brain like mulling bats. It filled my mind until it seemed I had no mind. Grimly, with great burning intensity, I held onto my sanity as reality flew apart inside my head and out of it. I screamed again. I must have screamed for I heard a voice echoing amongst the black and uneasy stars that pressed in from all sides. The walls of the room were gone. And when I looked up, there was no ceiling, there was no roof above, only the inverted sickle of a scarlet moon dripping its black blood onto my face.

Later, after my neighbor called 911, I was stitched-up—much against my feeble will. My neurotic soul sought death and death was denied it. So be it. I was held in the psych ward where I regularly had to be heavily sedated and restrained because I saw the haunted onyx eyes of the cold dead thing in the tub and they created a grim alchemy in my brain. I told the staff feverishly about *The King in Yellow*, how Act II had thrown open the doors of nightmare perception and plunged me screaming into a phobic void. But they would not listen. And the more they would not hear my words, the more certain I was that they already knew them.

I was incarcerated, of course. While the courts decided what to do with me, I underwent some two months of recuperation and intensive therapy. At the close of which, I was brought before the police psychiatrist for yet another interview.

"Why?" he asked me. "Why did you do it?"

"If you have to ask that, then it's beyond your understanding."

He smiled gently as if I was something to be pitied. "Enlighten me."

"Enlightenment is dangerous."

He had no idea how close he was to the abyss and I would not be the one to give him the final push. I studied the scars on my wrists. They had healed into pink whorls, spiraling pink whorls that captured the eye and drew it deeper into Archimedean complexity. It was there that I saw that which no man or woman should ever see: the Sign. It was sketched on each wrist in an intricate weal of healed flesh. Once my eyes had discovered it, I could not look away. It owned me and I knew that my service to the King had only just begun.

The police psychiatrist pegged me with questions, of course. He was intrigued that Marcus's father—dear, lost David—had committed suicide and that I had no family and no friends. He was only doing his job and I tried to be helpful. I did not want to involve him in the greater cosmic horror of the things I knew to be true, the things that had forced David to put a noose around his throat. Keeping with that, I kept my wrists out of view and when he asked questions whose answers might be dangerous to him, I remained mum. But he was insistent. As he jabbed, I parried. It was exhausting subterfuge, but in the end I would not confess the secret of the Hyades.

My next stop, of course, was prison. I was sentenced to ten to fifteen years. I was not alone there; many of the women had killed their own children and some had killed the children of others. At night, they would rage and cry and beg God for deliverance but there was never any deliverance. There was only the cool concrete silence winding out interminably.

One night, as I lay there beaded in the sweat of fear that the darkness always brought, a drug trafficker named Mother McGibb started calling out to God for forgiveness. Not just for herself, but for all the animals in all the cages squatting in the dirty straw of their lives. And maybe He heard her because a violent storm gripped the prison in its teeth. The more Mother cried out for divine intervention, the more the torrential fury outside built. The wind screamed and sheets of lightning flashed in the sky as rain lashed those high gray walls.

"SISTERS!" cried Mother above the cacophony of the storm.

"SISTERS! HEAR WHAT I SAY! THE LORD IS VENTING HIS WRATH FOR WHAT WE HAVE DONE AND THE SIN IN OUR HEARTS! BOW YOUR HEADS AND MAKE PEACE WITH HIM SO THAT HE MAY COME UNTO YOU IN THE FINAL HOUR!"

Some of the women cried out for her to shut up and others rattled tin cups and hair brushes against the bars of their cells. It was quite melodramatic. Soon, it seemed, everyone was awake and frantic, crying out in anger and remorse as the thunder boomed and the prison shook like a wet dog. The wind was howling and I was certain it was calling out the names of the incarcerated. The scars at my wrists burned interminably.

"HE HAS A PLAN FOR THIS WORLD!" Mother shouted. "AND HE WATCHES ALL FROM HIS LOFTY THRONE IN THE HYADES! HE WILL ALIGN THIS WORLD WITH ALDEBARAN, FOLLOWER OF THE SEVEN SISTERS! MAKE HIM WELCOME! TREMBLE BEFORE HIM! ACCEPT THE LIVING GOD SO THAT HE MAY LAY HIS HANDS UPON YOU!"

The lightning was flashing interminably by this point and rolling thunder echoed down the sullen corridors of the prison, punctuating the fearful voices of the incarcerated. I was shaking, mouthing the words of Mother McGibb even though they tasted like poison on my tongue. It was then that my cellmate, Gretta Leese—doing twenty-to-life for multiple homicide—took hold of me, wrapping her arms around me as if I were a child frightened of the dark and what lurked in it (which was very true).

"Don't listen!" Gretta said into my ear. "She's a false prophet and her words are iniquity! The god she calls out to is not the god of anyone sane or righteous! Don't listen! Do you hear me? *Don't listen!*"

But even though Gretta clamped her hands over my ears, I could hear the words of Mother McGibb just fine, as if they were spoken in the hollows of my skull.

"WE SHALL LOOK FOR THE SIGN, SISTERS! HIS SIGN! THEN WE SHALL KNOW THAT WE ARE AT ONE WITH HIM! THAT THE SON OF HASTUR WALKS THESE LANDS AND THE BROTHERS AND SISTERS OF MAN SHALL BOW THEIR HEADS AS HE KNOCKS AT THE DOOR! WE SHALL BE BROUGHT FORTH INTO THE BODY OF THE PALLID MASK AND WE SHALL MAKE OFFERINGS ONTO HIM AND GIVE PRAISE TO THE KING IN HIS TATTERED MANTLE!"

By that point, the guards had had more than enough of it. Mother McGill was told to quiet down and when she didn't, they hauled her down to solitary where, I heard, she continued to rant and rave. But I didn't need to be told that—the stigmata of my wrists burned throughout the night.

Month after month, the prison psychiatrist picked and pecked at me in search of some tasty red meat, trying in vain to understand my inner workings, the motivation for my crime and (what she called) a deep-set delusional disorder. She was convinced the wellspring of it all was David's suicide. Although I advised against it again and again, she insisted on hypnotherapy. Our first few sessions were a complete bust. Then, on the third or fourth try, I came out of it and she began asking questions that I dared not answer. She had jotted down things I said while under—"the Pallid Mask" and "darkest Carcosa" and "Cor Tauri, the Festival of the Bloody Heart"—but I refused to comment on any of it. In fact, to my credit, I acted as if I had never heard of such rot and practically accused *her* of multiple delusions.

But I was not completely stubborn. I tried to be cooperative when and where possible. The psych badly wanted to understand me and my psychosis. The way she spoke of the latter, you would have thought it was a living, breathing thing like some immense, fear-swollen parasite or an evil conjoined twin. She found it perplexing that I, an apparently loving and kind single mother, well-educated, well-bred, and quite successful, could commit such a crime, as if status precludes one from darkest folly. I parried with her a bit, telling her that when things were so right they had a way of going so wrong. But she was no fool. She wanted answers and she planned on having them, even if that meant slicing my brain wafer-thin and putting it under a microscope. She had a great deal of passion for my dilemma and I was pretty certain that she had some scientific paper in mind that would win her accolades amongst her peers. I understood ambition. She wanted to know the root cause and I explained it to her (in the most general and antiseptic way). It was the book, *The King in Yellow*. I had discovered it in the historical collection of St. Aubin's College. As a full professor of Medieval History, I had access to those things which were denied others. I read the book, knowing quite well its fearsome rep-utation, and suffered the consequences. She claimed that the book did not exist and its namesake, the King himself, was a fantasy. I explained that for those who were chosen (*cursed*, might be a better word), he was occa-sionally visible in the distorted glass of certain antique mirrors or in pools of October rain. I had once glimpsed his numinous shadow at sundown, an immense and ragged form hovering over the city. I could tell her no more. Already, I knew, the ether of this world was beginning to fracture.

That the King was close, I did not doubt. That he was reaching out for me was a given. That became very apparent to me one summer day as we trimmed weeds amongst the graves at the prison's potter's field. Here were acres of withered crosses and crumbling sandstone markers invaded and sometimes engulfed by infestations of devil's gut, hairweed, and woodbine. We spent the better part of a week cleaning it all up. Creepers had even grown up the wall of the little stone mausoleum. I was one of those who peeled the knotty growths free and when I did, revelation of the worst sort awaited me. For there, etched into the wall, was the very image I had drawn on the bathroom wall in my own blood that terrible night: the King. He was a stick figure and nothing more, but as I stared upon him, he became three-dimensional, fleshing out like a flower blooming until I could see the juicy running orbs of his eyes that bled like crushed berries and the vibrant colors of his tattered mantle drew me in closer and closer until I heard my own voice say, *"Oh, please, King, not again, not so soon."*

I have no idea how long I stood there, transfixed, but soon enough a guard came. "What do you think you're doing? Get back to work."

I pointed one trembling hand at the wall. "But . . . but *he* won't allow it."

"There's nothing there, can't you see that? Get back to work."

Oh, the rapture of ignorance. The guard did not see what I saw and how I envied the sheer simplicity of his mental processes. Simplicity, I began to believe, was close to divinity. I dreamed of it and wished for it, but once you have opened the book and seen the dark star and the hollow moon there is no going back. No one can ever close that staring third eye that shows you hidden things in this world and beyond.

I could go into great, prolix detail about other such occurrences, but I present only the latter to illustrate my point. The penumbra of the king was creeping closer and it would compel me to do the most awful things.

All of which brings us to my last night in prison. After some six years, I was paroled. And the only reason I was paroled was because I was clever. I kept my nose clean, yes, but there was more to it than that. After a time, but not too soon as to appear suspicious, I accepted what the prison psychiatrist told me and volunteered for therapy sessions. That made her happy. I accepted all that she told me, sometimes repeating verbatim what she said, and that made her even happier. There was no book and no King. It was all delusion and fantasy. And that was how I won my early release from the cesspool of the prison.

But let us consider my last night there for a moment.

Sometime, in the dead of night, I opened my eyes. There was something in the cell with me and it was not Gretta. This was something born from the womb of dark and secret night. I could hear it breathing like wind in a chimney flue. It was standing near to me. Its body was a grotesque, heaving sack, its face white and soft, glistening like a mushroom damp with dew. I could see little of it and I was grateful for that. When it spoke, its voice was mucid, almost gelatinous: "You have found the Yellow Sign?"

"No," I muttered. *"No."*

Then a single pulpous hand like a flaccid starfish touched my wrist and the scars there burned like phosphorus. "It has been sent and you have found it."

I was released with very little fanfare. My parole officer was a man named Meecham who I instinctively did not trust. He was a smallish man, thin as a swamp reed, with a chin so sharp you could've sliced cheese with it. His right eye was blue, blinking all the time, but the left just stared. It was oddly large and green, but not a good sort of green, but the green of stagnant ponds and mildew. Frogspawn. It was gummy and jellied-looking.

"What I want you to keep in mind," he told me, "is that what happened is over with and you have a new life now. A new purpose. I will help you fulfill that purpose. Do you understand?"

I told him that I did. At which point, he pulled out a large envelope and out of it he took the book.

"Do you know what I have here?" he said.

I was trembling. "I don't want to see it."

"But you must, you must. You see? It's no book at all."

What I was looking at was not *The King in Yellow*, but only a sheaf of papers that I recognized instantly. These were the doodlings I had done after finishing Act II. The work of a madwoman, certainly. Drawings of stars and distorted planetary bodies, surreal landscapes and cities with misty towers etched against the face of a rising moon. All of it was dominated by mindless scribbling that looked like the work of a child and numerous spiraling forms that seemed to connect it all together.

"There is no book. There never was a book. Do you believe that?"

"Yes," I managed, turning away from those awful spirals that made my wrists burn. "Yes."

He slid the papers back in the envelope. "Excellent. Then we can begin to craft the new you. And you do want that, don't you?"

I told him I did. I was afraid not to. He was playing a merry obscene game and I knew it. For even as he spoke, I noticed that the edges of his mask were beginning to fray.

Over the next few weeks as I settled into my role as ex-convict and former child murderess, there were things that did not sit right with me. I had the most disquieting sense that the world was no longer spinning safely and smoothly on its axis. Something had changed. I told myself it was only my perception of the same, but I was not convinced. Whomever or whatever had been in control of the universe before was in control no longer. Guardianship had changed hands. Maybe others were unaware of it, but I saw the signs immediately. They were subtle, but apparent— the arcing of sunlight at the horizon near dusk, the misaligned curvature of certain angles, the gathering of immense pale moths outside my window, and (the most telling) the frightening progress of a certain shadow that was getting closer by the day.

Meecham settled me into a halfway house with the other ex-cons. It was a unisex place, the men's quarters up the staircase to the left and the women's up the right. Regardless of gender, they shared one thing in common: the stare, that awful almost cataleptic sort of stare as if they were looking at something far in the distance no one else could ever see. The majority of them stayed in their rooms, pacing back and forth as if they were still in their cells, uncomfortable with the outside world. I suppose the higher physics of unlimited space was beyond their comprehension after being caged so long. One of the women, an old lady everyone called Marge, hanged herself my first week there. She left a suicide note that said simply, ONLY THE LEFT EYE MAY SEE. But before she slipped the noose around her throat, she took an apple corer and took out the offending orb. She set the bloody glob in a teacup and then killed herself. And so very quietly that the woman in the next room didn't even hear her.

THE PENUMBRA OF EXQUISITE FOULNESS

The woman next to me cried a lot at night. She had dead eyes that reminded me of pools of gray rainwater. It was said that she had murdered her own child. I understood her pain. Sometimes in the middle of the night, I would wake up thinking Marcus was crying and I had to feed him. My breasts would ache incessantly, but then I'd remember that Marcus was dead and that I was alone. *Oh, David, you do understand, don't you?* Often, I'd stare out the window, certain I could hear a baby crying somewhere in the night, lost and alone. But it was all in my head. More than once, I was certain I had spied Marcus in a baby carriage. But that was impossible . . . unless the time had come.

Next door, night after night, I could hear the crazy woman rocking back and forth in her chair, squeak, squeak, squeak. Sometimes it went on until dawn. She often sang lullabies in a shrill, scratching voice that made my skin crawl. I wasn't truly terrified until I heard a baby crying over there. It wasn't possible. I knew it wasn't possible. Yet I heard it and there was no mistaking it or the moist sucking sound of an infant feeding.

Finally, after too many haunted and sleepless nights, I inquired about my neighbor. "She can't have a baby in there," I said to Kim, one of the other girls. "She killed her baby."

"Hell are you talking about? You're the one that murdered your baby. Only you."

That was only one of many items that convinced me the world was lopsided and stretching itself inside out. Let me tell you of another. I woke one night quite late certain that I was not alone in my room. A search proved otherwise. I went to the window, staring at my reflection in the glass. And it was then that I saw not my room reflected behind me but some deranged seesaw landscape with an immense lake over which dangled black, guttering stars. On the shore of the lake I caught sight of some tall, crooked figure in scalloped tatters that blew about it like a shroud. I knew who it was. It could only be the King in Yellow and he was striding in my direction.

That was enough in of itself, but it was not all. You see, the spiraling scars on my wrists that revealed the Yellow Sign were spreading. It was not possible and I knew it, but the evidence was all-too apparent: the intricate pink whorls had spread up my arms and down onto my chest. I traced them with my fingers and they were upraised like burns and unbelievably intricate. Their geometry was not only Archimedean in nature, but hyperbolic or inverse. If the eye followed their vortexual progression, the Yellow Sign was always revealed. And when it was seen, you could look beyond it and see the skeletal towers of Carcosa rising into a red-hazed sky through which Aldebaran and the Hyades peered through sickly yellow cloudbanks like swollen, diseased eyelids.

After that, I must admit my memories are not as lucid as I would like. It seemed that everything started to get obscured. My world was leaning a little too far this way or that and where the angles met, I was afraid of what I might see. It was like looking through cellophane, everything became oblique, obscured, inverted. The King was turning my world upside down as he crept closer, ever closer to claim me as his own.

Now to the next few items on my list.

I awoke another night and I could hear whispering voices next door that disturbed me greatly. After a time, I pressed my ear against the thin wall and listened. This is what I heard: *"You won't be the one, you know. It is I who'll wear the crown . . . not you! I have been made ready by His hand and the crown was promised to me in a dream of withered roses! I alone have plumbed the black depths of Lake Hali and I alone have climbed the towers and cried out the sacred names above the hill of dreams! All will soon bow down before me, the child of Hastur!"*

Whether it was the crazy woman speaking or the child itself, there was no way of knowing. I wanted to go over there and make them stop, but I did not dare. I knew if I opened that door, I would see a fleshy spiraling that would suck my mind from my skull.

One afternoon after stepping off the bus, I stood on the sidewalk before the halfway house, trembling with fear. It was changing like everything else. It was no longer some simple, shabby three-story house but a cyclopean, rising black monolith that wavered and shuddered as if it could no longer hold its shape. I watched as it rose before me, filling the sky, its icy shadow enveloping me in the icy cerements of the King himself.

But it did not end there, oh no. When the house became nothing but a house again, I went to my room. After lying on my bed for an hour or so, I went to the window and I saw not my world but the scarlet-litten city of Carcosa with its forest of twisted, rising towers overlooking a warped anti-world of clustering black ruins. I could see the Lake of Hali, its dark flat waters reflecting an immense moon of blood. On the shore stood the King in Yellow beckoning to me amongst the crushed shells of a thousand disciples.

I pulled the shades so I did not have to see the twisted nightmare vistas of that anti-world and particularly its king. For three interminable days and three torturous nights I hid there in my boxlike room, waiting for a tread on the stair or, worse, for the gossamer material of this world to wear thin from its constant friction against that intrusive other which threatened to intersect all that we know. The penumbra of the King's shadow grew closer and closer by the hour. My second day of self-imposed isolation, I dared peek around the drawn shade and what I saw was the shadow edging closer to the house. Of course, others would say it was only the shadow thrown by the looming building across the street, but I knew better. For each evening at dusk I watched its grim approach, I clearly saw that diabolic penumbra creeping ever forward on a thousand tiny legs.

By the night of the third day, I knew that I was trapped. I should have escaped while there was time and maneuvering room. The reality I had known my entire life was fragmenting, giving way to the tidal thrust of a limitless blackness without form. Each time it began to come apart I heard something like a crackling or sizzling and awful pains swept over me . . . following, yes, *following* the exact patterns of the spiraling cicatrisation that covered my entire body now much as electricity will follow the path of a copper wire. When the pain ceased, I would see—if only momentarily—my room turned topsy-turvy and inside out, remade by the hand of another into some poor, crude replica whose walls oozed a mephitic pink slime and whose ceiling was loose and spongy. Dear God, even the floor was like some nasty jelly as if I were not squatting on tiles but on the accumulated soft putrescence of dozens of over-ripened corpses.

Then it would pass.

But I knew, given time, it would engulf my world and there would be no going back. For three nights I watched the moon hanging above the city like an immense peeled eyeball studying the nocturnal scrambling of those creatures who would soon tremble before a new and malefic god. It throbbed like a heart, pulsing with each abnormal beat, filling itself with blood, getting stronger and larger, fleshing itself out for the final act.

There were things that needed doing and only I could do them. I plotted carefully and waited. When I heard that poor demented woman slip downstairs, I went over there and found the door ajar. It smelled strange in there, hot and briny like tidal flats on a scorching summer day.

Passing by the bed, I went to the bassinet under the window, pushing aside the flowing lace. The baby stared at me with curiosity and innocence.

"Again, oh King, must I do it yet again?"

The moon was peering through the window and looking at its face I saw voids, glistening depths, and some demented stygian dead-end space where black stars shiver in a nightmare cosmos. Soon, I would travel there.

As I hesitated in my sacred task, the penumbra of the King in Yellow crept ever closer. I heard the crackling-sizzling sound and the stigmata of my elaborately scarred body went electric with pain. Right away, the room began to alter. It mutated, morphed, going liquid like hot corpse fat and cooling into something perverse and insane. It was a room as envisioned by a lunatic, a surreal, anti-real, expressionistic tangle, a black and red framework of pitted bones and jagged shards of glass, warped doorways that led into black pathless wastes and windows that looked into the pulsating face of the grinning, sardonic moon.

But I completed my task and when they charged into the room, I held up the blood-dripping, mangled offering to the King. I saw then that there were no secrets between us. They knew that I had tied the noose that David hanged himself with—dear God, he had *begged* me to after glimpsing the book—and they knew I brought Marcus to term only to offer him to the mighty King at summer solstice. "I have won and now I ascend to the throne! It is my right as concubine of Hastur! It is I who shall wear the crown and I who shall rule over darkest Carcosa!" As they approached me, I tossed the offering at them so the King would know that I was righteous and pure. Then carefully, calmly, and with exacting precision I showed them the knife I carried. How the face of the moon glimmered along its blade. Then, with the finesse of a surgeon, I slit along the outer edges of my mask and began to peel it free so they could see what I hid beneath, the face the world would soon worship and tremble before.

Yield

C.J. Henderson

"The best way to get the better of temptation is just to yield to it."

—Clementina Stirling Graham

"Just give in . . . in the end, you know it's so much easier."

Yeah . . . easier. It's true. The easy way. The easy way out. Take it easy. Ease up, friend. Why resist? Why bother? Don't you know that no one cares if you put a lot of effort into your work? Why do you struggle so? What a waste of time. Stop being so damn stupid and just relax—

Take it easy—

"After all, a hundred years from now, who's going to know the difference?"

It's what the entire world has been saying to me my whole life. Well, no, not to me directly, no endless slacker choruses of hip know-it-alls, self-indulgents preaching a gospel of sloth outside my window as if I rated my own personal carolers of the Apocalypse . . . nothing so obvious, so easily spotted.

To tell the sad truth, that . . . that would have been something which I probably could have dealt with.

My name is Edgar Wilson. If you can believe that. I mean, who names their kid Edgar anymore? Thirty years ago was the rat's ass tail-end of the twentieth century. What were they thinking? I mean, honestly, "Brad" I could have understood. "Clint," or even "George," dopey but okay, I get it. But . . . Edgar. God Almighty—

I guess when the doctors told them I was going to be born healthy without any birth defects they decided naming me thusly would help curb any sense of entitlement I might develop along the way. Well, if that was indeed their thinking, they were certainly correct about at least that one thing. Credit where credit's due, and all—

"Really, why do you bother to resist?"

I had no good answer about my name, or to offer the eternal voice in the darkness whenever it questions me. I really do wonder myself. Why *do* I bother to resist? What *is* the point I'm trying to make? And, if I do have a point, if it even is *my* point, or just something someone else came up with first that I latched onto somewhere along the way—

"What does it get you?"

Another of the darkness's unanswerable queries.

What was I thinking? Hell, really, if I wanted to approach the problem in any way objectively, instead of just resisting because it's what someone, somewhere, once decided was supposed to be done in such situations, didn't I need to have some idea what it was I was even resisting? Which is what led me finally to summon up the courage to ask the voice within my head—

Really, just what is it you think I'm resisting?

I mean, tell me . . . what is it you want me to give in to exactly? Just tell me—chances are I probably don't give enough of a damn to keep it up. I mean, yeah, you're probably right. Okay—I'm willing to admit it. I don't know what I want, or why I do anything in this world. Most people don't think, they only react, and damnit, I'm as much a part of "most people" as anyone. And, in a hundred years I suppose it's not going to make any goddamned kind of difference.

And, I swore, knowing that for at least once in my life I was being honest with myself, I'm not trying to kid anybody because honestly I don't know what difference anything makes any more.

"Your brain, it's so cluttered, all those thoughts, ideas . . . so self-centered, self-absorbed . . . you know that's not right. Not the way people should be. Not the way people are supposed to act. *Who* do you think you are?"

Of all the questions the nagging voices whispered in the back of my mind, they went right back to the one that remained the hardest to ignore. I mean, honestly, how can you? How can anyone? It is one of the essential things about oneself anyone needs to know if they're going to advance at all.

Who do any of us think we are?

Children, of course, don't have to worry about such things. They're not supposed to. They're not capable. Indeed, if you can answer that question, you're not actually a child anymore. Maturity takes having reached the point where one is ready to assume responsibility for their actions. Children can't do that. They're too self-centered, which oddly enough, was what the voices kept saying of me.

And that's such a large part of what I don't get.

Me . . . self-absorbed. I know I'm not like that. I know it. Or, at least, I *believe* that.

And, maybe that's the trouble. After all, isn't that kind of denial exactly what a child would offer in the face of accusing authority—No, no . . . not me. I didn't do it. I'm not like that. Their inability to accept blame is one of the most frustrating, infuriating things about them.

About all of us . . .

Those that mature, we're (they're?) not like that. They've matured. But, and I think this is equally valid, matured into whom? Into what?

When the moment comes, when the child's eyes open, whatever tiresome, horrible, permanent shock finally comes along to rattle their endless, tiresome innocence into submission and release the growing suspicions of other realities, it's always the same—

The baby learns to talk, and immediately assumes the role of the superior, not understanding those to whom it is speaking are not learning of the discovery of spoken communication through them.

"Sounds like a break-through. . . ."

Is this where I'm at now? Just another of these early, formative points, merely another arrogant child's well-there-certainly-can't-be-anything-else-to-learn-ever-again-after-this moment self-deluding assumptions? Jumping jackasses, is that all life is, a never-ending series of lessons one can't believe they didn't already know, hadn't already learned, but now that they have they'll never have to do it again—

"Oh, yes . . . definitely break-through time. . . ."

But when does it end? Does it ever end? It certainly looks like its ends for everyone else. Everywhere I look, slack-jawed morons enjoying life, typing away on their phones, flitting from one fascination-of-the-moment to another, stuffing their faces with food they can't taste, listening to music they don't understand, discussing movies they're too dimwitted to realize are simply remakes of things they've already seen, pawing the controls to their televisions and game monitors like apes, thinking themselves masters of the universe as the world they actually inhabit shrinks to the size of something smaller than a standard prison cell—

Why don't I get any of that? When do I get to join in? Where's my ignorant bliss? When do I get to feel excitement watching millionaire thugs play children's ball games?

"Oh, he has to be at a breaking point now."

There are no answers, of course. Well, not for most. For the many. It's not possible. I almost want to add the qualifier, "anymore" but would that even be accurate? Was there ever a time there were answers, whenever anyone could figure things out, how they work, how they *really* work . . . I mean, answers they could see and understand and relate to others? A moment when all clarity is revealed once and for all?

Was there ever anything like that for anyone? I mean, before the play? Oh, man . . . I mean, all I can say is, thank God for the play. If there is anything that has brought even the slightest bit of peace and understanding to my life, that's it. Thank God for *The King in Yellow*.

"Tell us about it."

I don't even remember when I saw it. That's funny, right? Well, I don't mean "when," I mean where. Where I saw it. What a night, what a freeing, cleansing, perfect night. Whoever it was that I saw it with, that went with me . . . it's like they just didn't get it. In a way, it seemed like the whole damn theater didn't get it. But me, little Edgar Wilson, son of Mark and Patty Wilson, little Eddie got it. In spades.

It's kind of funny actually, I mean, the fact I can't really remember when I saw it, or where, or with whom, or even why I went. But, it's not. That kind of stuff is important to those who haven't got things figured out yet. I mean, there's nothing important about who I saw the play with. Nothing at all. Especially if they didn't get it, when they didn't understand what they were watching. No—watching isn't the word. Not with *The King in Yellow*.

"What would the word be?"

You don't watch the play, that play, you . . . I kind of want to say "experience" it, but that's still not enough. Too shallow, too imprecise. The kind of word some college freshman would use to make themselves sound smart . . . no . . . it's close, a shade of pale just one removed from the final coat—

You "live" it. That's what you do when you see *The King* . . . you just goddamn live it. You're not removed from the action, not by any fourth wall, not by the edge of the stage . . . nothing separates you from the action. You don't hear the lines, you speak the lines, and I don't mean simultaneously, no one else is speaking—

"You mean, no one is saying your part at the same time that you are?"

No, no—there is no part, there are no lines, there are no actors . . . it's just you, living your role, being in the moment the way we were always intended—

"Intended by whom?"

And that was when it hit me. They didn't know. Whoever they were, whatever they were, the voices in my head, in the darkness, the probers, the yammering noise, the outside grabs . . . *they didn't know.* All my life I thought they had some kind of authority, or insight, or . . . or something. But they didn't know anything. They were just smart enough to keep me off balance, to learn from my mistakes, to observe and comment without acting, without offering solutions—

The King had taught me so much, without even trying. No wonder people called it madness. Said it created madness. This was the kind of truth that the world can't handle. The kind that makes mediocre knowledge so useless, so worthless. I get it now. When I saw it, where, why, with whom, for what reason, the usual push-pin limits trying to uncurl the edges of a notice they honestly believe they want to show the world, but which they're trying to pin on a placard posted in the dark, I moved past all that.

The King In Yellow is a release. Not from social conventions. I can remember the important facts, the thing that everyone was all in whispers that seeing the play made people go mad. All these nonsense stories about every time the play was presented the audiences would be left gibbering and drooling, running through the streets, wild-eyed, murderous, suicidal . . . blood everywhere. . . . God, what rubbish—it was nothing like that.

Nothing at all.

No one was left in their seats staring off into space, spittle dribbling down their cheeks, or scrambling to the lobby in search of a fire axe or some other object of destruction—compelled. Irrational. That kind of mundane fourth act was something only the laziest of hacks could believe would follow such a glorious moment. No, it was ever so much, much more.

I remember clearly—everyone was moved. Everyone was quiet. There was no mandatory standing ovation, no applauds at all. Just silence. Both human and electronic. No cell phones chattered, no cameras recorded—the trivial reality pretending to exist in the ether receded, illuminated as both foolish and unnecessary in a moment.

And, instead their remained the overwhelming roar of an intense silence, a penetrating, necessary quiet, one which the actors not only understood, but appreciated. Expected. Did more than their fair share to create. The silence only complimented their achievement, and you could see it in their smiles as they took their bows. They *knew*—

"What did they know?"

What we all knew. What the play had taught them the first time they read it, what it taught all of us when we became a part of it, what it has sitting there within its essence, waiting for all brave enough to face that part of themselves to which the play called out in the first place. You know. . . .

Don't you?

That was when I realized that they did not know. The voices that had hounded me for all those years, questioning, guiding, scolding, second-guessing me from the darkness, the carping, annoying, pestering building blocks of conscience and fear, bullying me into accepting whatever the latest norm was for socially acceptable behavior. The dispensers of each week's guidelines—not followed at one's social peril.

Those shallow sad little souls—they didn't know anything. They certainly didn't understand that there was no absolute truth toward which anyone could be guided. The very concept was a shell shuffle with an infinite number of shells and no pea under any of them.

The game of civilization was rigged, not from the top down as if the rich and powerful were standing on the necks of the rest, but from the bottom upward. Every possession was a buckling strap, every dollar, each pot and pan, every trinket yet another weight welding one in place. But *The King*, seeing *The King*, having its own peculiar truth presented so one could pull their own understanding from within it, *The King* revealed all.

In the Court of the Yellow King

The King, one of the three primaries, so vast and multi-colored, so wrapped around everything, his power and influence in every yellow hue—how could it not be obvious? How could anyone not see him when he reveals himself everywhere? Of course, the answer was that he was known. In the same way the sky was known. Is known. So obvious is the sky, so always present, it is not noticed. One only notices the sky—filled with our atmosphere—when it is gone.

So too, once one sees *The King*, it becomes obvious that he too is everywhere, his hand on every shoulder, his breath within all lungs, unseen only because he is so large he can not be comprehended by such mundane senses as sight and touch.

In the beginning, when thoughts first solidified in reproducible form—stone tablets, crushed reeds, animal skins, whatever—in every corner of the world the first play written was always his. Men called them bibles or commandments or other lesser titles to encourage familiarity, if not understanding, but it mattered not. It was all his truth, and it has crawled forward toward mankind over thousands of years—

Waiting for humanity to become conscious enough to grasp its presence.

The King In Yellow is nothing more than the core truth revealed. The universe making witness—giving testimony to the fact that it has secrets, and that they are easily understood.

Madness . . . to call the clearing of one's eyes to all that is irrelevant in life insanity is so very tiny. And, to not understand the place of all that is tiny, is so very sad.

Sadness and all its terrible siblings will disappear, though—it is foretold. To say that such will be soon would most likely be misleading. The King but showed the barest of interest in the Earth and the paltry few planets around it but a moment ago to his own reckoning. Think of it as if you had taken note of something in the morning paper. While at work, you allowed the notion to inhabit the back of your mind. Arriving at lunch, the nagging little thought returns to where you finally consider it. That is the history of The King and mankind.

Some ten thousand years ago, his attention flickered past our random little globe. Millennia later, he has actually begun to exert some small desires concerning our small reality off in the corner of existence as it is.

A distraction is all we are to The King.

"Just give in . . . in the end, you know it's so much easier."

Yeah . . . easier. It really is true. The easy way. The easy way out. Take it easy. Ease up, friend. Why resist? Why bother? Don't you know that no one cares if you put a lot of effort into your work, into your life? Into anything—

Why do you struggle so? What a waste of time. Stop being so damn stupid and just relax—

Take it easy—

"After all, a hundred years from now, who's going to know the difference?"

It's what the entire world has been saying to me my whole life. In so many ways, a part of me wants to struggle, to fight onward. But to what purpose? When is the lesson finally learned?

If you want to know the day I learned I had been wrong so very long, to believe in humanity, in the nobility of the grunting apes to every side of me, just read the date on my ticket stub. The play is the thing, they say.

They're right.

Homeopathy

Greg Stolze

het's posture was entirely that of a man trying to relax. He sat in the corner of the sofa, self-consciously leaned back against its yielding floral-print pillows, hands in his lap, then off to the sides—cushion and arm—then back, but folded instead of resting on his thighs.

"So," he said.

Connie, the therapist, smiled reassuringly.

"What shall we talk about?" she asked.

He laughed, nervously. "Um . . . I don't know. I mean, things are OK. They're all right. My . . . wife, my children it's all . . . fine."

"Kids getting good grades?"

"Brett kind of struggles with motivation."

"Hm. No work troubles?"

He shrugged. "If a job was fun, they wouldn't have to pay you to do it. My dad used to say that." He looked away.

"Is that my cue to say 'tell me about your father?'"

She chuckled. He smiled back in reply.

"What did your dad do? For a living, I mean," she asked.

"Oh! Well, he put together washing machines in a factory."

"That does not sound like a fun job."

"He did his share of complaining about it."

They trailed off into silence.

"And you?" she continued. "What do you do?"

He explained. It had something to do with mathematics, computers, and insurance. Connie didn't really follow it.

"You like it?"

He shrugged. "Beats working on a loud, hot assembly line. It can be tedious but . . . I like tedium, maybe? I handle being bored better than a lot of people." He sat up and forward. "I mean, I guess that I have a tolerance for problems and tasks that are *just the right amount* of busy work? Not really really hard problems, but the kind of thing that you know will . . . that you know you can solve if you just, like, keep chiseling away at it."

She nodded.

"How are you sleeping?"

He sighed.

"Well that's it, isn't it?" he said.

After their first session, Connie's secretary Griffin wound up calling Chet's insurance company.

"Hi," Griffin said. He had a beautiful phone voice, deep and resonant. "I'm calling from Stearkwether Therapeutic Associates?"

"Hello, my name is Jennifer," said a voice with a thick Bengali accent. "How may I help you today?"

"We've got a new client, he's insured through Allied Health Programs."

"Can I have his account information please?"

Griffin gave it, the name 'Chet Wegler,' his Social Security Number, his account number, and the Single-Payment Service Identification Code.

"Was Chet Wegler's referring physician Dr. Weinbaum?"

"I don't know. Dr. Weinbaum isn't in our office."

"Can you describe the therapy Mr. Wegler is receiving?"

"Of course I can't, c'mon. Patient confidentiality precludes."

"I'm going to transfer you to my supervisor."

Her supervisor ("Jeremy") had a Punjabi accent and asked for the client's name, SSN, account number and Single-Payment Service Identification Code.

"And he is taking the therapies from Dr. Constance Stearkwether?"

"She's not a doctor," Griffin said, "But yes, Connie Stearkwether is his therapist."

"And what sort of therapy does she do, please?"

"Traumatic association reductive therapy."

"Please hold."

The music was an R.E.M. song from the early 1990s. It played twice before breaking off.

"Hello, my name is Anthony," said the man with the Marathi accent. "Can I have the name of the client please?"

Griffin sighed, but he gamely provided name, SSN, account and SPSIC again.

"The code you provided is for psychotherapeutic services," Anthony said.

"Yes. That's what Mr. Wegler is getting."

"But Constance Stearkwether is not a psychiatrist, nor is she a psychologist."

"She's a counselor."

"What is it that she does, again?"

"Traumatic association reduction therapy."

"And what is that, exactly?"

"She reduces the traumatic associations between memories," Griffin told him.

". . . we don't have a code for that."

"It's a new therapy."

"I'm afraid Mr. Wegler's insurance does not cover experimental therapeutic modalities."

"In process, they sit and talk. It's no more 'experimental' than any other talking cure."

"I'm going to have to transfer you to a mental health expert. Please hold."

Griffin sighed.

They had several sessions, talking about Chet's dad, before Connie asked, "How much do you know about the brain chemistry of memory?"

"Um . . . very little."

"It's interesting how many different tasks we talk about when we speak about remembrance. Your son's name is . . . Brett, right?"

"Yes."

"I didn't consult my notes," Connie said, with a little smile. "I accessed recollection—I drew up the fact from within the pattern of electrochemical signals in my brain, right? And when you hear the name 'Brett,' you don't have to dredge it up to know it's your son's name, you instantly feel its rightness. That's the difference between recognition and recollection. One's active and one's passive."

"Okay . . ."

"It's not that difficult," she insisted. "There are memories you have to work at, and there are memories that jump out and surprise you because something triggered them, like a photo or a turn of phrase or a smell."

"The taste of a . . . oh, what are those cookies in that French novel?"

"Don't remember?" she asked.

He smiled back.

"Madelines, from *A Remembrance of Things Past*," she said.

"I bet you talk about that book a lot, in your line of work," Chet said. He finally seemed comfortable on her sofa.

"A fair bit, yes. I'm also a fan. But if you think of it, reading—where you blast past the words so quickly that meaning builds up through their collective action, not from individual letters—is different from writing, when you're going much slower and trying to find just the right word for this or that situation."

"Got it. Some memory is automatic, some you have to fight for."

"Right! The division between directed memory and reflexive memory is an important one. But if those are the X-axis of the chart, there's also a Y-axis. Make sense?"

"Rows and columns, oh yeah. I spend . . . a *lot* of time with spreadsheets. What's the other axis then?" Chet asked.

"Some memories are functional—remembering how to ride a bike or juggle. Those usually start out conscious, like when you're picking out notes on a piano or letters on a keyboard, but become instinctive over time."

"Got it."

"Other memories are emotional."

"Oh, now we're getting to it."

"These different categories are largely disconnected from one another. Someone with total retrograde amnesia, where they don't even know who they are? They retain skills, *Bourne Identity* style."

"Now there's a story I know better," Chet said. "The movie, anyhow."

"People who've damaged their ability to form new memories, or who've lost old ones, often *recognize*," she said, drawing attention to the word, "People from their past who were important to them. A man who couldn't tell you his own name or where he was from knew he loved his wife when he saw her. Similarly, some experiments with electroconvulsive memory erasure indicate that patients feared the doctor even when they didn't and *couldn't* consciously know her name or what she'd done with them previously."

"That's kind of spooky," he said. "It also sounds like bad news. I mean, isn't it? My . . . baggage . . ." he twisted away in the sofa, looking out the window.

Connie reached over and took one of his hands, tugging lightly until he turned to look at her.

"Your problem is that you have deep, traumatic emotional memories," she said, staring deep into his eyes. "They are reflexive and they are set off by commonplace stimuli—lying flat in bed, darkness, late night. You are re-experiencing old abuses."

Chet eyes were reddening, but he didn't look away.

"*I can break that, Chet.*" She let go and leaned back, but held his gaze.

"How?" he whispered.

She handed him a box of tissues.

"There are stimuli that have profound impacts on the mind," she said vaguely. "In the past, they've been applied haphazardly, or accidentally, or . . . um, recreationally. But I believe these factors can be used with precision. They can alter your sense of what life is and what life can be."

"What sorts of . . . I mean, how would that work? I'm not sure I want to get my mind rewired. I just want to not have to think about . . . you know."

"I know Chet. Look. Emotive memory is stored in the amygdala," she said. "Procedures are spread throughout, which is why they can be so resilient. Visual, intellectualized data resides in the hippocampus. But all memories—functional, feeling or fact—are plastic. We trust what we know as if it was iron, but it's actually as supple as rope."

"How can that be possible?" Chet asked. "I *know* what happened. I was *there*, I wish I could forget or misremember, but it comes back *exactly the same every time*, it's like a broken record, it *never* changes, I'd rather be delusional than be stuck in a loop with what actually went on!"

"It's an illusion," she said steadily. "Memory is the graveyard of facts."

"That's crazy! God, how can you tell me that I don't even know what happened when I was there and you weren't?"

"Because *all* memories are illusions. Your father isn't here right now, is he? He died in . . ."

She checked her notes even as he said, "1997. I'm not wrong about that, am I?"

"No."

"Then how are you going to convince me that I'm wrong about the . . . the rest of it?"

"You don't have to be right or wrong," she said. "We just have to convince your amygdala that it's not happening *right now*. Because we can agree on that, right? That it's not in the present, but the past?"

"Who said, 'The past is never dead. It's not even past'?" he asked.

"I'll have to look that one up," she said.

When he checked out, he asked Griffin about the insurance situation. They spent a few minutes going over it.

"Today," Constance said at their next appointment, "I'd like to talk about homeopathy."

"It's interesting," Chet said. "Of all the therapies I've tried, and most of them were the 'talking cure,' this is the first time I feel like I've done the minority of the talking."

"Is that a problem?"

"Kind of a relief," he admitted. "But—excuse me, please, don't take any offense—it does make me skeptical."

"I'm not offended." Constance had a pretty smile. "Look, this *isn't* like other therapies. They're a process to help you construct mental and emotional tools for living your life. Like . . . like a seamstress who won't make clothing, but who talks you through every step of measuring yourself and threading the needle and putting it together?"

"Um . . ."

"Sorry about my metaphors," she said. "Let me conclude this one. I don't want you to have a bespoke suit of psychological techniques. I want to hand you a set of one-size-fits-all pants to, um, go over the naked memories that are troubling you."

"So you're a specialist."

"A very narrow specialist, which is why I don't have an M.D. or a Psy.D."

"Which is why the insurance company is having a conniption," Chet said.

She grimaced a little. "Sorry about that."

"Look, it's fine, if this works I'll happily pay it out of pocket. Though, again . . . that's a reason for some . . . concern? I guess?"

"Memory is plastic," she said. "Every time you remember an *event*, you edit it and consolidate it. Often, several similar scenarios are melded together."

"See, that's the part that I can't . . ."

"How many times did your dad do it?" she asked.

He moved back into the sofa as if slapped.

"Too many," he said at last.

"You do not remember an exact number."

"Well, it's . . . you can't . . ."

"You recall several archetypal encounters, and those are probably the result of multiple events being compacted together. Anything you remember with particular clarity, I'm guessing had some extraneous element involved."

He was quiet for some time.

"The scent of gingerbread," she said quietly. "The Christmas episode. That one stands out. Doesn't it? You said."

He nodded.

"Because that time was a little different, it didn't get combined with the times that were all the same."

He said nothing, just stared, blank.

"I'm not trying to belittle your suffering," she said, leaning in and putting a hand on his knee. "I'm not trying to tell you it wasn't every bit as awful as you think. *But you did change them.* The memories *did* get loose from the actual events. Can you agree to that?" She bit her lip.

"I guess I have to," he whispered.

"It is hard to admit that we not only don't know something, but that we can't," she said, reaching out to take one of his hands in both of hers. "But this means that you can alter how you respond to those memories. *You can change it.* You can take control of your past."

He nodded.

"Do you believe me?" she persisted.

He nodded again. Satisfied, she sat back and let him withdraw his hand.

"So," he croaked. "Homeopathy? It's some kind of . . . New Age thing, right?" Chet asked.

"Actual homeopathy is, yes. Sure. The theory says that if an ounce of the chemical irritant from poison ivy causes an itching rash in a healthy person, a hundredth of an ounce of it would heal a sick person's rash. Or, something that makes you nauseous when you take it healthy would—if carefully diluted down to a fraction of its initial intensity—settle your stomach if you were already throwing up."

"Okay, how is that even *supposed* to work?"

She shrugged. "I'm not claiming it works for snakebites, although exposure to small doses of venom can let people build up immunities. Really, if you think about it, the process of getting vaccinated with a small sample of dead disease cells sounds very similar to homeopathy. But I'm not trying to sell you on it for the body, but for the mind."

"I'm not sure I'm following you."

"Think of psychoactive chemicals. If you give lithium salts to a healthy person, the bad effects are going to outweigh the positive ones. Give the same dosage to someone suffering mania, and it can be, can be very helpful."

"All right," Chet said slowly. "It's like . . . like that stuff Adderall? Or am I thinking about Ritalin? The stuff that makes normal . . . normal people hyper, but makes hyper kids more normal?"

"That's quite an oversimplification," she said, "But that does speak to the fundamental theory at play here. A stomach, say, that's functioning just fine might be thrown out of balance if you add too much of an acid to it. But if it has insufficient acid, adding some might restore it. Something that has an effect is a better starting place than something that has no observed effect."

"I thought you didn't prescribe medications," Chet said.

"I don't. Have you ever heard of *The King in Yellow?*"

"We think our memories are like pictures," Connie said. "When we think of our first kiss, it's usually an image, even though we probably had our eyes closed. We see ourselves from outside, very often."

"So that's another example of how we change our memories?" Chet asked. "I was in 'first-person view' when I got married, but I imagine it in third-person because that's how I see the wedding video and pictures?"

"It's partly due to those reinforcers, and partly due to our tendency of make narratives, with meaning, out of events, which are merely observed. But memory isn't really like a picture, because pictures don't change. We *want* it to be fixed and steady, but it's not."

"If I wanted my memories to be unchangeable, I wouldn't be here," Chet said.

"Very true." Constance stood, produced a key from her pocket, and unlocked a gray metal box on her desk. Inside was a small Tyvek envelope, which she set aside. Under it was an old book, in rather poor condition.

"*The King in Yellow,*" Chet said, staring at it.

"Memory is more like clay," Connie said, sitting with the book in her lap. "Think of an unfired statue, in a dark room. To find out what it's like, you have to feel it. But because it's still soft, each touch makes tiny changes. That's memory. Every time you call something up, the fingers of your mind leave streaks or imprints on it."

"So you think things weren't really as bad as I remember them?"

"In many ways it *does not matter* objectively what 'really' happened. The flexibility of the mind—the plasticity of recall—lets you choose a better reaction."

"Tell me again about the book," he said, lips dry.

"No one's sure why *The King in Yellow* produces drastic effects on consciousness. It seems to operate almost like a hallucinogenic drug."

"Yeah there's . . . there are some scary stories about it, on the Internet."

She waved her hands. "Oh, the *Internet*. They must be true, right?"

"Well, nothing is, is it? If our memories are all plastic?"

"Something that changes isn't necessarily *false*," she said sharply.

"It's just, people talk about it like it's a drug. Or a religion. That everything changes in the, what's the phrase, 'in the shadow of the King.' People say they get their wishes coming true, or that people with masks chase them out of paintings. Crazy stuff."

"Let's assume this literature has the ability to alter memories," she said. "If you didn't know that's what it did, what would that feel like? It's not unusual for confabulated memories to be weirdly dramatic, even horrifying. If you accidentally reworked your mind so that you remembered a nightmare of a past, wouldn't normalcy seem like a granted wish?"

"Once again, we come to the idea that my memories are false . . . ," Chet said.

"I don't care if they are! Real, fake, something in between, if they're hurting you I want to make that stop."

"So the guy who said everyone around him had a mask on over their real faces and was trying to rebuild his house to convince him he was still on Earth and hadn't been kidnapped to some weird lake somewhere?"

She shrugged. "First off, the Internet is full of freaks and weirdos."

"I'll give you that one," Chet said.

"Even if he wasn't just hoaxing you, are you going to hold up a guy who remembers nonsensical assaults as proof that *The King in Yellow* does *not* alter perception and recall?"

Chet opened his mouth, closed it, then said, "No, but he might indicate that it's a bad idea."

"They're just words, Chet."

"So's *Mein Kampf*."

"There's a difference between mnemonic effects and political incitement," she said, folding her arms and giving him a stern look. "I do know what I'm doing. I'm taking every possible precaution to limit the alterations to only malignant memories."

"How does that work?"

"*The King in Yellow* and some associated materials seem to powerfully disconnect the mind's ability to keep its memories structured. If you go with the statue metaphor, it takes the clay from being mostly-dry to a . . . muddier state. Changes become much easier. There was a man named Castaigne, did you come across his name in your research? He was treated for what was probably frontal lobe damage before being accidentally exposed to the book."

"Did it homeopathically fix him?"

The therapist shrugged. "No way to know. Without it making his personality more labile, he might have just been one of those spaced out, nodding, lost-mind cases, like someone with late stage dementia."

"What happened instead of that?"

"He fell in with another fellow, a Mr. Wilde. While Wilde isn't *known* to have read the play, he was reputedly in possession of, um, ancillary material that had similar effects."

"Wait, you mean the 'Yellow Sign'?"

Her eyes flicked to the envelope on her desk.

"Yes, among other things."

"That's supposed to be the really fast version, right? You see it once and it gets in your head?"

"It does seem to work much more directly on some people, possibly because it doesn't have to go through the linguistic centers of the brain," Constance said.

"Yeah, one guy said that once you see it, you start seeing it over and over again, everywhere."

"A more rational explanation is that, given its impact on the brain, one begins to *hallucinate* seeing it everywhere, like when you see faces in clouds. Or that one falsely remembers sightings, when in fact one was only experiencing an emotion associated with it. But that's really not relevant, Chet! You," she said, "Are not getting anywhere near the Yellow Sign."

"Okay." He sat back. "These symbols and ideas are really that powerful?"

"They seem to have affected Castaigne and Wilde, not to mention the reports about Bundry and Hollis in the 1970s and the New Bristol episode in 1986."

"What were those?"

"Oh, Bundry and Hollis tried to put on a performance of *The King in Yellow* at their college but wound up leaving school and kind of disappearing for two years. There was a big media buzz over them vanishing without telling anyone, but they were eventually found in Florida living as 'Camilla' and 'Cassilda,' their characters from the play." She shifted her eyes away from him. "Wilde styled himself a 'repairer of reputations.' That's a phrase that's *fascinating* to consider . . . 're-pair' suggesting to take things that have been disconnected and join them once more, very reminiscent of the word 're-member'. Memory language is full of the idea of return . . . when we 're-call' we summon ideas together, or 're-collect.' And then we have 'reputation,' descended from the Latin *'putare,'* to know. A reputation is that which is known again. To repair a reputation is to shuffle the connections, knead the clay, and connect old things in a different way."

"All that from a play?"

"You're not going to enact the whole thing over and over, like Hollis and Bundry," she assured him. "You're only getting a safe, small dose. Just enough to jar some things loose, or soften them up."

He nodded. "How do we start?"

"We start with the hardest part," she said. "I need you to remember, and describe to me, everything your father did."

Nervously, he tapped on the full box of tissues on the table by the sofa. He was quiet for a second. Then he nodded, and began.

He was still when he stopped talking. Unnervingly still, like a clay model himself, heavy and inert.

"Read the book," Constance said quietly. She handed him a sheaf of photocopied pages, and he listlessly took them.

"This isn't . . ." he said.

"Shh. Read."

With narrowed eyes, he did.

"I don't feel anything," he said, when he handed them back.

"It doesn't work all at once, I'm afraid."

"Should I read more? I mean, I don't really get what the big deal is. I don't care about Cassilda and Camilla and the city under black stars."

"You've only read the first act," she said.

"Well so what? I mean, what am I supposed to get out of part of it? If I looked at a third of a painting would that be worth, what, three hundred and thirty-three words?" His inertness was wearing off, turning into a truculent anger.

"Are you familiar with what happened after the first performance of *The Rite of Spring*? Or with the rash of suicides patterned after *The Sorrows of Young Werther*?"

"No, I'm not and I don't see why you are," he said crossly. "Are you a psychologist or an English professor? Or, wait, you're not either, are you?"

"This anger is good, Chet. It shows that your amygdala is involved."

"Oh whatever."

"I'd like to schedule for twice next week."

"Yeah, since I'm paying out the nose . . . you want cash or check?"

"We'll do Act II next time."

"Oh great. I'll finally find out what's up with the Stranger."

He was calm the next time, and apologized, and she said it was fine. She'd brought fresh-baked gingerbread, and a basin in case he threw up.

They talked through the Christmas episode, and then he re-read Act I and read Act II.

"Oh my God," he said afterwards. He was staring into space, blank.

"Breathe, Chet."

"What if I forget how? What if I forget I need to? It's . . . what happens in Act III?"

"I don't have Act III."

"*What?*" He practically lunged out of the sofa's corner. "How can you not have it? You mean you haven't copied it, right?"

"No, the book I got is damaged. Only the first page of Act III is present."

"Let me read that!"

"Chet."

"Okay, okay," he said, settling back. "Wow though. *Wow.* I mean, I can see now why you thought this would change memories. It feels like reality itself is reshaping." He gave a slow blink. "It feels like I could re-make the whole world."

The next session, Chet reported feeling more confident, more in control of his life than ever. He'd been sleeping well. His wife, he said, had definitely noticed a difference. Even his kids were treating him more respectfully.

(The insurance still wasn't covering his treatment, though.)

The appointment after that, Chet showed up with a small Tyvek envelope folded in his jacket pocket. He and Griffin called Allied Health Programs immediately after, and then brought Connie out to explain her process to a man with an accent that was almost perfectly Standard British. While they were distracted, Chet exchanged his envelope for the one in the lock-box.

He didn't know for sure that it was a copy of the Yellow Sign, but he suspected.

When he got home and finally viewed it, he knew it could be nothing else.

"Thank you for calling Allied Health Services, this is Janet, how may I help you?"

"Hi. My name's Chet Wegler, and I've put in several reimbursement requests for treatments from Stearkwether Therapeutic Associates?"

"Can I get your account number, and the Single-Payment Service Identification Code?"

"Certainly. My account is 33-J-20177. The code is 31-R30-S1, traumatic reality reductive therapy."

"I'm not seeing it."

"I remember," he said patiently, "That the code is on the list for full reimbursement. Please check again."

"Oh, there it is!"

He made a small noise of satisfaction.

"That's with Constance Stearkwether?" she asked.

"Dr. Cassilda Stearkwether," he corrected.

"Of course, of course. Cassilda. How silly of me!"

"It was always Cassilda," he said.

Bedlam in Yellow

William Meikle

t was a Friday night in the hottest July in London I could remember, and Carnacki had the windows open to let a breath
of air in, although what breeze we got proved to be hot and
dry, and tasted of an overly heated city. The heat had drained our appe-
tite, and we had partaken of only a light meal of trout and green vegetables. As a result we were earlier than usual in retiring to the parlor, and
had taken our normal seats, with our drinks charged and fresh smokes
lit well before eight.

Carnacki wasted no time in getting to his tale.

"It is as well that we have some warmth, old friends, despite the
slight discomfort it might bring," he began. "For my tale tonight is a chill-
ing one indeed, and I fear you will be glad of the heat by the end of it."

"It started last Monday, with a telegram requesting my attendance
at Bethlem Asylum in Southwark. The note intimated that it was a matter of some delicacy that required my particular skills, and that I would,
of course, be suitably remunerated for my time. I was intrigued enough
by the request to make my way by carriage to a meeting with a Doctor
Donaldson, the chief medical officer of the facility.

"We are all aware of the moniker given to the Asylum by the general
public—a reminder of its earlier days when the treatment of the mentally
ill was not as enlightened as it is today. And like you, I have heard all the
tales of mistreatment and torture, chaos and confusion. But despite any
qualms I might have had about visiting the place, I was met with a calm,
almost serene establishment of quiet, whitewashed corridors and nurses
in clean, starched uniforms efficiently going about their business. It is a
fine, well-appointed building, and Doctor Donaldson's oak-lined library
and office would not have seemed out of place in any of your town clubs.

"The doctor himself, however, was clearly in some distress, and his reason for contacting me all came out of him in a rush.

"'It is the top floor, Mr. Carnacki,' he said. 'I cannot get the staff to go upstairs, especially after dark, and any patients we leave there for more than a day come away with their mental state even worse than anything they might previously have been suffering. Something strange moves through the corridors up there of an evening. There is talk of it being a *haunt*—and I can't say as I disagree with them, for I have even seen something myself, although as a man of science I am loath to give voice to it being anything of a supernatural nature. I have heard that you have experience in such matters, and that you are most discreet—can you help us?'

"You chaps all know that I cannot turn down a genuine request for help—or the chance to pit my wits against a denizen of the Outer Darkness, so I gave the man my word that I would look into the matter. We shook hands on it and that same afternoon I began my investigation."

"The top floor of Bethlem is a light and airy place by day, with high ceilings and sunlight streaming through skylights that run the whole length of the building. The walls are white and clean—almost sparklingly so, and my footsteps echoed on a polished hardwood floor as I topped the stairs and entered the main corridor. Doctor Donaldson had come up with me, but he stayed at the top of the stairs, not venturing into the hallway.

"'I can leave you to it then?' he asked and it was plain that the man was bally terrified, so I took pity on him.

"'I will call into your office before I leave,' I replied, and he was off and away down the stairs almost before I had finished speaking.

"I was left alone in the corridor, and as the sound of Donaldson's footsteps descended away from me leaving silence behind, I became aware that there was definitely something strange in the air. I have developed a sense for these things, as you know, and I felt it straight away—a thick cloying miasma despite the sunlight, a tingling at the nape of my neck and a throbbing in my guts that all told me there was a presence here.

"I walked along the corridor, slowly, trying to intuit what it was that was affecting me so. As I reached the farthest room from the stairwell, I heard a soft voice, little more than a whisper, reciting a passage I did not recognize but which chilled my blood.

"'*Strange is the night where black stars rise,*'

"'*And strange moons circle through the skies.*'

"They were only words, but spoken as they were in a stilted cadence, and in a whisper that still managed to echo and ring around me, they gave me pause in my exploration. The voice came again, and I pinpointed a source, a room on my right. I stepped forward and looked though a small eye-level window. A thin, almost skeletal, chap sat curled in the far corner, wrapped tight in a stitched canvas jacket bound such that his arms were hugged close to his chest. He stared upward, to the corner of the room, as if watching something only he could see. He was still reciting.

"'*Song of my soul, my voice is dead,*'

"'*Die thou, unsung, as tears unshed.*'

"Despite it being full daylight, with sun still streaming in from above through the skylight, it was as if the room beyond the small window lay in dim twilight, with the shadows hanging particularly darkly around the hunched figure in the corner. I must have moved, or made a sound, for the occupant stopped in his recital and looked straight at me. I looked into the flat empty eyes of a mind gone elsewhere. The dark around him seemed to swirl and thicken.

"'*The shadows lengthen in Carcosa,*' he said, looking straight at me."

"Five minutes later I was back downstairs in Doctor Donaldson's office. He took one look at me and poured snifters of brandy for both of us. He smiled thinly as he passed me the glass.

"'It seems you will need little convincing,' he said.

I took a stiff drink before replying.

"'The man at the end of the corridor—he is at the heart of the matter?'

"The doctor nodded. 'So it would seem. His name is Jephson, and he is—or was—an actor of some note before coming to us. He has been here for a month now—as have the nightly disturbances on the top floor. Can you help us?'

"I said yes, although in truth I was as yet unsure as to how to proceed.

"'Can I talk to the chap?' I asked.

"Donaldson downed his own brandy in one gulp, like a man well practiced in the procedure.

"'If you must,' he replied. 'You will get little out of him but that doggerel he spouts. And we cannot unbind him, for he is a danger to himself if his hands are freed—he has made several suicide attempts.'

"We reached an agreement that I could interview the man on the Tuesday afternoon, and I returned here to Chelsea, hoping that my library might provide me with a starting place in my investigation.

"I was to have little luck. I could find no reference in any of my books to a place called Carcosa. The mention of 'black stars' had struck a chord, mirroring as it did some of the descriptions of the outmost realms of the *Outer Darkness*, but I was still little the wiser by late afternoon. I decided to try a different tack, and headed for the West End, and *The George* bar in the Strand.

"I was in search of actors, and as you know, *The George* is one of their favorite watering holes. By admitting I was willing to buy ale in exchange for information, it did not take me long to find someone who knew someone who might be able to help me. Sometimes this little dance leads nowhere, but on Monday night I was lucky, and an hour after entering the bar found myself in a quiet corner with a rather voluble Irishman who not only knew Jephson, but had worked with him in the recent past.

"'It was that damnable play,' the big man said, wiping ale foam from his whiskers, and off we went on a long involved story that I will not bore you chaps with, for it would take too long in the telling. There are only a few pertinent facts in any case, for the big man was most adept at elaborating his tale, spinning it out in order to receive more ale for his trouble. The facts, as I saw them, are these: Jephson had been commissioned to work on a play, and he was the first of the actors to receive the script. The Irishman had got a glimpse of it—a leather-bound volume that was purported to be the only copy and which Jephson was under instruction to keep secret and close to his person. Jephson had read the play—and had almost immediately been driven quite mad. As for the book itself, the Irishman did not know what had become of it—indeed he knew nothing of it beyond the title

'*The King in Yellow*.'"

"I did not see how this new information would help me, and a further search of my library that night for anything about the play proved fruitless. I was rather disgruntled, and somewhat bemused, when I returned to Southwark on Tuesday for my meeting with Jephson himself.

"You will remember that it was a scorcher of a day, and the ground floor of Bethlem was indeed as hot and muggy as the rest of the city. The top floor, despite the preponderance of windows being bathed in full sunlight, still felt like walking past the door to an icehouse.

"Jephson had been raised from his place in the corner and sat on a chair in the center of the room, although he was still tightly bound, and he still stared, flat-eyed at a point in the upper left corner. He muttered continually under his breath, although I could, as yet, make out no words. A nurse put a chair inside the door for me, refusing to enter and backing away as soon as I thanked her. The door shut behind me with a clang and I was left alone in the room with a madman.

"Only we were not alone—not entirely. Strange shadows crawled and capered in the corners, and once again I felt the tingle at my neck and roiling in my gut that told me there was more here than meets the eye.

"Jephson would not look at me, merely kept staring into the corner and mumbling.

"'I know about the play,' I said, but if I was hoping to get a reaction, I was to be sorely disappointed. His gaze never wavered from the corner.

"I talked about the Irishman, about the play, about *The George*, but nothing got a twitch from the chap. It seemed my trip had been for naught. Then I said one thing, one small sentence that changed every-thing.

"'Tell me about Carcosa.'

"He turned his head, ever so slowly, and that dead-eyed stare fixed on me. The temperature dropped alarmingly, and it seemed to my eyes that the darkness gathered, swaddling the man in shadows every bit as constricting as the stitched jacket. He recited again, a singsong whisper that had more than a touch of the rhythm and cadence of a chant.

"'*Songs that the Hyades shall sing,*'

"'*Where flap the tatters of the King,*'

"'*Must die unheard in dim Carcosa.*'

"At the mention of flapping tatters, I heard it for myself—a sound like cloth being taken and slapped by a wind. It lasted mere seconds before Jephson went back to staring at the corner. The shadows stilled in their dance, and the actor returned to muttering.

"A warmer breeze hit my face, reminding me of the season.

"And that was that, for a while at least. I could get nothing out of him. He was lost, in a far-off place—his Carcosa at a guess. Wherever it was, it was out of my reach at that moment.

"I knocked loudly on the door and, after a wait that almost had me wondering whether I was to join Jephson in his seclusion, the worried nurse finally let me out. I took the chair down the corridor a way, sat down, lit a smoke and waited to see what nightfall might bring."

"I sat there for several hours. The nurse brought me tea and biscuits around six that did much to improve my mood, and several smokes calmed my nerves, frayed as they had been by the encounter in the room.

"I was still no nearer to discovering the nature of the thing I had come to investigate, but I got a clearer idea of what I was up against just after the sun went down. Darker shadows crept in the long corridors of Bethlem Asylum, only to be dispelled by gas lamps lit by an elderly janitor who scurried away as soon as the job was done.

"Several seconds later Jessup started whispering again. As before, the strangeness started with his reciting—I was coming to believe it must be passages from *The King in Yellow.*

"'*Strange is the night where black stars rise,*'

"'*And strange moons circle through the skies.*'

"I instinctively looked up through the skylight. There were no black stars, no strange moons, although if there had been I might have taken a blue funk and fled there and then.

"The corridor dimmed and darkened despite the gas lamps. It got colder fast, a layer of fine frost running along the hardwood flooring and up the walls. I happened to be looking along the length of the corridor, so spotted what occurred almost immediately.

"Something flowed out through the door of Jephson's room—I know that is hardly much of a description, but I have no other words for it. It was at eye level and looked at first little more than thin smoke, but it quickly coalesced, going from gray to yellow, and solidifying into an object that spun in a slow circle, hanging in mid air. As I said, it was a deep yellow, almost golden, and was a solid representation of a pictograph or hieroglyph—three curved and distorted arms reaching out from a globular central hub. The symbol was neither Babylonian nor Egyptian—indeed it did not resemble anything I had ever come across in all my reading in the field.

"The yellow sigil spun in time with Jephson's recital.

"*'Along the shore the cloud waves break,'*

"*'The twin suns sink behind the lake,'*

"*'The shadows lengthen in Carcosa.'*

"The spinning sign made its way along the corridor, heading straight for me. As it passed by them, yells, groans and screams came from the previously quiet cells, tortured souls pleaded for mercy, others shouted their joy, and some laughed, too loud, as if they would never stop.

"I heard the noise I had heard before, the sound of cloth being taken and slapped by a wind.

"*'Where flap the tatters of the King.'*

"The yellow sign spun faster. The corridor behind it seemed to melt and fade, like wet paint in heavy rain, washing away until I could see through, see beyond.

"And suddenly I was not looking at corridor walls and hardwood floors. I looked out from a high vantage to a moonlit scene—three pale yellow moons floating amid black stars, and a stunted forest along the banks of a black lake that drew the eyes to a castle, huge and decayed, perilously perched on an outcrop of crystal. And although it was far off, a figure clearly stood there on the highest battlement, long black robes flapping in the breeze. It turned towards me, a wrinkled yellow mask with no features.

"The King in Yellow fixed his gaze on me.

"I fled, screaming."

Carnacki paused at this point, which we all knew was a sign to refill our glasses and get fresh smokes lit. No one spoke. Arkwright, as usual, seemed almost bursting to ask a question, but Carnacki looked sterner than his normal ebullient self, and gave Arkwright a stare that would brook no discussion.

"Before I go on I want to say something about what I have just related. You chaps have heard me expound many times on the Outer Darkness and the entities that dwell there. What I believe I saw was a direct vision of those realms, a place where dream, myth and reality are not separated by rationality as they are here in the inner microcosm. Somehow Jephson's madness was inextricably linked to that place, and the connection enabled it to draw close, so close that the veil was parted. I could see through—and be seen. I have no doubt that *The King in Yellow* exists, over there in his high castle—for if we have royalty here on this plane, why not there?"

Once again Arkwright looked ready to ask a question, but Carnacki waved him away and headed for his chair. It was a matter of seconds before we were all settled again, and Carnacki took up the tale immediately where he had let off.

"I came to my senses sitting on a chair in a room on the ground floor with two nurses fussing over me, and feeling like a damned fool, although my nerves were not sufficiently strong to allow me to go back up to that corridor right away.

"You chaps know I am not prone to taking a funk without rather extreme provocation, but I am not afraid to tell you that I was rather severely spooked, and in need of a stiffener. I found Donaldson's brandy in the desk in his office—the man himself had long since gone home for the evening—and helped myself to a double. After that, and a smoke of my pipe outside in the hospital grounds, I began to feel more like my old self, but even then I knew I would not be able to make myself go back to the top floor—not without the proper defenses.

"I had one of the nurses call for a carriage, and made my way back here, where I picked up my box of tricks and returned in the same carriage, arriving back at the Asylum just before midnight. I paused long enough for another leisurely smoke then carried the box up to the top of the stairs.

"It was time to pit my wits against whatever walked those corridors."

"The top floor was once again quiet and still. Thin moonlight came in from high above but the flickering gas lamps kept any shadows at a safe distance. I stood there for several minutes in the silence, ready to flee again should an attack come before I was prepared, but it seems I had arrived at a lull in proceedings. I set about readying myself. I drew my circles in chalk on the hardwood floors, knowing that should nothing come of them, I was earning myself a telling off from the same nurses who had tended to me earlier.

"I need not describe the nature of my defenses—you all know of the ritual circles and the electric pentacle—although Arkwright will be most interested in my newest battery, for it has a greatly increased life, and provides a much steadier power output than any I have tried previously. It was about to be put to its greatest test yet.

"I switched on the pentacle and stepped into the circle. The valves washed the corridor in an aura of rainbow colors, and the faint hum of the battery was the only thing breaking the silence.

"I stood in the center, lit up a smoke, and began my night watch."

"I did not have long to wait. I got my first intimation that something was happening when the blue valve brightened considerably. At almost the same moment Jephson started in on his recital again, his whispering voice clearly audible even above the hum of the battery.

"'*Along the shore the cloud waves break,*'

"'*The twin suns sink behind the lake,*'

"'*The shadows lengthen in Carcosa.*'

"Thin yellow smoke came through the door of the man's room and began to thicken and solidify in the corridor. The temperature dropped markedly and once again frost ran along the floor and walls, although this time I remained warm, almost hot, inside my protective circle.

"The blue valve began to pulse in time with Jephson's voice, flaring ever brighter as the yellow sign drifted closer.

"'*Strange is the night where black stars rise,* '

"'*And strange moons circle through the skies,* '

"'*But stranger still is lost Carcosa.* '

"The occupants of the other cells woke, and once again there was a chorus of screams, laughter and howls of pain and anguish to accompany Jephson's voice. The blue valve pulsed in sympathy.

"The yellow sign floated ever closer, coming to a halt in the air not three feet away from the edge of my defenses.

"And now I did indeed feel cold—a biting chill that seized at my calves and began to work its way upward. Jephson's voice grew in strength and volume, echoing along the length of the corridor. The yellow sign flared brighter and spun in time, its glow threatening to overwhelm and consume the glow from the pentacle.

"'*Songs that the Hyades shall sing,*'

"'*Where flap the tatters of the King,*'

"'*Must die unheard in dim Carcosa.*'

"The corridor behind the sigil melted and swam and I was given another glimpse of the forested landscape beyond. The robed figure still stood on the battlements of the high castle.

"And once again *The King in Yellow* turned his masked gaze upon me.

"Despite the protection provided by the pentacle, I felt cold creep into my very spine. Jephson's whispering seemed to come from somewhere inside my own head, burrowing its way into the dark recesses of my mind.

"'*Song of my soul, my voice is dead,*'

"'*Die thou, unsung, as tears unshed,*'

"'*Shall dry and die in lost Carcosa.*'

"The yellow sign drifted forward again to touch the edge of my defenses. As if I had suddenly focused a telescope, the robed king seemed to fly forward towards me until he stood there in the corridor, grim and tall in tattered robes, just beyond the sigil. His clothes flapped and fluttered in time with Jephson's voice. The blue valve flared and pulsed, attempting to combat the yellow, trying to force it away into the darkness.

"The robed figure stepped forward and put his hand on the sigil, pushing it ahead of him, forcing it to clash with the pentacle's defenses. The corridor lit up like a lightning storm in flashes of blue and yellow. Electricity crackled all around me.

"Jephson's voice rose to a shout.

"'Unmask!'

"The figure reached up to the wrinkled cloth over his face, at the same instant pushing the sigil, hard, towards me with his other hand.

"The blue valve blazed, flashed and exploded in a bolt of azure lightning. The yellow sign fell apart in a myriad of fragments that glittered and danced, vanishing before they hit the floor. The robed figure reached for me, the yellow mask the last thing to disappear as it faded into wispy smoke. Then it too was gone.

"Jephson screamed, one long despairing cry of agony that cut off sharply.

"My battery hummed slightly louder, then died, the pentacle falling dark.

"Silence fell in Bedlam."

"I checked on Jephson once I was completely sure all the excitement was over. He lay on his back in the center of his room, gaze still fixed on the same spot in the corner of the ceiling, but he was quite, quite dead.

"The nurses took over as I cleared away the pentacle, and by the time I had the box ready to transport they were already moving the other patients away from the top floor.

"Most of them seemed to be in some kind of catatonic state, but one chap appeared to take an interest in me. He looked me in the eye in passing, and once again I felt a chill pass through me as he spoke.

"*'The shadows lengthen in Carcosa.'*"

Carnacki sat back in his chair, his tale obviously done.

"Dash it, man, "Arkwright said. "What the blazes was that all about?"

Carnacki smiled.

"I cannot rightly say. But I believe I have had a damned close shave, for if I had caught even a glimpse of what was beneath that yellow mask, I might well be replacing Jephson in the vacant room. Just be thankful the peril seems to have passed gentlemen. And if you ever come across that blasted play—do not read it."

He ushered us to the door without further explanation.

"Now—out you go."

A Jaundiced Light at the End

Brian M. Sammons

illie, just keep talking to me," Frank said into his headset as he cracked open another Mountain Dew while watching the Lakers game on the muted television to his left. "Come on, you called because you wanted to talk, right?"

Billie was one of the regulars at the suicide prevention hotline Frank volunteered at. He usually ended up talking to the perpetually depressed seventeen-year-old girl two or three times a month. She never seemed sincere about taking her life, just very sad. Still, it was hotline policy to never, ever ask anyone who called if they were serious about suicide. Everyone had to be treated like they were literally out on the ledge at the moment of the call, even if most of them, like Billie, were just lonely and desperate to have someone listen to them, if just for a little while. Still, it's always better to be safe than sorry.

Frank knew all about sorry.

He shot a quick glance at the black rubber bracelets on his wrist as he pulled the can of Dew from his lips. He felt too old to still wear such gaudy things, but they did a decent job of covering up the scars.

A soft, wet sob came through Frank's headset and that caused him to stop drinking the sugary go-juice mid-swallow. While Billie always sounded sad, she had never cried before.

Better safe than . . .

"Billie? Talk to me, girl, what's got you so upset?"

Low sobs was all he heard.

"Come on, no matter what it is, if you talk to someone about it, you'll –"

"Bullshit." It was a thick, phlegmy word.

"What's bullshit, Billie?"

"All of it. Everything. Life," Billie said and then snuffled.

"No, life is not bullshit, Billie," Frank said, the hairs on the back of his neck starting to rise. *Is she for real this time?* he asked himself, while he continued, "life is all we've got and it's a beautiful thing. So whatever—"

"Oh bullshit! You don't know. You don't know where I've been, what I've seen."

"No, no of course I don't," Frank said on autopilot as his mind raced behind the scenes. *She sounds really bad. Do I hit the panic button and let the cops handle this?*

All calls to the suicide hotline were routed to the volunteers at their homes from a central hub downtown. There was no office where people went and took calls at a switchboard. Not in this modern, wireless, and always connected age. Everyone who helped out on the hotline had a laptop provided to them, and the calls were sent through it. At a press of a button, Frank could send the caller's phone number directly to the police where they could hopefully trace it back to an address, or use the cell phone's GPS, if they had one. Frank was only supposed to hit this "panic button" if he felt the caller was beyond being talked down from the metaphorical ledge. Since he had started volunteering on the hotline over a year ago, he had never had to press the button.

Shit, what do I do?

"See, you're not even listening to me," Billie whispered.

"No, no, I am, I swear it. It's just . . . look, I know what you're going through. Really, I do. I've been there myself and well, I made a bad decision once. A real bad decision, one I hope you don't ever make. That's why I do this now. I want to help others so they don't do what I did, because I got lucky, but many don't get a second chance like I did."

Frank stopped to let Billie respond, but for a long, cold moment, all he heard was the girl's breathing. Then, "So how did you do it? And how did you fuck it up?"

"That's not important, I just wanted you to know that I do know what you're—"

"Tell me!" Billie shouted. Then, in a whisper, she added, "Please."

"I slit my wrists." Thinking about it always made Frank's scars itch. He was sure it was some weird psychosomatic crap, but knowing that didn't do a thing to stop the itch. "I got lucky, because the woman who was leaving me at the time happened to come by to pick up some things she had forgotten when she moved out, and she found me."

"You tried to kill yourself over a woman?" Billie said with a hint of a grin in her voice. "That's pathetic."

Good, keep her talking, joking, anything. Frank thought. "Yeah, I know that now, but at the time I was in a very dark place. Who knows, it might have been a cry for help, attention, I don't know. My shrink thinks I was trying to guilt my ex into staying with me, and if so, I can say now that was pretty lame on my—"

"So . . ." Billie interrupted and then stayed quiet for a long time. "When you did it . . . when you were dying, did you see anything? Like a light or something?"

Frank's stomach became a cold, hollow pit as unwanted memories came flooding back to him. "What?"

"A light? A color? Anything?" Then in a monotone devoid of any humanity, Billie added, "I would give anything to see some color. Everything is so damn gray now . . ."

Frank heard a clunk and recognized it as the phone being put down on a table or counter. He called out to Billie, but got no answer. He heard metal scraping on metal and the sounds of whipping wind. Another memory rose to the surface of Frank's mind, something Billie had offered on one of her first calls into the hotline: she lived on the ninth floor of an apartment building. "Billie!" Frank shouted into his headset as his finger jammed the panic button. Then a scream came over the phone. It was high-pitched, full of fear and tinged with anguish. As Frank listened to it, yelling the girl's name into his headset, he heard it fall away and then suddenly stop.

Afterwards it was about how Frank always guessed it would be, should something like that happen. First the police had come and asked a bunch of questions. Chief among them: they wanted to know if he recorded the call. When he told them no, they wanted to know why not. Having to explain the law to cops was always weird, and they never liked it, but Frank had to tell them that if they recorded the call, they would have to let the caller know that they were right at the start. When other suicide hotlines had done that in the past, most of the callers hung up. So no, it hadn't been recorded.

Next came those that ran the hotline. Two together in person, lanky, always smiling Matthew Carpenter and pretty, red-headed Lacy Dwyer, who together had co-founded the hotline, and two others, Jamie and Amber, individually on the phone. None of them blamed Frank for what happened, or if they did, they didn't say it to him. They were sure he had tried his best and had done everything by the book. They asked if he wanted to talk to a counselor about "the incident," as they all called it. That was such a nice, neutral phrase they were no doubt instructed to use whenever this happened. The hotline even offered to pay for the therapy. Since Frank was already seeing a shrink every other week, he politely declined. That didn't stop them from pressing the issue. Someone even told him that "an incident" like this happened to another hotline volunteer just last week, and she found the counseling very comforting. Still, Frank said no.

That night, after everyone had gone and he was alone again, the bad dreams started. He was expecting them. After all, he had just heard a young girl kill herself, and despite what the hotline people told him about not feeling responsible, he did. How could he not? He supposed that was a good thing. A very emotional, human way to feel, but that didn't make it suck any less.

Thankfully he didn't remember the dreams. He just kept waking up all through the night feeling uneasy and sick. He would then toss and turn in his bed for an hour or more before drifting back off to sleep, only to wake up after a few more fitful minutes to start the cycle all over again. The one thing he did recall from his failed attempts to sleep was something Billie had said: "When you were dying, did you see anything? Like a light or something?" That was the thought he woke up to every time, because yes, he had seen something back when he slit his wrists. However, he had spent more than a year convincing himself that what he saw that night was nonsense. Just synapses misfiring in a dying brain, isn't that what the doctors and scientists said about all near-death experiences? Still, the memory was there, itching in the back of his mind.

Three days after "the incident" and the weather outside had changed to match his mood. Gone were the famous blue skies of L.A. In their place was a dull, dripping, gray more suited to Seattle.

Frank sat at his desk, a cold can of beans with a spoon sticking out of its open top to his left, a piss-warm can of Mountain Dew to his right, with plenty of the soda's empty brothers lying scattered around his feet. A new addition to his desk was an ashtray already filled to overflowing with crushed-out butts. He had quit that nasty habit three years back when his apartment building had done the very Californian thing and gone totally smoke free. It was now easier for him to buy and smoke marijuana in this city than tobacco, and that was a thought that would have caused him to laugh just a week ago.

Tonight was Frank's return to the hotline. The people who ran it had originally told him to take some time off after "the incident," a couple of weeks at least, but today Matthew from the hotline had called. After a few awkward moments of "How you doing?" he sheepishly asked if Frank could cover a shift tonight. One of their volunteers had taken some unscheduled personal time yesterday and another simply didn't report in for her shift tonight. That left the hotline in a lurch, and so if Frank was feeling up to it . . .

More to prove something to himself than out of any loyalty, Frank now had his headset on and was staring at the open laptop. Dread slithered around in his guts like an eel, and his recent diet of whatever he could find in a can sure wasn't helping matters. Then the first call came in. It was Martha, a retiree and prisoner – to hear her tell it – at an old folks' home. She was much like Billie had been: a lonely soul looking for some kind of companionship, no matter how brief and impersonal it was. Thankfully, that's where the similarities between Martha and Billie ended. The call lasted twenty-two minutes and ended without incident.

Thank God, Frank thought as he leaned back in his chair with an almost forgotten expression on his face: a smile.

Eleven minutes later he got a second call.

The man called himself Tyler and he sounded young, maybe still in his teens, and right from the start, Frank had a bad feeling about it.

"They took it all away," Tyler mumbled into the phone after Frank got his name and asked how he was doing.

"Took what, Tyler? And who?"

"The colors, man. Everything bright is just . . . gone. It's all gray now. Everything and everyone is gray. Even the textures. Whatever I touch is cold, lifeless, and filthy. Whatever I eat or drink is flavorless. I'm stuck in a fucking world of gray."

"Okay, Tyler, I'm going to ask you something, don't take offense, but I have to ask: are you on anything right now?"

"None of that shit works anymore," Tyler wailed in despair. "Man, I've taken every sort of upper I could get my hands on and nothing changes. I still feel like I'm all used up inside and I'm just too stupid to lay down and die. And everyone I see around me is just like me: a hollow, rotting shell. Ashes, man, ashes and dust everywhere. Because everyone's already dead—you, me, everyone, but nobody gets that."

Frank's hand shot up and hit the panic button. *Keep him talking, don't let this one slip past you,* he thought. "Alright, I hear you. So tell me how all this started. When did you notice—"

"I just want to see something bright again, it doesn't have to be beautiful. I just want to feel . . .something. Shit, even my blood is just cold, gray sludge and there's no pain . . . no pain. . . ."

"What?" Frank's voice croaked out.

"I've been looking up how to do it online for days, and everyone says that if you're going to slit your wrists, do it in a tub of cold water to numb the pain. Fuck that. I wanted the pain. I wanted to feel something, damn it. So I did it right here on the couch. I got my left wrist good, cut it right to the bone, and I did it right: up and down, none of that sideways, sissy-shit for me, man. Hell, I did it so good that I can't use that hand no more, so I had to put the knife in my teeth to do the right wrist. That one's not as deep, but it's still bleeding good. And you know what, I didn't feel nothing. Not a goddamn thing. So I know for sure that I'm already dead, dead and gone, just like he told me."

"Jesus Christ," Frank whispered as both of his wrists started itching again.

"No, not him. I've been praying to him for days and the fucker never returns a call," Tyler mimicked a laugh totally devoid of joy. "No, it's that other guy, the yellow bastard. Been watching me for days. Whispering to me. Showing up in my dreams. He's the only bright thing left in this shitty world, so I figured, why not join him? I mean, anywhere has to be better than here, right?"

"Who, Tyler? Who told you that?" Frank said and thought, *could someone have talked him into doing that to himself? That's murder or manslaughter or something, right? Got to find out who, the police will want to know that for sure.*

"It was the king. The one in yellow. The one . . ." Tyler's voice trailed and Frank noticed the sluggish, sleepy sound to it. ". . . who waits at the end. . . ."

Frank's finger mashed the police alert button again and again. He knew that like an elevator call button, all he had to do was press it once, but that didn't stop him. "Tyler!" he shouted into his headset. "Come on, stay with me!"

"Have . . . have you sss . . ." The voice on the other end of the line was a slurred whisper.

"What?"

". . . seen it? Have you seen the yellow . . . the yellow . . . sssss . . ."

Frank next heard the clunk of the phone hitting the floor, and no matter how loud he screamed, no one answered him.

Repetition followed.

First came the police with the same questions as before. Frank answered them, only with more grunts and nods of the head than words this time. He didn't bother to tell them about the mysterious "yellow king" Tyler had mentioned. It very well could have been the kid's dying mind playing tricks on him. Frank knew that much from firsthand experience. Besides, without any real info on the mysterious monarch, it all seemed pointless. So goddamn pointless.

Then came the people from the hotline, but this time they called on him only by phone and there were just three of them, pretty Lacey had quit a few days before. According to Matthew, she took off without saying anything to anyone. No one had heard from her since. Matthew thought it must have been all the stress, and he hinted that things were not going well with the hotline, but he kept the specifics to himself. Also no one bothered with euphemisms this time. The incident was referred to as a suicide.

And of course, there were the nightmares, which were always the same. He was in a dark tunnel with only a feeble glimmer of light at its end. Even Frank's slumbering mind recognized what that light was supposed to represent, and part of him remembered seeing it before, but it wasn't the warm, welcoming brightness he associated with heaven. It wasn't even the fearsome, fiery glow he expected from hell. It was wan and sickly, a creeping, seeping light. It was joyless, lacking any comfort or warmth, the color of an old bruise and jaundiced flesh. As he got closer to the end of that tunnel, he could see something moving in that cold light, a tall figure in a tattered robe with something on its head and a beckoning hand. . . . That's when he would wake up, always with a scream, and once with blood on his hands after he had scratched his wrists so much during the night that he had split the scarred flesh.

The days that followed fell one into another and another until each was indistinguishable from the next. Frank would wake, eat something, lay on the couch and watch TV, eat something else, then go back to bed. Since he didn't go out, bathing seemed pointless, as did cooking. He stayed on his strict all-canned diet, and food became an indiscernible paste he would force himself to swallow only when his stomach growled its loudest.

The phone rang a lot for the first few – days? weeks? – but he figured it was either that special slice of cubical hell he called a job or the hotline, and since he didn't want to talk to either, he didn't. The phone was now mercifully silent, as was his constant companion, his television. He had kept it on night and day, but it had been mostly a white-noise generator, a flashing and hissing rectangle in the background; something to keep his mind sedated and away from unpleasant truths. He did recall something from the dull images and monotone drone, the word epidemic. Frank never thought he would see that word linked to suicide, but that's what all the talking heads on TV were calling it. The same dead-eyed faces spat out different reasons behind it all, but Frank could not bring himself to give much of a damn. He did remember snippets of the various stories, the cold details of a young life cut short here, some parents crying for the cameras there. The only thing that still flickered with any light in Frank's memory was the video that showed Amanda Dwyer killing herself. The one that YouTube kept trying to take down, but nevertheless kept popping up on the web, as if the fifteen-year-old's death had taken on a life of its own. In the phone-captured video, the cute, chubby girl was standing in front of a coffee shop, already wet with gasoline. "I always wanted to be famous. Do you think this will do it?" She said through a sad, twitchy smile. She added, "I hope the fire will be bright. That would be nice," before flicking the lighter and immolating herself. The thing that made Frank remember the video was the fact that he was sure he had seen the girl before. More than that, he knew her from somewhere.

Wait, isn't Lacy's last name Dwyer? Frank came to a half-formed conclusion, one he had reached several times before but always let slip away. However, this time his mind spiraled in a new direction, *and that wasn't on TV, I saw that on the computer.*

With that thought, he looked across his dark apartment, past the empty cans and crusty rags he used for his itching wrists, through the cloud of cigarette smoke and buzzing flies, to his open laptop. The screen was dark, gone was his exotic island wallpaper, but the monitor wasn't completely dead. Not yet. Not like everything else. In the upper right corner, something amber flashed. It was the icon telling him that he had a call waiting for him on the hotline.

"God damn it, leave me alone," Frank grumbled, picking up an empty tuna fish can from his lap and tossing it at the computer. He missed by a mile, but the action did make him feel the slightest bit better for the briefest of moments. He looked for something else to throw, but all the other cans were at his feet, and that realization murdered the thought of more missile fire. Leaning back onto his sweat-soaked couch, Frank's eyes went back to the flashing yellow light on his laptop screen. *Just like a bug, now I get it,* he thought as he was drawn to the dull flicker. More memories stirred in him, a scream that faded and then suddenly stopped, the *thunk* of a dropped phone, the *woosh* of a sudden eruption of flame, a voice whispering, "Come and see what awaits. . . ."

Frank shook his head to clear his thoughts and found himself sitting at his desk, in front of his hotline-provided laptop. He looked back at his couch, confused and half expecting to see himself still lying on it. Instead all he saw was the dark room and the cold, gray light outside the window on the opposite wall. The ceaseless rain was still coming down, leaving dirty streaks everywhere, and Frank could not bear to look at it anymore. So he turned to the computer and pressed the button to accept the call.

"Yeah?" he croaked out in a voice that had gone days without talking to anyone.

Static hiss was the only sound that answered him, so Frank stretched out a hand to hit the disconnect button, but froze when a lifeless, sexless voice mumbled into his ear, "It's the alignment, you know. . . ."

"What?" Frank said, and then remembered some of his hotline training, and added, "Who am I talking to and how can I help you?"

"Alignment," the voice repeated, "the angles, phases, stars and all that shit. Aldebaran is ascendant and things have lined up so that right here, right now, two kingdoms border each other. That event allows the huge falsehood we call reality to be washed away for a little while, so that we can see the truth of things. No, not everyone can see what really lies behind reality, but we can, because we're sensitive to it. We're special. We've either tasted it before, or longed for it in our deepest dreams. We're the chosen, lucky few."

"I'm not following you. . . ," Frank said, but he knew that somehow, in some way he didn't understand, he was lying even before the voice called him out on it.

"Bullshit. You know exactly what I mean. You've been there, you've seen it, I know, you've told me as much, so no more bullshit, okay?"

A memory sparked to life inside Frank, "Billie?" he whispered.

There was a brief silence and then the caller continued. The tone of the voice remained the same, but something about it had changed. The cadence? Pitch? "He told me all about it, man, the Monarch of Carcosa, and he'll tell you too, if you'll only listen to him."

"Tell me what?" Frank said, his left thumb starting to rub his right wrist.

"He tried to tell you before, don't you remember? But you wouldn't listen to—"

"Shut up," Frank pleaded.

"This *life*," that second word came out a mocking hiss, "is a lie. Death is reality. It's all 'round us, the very air we breathe is loaded with dead things. Everything you eat is dead. Man, everyone you see is slowly dying, decaying right before your eyes. They're all just hollow, rotting shells, nothing more. That's not all. The building you live in, the clothes on your back, the computer before you, all of it, everything, is rotting, falling apart, breaking down, becoming heaps of ash and dust in a meaningless world of gray. Even the cosmos, since it first exploded into being, has been dying, aeon by aeon and minute by minute. Entropy is the only universal constant. Deep down, everyone knows that, but only a few have the courage to admit —"

"Stop it." Frank commanded.

"So the question becomes, why drag it out? Why play the stupid game? It's all rigged, no matter what you do, you're going to go bust. The house always wins, man. With that in mind, the only sane thing to do is to play by your own rules. Become master of your own fate. Decide when, where, and how you cash your chips in. Don't mess around with that sissy-shit, just be a man and —"

"Stop it!" Frank shouted, ripping his headset off and throwing it across the room. As he did, it came unplugged from the computer, so what was said next, came out of the laptop's speakers, after a long moment of silence.

"There is something you can do, if you're not ready to face the ultimate truth to everything, if you're still afraid, or if you're feeling benevolent."

The caller continued to talk to Frank for a while, laying out plans that seemed to make all sorts of terrible sense.

"Oh God," Frank moaned.

"Nope, that's another lie," the caller mocked, the voice changing once more in a way so subtle it was nearly indistinguishable. "Come on, you tried touching the truth once before, you just needed more conviction. That's why I'm here, to help you, to guide you. To save you. And who knows, if you do it right, it could even make you famous."

Once again, there was pounding. Not in his head, that was a constant, but at his door. Frank had heard that a lot lately, and all the times before he had ignored it, but this time he didn't. This time he knew who was knocking, his last caller had told him. "Come in," he said.

The apartment door slowly opened, pushing over a pile of unread mail and official red-stamped notices that had been slipped through his mail slot. Matthew from the hotline walked in. "Frank, are you . . ." he began, before the stench hit him full force, causing his nose to wrinkle, eyes to water behind his glasses, and his hand to come up to his face in an impromptu mask. "Damn, what's that smell?"

Matthew's other hand went for the light switch on the wall, and after clicking it up and down few times, he muttered to himself, "Oh yeah, right," before shouting, "Frank, you in here?" and peering into the apartment's gloom.

"I'm over here," Frank said, watching the lanky silhouette slowly find its way towards him through the gray waste of his cluttered hallway.

"What happened here? I ran into your landlord downstairs and she's pissed. She said you haven't paid your rent in over two months, your neighbors are complaining about the smell, and you won't answer your door. She said that your lights and water were shut off weeks back because you haven't paid those either, and she wants you gone. She's even called the cops to come and evict you, only with all the craziness happening out there, they haven't had time. . . ." Matthew trailed off as his eyes finally adjusted to the gloom and he saw Frank, sitting at his desk, in front of his laptop, with his headset pulled over his greasy, matted hair. "Wow, Frank, you look like crap. Sorry, but that's the truth. What happened to you, and why you just sitting here in the dark?"

Frank smiled through a weeks-old, food-specked beard as his lips dragged over dry, rank teeth, "Just talking to people on the hotline. You know, listening and helping."

"Uh-huh. Frank, you know the hotline has been shut down for weeks, right? The police are taking all the suicide calls now. Besides, like the lady said downstairs, you don't have any power, so how can you—"

"They're still calling, they're still dying. That never stops . . . never stops. . . ." Frank whispered as the husk took another step closer, a look of some sort on its cadaverous face. Was that concern? Repulsion? It didn't matter. Emotions, like everything else in life, were utterly meaningless.

"Frank, I'm worried about you. I think all this . . . whatever the hell is going on, got to you. It's alright, buddy. A lot of the volunteers have had it rough during this. Hell, before the cops killed the hotline, I was pretty much running it by myself. So you're not alone, and I don't want to see you . . . get hurt. That's why I came over, and I'm glad I did. So come on, and let me get you out of here and I can help you."

Matthew placed his cold, dead hand on Frank's shoulder. His withered lips curled back into an unrecognizable expression to Frank. It was familiar, yet alien. The sunken, hollow eyes above it remained flat, lifeless.

"No, Matthew, let me help you." Frank said, and in his muddled memory, the voice of the caller came back to him, explaining its plan as it had the first time, and every night since. *There is something you can do, if you're not ready to face the ultimate truth to everything, if you're still afraid, or if you're feeling benevolent. You can always help others, all the poor fools that don't see the truth behind the life that's been pulled over their eyes. All the people walking around that don't already know that they're corpses.*

You can save them from the slow, painful decay of life. You can spare them the sagging of flesh, the dulling of the senses, the weakening of bones, the failing memories, the uncontrollable bowels and bladder, and the loss of all that they loved. Save them from all the little deaths that need to pile up around most people before they finally give in to the truth of things. In helping others bypass those indignities, you might fool yourself with moments of pleasure in your own, so-called life. Many people do, more and more every day. And after all, you've tried your own death and found it unpalatable, or perhaps you were just too much a coward to face what's waiting at the end? Maybe sampling someone else's death would taste sweeter to you and give you the courage that you're obviously lacking.

Frank's hand swept up in an arc, the kitchen knife he held in it was filthy but sharp, and it cut through the dull cloth of Matthew's shirt, and the gray flesh behind it, with ease. A gout of dark fluid gushed out and something uncoiled from the dead man's stomach, and in that briefest of moments, Frank saw red. Bright, hot, glorious red, a single flash of something he had almost forgotten. Likewise, it made him do a forgotten thing, a mirror of what had been on Matthew's face before shock and pain had replaced it, Frank smiled.

In a span of a few blinks, Frank's twitchy rictus was already starting to fade as the lanky shadow in front of him gasped and shrunk back. The beautiful red flash was gone, it had only been a tiny spark of color in a world of gray, but it was enough for Frank. Now only the cold sludge that dripped from Matthew's guts and pooled on the floor beneath him remained. Luckily for Frank, he knew how to make that flash return.

The frightened husk turned and shambled for the door to the apartment, his glasses falling from his face and feet slipping over the weeks' worth of cans and wrappers on the ground, with Frank rising, chasing, and slashing behind him. Flash after beautiful, red flash filled Frank's eyes as the knife swooped through the air. He heard a weird thing as he continued with his wet work, not the screams of the dead man before him who stubbornly clung to the lie of life, but another long forgotten thing; laughter. *Is that me?* Frank thought with something approaching joy as his blade now descended in powerful, white-knuckled thrusts.

Then, all too quickly, it was over. The empty shell lay at his feet, silent and unmoving. Sticky, gray fluid was everywhere, and no matter how many times Frank's knife plunged into the shapeless mass, the beautiful sparks of light did not return, nor did the feelings they had elicited. Once more Frank was cold and his world colorless. Not even the fading thought that he had saved his friend from the cruel lie of life brought him any . . . what was the word again? Oh yes; joy. But just like the spark, Frank also knew how he could find that again.

But first, he had to be careful. As dull and lifeless as this world was, he still had to be cautious in it. Those who were slaves to the lie clung to their delusions and punished anyone that tried to show them the truth. So Frank went to the door of his apartment and looking into the hallway to see if anyone had heard him. However, instead of the gray hall of his apartment building, Frank saw the dark tunnel that had haunted his dreams for so long. And like all the times previous, far down at one end of the tunnel there was a cold, tawny light seeping in, and a tall figure dressed in tattered yellow robes with a golden crown on his head. The Lord of Carcosa was no longer beckoning him to come forth, instead he inclined his regal head ever so slightly in a nod of approval, and Frank knew that behind the pallid mask that the monarch wore, the King in Yellow was smiling at him.

And that caused Frank to smile back.

THE YELLOW FILM

GARY MCMAHON

Sarajevo, 1993

The city is a warzone. There isn't much time. He must retrieve what it is he came back for and then go. If he stays here too long, he will be discovered, and he will pay for what he has done. There are forces at work here that even he cannot understand.

He walks across the bombed-out ruins of the building and stands at its centre, staring up at the sky. The clouds are low and black, obscuring the moonlight. Directly above him, the atmosphere seems charged with energy: a slow-spinning vortex, perhaps created by the bomb blast, has created a vague whirlpool in the sky.

He smiles.

Then he picks up the camera and inspects it. The case is damaged, but the apparatus itself seems to be okay. The film, it appears, is safe inside.

Still smiling, he makes his way to the outer perimeter of the bomb site, where a jeep is waiting with its engine running. The driver does not look at him; the man is silent; his face does not move beneath his balaclava mask.

He sets down the camera on the rear seat and climbs into the jeep, resting one hand over the camera as he puts on his seat belt. Glancing one last time at the bombed-out wreckage, he nods. The jeep pulls away, wheel-spinning in the dirt.

Moments later, something in the bomb-debris stirs. A shattered piece of concrete shifts, a shard of glass breaks, what looks like a thin yellow-skinned hand emerges from the rubble and clenches into a fist against the night.

For James Fontaine, it started with pictures of other people's tattoos on the Internet.

He was planning to make a documentary about tattoos inspired by films. Portraits of characters, actors, inked text from film quotes . . . whatever he could find. It was a vague idea, admittedly, and one that he was starting to think might not have much mileage. And when the hell had he ever taken a personal project to completion, anyway? It seemed like he spent his whole time researching and never actually creating anything of value, just the dull work projects he took on to pay the bills.

But then he found a photo of the tattoo titled "The Pallid Mask" and something inside him shifted, like a lever moving or a switch clicking gently into place to set off a chain of mechanical events towards an unknown purpose.

It was a single jpeg image, used as part of a brief blog article written a long time ago about a short film made over two decades in the past. There was a photograph at the end of the piece, and it showed a small man – was he a dwarf, or a midget? – with a disturbing, almost featureless yellow face tattooed across the skin of his chest. The tiny man was naked, pictured from the waist up, and standing in the time-honoured bodybuilder pose, flexing his guns. The camera lens must have been focused explicitly on the tattoo because the detail showed up so well while the man's face was blurred by shadow. The inked image depicted a torn and tattered face wreathed in smoke, the flesh peeling away to reveal nothing but more smoke beneath. The eyes were blank. The mouth was just a gaping hole.

There was something powerful about the image. James was unable to look away. The caption under the photograph said "Tommy Urine, actor/inmate."

"What the hell kind of name is that?" It was amusing but for some reason he didn't feel like laughing. He dragged his attention away from the tattoo and began to read the article.

The Yellow Film

In 1993, during the Bosnian War, an underground filmmaker calling himself Phantomas Ulna apparently used the inmates from a Bosnian asylum to create a short film called "The King in Yellow," which was an adaptation of a fictional play invented in a book of short stories by the cult author Robert W. Chambers.

Ulna (whose real name is not a matter of public record) used his (probably bribed) connections in the war-torn city of Sarajevo to gain access to an unnamed mental institution and the patients kept there. Over one weekend, he shot a reel of footage that came to be known as "The Yellow Film." The footage has never been seen, and has in fact taken on an air of legend Phantomas Ulna was never heard of again – many people say that he vanished, or was killed as he made his way across the city after leaving the asylum (which was bombed a few hours later). Nobody involved in the filming has ever come forward to tell of what actually happened over the course of that weekend. It is rumoured that everyone who appeared in the film died in the blast or disappeared into the chaos of the city, but it is impossible to substantiate these claims. This is not a very well documented case, and even on the Internet it's difficult to find any further information.

I suppose we'll never know the truth – or see anything of – "The Yellow Film." My guess is that it probably never existed in the first place, and the story is simply one of many fictions to come out of a besieged city during a time of great and violent conflict. The photograph shown below is possibly a fake, but the anonymous person who sent it to me claims that it is the only surviving still from the supposed Sarajevo shoot.

The part of James that always believed he could actually complete a project came out of hiding, sniffing at the air like a dog catching the scent of something tasty. There was something about this story that caught his attention. He scanned the blog for contact details, and found an email address: weirdflix@gomail.com

James typed out a brief query requesting more information about the Sarajevo shoot (as it was called in the article), and fired off the email. Almost immediately, it was bounced back by the server. No known email address. Typical. If he was honest, though, he had not expected the email address to be current. This seemed to be the only entry on the blog, and it had been uploaded five years ago according to the date in the header. The Internet was full of stuff like this: dead websites, gathering cyber-dust and not viewed by anyone since they'd first appeared online. Behind the popular websites and billion-user social forums, there was an information graveyard; a virtual space filled with decaying ideas and interests into which hardly anybody ventured.

James went to his bookshelves. He had a copy of that Chambers book, had read it a few years ago. It took him a few minutes to find the book, but when he did he pulled it off the shelf and flicked through the pages. It was just a collection of short horror stories – and a good one, as he recalled. No matter how entertaining the stories were, there was nothing here that could lead him to the film.

Picking up the phone, he dialled a number.

The voice that answered was grumpy, still half asleep: "Yeah."

"Burke. It's me, Fontaine."

"Oh . . . hi. Bit early, isn't it?"

He glanced at his watch. It was almost noon. Being of a nocturnal bent, Burke often slept in till teatime. "Sorry, man. I need some info."

The voice was now wide awake: "Hit me."

"Obscure European film director. Goes under the unlikely name of Phantomas Ulna. Apparently he made a short movie in Sarajevo, during the war."

"What war?" If it wasn't a film or a video game, Burke had no idea.

"Doesn't matter. 1993. The film was called "The King in Yellow". He made it using mental asylum inmates."

"Wow . . . I've never heard of this. That name, though – the director. No way is that real. Give me a minute." The phone went silent, just dead air whispering in his ear.

"Okay, I'm back."

"That was quick."

"You know me. Always quick on the draw. Okay . . . Phantomas Ulna. It's the name of a character in a German TV drama. Made in 1974, directed by someone called Werner Lenz. He was a schoolteacher. Never made another film after that. Interestingly, he spent some time in Sarajevo in the 1990s, teaching media studies in several colleges and Universities."

"Interesting."

"It's all I have. Give me a few days and I'll have a snoop around, but none of that other stuff rings any bells. Is it an urban myth? Like the Nazi demon footage from Dachau?"

"I'm starting to think so."

"Lenz is still alive, btw. He lives in Berlin. I can't get a phone number or an email address. These old guys, a lot of them never use the Internet. I have a physical address, though, if that's any good."

"Okay. Give it to me. You never know. . . ."

"You never know," repeated Burke. Then he dictated the address.

That was how, three days later, James found himself standing on a quiet, affluent street in the Pankow district of Berlin. He wasn't quite sure why he'd been so proactive, but coming here directly, to try and speak with Werner Lenz, had seemed like the best thing to do under the circumstances. He had not been on holiday for years, had some money sitting in the bank, and wasn't due to start any work for at least three weeks when the budget came through for a series of government safety films he was contracted to shoot and edit.

But at a deeper level, he knew that he wanted to pursue this because it represented something that he had not faced in a long time. He wanted to make something that was his own – a project that nobody else could do, and only he could see through. Something about this mysterious footage had woken something within him. Call it passion, call it desire. Whatever it was, he had not believed in anything so completely since his college days, when he had considered himself a fledgling artist.

He walked along the footpath and stopped outside the house that matched the address he'd been given. It was a modest two-storey town-house, with wooden shutters at the windows and well-tended planting beds flanking the concrete steps that led up to the front door.

Now that he was here, James began to doubt his actions and feel exposed. He glanced along the street, but nobody seemed to be paying him any attention. Not the elderly woman carrying her shopping bags, nor the middle-aged jogger moving in the opposite direction. He looked again at the door, unsure of what to do next.

There was a café across the street – a low-key place that provided a good vantage point from which he might watch the house. He crossed the street and went inside, sat at a table by the window but not *in* the window: he wanted to watch without being seen. The waitress spoke good English, and recognised him as a tourist, so he ordered a pot of coffee and waited.

He did not have to wait long.

After thirty or forty minutes, a small white Fiat pulled up at the kerb outside the townhouse. There was a short pause, and then the driver's door opened. The man who stepped out onto the kerb was small and broad. He was wearing a knee-length overcoat and a crumpled fedora hat, but still James recognised him from the photograph on the website. This was a man who had allegedly appeared in the footage shot that weekend in Sarajevo; it was also the man who made a film featuring a character called Phantomas Ulmer, which was also the alleged name of the man who had filmed the adaptation of *The King in Yellow*.

A thrill of something that might have been excitement, or possibly terror, made its way through James's body. He put down his coffee cup but gripped it tightly, trying to cease the shaking of his hands.

The small man opened the door to the townhouse and went inside.

James stared at the door, wondering what he was going to do next, and why the hell he had come here. Beyond the initial mystery of the footage shot in a Sarajevo asylum, there was a deeper puzzle to solve. He had only just glimpsed its edges, but he wasn't sure if he wanted to dig any deeper. He had no doubt now that the film existed – it was not a myth. There was no evidence to support his belief, only the certainty that he felt inside. He had not been so certain about anything for a long time. If he was honest with himself, he'd be forced to admit that for the first time in years he actually felt alive.

There was something going on here. Something that might lead to the creation of a project that people would talk about for years to come. And wasn't that the whole point of all this: to make his mark and force people to notice him?

He left some money on the table and left the café, crossing the street to the townhouse. He climbed the steps and knocked rapidly on the door. Only then did he regret being so impulsive. He had no idea what to say, what to do, when the door opened.

Just as he was about to flee, the door did open. The small man stood there smiling. Without the fedora hat, he looked even more like the image in the photograph. In fact, he had barely aged at all.

"Hello," said James, feeling heat in his cheeks. "I'm sorry."

"Don't be sorry, James," said the man in a cultured European accent.

"I have been waiting for you." He pulled the door wider, brushing back shadows, stepped aside, and motioned for James to enter.

"Do you not think I monitor that website, the one with the article?" Lenz moved quickly and lightly across the cluttered room. His economical gait suggested that he floated rather than walked. He'd taken off his jacket to reveal a sturdy torso wrapped in a white long-sleeved shirt. His arms were wide, as if he worked out regularly with heavy weights.

"But how did you know my name?" James was sitting in a large armchair with a glass of whisky in his hand. He watched Lenz as he fussed with a pile of books on a low table, arranging them into a neat stack.

"Nobody has sent anything to that email address in years so it was flagged immediately. I simply did a little research and discovered that you were indeed a fellow filmmaker." He smiled. His teeth were short, stunted. They weren't very clean.

"So . . ." James put down his glass on the floor at his feet. "You're all of them. Tommy Urine, Werner Lenz, Phantomas Ulner. They're all you."

"Yes, that is correct." His clipped accent gave him a sinister air, but James wasn't afraid. Not of this tiny man.

"I'm not sure I understand any of this. Why the different identities? Who are you hiding from?"

Lenz sat down on a small dining chair against the wall – one that was probably meant for a child. He crossed his legs and smoothed his trousers with a small, dainty hand. "I'm sorry for the . . . secrecy. The obfuscation. Sarajevo was a strange time. A dark time. There were many evils abroad. When I made my . . . my little film . . . I was a different man, under the influence of all that evil. I've tried to keep the darkness at bay ever since."

"What happened back then?" James moved forward in his chair. "Don't lie to me. I know you filmed something . . . something that you shouldn't have?"

Lenz stared into James' eyes. His face was stiff, like that of a doll. "What I filmed was . . . in all honestly, I still do not know what I filmed. We only got a short piece of footage, a few minutes, before trouble outside the institution disturbed our shoot. What I saw through the camera's lens in that time was confusing: a soft billowing of something yellow, a thin, bony hand, someone very thin running towards the camera. Then darkness."

James glanced around the room. He had the feeling that it contained more than the little man's possessions. Somewhere in here, there hid memories and he wanted to access them, to dust them off and bring them out into the light. "Come on, man. This sounds like something from the Twilight Zone."

"Ah, yes," said Lenz. "That was one of my favourites. I did enjoy those American shows."

James felt tired. The travelling was catching up with him. He rubbed at his eyes with his hands; they felt dry and itchy. He yawned. "I'm sorry . . . I didn't realise how exhausted I was."

Lenz was smiling. His grubby teeth looked ugly, but his eyes were kind. "I know. And I'm sorry." He stood, took off his shirt, and pushed out his chest to show the tattoo: The Pallid Mask. Now that he saw it in the flesh, James could make out the colour. It was yellow.

"What is this?" He tried to get to his feet, stumbled, went down on his knees.

"The oldest trick in the book, my friend." The tattoo seemed to be speaking, not the little man upon whose chest it had been inked. "I lured you here, drugged you, and now I am preparing to use you for my own means."

James felt like screaming but his mouth was sealed shut. He couldn't believe he had been so stupid.

When he awoke he was strapped into an upright framework of steel tubes, like scaffolding built for a hanging. He was naked. He tried to blink but nothing happened. Then, taking in his surroundings, he re-alised that there was a long mirror on the basement wall opposite his position.

His body had been shaved clean of hair and strange symbols and shapes were daubed on his flesh. The bald, bloody, shivering man hanging by his wrists from an inverted cruciform structure was himself. He was unable to blink because his eyelids had been sliced off. There was no pain. He was too drugged-up to feel anything at all.

Puzzled, he stared at his own haggard face and tried to see some kind of light in the panicked eyes.

"I really am sorry." Lenz stepped into view. He was naked and sporting an erection that was disproportionate to his body size. He, too, was bloodied, and James knew exactly whose blood it was, where it had come from; his veins longed for its return. "But I cannot have anyone trying to get their hands on the film."

Lenz smiled: yellow baby-teeth in a tiny skull. "I went back there after the asylum was bombed, you know. The camera was still intact. Do you want to know what was inside when I opened it up?"

James could only shake his head. *No. No, no, no. . . .*

"No film . . . not that. It was gone. Instead, there was a roll of faded yellow material, like a ribbon, and written upon it in delicate black lines was a set of instructions. A map, if you will: a map to Carcosa, the land that only exists within the imagination of a long-dead writer of weird fictions. I've spent years trying to translate what was etched onto that strip of cloth, copied it onto the flesh of so many sacrifices in an attempt to access the roads and territories on the map so that I might journey there and meet the Yellow King. I have risked so much, but nothing has worked. So I continue to try, but only when an opportunity presents itself. I grow too weary to seek out fools like you. These days I wait for them to come to me instead."

James shook his head again. He wept red tears into a gaping yellow abyss.

"An opportunity just like this one, dear friend . . ." Lenz raised his hand, showing James the knife. The odd double-handle was made of what looked like bone – a small human arm, to be exact: the radius and ulna still attached together, or perhaps fused in the intense heat of something like a bomb blast. The long, thin blade was a dull yellow.

"Perhaps this time," said Lenz, advancing. "Perhaps this time, it will work." He didn't sound convinced.

The little man stopped in front of James, cocking his head to one side. He seemed to drift, his mind going elsewhere for a moment. "The atrocities I've committed, the lives I have wasted . . . so much blood I have spilled, in fact, that sacrificing you will barely even register on my conscience. Like a fart in a wind tunnel. I wish that I could grant your end more of a sense of occasion and make it signify something better than a banal rite in an underground room. I really do. But I cannot. It means nothing to me . . . unless this time something happens, of course . . . something *numinous.*"

Lenz snapped back into the moment, focusing on James.

"Truth be told, I very much doubt that it will. I commit these acts now more out of habit than the hope of something happening." He blinked, as if caught in a moment of self-realisation. "*Habit* . . . and it is such a tough one to break."

Lenz's shadow elongated, mocking the dimensions of his body. It crawled along the walls, old and sleek and monstrous.

James stared at his own face in the mirror. He barely recognised himself. Then, as his diminutive murderer moved in swiftly with the blade, he stopped seeing himself altogether and focused only on the slight billow of yellow he saw momentarily reflected in the grubby glass.

Berlin, 2004

The city is too dangerous. He can no longer stay here. He packs up his suitcase and waits for the taxi to come and take him to the airport.

The Yellow Film is locked away somewhere safe.

The map to Carcosa, those teasing instructions whose meaning remains tantalisingly out of reach, is held in a safe deposit box in a bank in Zurich. But he does not need to go there. The strange words and symbols are engraved upon his soul. He sees them whenever he closes his eyes; he dreams about them on the few occasions he is able to sleep. He has written them out time and time again on the shaved and purified skin of his victims.

He walks outside and sits down on the sidewalk. The taxi will not be long, and then he can leave this place. He listens intently but cannot hear anyone talking in the dark. The basement cell will never be found. The bodies shall not be uncovered. With that last one, he could have sworn that he saw something: a billowing movement, a flash of yellow, like something caught in his retina, as he dug into the wet cavities and exposed their internal secrets.

Perhaps he did.

Or perhaps not.

Maybe next time things will become clearer and he will finally be given access to the place where he belongs, the city that he no longer believes exists outside of an old book of stories that he once tried to put onto film.

But even this realisation isn't enough to break the habit of a lifetime.

The taxi pulls up at the kerb. Without even a backward glance, the small man with many names climbs inside and waits to be taken somewhere else.

Lights Fade

Laurel Halbany

ulia's reflection raised its arms. It rippled in the yellowed, uneven glass of the mirror. It turned slightly at the waist and gestured at something unseen to its right. It took a half-step, awkward and hobbled, a bird with an injured wing, and then Julia's foot twisted under her. She flailed into the heavy wooden frame of the standing mirror and knocked it over, landing flat-out across the glass. She looked down at her reflection; for an absurd instant she worried that it might be hurt. A dull bead of blood dripped from the point of her chin and splashed the mirror.

Someone shoved the heavy back curtain aside and the other actors of the company crowded into the space. Nicole, the tallest woman in the group, did not so much shove them aside as move them by the aura of her angry presence. She looked down at Julia. "What happened?"

Julia awkwardly rolled over and sat up. "I was doing warm-ups in front of the mirror —"

"You're not supposed to be practicing your *dance*," Nicole said, practically hissing the last word. "You should be practicing your *lines* and practicing them *sitting down* until your ankle heals. We are putting on this play with a skeleton crew and nobody has time to be your understudy. Is that clear?"

Nicole spun and stalked away without waiting for an answer. The other actors milled around, avoiding her eyes. Only Kai stepped forward, regal, beautiful Kai, helping Julia to her feet.

"Sorry about that," Kai said. She smiled an apology. "Jarré hasn't sent any new pages of script in days and Nicole's very upset."

You don't have to apologize for her just because you're sleeping with her, Julia thought, but did not say. She mimicked a smile back, and nodded, and said nothing at all. She resisted the urge to go back and check on the mirror before she left the theater.

Julia spent the next two days sitting down. She didn't bother to practice her lines, because there were only two. She passed the time re-reading Abelard Jarré's other plays, the ones she had hunted down in the basements of used book stores and read to tatters when she was a drama student: *Memorial Sand*, *Anticlast*, *Hour of the Oxen*, even *Indolence*, his first and least-regarded play that was nonetheless her favorite. In the thirty-five years since releasing *Manifenêtre*, Jarré had written nothing. He gave no interviews and appeared in public rarely; many speculated that he was dead. Through some chain of friendships or remote relation that seemed hazy to Julia, Nicole had gained his rare favor, and Jarré picked her tiny, all-woman theater company to stage his new play *Carcosa*. Julia would have believed it a hoax or publicity stunt if she hadn't seen the first pages of the partial script herself, read scenes described through Jarré's searing vision, impossible to imitate. She still had trouble truly believing that she had a role, even a small one, in his play. It was a gift that even Nicole's hostility and arrogance could not tarnish.

Julia had read to the point that she feared any more would make her bored and tired even of Jarré's writing. She went to the theater and slipped in to the back, picking a seat far back in the shadows where she could watch the rehearsals unnoticed. Even the choice of theater was odd, if not surprising for Jarré: a jewel box of a building from the turn of the century that seated perhaps a hundred patrons. It fell into disrepair after World War Two, but in a spurt of local philanthropy, had been renovated to a state that echoed its old glory. Julia privately hoped those renovations had included meeting modern fire codes. Whoever had dictated the renovations failed to match their nostalgia for a historic theater with modern practice; the seats rose in steep tiers, but the stage was raked, tilted forward toward the audience, a trick from the early days of theater to make actors upstage visible to the groundlings. Julia had twisted her ankle because of the unfamiliar angles of that tilted stage.

Onstage, Kai and Catherine were practicing Scene Four, the lovers' spat that turned from sensual flirtation into a violent, erotic brawl. Nicole rose from the front row of the audience. The actors scrambled apart. They spoke, their voices too low for Julia to make out the words, but their tone of voice clear: Nicole furious, Kai and Catherine abashed. Julia wondered whether they had botched something in the script – a forgotten line, or an intonation departing from Nicole's rigid interpretation of Jarré's artistic vision – or whether Nicole was jealous, suspicious that the passion between her lover and Catherine heralded something other than the demands of the play.

Nicole sat back down, vanishing behind the tall back of her chair, and the women onstage began the scene from the beginning. Julia lost interest in watching the drama, either within the play or outside of it. She slipped out of the back row and along the shadowed aisle that led to the stairs going up. She decided to explore the old box seats first, and then, when the others took a break from the rehearsal, to look around backstage. Something about the old theater intrigued her: the oddity of its architecture, its strange partial renovation, the odds and ends of props and costumes left behind by other troupes years ago.

There was little backstage proper that she hadn't already seen. The tall mirror had been shoved into a far corner, next to rolls of canvas crusted with ancient paintdrops. Thick layers of dust rose and made her sneeze. She wandered through the near-maze of pallets and backdrops and cheap furniture sets, her interest in exploring the theater waning. In turning to find her way back out she stepped on a knob of metal sticking up from the floor. She crouched down and gave it an experimental tug. It came up, attached to a thick cord that might once have been white, before it abruptly stopped. Julia pulled harder. A section of the floor swung up and over, like a utility door in an attic. Beneath it a set of haphazard wooden stairs led down. The air rising from the hole smelled stale.

Julia tapped the flashlight icon on her phone and shone the beam down the stairs ahead of her. Splinters dragged at the fabric of her shoes. She picked her way down a wooden staircase that was little more than a wide ladder. Even with her careful balance, the absence of handrails felt dangerous, as if putting a foot wrong in the slightest would send her flailing over the side. The weak, dusty sunlight barely filtered down to the room below, and she shined the flashlight ahead. It was hard to guess exactly where the room was relative the rest of the theater; perhaps under the stage, but wouldn't that all have been cleaned up during the restoration? Cold leached through her thin shoes. The floor felt hard, uneven, like packed dirt.

She turned the flashlight up toward the low ceiling. White ceramic knobs looped with wire dotted the crossbeams. Julia frowned. It was hard to imagine that restoration work would have left old wiring in place, especially in a theater, where concerns about fire bordered on the paranoid. *They restored the whole place, top to bottom,* Nicole had told them; either Nicole was wrong, or there was some other reason that an electrical system a century old was still in place.

Julia held up her phone so that the beam of light shone along the wire, which turned sideways and ran left along the seam of wall and ceiling, into the darker recesses of the room. She followed it a ways until it struck a wall, curved down, and paralleled a doorframe, disappearing through a hole drilled into the wood of the frame. The hole was fringed with some kind of sticky cloth, protecting the wood from the electric wire. It was too close for her to peer through to the other side. She moved the light to the door and illuminated dark, heavy-grained wood. Light sparkled on an old-fashioned glass doorknob, its facets caked with gray dust. Julia turned the knob, expecting the mechanism to be rusted shut, the door warped into its frame. To her surprise, it moved. She tucked the phone into her back pocket and used both hands to twist the knob harder. There was resistance, and then something metallic snapped, letting the knob spin all the way over. She tugged at the door. It opened with surprising ease, the old hinges grating but doing nothing to hinder her.

Without thinking she reached inside the door for a light switch, felt something under her fingers, and flipped it up. There was a humming, crackling sound overhead and the room flooded with dusty yellow light. Julia stared up at a light bulb, the size of her fists put together, mounted in the ceiling inside a faded green-bronze dome of metal. Not only had the old wiring been left in it place, it still worked. Possibly the electricians just hadn't gone this far into the building.

The light in the ceiling was hardly brighter than her phone's light, but at least it left her hands free. The secret room was disappointing; more of a storage closet than a proper room. The damp-dog smell of old books, poorly cared for, was everywhere. Sheaves of paper overflowed rickety wooden shelves. Julia flipped through a few, saw nothing of interest, put them back haphazardly. Other than the usual copies of Shakespeare, they were plays she'd never heard of, none dated any sooner than fifty years ago.

The room was poorly ventilated and uncomfortably hot. Julia pushed a stray wisp of hair out of her eyes and left a streak of dirt and sweat on her face. She wiped her filthy hands on her jeans and reached for the switch to turn the light off as she went out. Her gaze rested on a cardboard box that she hadn't noticed before, high up on a shelf, pushed so far back that it was barely visible. She stood on tiptoes to reach it. Her fingers just brushed the corners of the box; she stretched up, using her fingertips to inch it towards her little by little, and before she could get her hands fully around it the box tipped forward, showering her with musty paper.

Julia stood, stunned, the now-empty box in her hands. It was perhaps three inches deep. Its dimensions were slightly unfamiliar, not quite right to fit a standard piece of paper. She kneeled down to start gathering up the papers that had tipped out, and saw that they were also odd-sized, maybe a European size, or paper so old that it had come out before standard dimensions. They were yellowed and crackled under her touch.

She turned the papers written-side up. At first glance she thought they were sheet music, covered in long, lined boxes that looked like musical staves; on a closer look, the markings on the staves weren't musical notes, but stick figures. If it was dance notation, it was a form she'd never seen before. The figures moved up and down on the grid behind them, and the staves had seven lines, not five. Their limbs and posture contorted in positions that didn't flow from one movement to the next. *Twisted in pain*, she thought, then dismissed it as fancy. No system of dance writing illustrated how uncomfortable any position would be for the dancer.

There was tiny, faded writing everywhere around the papers, too; some neatly printed above and below the figures, some in the margins. Entire paragraphs of dense scribbling were crammed between staves. Most of it was illegible, possibly not even in English. Julia sighed and piled the papers back into the box. There were no page numbers or titles, no way to find any sensible or orderly arrangement of their proper sequence.

Julia picked up the last stray sheet and dropped it back on top of the others. Printed squarely in the center of the page, surrounded by a margin of white, was the word CARCOSA.

She squinted at the page. She couldn't tell whether the word had been printed in the only block of available space, or whether it had been put there first and the other writing around it. The scribbles did seem more compressed at its margins, almost as if they were crowding away from the word.

Julia carefully fitted the grey cardboard lid back over the warped edges of the box. She decided that she would look it over later, after she'd had some rest and wasn't squatting on the floor of a dingy and probably dangerous old storeroom, working herself up into a melodramatic lather over an obsolete stack of papers that had nothing at all to do with her current work. For all she knew, it was some long-dead choreographer's idiosyncratic notation for *Swan Lake*.

On the way back up the stairs, box tucked under her arm, she paused to shine her light on the near end of the wiring system, tracing it up to find where it tied into the building's electricity. At the last knob, the wire hung loose, its end frayed, attached to nothing at all.

The sounds through the cheap walls of the hotel room were not soothing, but they were predictable. Through one wall of Julia's narrow room, Nicole's voice rose and fell like the surf as she berated Kai, for some failing in the day's rehearsal, or perhaps for showing too much enthusiasm in her scene with Catherine. In the room that shared the opposite wall, Taylor was practicing her monologue from Scene Two, halting mid-sentence, starting over with a different intonation, hours of the same two minutes of speech, a broken record that would continue until nearly midnight. Outside, breaking glass heralded drunks pitching empty bottles into the nearest dumpster. Julia had learned to ignore the sounds as best she could. Neither the company's budget nor Julia herself could afford any better living accommodations.

The floor was strewn with the papers she had found in the theater basement. Ever since returning to the hotel, she had puzzled over the dance notation, trying to find their correct order, to spot a page number or direction that would permit her to see the full pattern of the dance. The noises from the rooms next to hers did not help her concentration. A few times she thought she could discern a connection between the end of one stanza and the beginning of another page, but when she looked a second time there was no consonance; she could not imagine why she had placed those pages together.

To her left, a repetitive thud against the wall: the headboard of Nicole and Kai's bed punctuating their post-argument lovemaking.

Julia gave up. She picked a paper at random and taped it to the mirror that backed the door of her hotel room. It was hopeless to expect that she could properly reconstruct the entire dance; perhaps rehearsing at least one of the pages would give her a sense of what sort of dance it was, a clue to what movements would logically follow. She spread her arms, wrists canted, mimicking the posture of the first stick figure on the page. It was slow work, stopping and adjusting her position, sometimes painfully, none of the movements recalling any dance familiar to her. Julia concentrated on matching each stance before moving to the next, the sounds of the women to either side of her a bizarre metronome to her efforts.

Halfway through the page she broke out in sweat; before the final stanza she stopped and let her arms drop to her sides. In spite of the aches and exhaustion, she felt elated. It was a distraction from the tedious personal drama around her, but more than that, the excitement of learning something new, something difficult but promising, something that with enough effort and practice, she could understand, perhaps even master.

She looked down at the floor and her eyes lit on one of the papers scattered there. She recognized it immediately as the next in sequence, the position of the first dancer clearly the natural progression after the last one in the page on her mirror. Julia couldn't imagine why she had not seen it before. She taped the new page next to it, paused to drink a glass of water, and began again.

When she arrived at the theater the next morning Nicole was, to her great surprise, waiting for her. Less surprising was Nicole's cold fury.

"Where have you been? We've been rehearsing for hours. Jarré sent more changes last night." She thrust a paper-clipped script at Julia. "You have a few more lines. Learn them."

Julia eased herself into the nearest seat; under Nicole's sharp gaze, she did her best to hide her stiffness and aches from her work the night before. She had a few more lines, true, but none of them were very good, the dialogue not merely short, but banal. She glanced up at the other women; they seemed to share her view, though Kai was careful to wipe the surprise off her face before Nicole saw it.

"What *is* this?" Madison asked. She tapped one long white-tipped fingernail on the page. "Iambic pentameter? Bad poetry? Is he writing this stuff drunk? It's awful."

Nicole's mouth twisted. "This is what he sent. Perhaps it was meant as satire. It's what we have. The man is a genius playwright, who do you think you are to criticize him?"

"Someone stuck having to memorize this crap," Madison said, but the fight had drained out of her voice. All of them were nervous and off-balance. Their excitement at being chosen to act in Jarré's first new play in decades, even with a partial script, gave way to anxiety about his delay in finishing the material. Now their relief had turned sour.

Julia broke the silence. "We shouldn't rehearse today until everyone has time to look over the new material. Right? Why don't we all take a break. My ankle's better, I can practice some of my dance. It'll be easier on an empty stage."

She was surprised to hear the confidence in her voice; almost as surprised to see Nicole respond with a curt nod and a gesture herding the other actors out of the theater. Julia rarely spoke when the director was around, and certainly never told her what to do; even hesitant suggestions were ignored, or shut down with disdain. Perhaps it was the uncertainty over the new material that distracted Nicole, but at least it meant that Julia had the stage to herself for practice. She planned to add some of the new steps from the manuscript to her routine, and it would be easiest to do that without anyone telling her to move this way or that to accommodate the other players.

This time, the tilted stage gave her no trouble at all.

Everyone's nerves were stretched by the end of the week. Jarré made daily changes to the script, sometimes adding entirely new blocks of dialogue or throwing out difficult lines that the actors had finally mastered. Taylor's monologues next door were more subdued. Kai and Nicole's arguments were longer and punctuated by tears; sometimes there was silence, as if the women had gone to bed without speaking.

Julia hardly noticed. She had assembled more than half of the manuscript in what she was sure was the correct order. She could no longer see her mirror, covered in paper taped neatly together, the pages spilling around the corner to the adjacent wall. The movements were still difficult at times, even painful, but they formed a cohesive whole. With more of the dance assembled in its proper order, Julia could see that there was more than simple choreography. It told a story, one that she could only glimpse in fragments, conveyed through even small details such as the angle of an elbow or the tilt of the head. She might have called it *interpretive dance* except that the dance was the language, itself; the dancer was the interpreter, the conduit for the power and meaning of the dance.

The other thing Julia realized was that the drawings illustrated the movements not of one dancer, but two.

This took her by surprise — the figures were so similar that she did not realize there was more than one until she had assembled many pages. So many revelations in the dance were like that: utterly opaque until enough of them were placed together, and then the pattern was so obvious a child could have seen it. It seemed less choreography than a wonderfully complex puzzle.

The second dancer appeared early on, simply materializing halfway through a stanza, the first figure accommodating its presence as if it had always been there. The second figure grew more prominent until the two were virtually indistinguishable. Julia could not put her finger on why she believed there were two dancers when only one was drawn, but she was nonetheless sure it was the case.

By the last page, only the second dancer remained. It was difficult to tell if the first had simply been removed from the manuscript, or was still present, the second dancer superimposed so that they had . . . merged? Julia hoped that the solution would reveal itself once she assembled the entire dance.

Her exhaustion and soreness were partly the fault of trying to dance both parts at once, when she had mistakenly thought there was only once dancer. She began with the first, then switched to the second when it appeared. Technically it appeared more difficult, yet as she practiced it became easier, or at least, less stressful to her body; she was able to get through two or three pages at a time without having to stop to rest.

Julia's one frustration was the text. No matter how she turned the pages or peered at the words, nothing was coherent other than the single word, CARCOSA, that she had seen in the theater basement when she first discovered the play. She could pick out a letter here or there, and very occasionally, groups of letters that turned into nonsense words: DEMHE. PTAHYL. There was meaning here, words at the edge of her memory like the name of a forgotten friend.

She sighed and stretched her limbs. It would become clear to her, in time, just as the strange notations of movement had been incomprehensible at first and then so obvious that she wondered she could have ever failed to understand it. Until then, she would master the dance.

When Julia wandered into the theater late the next morning, there were so many new pages that the play was almost a different script, and Nicole was on the verge of tears. "I don't understand what he's doing," she repeated, as the actors bickered and complained about days of wasted rehearsal, wondered aloud whether the bad writing was some kind of Dadaist feint, the play's true brilliance reserved for the yet-unwritten

Act Two, or whether it was nothing more than Jarré's descent into alcoholism and dementia.

Julia picked up her copy of the new script and turned to the final scene of Act One. Her brief exchange with the Queen had become a conversation; her insistence that something was wrong growing more strident, the queen's commanding words turning fearful. There was a mistake, she thought; writing in a hurry, Jarré had confused his pronouns, muddling when the Queen addressed the Dancer and when she spoke to the Masked Stranger. She pointed the lines out to Nicole, who merely shrugged.

"I have a suggestion," Julia said. "I've been practicing a new dance routine, I think I should do more than a few steps on stage during the masque. A real dance, since I have more of a part now. It will make the masque seem more believable."

Nicole looked at her, opened her mouth, then turned her gaze away, as if she thought better of her reply. No one, other than Julia, rehearsed that afternoon.

There were no more changes the following day, which muted some of the grumbling about the poor quality of the script. They worked their way through the leaden dialogue, some with better humor than others. Julia hardly cared. Her lines were perhaps not as bad as those of Kai, who played the Queen, or Taylor, whose monologue was almost now a comedy; and besides, the important thing was the dance.

Nicole stood up quickly and interrupted Kai halfway through a line. "Julia, we have a real problem here. I'm stopping rehearsal for the day so that you and I can go over this one-on-one."

Julia looked at her with mild surprise. Nicole seemed less angry than . . . afraid? Kai, too, noticed something was wrong, her gaze flickering from her lover to Julia as she reluctantly filed out of the theater with the others.

Julia sat down cross-legged at the edge of the stage and waited patiently.

Nicole paced back and forth. "The play—" she said, and then seemed to reach a decision. She stood in front of Julia and looked up at the smaller woman. "It isn't Jarré."

"Of course it's him. That first scene, nobody else could have written it."

"The first scene *was* his writing. All his. And so were parts of the others." Nicole glanced over her shoulder at the entrance to the theater, as if she feared eavesdroppers. She lowered her voice almost to a whisper. "You understand, Julia, he was not a very pleasant person. He is – he was – almost eighty, and he managed to piss off a lot of people over the years. I was the only person left he didn't have to pay to deal with him or his problems."

"Was?" Julia said. She stared at Nicole, not quite sure if she thought she had heard correctly.

"Very few people knew where he lived. He was a recluse, everyone knows that. He hated e-mail and faxes. All of his new material, he mailed to me. When there was nothing, for days, I drove out to his house. I thought he'd gone on a bender or had some kind of artistic fit. I thought if I met with him face to face, I could bully him into getting his act together." Nicole smiled without humor, her eyes looking to one side of Julia as if just remembering something. She gave herself a little shake. "I knew something was wrong as soon as I arrived, the house—the lights were all on. He was notoriously cheap. When it got dark he'd only have one room lit at a time, to save on his electric bill."

"And he was dead," Julia said quietly. She didn't believe the words as she said them, waiting for Nicole to snap at her for jumping to conclusions.

"I knew when I opened the front door. The smell of the place, you can't imagine. I found him in his study, behind his desk. I don't know what killed him. Probably a heart attack, or his liver finally giving up.

There were some papers stacked on his desk that looked like they were part of *Carcosa*, so I grabbed them and got out of there."

"What did you do with him? Did you call the police?"

"So that everyone would know he was dead? What do you think would have happened to the play? To *us*? Do you think anyone would come to watch a bunch of struggling nobodies put on half a play, and that half not even finished?" Nicole's gaze shifted. "I thought I could use his notes to finish *Carcosa*. I've known Jarré since I was a teenager, I thought I could . . . imitate his style, fill in the gaps. But his notes were garbage. I couldn't even read most of it, he was probably full of tequila when he wrote them."

Julia took the wrinkled papers from Nicole's outstretched hand and smoothed them out. Spiky handwriting slashed across the pages at a steep angle. Nicole craned her neck and tried to point out a few legible words. "This is all I could make out—something about the Masque. That's why I added some more lines for you, I thought that's what he wanted. The rest of it . . . let me show you."

Julia leafed through the pages. She understood now why Jarré had bragged in interviews about using his father's manual typewriter; the man's handwriting was all but illegible, ordinary poor penmanship dragged into ruin by his advancing age and years of heavy drinking. She frowned. Here and there she could make out a few letters, almost a word—

Demhe

Ptahyl

Carcosa

Nicole stared at her with frank desperation. "Look, I know I've been harsh, but . . . I've watched you dance on days when we cancelled rehearsal. Whatever you're doing, it's like you understood something Jarré tried to write in his play, or . . . I can't fake this anymore, Julia. If you can help at all . . ."

Julia set the pages to one side. She hardly saw Nicole. In her imagination the skittering text between the stanzas unfolded itself, like a flower opening through too many angles to be properly seen. All she had to do was sort them into the correct order; she marveled at herself that she could have missed it before.

"Let's head back to the hotel," she said. "There's something I want to show you."

Julia was no playwright. Reading the words on the manuscript was one thing; making them into coherent speech, and crafting them into dialogue or plot was beyond her. For that, she used Nicole. The two of them sat on the stained, worn carpet of Julia's hotel room, surrounded by pages that Julia had carefully removed from the walls. She didn't need to number them or mark their pages; the correct order was plain to her now. She pointed out words to Nicole that she thought were important. When Nicole admitted she couldn't make sense of them, Julia read them out loud, or cleared the papers away to perform a few steps of the dance, to show Nicole the *essence* of the words. Nicole wrote everything down in a small notebook, her pen skittering across the page, her handwriting, from Julia's upside-down perspective, growing as tangled and unreadable as Jarré's had been. As the manuscript had been, before Julia finally understood.

This time it was Nicole who arrived late, while the troupe milled around sullenly and wondered whether she'd quit. She handed each of them a thick stack of pages, still warm from the printer: the script, all but the first scene completely rewritten.

"You must have been up all night working on this," said Kai. Her gaze was fixed on Julia.

Nicole ignored her. "We need to step up our efforts. We're short on time. I suggest we start with readings to familiarize ourselves with the dialogue. Start from the beginning, we'll work our way up to just before the mask." Her eyes were bright with excitement and fatigue.

Julia listened to the rehearsal with half an ear as she read through the script. The dialogue was still banal, the scenes still disjointed, but the phrasing was more like Jarré's; something hidden under the bland surface of the words, a predatory shadow, barely glimpsed out of the corner of the eye. The tension rose throughout the first act. There was no Act Two, not yet. Julia thought there must have been something, an outline, or at least rudimentary notes, among the papers Nicole salvaged from Jarré's desk.

She wondered if Jarré were really dead, if Nicole had told the truth that he was unmistakably a corpse. He could have been blacked out, unconscious drunk, or simply sleeping on the floor, exhausted from his driven schedule. Or, she thought, perhaps Nicole had killed him? She imagined Jarré dismissing Nicole and her little company on a whim, bestowing the honor of acting out his glorious return to the theater on some other, newer favorite—

Maybe he refused to finish the play. Julia pictured it as clearly as if it were real: Jarré an old man with the mind of a petulant, spoiled little boy, his desk cluttered with the half-formed remains of plays that he had begun and discarded when he tired of them, dismissing Nicole's stuttered protests with a sneer, turning away from her in disdain, and the heavy liquor bottle on his desk right at hand. . . .

The theater was quiet. Julia closed the script and stood up, stretching. She had been so absorbed in her silly fantasy of Nicole as a murderer that she hadn't even noticed that everyone else had left.

The play would be finished, she knew. It only waited for the right time to reveal itself.

When Julia returned to her hotel room, Kai was waiting. Julia nodded and slid her key card into the door. Before she could shut it behind her, Kai had pushed her way in.

"What are you doing to her?"

Julia looked at her, puzzled. "Nothing. Are you jealous? We're not lovers, Kai. If you two are having problems it's nothing to do with me."

"That's not what I mean." Kai shoved the door closed. "Nicole's not herself. She acts like she has a fever, she isn't eating, she has bags under her eyes, she looks like *you*."

"Like me?" Julia turned to her mirror. She had gotten out of the habit, since for several days it had been obscured by the slowly accumulating pages of the manuscript. Her reflection startled her. Dark rings smudged her eyes and shadowed her orbital bone. The planes of her jaw and cheekbones stood out in sharp angles. There was a slight tremor in her lip that she'd never seen before. Fear rose in her throat and threatened to choke her.

"When did you last eat, Julia?" Kai said. The anger in her tone softened. "You're obsessed with this stupid play. I don't understand, I know this Jarré guy is an indie favorite, but the play isn't all that good. It's not worth what you're doing to yourself. I won't let you pull Nicole in."

"*Demhe*," Julia said. "*Hali*." The words calmed her and she turned away from the mirror. "No one will see my face under the mask, anyway."

"What mask?" Kai looked at her in bewilderment. "And what are you saying? Are those more of his stupid plays?"

Julia bent over to pick up some pages and taped them back over her mirror. She looked at the one in her hand; it was the page where the second dancer first appeared, insinuating itself next to the first.

She straightened up and put the manuscript aside. "You know what, Kai? I think it would be easier if I just showed you."

"Where the ever-loving hell have you *been* all day?" Taylor said. "And where's Kai?" Everyone but Nicole was arrayed on the stage, scripts in hand: the scene that opened the beginning of the Masque.

"I have no idea where Kai is," Julia said, and in a way it was the truth.

The women looked furtively at one another and would not meet Julia's gaze. She ignored them. She was ready to rehearse her dance, her lines, in full for the first time. She made a beeline for the cabinet backstage where the smaller props were stored; the Queen's crown, the musicians' chimes, an ermine robe daubed with fake blood, a pair of torn slippers. Julia shoved them out of her way and dug through the cabinet until her fingers closed on the smooth porcelain oval of her mask.

It fit her perfectly.

She beckoned to Nicole. With Kai gone, someone had to take the role of the Queen, and who else knew everyone's lines so well? Nicole set her glasses and her notebook on the edge of the stage and hauled herself up over the edge, moving instinctively to the center, where the Queen stood when the Masque began.

Julia danced. A part of her wondered how she could possibly have tripped and hurt herself that first day of rehearsal; the raked stage was perfectly suited to her movements, and the shifting patterns of the other actors as they moved around the Queen, remarking on the fearful movement of the stars above, or feigning merriment to hide their terror of what was to come. Their feet moved in awkward, reluctant time to Julia's dance, as if they meant to stop themselves from joining her.

Slowly the circle turned and contracted around Nicole. The others scuttled away as the dance brought Julia to stand in front of her, with a low, grave, exaggerated curtsey.

Nicole spoke to her, the words obscure and distorted as if they were underwater. Julia's part came back to her in a rush and she remembered her cue.

"I wear no mask," she said, and it was true. The pallid oval *was* her face, the lips moving as she spoke. She turned her impassive, terrible gaze to the empty audience. A heavy mist rose up around their seats and swallowed them into obscurity. Above them, the stage lights winked into stars.

The subtle dread that had built through all of Act One swelled to the point of bursting. Julia could no longer pretend to wonder what might be written next; they rose in her mind as clearly as if they were lines she had memorized herself. Her body arced without conscious thought into the opening steps of the dance. The awful words of the second act poured from her mouth like the clang of a tocsin.

Julia was distantly aware of the other women around her. She could not remember their names. One lay on the floor, weeping in terror next to a corpse with a twisted neck. Another crawled on her belly, a smile of idiot ecstasy plastered across her face. Yet another had found Nicole's pen and used it to puncture one eardrum. She carefully twisted it into the other ear and sighed in relief as blood trickled down her neck.

Julia turned her back on them all. The lake stretched out before her. Where the mists parted, the light of an unfamiliar moon reflected from the water. She extended her arms in the final position of the dance and stepped from the edge of the stage, embracing the sly, reflected spires of Carcosa.

Demhe, she chanted; *Ptahyl, Uoht*, until the waters of Hali filled her throat and carried her under.

Future Imperfect

Glynn Owen Barrass

White sky, black stars, a moonless nighttime in negative above a horizon of twisted towers and minarets. The view was surreal; the closer scene, that of a grey, lichen infested, cobbled square flanked by a squat, crumbling, granite wall. . . .

Horrendous.

Crouched on their knees, their hands behind their backs and their heads bowed in supplication, were eight *things* lined in a row. Tall, bald, gangly humanoids, their naked yellow flesh was covered in scabrous patches. Not all were supplicants however. A female specimen, bald like the males but with pendulous, flaccid breasts, looked in Campbell's direction with bulging grey eyes, licked her lips with a long, vein-filled black tongue.

A red dot appeared near the centre of her forehead, and the back of her head exploded in a cloud of atomised skull and brain matter. Campbell shuddered as if he'd heard the gunshot, but the video, now as it was at the beginning, was completely silent. Whoever held the camera shook a little, backed off as the dead female slumped forward. A momentary close-up returned. A gore-filled crater replaced the back of her head, a protuberant twist of spine poking up behind it. Her hands, tied with a black plastic cable tie, bore obscenely long, twisted fingers, the jagged nails thick with dirt.

The camera zoomed out. A male form dressed in black combat fatigues, a ski mask and tactical vest, replaced the corpse. He held a Glock 12 in his gloved hand. Kitted out for combat, and murder, he lifted a sheet of cardboard towards the camera.

Black letters read:

Revenge is Sweet

The man stepped away, and following that cold, clinical first kill came a barrage of gunshots that tore the defenceless things asunder, the shuddering bodies ripped to shreds while silently screaming faces blossomed with new orifices and screamed no more. The screen turned blank. Further darkness follows as Campbell closed his eyes, numb with disgust. *What the hell is going on here? A rival agency or some foreign power in competition with us?* He was sure Analysis would have a field day with the video, but had decided to keep this his secret.

Campbell opened his eyes and stared at the screen. It made no sense. He was accustomed to seeing the things, had been in the Carcosans presence off and on for eighteen months now. But he never thought he would see them die; didn't think they *could* die. *Do I speak to The King about this?* His superior in the Bureau, Mr. King, would be suspicious as to why he'd kept this alien snuff film to himself. Two days earlier, Campbell had found the dirt-smeared, yellow object in his jacket pocket, and, considering its contents, could only assume it had fallen there from the sack of offerings he'd carried from the summoning room after the last Carcosan Event. His instinct told him to remain quiet.

He checked his watch and sighed. It was almost time. He pushed the chair back from his desk, pulled on his jacket, and halfway to the door returned to his desk, removing the memory stick and pocketing it before powering the computer down.

Revenge is sweet. Campbell pictured the slaughter. Yellow corpses, dirty cobbles pooled with black blood—with difficulty, he shook the image away. Standing with Gibson, a short, female, blonde fellow agent, the tall, bald headed King and two armed, buzz-cut blonde guards wearing khaki combat fatigues, a palpable fear filled the elevator's small confines. Whenever Campbell was in close proximity to the summoning device, he needed to be somewhere else, anywhere else. By the looks on

the other men's faces and the sweat beading Gibson's brow, he guessed
they suffered similar thoughts. He didn't envy The King's role in this, the
man holding the black cloth-covered device with his arms outstretched
as if it were a bomb. The device was an artefact from the Roswell Event,
one rumour went. Another said it had been discovered in Egypt, stuffed
inside a Mummy. Whatever its origin, the device was bad company.

The elevator continued its descent, to a floor unused by anyone but
the score of members belonging to Project Yellow Sign. Officially, The
King's agents belonged to the F.B.I.'s Facilities and Logistics Services
Division. That's what it said on paper.

Campbell grew lost in thought again, his mind drifting back to the
blood, the death. The memory stick felt heavy in his jacket's inside pocket.

An almost unfelt shudder, the elevator touching the basement floor,
returned him to the here and now. The doors parted and The King strode
forward, flanked by the guards. Campbell followed them down a grey
basement corridor lined with rusted pipes. As The King and his retinue
walked, ceiling tubes flickered above their heads. The group turned left
at an intersection, and contrary to the unkempt state of the remainder of
the floor they now faced a relatively new, reinforced steel door flanked by
two armed guards. "They're in there," the guard on the left said, and tilted his head towards the door. While the rest paused, the petite Gibson
stepped forward and with quick movements slid a card key past a reader
at door's midsection. A loud beep followed and the door fell forward a
few inches. Gibson backed away, gave Campbell a nervous look as The
King moved forward.

He nudged the door open with his shoe and revealed a familiar,
frightening room.

Bare, dirt smeared white plaster walls, a cracked concrete floor, fluorescent tubes starkly illuminated the room. The offerings flanked the
door. Sedated, strapped to gurneys, two Death Row criminals awaited
a doom far worse than death, and they deserved it. Campbell had read
their sheets. One, a man named Devon 'Dee' Dewitt, had supposedly

been executed two days earlier, for the multiple rape and murders of eight women in North Carolina. The other, Allen Stuart, 'executed' by lethal injection but instead retained and sedated by Campbell's team, had murdered four people during a robbery at a Chuck E. Cheese. The FBI procured them easily. Monsters, scum, Campbell had witnessed what the Carcosans did to their 'subjects' for they occasionally dumped their leftovers when collecting fresh offerings. Why? Because they were evil, sadistic bastards.

"Okay, let's get this started," The King said, his pockmarked face betraying only a hint of nervousness. "Campbell, close the door. You two push the offerings towards the back wall." This was directed at the guards. They shouldered their rifles and reluctantly wheeled the squeaking gurneys to the rear of the room.

Campbell pushed the door closed and heard it click as it locked. The way he felt, utterly trapped, was mirrored by Gibson's strained expression, the woman's eyes wide with anticipation. Beyond Gibson the guards returned, passing The King who now crouched on the floor with the device uncovered. He shoved the cloth in his jacket pocket, stood and backed away. The device, an amber, roughly triangular blob, released a mellow glow Campbell knew from experience would fill the room when the lights went down.

"Lights," The King said and Gibson followed his instructions. Campbell placed his hands behind his back and clenched his fists. His throat dry, he swallowed loudly with fear and anticipation.

The device, now a yellow blob of fire, revealed an object embedded in its depths, a bulbous black cylinder surrounded by three twisted spokes. The King's body became a black silhouette before it. Within the device's apparently solid matter, the spokes moved with a sinuous life of their own.

"Here we go," Gibson whispered, and reality shifted.

Blasts of wind, accompanied by wild, animal roars, appeared as the walls and ceiling disintegrated, revealing a blurred white sky spotted with obsidian stars. A too familiar scene. The chaotic air buffeting Campbell smelled of cinnamon and over-ripe fruit. Everyone but The King ducked at the gusts pounding their bodies. He stood stolid, his arms folded as the gurneys rattled around him. Where the walls had stood, just beyond the concrete floor, a world of sandy desert surrounded the group. Although the air shimmered, the wind only assaulted those within the remains of the basement.

Campbell stood straight, tried composing himself to match The King's firm countenance. He shuddered when he saw they were no longer alone. As if from thin air they'd appeared, too many figures to count. The things, the Carcosans, were everywhere, spotting the sand dunes into the distance. Campbell shuddered, the guards stood alert, and Gibson turned and said something that was lost in the wind. Campbell was distracted anyway, for a tall, spindly male creature now stood facing The King, its ugly, elongated form matching those surrounding them, matching those things he had seen murdered on video.

Fingers reaching past its knees twitched on multiple joints as the Carcosan bowed before The King. Its face, small and withered within a bulbous head, bore a grin of huge black teeth, its eyes glazed and unfocused. It spoke and Campbell shivered, the ugly voice resembling scratches on a record. It didn't speak English, yet the words appeared in his brain as such.

"You bring things? Good things yes?"

The Carcosan raised its head and giggled like a child. Its voice filled the air as it looked to the sky, its chest convulsing at it laughed at some private, alien joke. It looked to The King and nodded. *"Good things."*

Movement in the corner of Campbell's eye shifted his gaze to the gurney on his right. Another Carcosan had stalked closer, now looming over Dewitt. Unlike the others, this one, a female, wore a diamond-shaped, bone-coloured mask over its face. It stared down from narrow eye slits, teasing its hands across Dewitt's prone form like a pianist. Then Dewitt awoke. His screams filled the air, louder than the chaotic wind as he rocked in his gurney, twisted against the straps. The female Carcosan pressed a spidery hand against his mouth and muffled his terror. More movement – to his left Campbell saw another masked female interfering with the Stuart man.

"You return to your blue world now. Live blue lives," the male Carcosan said. The King looked small now, insignificant before the being, and was he shaking? *"Goodbye day,"* the Carcosan continued, and in an instant Campbell's world became a void of black silence. Light-headed, his knees crumbled and he was on the floor, his quick reflexes saving him from injuring himself. The sight of his spread hands pressed against concrete replaced the darkness, and the room surrounding him stood whole again. Nearby, he heard one of the guards vomiting. Footsteps to his right followed, tender hands gripping him as Gibson helped him up from his knees. He looked around and found The King bent forward, pawing through a large burlap sack. The Carcosan had deposited this before disappearing—their payment for the offerings.

After he composed himself, Campbell approached The King with slow hesitancy. The gifts from the Carcosans varied in usefulness: boxes of costume jewellery, crumbling maps to unknown continents . . . once a map had been in French, titled *Carcosa: Chemins Le Fer.* The name had stuck, for the aliens.

"Anything useful?" Campbell asked.

The King shook his head and snorted. "Uh, pieces of half built technology. I don't know what but Tech will have a field day. Nothing living, thank god." These words brought some measure of relief to Campbell. The living things were always the worst, especially when they consisted of the mutilated, mewling remains of past offerings. Sometimes, the Carcosans deposited the corpses of *future* offerings, condemned criminals still alive somewhere in America. At least in those cases, locating and procuring the subjects proved simpler.

It was a relief to everyone it was over, the feeling palpable within the room. Still, leaving it felt even better, the King bearing the device before him with Campbell hauling the burlap sack over his shoulder. It was heavy, but not as heavy as the memory stick.

Campbell went home that night in a mental haze. Gibson had noted his disposition, even offered to drive him home but he'd refused. His fellow agent meant a lot to him, and he didn't want to show weakness before her. He drove to his apartment knowing that if he'd left his car at the Bureau, it would have meant her picking him up in the morning and more time alone with her.

He stepped into his apartment, flicked through the day's post, then slumped on the couch, drained of energy and also, feeling poisoned. The Carcosan's had that effect on him, every single time. A shower wouldn't clean the psychic stink from him, and neither would changing clothes.

A little later he plugged the memory stick into his computer, re-watched the movie, and was disgusted and confused all over again. Afterwards he put the offending object in his wall safe. The tiny object seemed offensive there, polluting the sanctity of his mother's heirloom jewellery, his safety cash.

He stripped, worked out on his treadmill for half an hour, then took a shower before going through a few glasses of Jim Bean, laid on the couch naked while watching television. At 11 p.m. he went to bed, masturbated, and fell into an uneasy sleep.

As with every day after a Carcosan Event, a 9 a.m. conference was held by Mr. King. Usually this was in regards to what the aliens had given them, and what they would do with information gleaned from their technology. Campbell was not looking forward to it. For a start, it would be the ideal time to admit to owning the memory stick. Secondly, he felt like shit. The night had been a long one, waking constantly from vivid dreams about Gibson intermingled with nightmares about the Carcosans. Still, he went through the motions of getting up at 7:30 a.m., showered and dressed. He was on the motorway and winding his way around slow moving traffic at 8:15, was in the offices with ten minutes to spare. When he left home he'd brought the memory stick with him. For some reason, he felt it was safer on his person.

When he stepped into the large, white-walled Conference Room B, sugar-loaded coffee in hand and his brain still foggy from last night's poor sleep, the tense atmosphere hit him like a sledgehammer, instantly clearing his head. Fellow agents were already seated at the circular, glass-topped table at the centre of the room. The King stood before the TV on the far wall, his scarred, stony face looking more cadaverous than usual. He turned to Campbell at his entry, as did the other agents. All looked worried, to a man. All men . . . Gibson wasn't present and this, for a start, seemed wrong – in Campbell's experience she had never been late for anything. Then The King spoke.

"They've taken one of our own."

Those worried faces stared at him. Campbell wasn't partnered with Gibson, but he did spend a lot of time with her, had formed a friendship, of sorts.

"Gibson," he said quietly.

The King opened his mouth, stretching his pockmarked cheeks to reveal white, perfect teeth. "Sit down Campbell," he said finally. "We have it on surveillance."

Campbell slumped into his seat, his coffee ignored as he watched The King fiddle around with a remote control.

"I just had this spliced together by the tech team," he said.

The screen came to life, revealing black and white surveillance footage of the reception room downstairs. The time code at the bottom right said 8:19 a.m. The King pressed fast forward, zooming two minutes ahead, and on the screen Gibson came walking through the doors into the reception.

Her hair in a ponytail, she wore a black trouser suit, her usual attire. For some reason she looked unusually flustered. Campbell, feeling a fluttering in his chest, looked around self consciously before returning his gaze to the screen. Another scene followed, Gibson walking down a corridor on the first floor.

"No sound on these," The King said, "but the explosion was heard throughout the building.

"Explosion?" an agent whispered and many nervous glances were shared. Campbell kept his eyes on the screen. Gibson entering an elevator, the next camera shot showing her stood inside the elevator. All looked normal, and then Gibson shuddered, spasming where she stood. This happened two further times, then she dropped her briefcase. Next, her head turned directly towards the camera. Her mouth opened wide, her head flicking back so brutally that Campbell flinched like he'd heard it snap. Gibson's eyes rolled back in her skull, leaving nothing but staring whites. She froze there, and the screen turned to static.

Silence filled the room until a few agents muttered to one another across the table. The King switched the screen off and sat heavily in his chair. Campbell noted this peripherally as he continued staring at the screen. He watched his own dim reflection and screamed inside.

"She never left the elevator," The King said.

Tortured and violated. Mutilated for sadistic, insane needs.

"Forensics have been over it with a fine tooth comb."

They'll deposit the remains in front of us, with a smile.

"Nothing. The explosion had no natural source. We believe it was just some part of the abduction transition."

An agent said in a panicked voice, "This could be an attack! It had to happen eventually."

Another said, "Any of us could be next."

Campbell rose from his seat. All heads turned to him, but the only gaze he acknowledged was The King's. He said, "We have to get her back."

The King had flatly refused Campbell's request. It went completely against protocol. Campbell had argued that protocol had been broken as soon as they'd taken Gibson. The King still refused. Campbell had gotten angry, shouted. The King had ordered him from the room or face suspension.

Campbell sat in his office and brooded, fingering the memory stick. *Revenge is sweet.*

He slipped off the end cap and examined the USB. It was still tarnished with black residue, despite multiple uses. With unconscious volition he brought it to his nose. *Sulphur, the stink of hell.* Campbell plugged the memory stick into his machine and found, as before, an .avi file. He clicked the link.

This movie was different. Impossible, but there it was.

Men in black combat boots and fatigues, their faces concealed behind black balaclavas, stepping over the Carcosan corpses. They were armed with MP5 machine guns, the preferred weapon of choice for the F.B.I's own Black Ops teams. The leader with the sign, for this was most certainly a continuation of the other footage, stood to the right, talking animatedly with another masked man.

Of those examining the dead, one nudged a corpse with his foot. The leader budged past him as he strode towards the camera's POV. The man he's been talking to dropped his arms dramatically in resignation. The sign was dropped, and the leader signalled to the one holding the camera. The view changed to that of the leader's head, armoured shoulders, and the terrible Carcosan sky. The leader raised a gloved hand and started pulling his balaclava up. Campbell saw a stubbled chin, then the leader had the balaclava past his lips and up over his nose and eyes, leaving the head past a thick tangle of unkempt sandy brown hair. Campbell gasped at the face, for his own, familiar visage stared back at him.

"How . . . What the hell?"

Impossible, it's impossible. No, not really, he realized, as offerings from the Carcosans had defied time's arrow before. Who was to say he couldn't do the same, at least if he was there, in their world?

He knew just what to do.

A betrayal, a betrayal of The King *and* the F.B.I., was what was required to retrieve Gibson. He couldn't just leave her there, suffering at the clammy hands of those terrible beings. *I can't*, he thought, sat in her office, a room already cleared of her personal belongings. It wasn't right. She had a family. What if he was next? What if The King was next? Would a retrieval be in order for *him?*

Campbell looked at the only remaining object on Gibson's desk: her telephone. He picked it up and dialled a little used, in house number connected to Project Yellow Sign.

"Yes?" answered a male voice.

"This is Agent Campbell. We need a small team for a Black Operation. I know this is out of the blue, but The King ordered it. Yes of course I have proof. Just get a team together. We're going through the incursion."

A barrage of expletives followed, giving Campbell pause. He bit his lip then said, "We're going through, armed. We're going to retrieve a lost agent. Be ready in twenty." More arguments followed, then Campbell added, "Bring a video camera."

He checked his watch. *One-fifteen, The King should be out.* Campbell rose from the desk, looked around the bare room wistfully, and steeled himself for the next part of his unsanctioned operation.

The King's office stood two floors above Gibson's, and after popping to his own office to collect a few folders, Campbell headed there trying to hide his nerves from those he passed in the corridors. As soon as he reached his destination, he was forced to deal with The King's secretary, Mrs. Bell, a small red-headed woman with a stern demeanour who told him flatly to come back when Mr King returned from lunch.

"He needs these files on his desk when he comes back," Campbell lied, waving his props in the woman's face. He ignored her further protestations and walked past her desk, into The King's office.

What could she do after all? Complain to The King when he returned? All going well, Campbell would be long gone.

The King's office was cream, with dark brown carpet tiles underfoot. A large pine desk stood against the north wall, against which stood a large cabinet stroke bookshelf filled with books and files. The one window, upon the east wall, was shuttered with a blind. He looked around briefly, then stepped towards and around the desk. Campbell sent the office door a look but the secretary didn't appear to interfere with him. He slapped the files onto the desk, sneered at the framed family photos stood there, then moved The King's chair, leaning down to reach the safe beneath the desk.

Five, seven, nine, two, he thought as he typed the numbers into the safe's keypad. All the agents connected to the project knew the code, just in case something happened to The King. No one would have thought of using it for this. The door unlocked, Campbell opened it and found sealed letters, a few files, a Glock 22 (he took this, pocketing it), and the device, wrapped in its black cloth. He hesitated over touching it, briefly, then he was barging from the office, past the shocked Mrs. Bell and towards either his doom or his destiny. He didn't know which.

It took taking the elevator to the basement, walking down those cold corridors, then entering the currently unguarded, summoning room before everything finally hit home.

Fuck, I'm going into their world. Their hellish world. And what if I'm already too late?

Campbell scraped his shoes across the concrete and stared at the reinforced door, left ajar for his team. The device was tucked under his right armpit, its presence not a comforting one. The Glock 22 in his left hand *was*. After a few minutes stood in indecision, the idea of backing out was taken away from him as he heard footsteps marching down the corridor towards the room. A quick check of his wristwatch told Campbell they were right on time.

Yes of course I have proof, he'd said, and hoped the object under his arm was proof enough.

The footsteps paused at the door, followed by silence, then the door burst open.

The King entered the room, his face red with rage. This unforeseen sight made Campbell gasp. The Black Ops team, their weapons trained on him to a man, followed The King, and his shock became fear.

He awoke from a dreamless void, his mind hazy, his sensations padded in cotton wool like he'd just come around on a dentist's chair. The comparison was apt, for Campbell found a plastic mask strapped tightly over his face. Laid flat, he blinked at the bright, nebulous vision above. Gentle noise surrounded him, distant waves crashing against a shore. Then, his vision cleared, his mind cleared, and he saw a looming nighttime sky in negative.

Campbell screamed into his mask. Fear overcame his numbed body with an impetus to move. He struggled but found himself strapped tightly down against . . . he knew what.

A gurney. The ritual. The Carcosan Event.

He twisted his head to the right; saw The King, other agents, stood solemnly in the desert. They *could* hear him. One of the agents, Barnes he was called, had his head bowed in shame.

Campbell screamed himself hoarse, begging, the foam from his pleading mouth soaking his lips. He froze his struggles as a thin shadow fell atop him, a shadow sourced by a cadaverous, Carcosan female. She was naked but for a diamond-shaped, bone-coloured mask with slits for eyes, a slit for a mouth. Long fingered hands stroked Campbell's chest and he voided his bladder in fear. The Carcosan laughed and said something in their twisted alien tongue. Campbell didn't hear the translation. The fear growing too much for him, he started to hyperventilate, shuddering uncontrollably

The Carcosan touched his crotch, stroked it intimately, then lifted her hand towards the mask. Unattached by anything visible, the mask came up easily. The shrunken face revealed, too small for the surrounding, swollen yellow head, looked down and smiled. The thing wore Gibson's face.

The Mask of the Yellow Death

Robert M. Price

oyt Hefti's ninetieth birthday was coming right up, and the founder of Layboy Enterprises and framer of the Layboy Philosophy was not planning to let the occasion go by un-noticed. He liked parties and held them constantly, filling the Layboy Mansion with curvaceous Laymates from recent years, as well as all the sports and cinema celebrities he could invite. The Big Nine-O would be special, far more exciting and extravagant than his other bacchanals. The occasion surely merited it, but that was not all. For Hef's fortunes had begun to fade, his gleam to tarnish, in recent decades. For one thing, the competition was fierce. At first he had to deal with rival sex magazines, more of them every year, and most of these did not bother with his own *Layboy*'s "tasteful" and "artistic" approach. His competitors tended to be down and dirty, going straight for the sex, the cruder the better. After all, what was the whole point of such a magazine? The interviews in *Layboy* were interminably long, the "party jokes" moronically stupid, the kitschy merchandise too expensive. No, the whole point was sex, and *Layboy*'s pages didn't have enough of it to satisfy your average masturba-tor, whatever his age.

But it wasn't just raunchy rivals *Townhouse* and *Rustler* that gave Hef's accountants headaches. There were attacks from the Left, crusades against pornography mounted by feminists and lesbians (weren't they the same thing?) who puritanically denounced skin mags as vehicles for the oppression of women, yada yada yada. *Layboy* had thrown them a bone back in the 1970s by including "fact sheets" on the living party dolls displayed on his glossy pages. While stroking one's member one could educate oneself in the fascinating matters of each model's turn-offs, turn-ons, favorite sports and movies, etc. See? *Layboy* cared about the whole person and would never think of reducing her to a mere sex object. But it didn't do much to satisfy his shrill critics.

So one might say the *Layboy* empire was falling on harder and harder times. The Layboy Clubs and ski lodges had closed down years ago, except for a few in Japan, where they savored the camp chic of the 1960s. But it was equally true of Hoyt Hefti himself, for he was, after all, growing increasingly wizened and infirm. Though surrounded by a bevy of nubile sex models, most of them blonde and nearly indistinguishable from each other, Hef gloried in the rays of their smiles and well-oiled breasts like an ancient potentate with a well-populated harem ostensibly evidencing his superhuman virility. But old Hef, to the considerable relief of his own harem, was these days more of an *im*potentate. His girls, some of whom had their own TV "reality" shows, were pure eye candy, arm candy. His dentures would not allow him to actually taste the candy. At most, his liver-spotted, claw like hands would occasionally reach out to fondle a luscious-looking boob, its buxom owner shuddering as she tried to think only of the salary ("allowance") she would receive.

But old Hef's brain was still pretty sharp and shrewd. And what he had planned for his birthday gala stood to meet both his needs.

The day of his blessed nativity soon arrived, and Hoyt Hefti stood on an upraised dais at one end of his vast banqueting hall, surrounded and supported by his favorite concubines (he forgot which one he had "married"). He liked to call them Camilla, Cassandra, Carmella, and Cassilda, and so their fold-outs read. Sporting his jaunty yacht captain's cap and wearing his trademark lemon silk pajamas, he welcomed a huge throng of guests who were even more stellar than his usual sycophants. There were government and military men, captains of industry, even numerous ecclesiastical leaders. Gallery owners, arbiters of taste, noted authors and poets, winners of Pulitzers and Nobel Prizes. A galaxy of stars. They had agreed to come once Hef's lawyers had convinced them of the Mansion's security arrangements, for there might well be certain activities that none could afford leaking to the public, who might not, with their bourgeois morals, understand.

"Welcome, welcome! My friends, as you know, I have asked that no one bring presents. You know the old saying about the man who has everything. I am that man, and this evening I want to share it with you, to give something back. Consider this shindig my present to *you*. Nothing will please me more than for you to have a roaring good time! I believe you've seen the instructions I've had passed out. And I see you've chosen your costumes from our wardrobe department. You look *great!*"

Hef was referring to a dazzling array of movie-quality costumes including leather and spikes, furry animal costumes representing various species (with a heavy emphasis on sheep, horses, and pigs), diapers, Catholic schoolgirl uniforms, pirates, cowboys, show girls, popes, etc. Most were cleverly designed to leave the faces, breasts, ass, and genital areas bare. The crowd was sprinkled with a number of wholly naked forms. And the grunts and bleats of real animals could be heard from adjacent rooms.

"But you're probably eager for the fun to begin! I know I am!" With that, Hef signaled his DJ, who sat at a complicated mixing board. There were seven rooms surrounding the great hall, each with its own name as if it were a restaurant or a club, and this man was charged with piping play lists of different musical styles, all of them near-deafening, into each room. He secured his headphones and began, as the vast crowd began to fragment, following their maps to the room of their choice. Some were young and lithe, veterans of countless hours in the gym. Others were old and flabby. No one seemed to notice or to be embarrassed. It was time, as Hef had said, to get down to business.

Hef and his beauties, all naked and gleaming, watched their guests disperse. The sense of envy was evident in the expressions of the girls until Hef broke the tension: "Well, what are you waiting for, ladies?

Go have some fun!" Off they went in different directions, with many a giggle and a jiggle. Grasping hold of his gold-plated walker, Hef stepped over to his diligent DJ and said a few words. Not wanting to distract him, Hef nonetheless wanted to make extra sure the many, many hidden video-cameras, long shot as well as close-up, were functioning smoothly. They were? Great!

And yet, despite such surveillance, none noticed the quiet arrival of a single uninvited guest. He had arrived already clad in costume, though one that left not an inch of flesh exposed to the eye.

The master of the house gave things a half-hour or so to warm up, then decided to inspect the festivities. First he shrugged off his pajamas and slipped back into his bathrobe, not bothering to tie it closed. His nurse, nearly naked herself except for her pert little nurse's cap and white silk stockings, helped the old man into his wheelchair and slowly pushed him toward the first of the consecutive party rooms.

The first was the Gay orgy room, called Planet Uranus. Most there were male, and the favorite costume theme seemed to be Village People, though there were a few Roman togas, too. Old-time Disco music blared from the lavender walls, pretty stereotypical, but no one seemed to mind. Nothing all that new here, but Hef had to admit these lads were energetic. There was so much changing of partners, one might have thought it a square dance. And his guess had borne out: both televangelists had made a beeline for this room, though they weren't engaged with each other, of necessity, as both were on the receiving end. But they weren't the only religious superstars here. There were a couple of Indian New Age gurus present, and a kabalistic rabbi with numerous bestsellers to his credit. An ecumenical event, then!

As his wheelchair passed slowly through the room, having to thread its way through knots of struggling bodies who sometimes appeared to come from nowhere into his path, he shook his head, politely declining more than one invitation. He passed no judgments but was an old-fashioned kind of guy. He felt sure they all understood.

Next Hef and his nurse, who paused to wipe herself of some splattered bodily fluids, crossed the threshold into the S & M chamber, Medieval Times. It was outfitted like a torture dungeon, though of course all the deadly mechanisms were stage props, nothing more. But the horsewhips, chains, and cat o' nine tails were real enough. One might have imagined oneself transported miraculously to Iran during the holy flagellation days of Muharram for all the whip-cracking and blood-letting. The main difference was no doubt the ubiquitous occurrence of orgasmic moaning among the sufferers here. No leather masks or hoods were allowed, because Hef wanted every face, every identity recorded for posterity. He hoped the revelers were not as annoyed as he was by the music of the rock group Om, which sounded like the Trump of Doom and gave one the sense of listening underwater like a fish retreating from an exploding naval mine.

Politicians and government bureaucrats were in the majority here, equally glad to be taking the punishments and dealing them out, just like in real life. He and nursey had to be careful, once or twice coming dangerously close to the bite of a stray leather tendril. Once again, it was not to Hef's particular taste, though witnessing others enjoying any sort of sexual sport was exciting to him. And that was the point of his little tour. A lash got tangled in one of his wheels for a few moments, but soon he was on his way again, headed for the next room.

Mainly to avoid befouling his bright yellow robe, Hef did not really want to enter the Copro-Cabana, where naked women down in recessed tanks to either side of a central runway wrestled in shit. Others ate it, while still others smeared it on passive partners and then sodomized them. Children at play. Hef waved as he passed by as quickly as he could.

The Play Pen was next, echoing with nursery rhymes set to music, alternating with classic selections from Alvin and the Chipmunks. Uncle Hef nodded paternalistically as he supervised the fun. Men naked except for urine-stained trench coats shoved their dicks up the assholes of women (and some men) dressed in plaid skirts, while others, garbed as Catholic priests, stuck theirs into the mouths of actual school boys and choirboys, dressed for the part. Hef had told them to BYOB. Again, he did not linger to join in, but the sight did its work, and his penis slowly tingled, thickened.

On through the Barn Yard, where some, dressed as farmers, pretended to rape pigs and sheep. One of the "sheep" was costumed as Shari Lewis' Lamb Chop puppet. Others preferred the real thing. There would be no trouble telling who was doing what to whom, thanks to the clandestine camera work. Hef could not help laughing till he gasped as the repeating loop of "Old MacDonald" played and played again.

The special effects were top-notch in Area Fifty-One. Screens filled the walls with space's starry voids and scenes from science fiction classics, featuring space aliens of all silly varieties. Several of Hef's stable of Laymates wore Cone-head bald wigs and had gray-green powder over their bare bodies. Strapped to operating tables before them were more of Hef's guests, face down, and enjoying rough anal probing from their unearthly captors, who wielded smooth rods emanating a mild shock. All this was accompanied by a hilarious soundtrack of weird background music from 50s sci-fi flicks.

The last stop on the tour was the Morgue. Hef's connections in the city had managed to get him the loan of a number of well-chilled cadavers who were probably getting more action now than they ever had in life. Soft, soothing organ music drifted from the speakers, and many of the bodies were laid out in coffins capacious enough for their "mourners" to climb in with them and try to pump a bit of rejuvenation back into them. Hef knew good and well that it would not be too long before he joined their ranks, and not just in pretense. It would not be long at all. Hell. He was ninety years old this very day! But he planned on making every day count.

The Mask of the Yellow Death

By this time, Hef's virtually vestigial member was throbbing like the old days. It had taken quite a show to build him up to this, but he could tell it was racing toward him now. So he had his nurse wheel him back to the banquet hall and then rang the bell signaling his guests to reassemble there. He found he could not wait for all of them, but most were there, distinctly annoyed, straightening their costumes and trying to shake off their recent berserker lust.

The nurse pulled the hems of Hef's robe aside and noted with pleasure the first solid erection her ancient boss had managed in many a year. She knew she dared not waste time, so she helped him into a large, stationary, cushioned chair, where she proceeded to sit astride him and lower herself onto his standing lance. This she did with increasing rapidity as the crowd looked on, some cringing, others applauding. At last Hef's orgasm exploded as the old man screamed. His cry of joy segued seamlessly into a death rattle as the exertion proved too much for his corrupt old heart. He slumped over, as his horrified nurse climbed off him, wiping herself with his robe. She had not counted on a necrophiliac lap-dance.

In the ensuing melee, with coated physicians and paramedics rushing to the platform (they had never been far from their aging employer), no one took much notice of one more figure making his way onto the stage. But as the men with the stethoscopes shook their heads and stepped back, this robed and hooded figure, sporting a color very close to the lemon yellow preferred by the late pornographer, stepped to the front of the dais and spoke with a clear, cold voice that seemed to carry everywhere without rising noticeably.

"Hoyt Hefti is dead."

Was this man, in costume like the audience, about to deliver a eulogy? Had this, like all the other bizarre details, been planned from the start? Was it all a skit, a cruel joke?

"Okay, who are *you* supposed to be?" shouted an Oscar-winning actress, her gown stained with semen and blood.

"I am the Phantom of Truth. I bring the truth to those who lack it."

"*What* truth?"

"And take that damn *mask* off! Show some respect for the dead!"

"And what are we supposed to do *now*? We can't have the police come in here to take the body! . . ."

His empty tones brought silence, perhaps from mounting fear: "I wear no mask," though his face did appear to be tightly bound in featureless white linen. "As to what you shall do, that depends. It is up to you. But first hear my truth. Your host contrived to film your unspeakable revels. He required money and planned to release the films to the media if you did not pay him great sums."

Eyes widened at this, brows wrinkled, faces reddened, mouths muttered agitation, indignation, nothing intelligible except for outrage and panic.

"But I have altered his plan." Some vague signs of relief followed this, a few smiles.

"I have seen to it that the cameras fed what they witnessed directly to the news bureaus. They have it even now."

There was weeping and gnashing of teeth.

"Perhaps you will dare to face opprobrium and censure and prosecution. But I have a way in which you may avoid it if you wish."

Though the terminal issue of *Layboy* did not carry the story, all other media outlets did. The once-billionaire magnate of Layboy Enterprises and his hundreds of birthday guests were discovered stone-cold dead the next day by a delivery man who rang the bell for minutes on end, trying to rid himself of a crate of sex toys and another, a case of absinthe. Looking through the nearest window, he beheld the carnage. It reminded him of that nursery rhyme with the phrase "We all fall down," only nobody here was liable to be getting up again. Autopsies were indeterminate.

THE MASK OF THE YELLOW DEATH

There were some indications consistent with poison gas, though no actual trace of any such substance could be detected.

The only corpse clad in yellow silk was Hoyt Hefti.

THE SEPIA PRINTS

PETE RAWLIK

y apologies, I did not mean to scare you. Most mornings I wake screaming. I have bad dreams, but those dreams, they help keep me sane. The fact that such things still terrify me, in an odd way I find comforting. My sister likes to say that I came back from the war changed, others nod and whisper words like "shell-shock," but it wasn't the war that did this to me. It was something worse, something far worse.

It was after the war—I was still in Paris working as security for the American delegation to the Treaty of Versailles. I was on leave following a disagreeable turn of events involving a strange estate on the outskirts of the city and a rather disreputable doctor who, like me, was from Arkham. The Major had given me some time off and I had squandered most of it by wandering through the streets of the city, searching for something, though what exactly I cannot say. There was a sense of ennui within my soul, a longing that cried out to be fulfilled, but try as I might I could not find what I needed. Unable to satisfy myself I instead indulged in more earthly delights.

It was thus that I found myself one night on the balcony of the hotel that many of our mission had laid claim to. I was intoxicated, but not incapacitated. I was enjoying the view—the balcony was five stories above the square, and provided an excellent point from which to observe the comings and goings of those below, without being too close to those sometimes maddening crowds. As I have said, I was intoxicated, lost in the drink and the beauty of the city, for suddenly I was no longer alone at the ledge. There was a woman standing next to me, staring wistfully out at the city lights and its people. She was an attractive young woman, in a European way, but she was also disheveled. Her clothes were ragged, some of her hair had broken free from where she had pinned it, and three of her fingernails on one hand were broken.

She was uncomfortably close, and when I cleared my throat to gain her attention she stared at me with such a wild look in her eyes, such madness and fear, I was suddenly taken aback. I recognized her, a girl from Guernsey, a singer, or at least a student of the art. She was fluent in both English and French, and therefore had been useful to us in the past. Her name was Evelyn—it seemed to me most girls from Guernsey were named Evelyn—and she looked at me with a touch of madness in her eyes.

Her voiced cracked as she spoke, "Have you seen the prints?"

I stuttered out a puzzled: "I beg your pardon?"

There was a book in her hand, a folio of some kind. She offered it to me. "The prints, have you seen the sepia prints?" The book slipped from her fingers and tumbled to the ground, its contents, photographs, spilled out and scattered across the stones of the balcony, like dry leaves in a light breeze, falling to earth, but with no intent of staying there.

My eyes caught hers, and there was a tear. "The prints," she whispered.

"Not to worry," I said kneeling down to gather up the images and the book itself. They were indeed sepia prints. As I crouched there by her feet I saw her weight shift. Her feet rose off from the ground. A shoe, black, shiny, but scuffed, fell back down. I put out a hand to catch it and as I did rose up as well, offering the errant shoe to the young lady like some prize, as if I were a conquering knight.

She was gone.

I was alone.

I searched the balcony, but to no avail.

A puzzled word slipped through my lips, "Where?"

I stood there, a woman's shoe in one hand, and half a dozen prints in the other. At my feet the folio blew open and more of the sepia-tinted prints leaked out. I was staring at the space where she had been, where she no longer was, and could see nothing but the spot on the railing that had once been covered with a fine growth of ivy, which now was torn and broken.

Then I heard the screams from below, and with a casual glance saw what had caused them. Evelyn was there on the square below, her arms and legs at impossible angles. Her other shoe was rocking back and forth on the masonry like a ship tossed on the sea. Her head had caught the garden fence and had been impaled with such force that it had been torn from her body. It stared back up at me with wide open eyes; eyes that I swore were still filled with fear and madness.

I didn't wait for the authorities. It would take time to deal with the local police, and they had no love for us Americans. They would have questions, but I had no answers. I didn't really know the woman, barely knew her name, had barely spoken ten words to her—was it even ten words? They would want to take the book, the folio of prints, but it was the only clue I had, and I needed it. If I were to figure this thing out, I would have to start somewhere. The book was as good a place as any. I cannot even today say why I did this thing. I just did it. As I have said, I was searching for something to fulfill myself, and this girl's death, or more importantly, understanding the impetus for her death, seemed to provide a taste of what I needed.

I gathered up the loose prints and the thin book that had once held them. I sprinted down the winding stairs, down the hall and out the back door. Leaving the alleyway, I slowed my pace and merged into the pedestrians that were moving along the street. The Mission had another house, a place several blocks away that we used to lodge dignitaries or visitors. I knew it was empty and made my way there, trying not to draw attention to myself as I weaved through the crowd.

In the safety of that anonymous townhouse I held the book and in the dim light examined it and tried to put it in order. It was bound in black leather, but that was faded in spots, frayed at the corners, broken in places along the spine. Traces of gold inlay revealed that there had been stamped letters on the cover once, but the majority of them had been worn away, leaving only a few specks of precious metal here and there. Even the letters themselves had nearly faded completely away. At first glance I thought that the repair of the book would take a significant amount of time, but I was mistaken. While the prints were all the same size, the stains and stray marks that rimmed the edges made matching each to the correct page much easier, and within hours the book was in order and intact once more, and I was able to examine it in its original state.

Investigations begin in odd ways, and no two are alike. The exact way to start is driven by the antecedent conditions, the style of those investigating, and the available clues. I only had two pathways to follow: I could investigate the woman, delve into her personal life and her work, or I could begin with the book. Reasoning that any conversation with family, friends, or coworkers would eventually be tied back to the book, I decided to begin there. It was, after all, already in my possession. It was perhaps the best place to start, and so I began my examination in earnest.

Though the letters on the cover were gone, the title page made it clear what the collection of photographs was. I did not even need to translate from French, for the title was repeated in English.

The King in Yellow
A Souvenir Collection of Images of the Cast

On the Occasion of its Premier
The Sixteenth of February, 1899

Palais Garnier
Paris, France

I knew the Palais Garnier by its more common name the Paris Opera House, a magnificent edifice, a cornerstone of Parisian society, albeit one that was occasionally drenched in a little blood. Since the building had been completed there had been rumors that it was haunted, and these rumors came to a head in the early 1880s with the strange affair of the Opera Ghost. That phantom was not the only scandal that had befallen the opera house, for there were still rumors of strange figures haunting the halls, balconies and alleyways of the edifice. Indeed, I recalled some mention of a fire that had taken the lives of an entire cast, and even some audience members.

Below the title there was a stamp in blue ink that identified the book as part of the collection of the Bibliothèque-Musée de l'Opéra, a library with which I was not familiar. I consulted a guide book and learned that the library-museum was attached to the Paris Opera House and served as an archive of both the opera house itself and of opera in general, holding thousands of scores and librettos, as well as costumes, props and memorabilia of performances themselves. This book, it seemed, was part of their archive and documented a lavish performance that had occurred almost two decades earlier.

Lavish was an understatement.

The costuming was magnificently decadent and purposefully grotesque. I had heard stories concerning the Opera's production of Don Juan Triumphant, but I could not imagine that it was any more extravagant or ostentatious than what was in these images. First, the set was decadently detailed, with great banners and glass chandeliers hanging in the background, while the foreground was reminiscent of the art deco style of designer Erte. There was hedonism rampant in every set piece, and through it all ran a hypnotic triple spiral motif that drew the eye and threatened to make me dizzy. That design, which was a kind of trimaris but only in the most abstract sense, continued into the costumes for each character. It could be found in the lace that trimmed the gowns of the twins Cassilda and Camilla, and in the crown of the regent Uoht, and his wife Cordelia's headdress. Aldones spectacles were three-lobed, and Thale's staff bore a triple spiral. It could even be seen in the pale cloak of the Phantom of Truth, and the bindings that held together the Pallid Mask. Only The Stranger seemed to be without any influence from the weird design, and this served to set him apart from the others, to make him an outsider amongst a society of the strange.

Each character was photographed in two costumes, one in a kind of formal attire, and then again in a kind of masquerade, each with its own mask, one simple, one ornate. Heavy makeup had been applied to all the actors which suggested that beneath their masks they were all horrifically scarred. The only exception to this was The Stranger, who had one simple costume and appeared to have only one mask, or perhaps none at all.

As I progressed through the images I began to develop a strange idea, a suspicion really, one that was confirmed with a single ensemble photograph. For each character there were two actors, one in common costume, and the other in fancy masquerade. The resemblance between actors playing the same part was astounding—indeed I suspected that some of them were twins or at least siblings—but there were subtle differences. There was a facial mole in one photo that was absent in another. One actor for Uoht had very different earlobes than the other. The actor playing the fancy Aldones was missing the tip of his left index finger. The girls playing the twins Cassilda and Camilla were no doubt sisters, or perhaps cousins, but certainly part of the same family.

All except The Stranger, of course—he seemed to be played by just one actor.

But then there in the photograph I saw something that suggested that my conclusion was mistaken. There was in that ensemble photograph of the entire cast in costume a plethora of arms. One arm too many to be precise, it was off to the left, and nearly hidden behind the cloak of one of the Phantoms, but it was there. It was right where it should have been if one were to balance out The Stranger on the far side of the photo. An errant arm existed, one belonging to an actor that had been cropped out.

I flipped through the pages more carefully this time and sure enough I found suggestions of him throughout the other images: A shadow figure in the background, a hand that didn't belong, and a boot that seemed out of place. It was then and only then that I realized I was missing a page. It had been excised, I could see where the leaf had been cut, and the line was smooth and tight to the binding. I had seen other books, rare manuscripts that had been vandalized, and those looked similar to this. Whoever had done this not only wanted to take the images, which could have been done by simply taking the prints, but to erase all trace of their existence and hide what had been done.

Reviewing the images and the death of Evelyn must have had a profound impact on me, for that night my dreams were invaded by the wildest of images. I was sitting on a stage, surrounded by the set from the images. The actors, or more precisely the characters from the prints, were walking around me, and seemed to be engaged in some great undertaking on my behalf, though what it was exactly was unclear. Aldones, the dwarf, seemed to relish what was going on, dancing around me to some strange staccato beat. The twins used me as a maypole, effectively binding me to the chair with ribbons. The giant Thale brought me coffee in an ornate silver cup, but when he saw I couldn't drink it, my hands being bound by the girls, he sighed and lamented about what he would have to do with the pie he had made.

It was the actions of Cordelia which most disturbed me. She paced nervously, gnashed her teeth, and clenched her fists as she did so. That she wanted to tell me something was obvious, for she started toward me on more than one occasion, but then seemed to think better of it and turned away. The Phantom of Truth, a gauzy thing with only the hint of a face, haunted her. It had eyes with which to see and ears with which to hear, but no mouth with which to speak.

If the phantom haunted Cordelia, then The Stranger stalked her, or perhaps he stalked the whole family. He lurked in the background, moving amongst the shadowed curtains. He had the run of the stage, and would disappear from one spot and then suddenly appear in another. These actions were most disconcerting to Cordelia and Uoht, but for the twins Camilla and Cassilda it seemed more of a kind of game. The two girls screamed, but then as they ran their screams turned to giggles which caused Thale to frown.

Eventually, in a sudden rush, Cordelia overcame her hesitancy and ran to my side. It was only then I realized that I was wearing the Pallid Mask. She looked into my eyes, grabbed me by the shoulders and brought her face up next to mine. I could smell the rosewater that she used as a perfume, and the sequins on her own mask nearly blinded me with their scintillating reflections.

Her breath was hot in my ear and her voice was panicked as she whispered softly and desperately the same words Evelyn had said to me before she killed herself. "Have you seen the sepia prints?"

I woke in a cold sweat, my heart pounding in my chest.

The next day I made my way through the crowds to the Bibliothèque-Musée de l'Opéra which was on the western side of the theater. I carried with me the folio, secured inside a leather pouch. From the outside the library was impressive, a kind of pavilion that was attached to and mirrored the design of the main structure. However, as impressive was the exterior, the interior was just as ghastly, for it was not only poorly lit, in a manner that only libraries seem to manage and the French have taken to an art form, but also unwelcoming. It was cramped: great shelves and cases lined the walls and extended up beyond the lamps into the darkness. There seemed to be a plethora of spaces at which one could work, but these were covered in manuscripts, papers and dust. As far as I could tell there were no other patrons. The library was empty save for me and the man behind the great reception desk.

He was old, perhaps an octogenarian, bent with age, smartly dressed, and by all evidence a well-educated man. He asked me if I needed assistance. His request was odd in that it came in English, and he laughed at my obvious surprise. "You Americans think that you look like us, or at least the British. You don't. Your clothes are cut differently. You're overfed. You walk oddly. You stand differently. You may look like us, but you aren't us, and we can see that."

I smiled at his candor and recalled how I talked the same way about European women. "I was hoping you could tell me about this?" I opened up my satchel, took out the folio and handed it to him.

"Young man I am Moncharmin, I am the curator here. If I cannot help you, no one can." He flipped through it, and though he did his best to conceal it, I could see that he was genuinely thrilled to be handling the object. He paused at the title page and made a hissing noise presumably at the stamp that identified it as property of the library. This was followed by a disappointing "Tsk," when he almost immediately saw the missing pages. With a flourish he closed the book and raised his eyes to mine. "Where did you get this?"

"A girl I knew had it," I said. "A girl named Evelyn. She killed herself yesterday. The book, the photographs, seemed important to her."

The old librarian nodded. "I knew Evelyn, a girl of some talent vocally. She came here often to read, and study the archives. I am sorry to hear that she is dead. Though given what she had been studying, her death is not surprising."

"Why do you say that?"

He closed his eyes and pursed his lips, obviously mulling over how much he was willing to tell me, if anything. "Please. You will follow me."

He stood up and pushed his way past me. I don't know why I followed him, but as he moved through the door and down the hall I seemed to have no choice. The old man had mesmerized me. Through the stacks we went, winding through the shelves and cabinets of books and papers. There was a door, a thick wooden thing with clasps of black iron. He unlocked it with a thick brass key that he pulled from his vest pocket. Beyond in the flickering light there were stairs leading down into the depths of the basement of the opera house. Great stones formed the walls and the steps, and the only signs that anybody had been down here in decades were the electric lines and lights that had been strung up using hooks pounded into the masonry gaps. As we descended he spoke, and I listened.

"Those were dark days. 1898 was a bad year for the Opera, for all of Paris, but for the Opera in particular. The excesses and scandals of the Third Republic had culminated in the Dreyfus Affair and public sentiment had slowly turned away from supporting the arts and literature. The Opera and its managers did things, and allowed things to happen that were not made public. The Opera was used for unsavory productions."

"Like this play, The King in Yellow?"

He nodded slowly. "You must remember that this was just three years after Jarry's Ubo Roi, an exercise in what he would later call pataphysics, the study of the laws of exceptions and the universe supplementary to our own. It was nonsense, of course, a first step into the absurdism and surrealism. The crowd on that first night, they rioted. There was a man, a poet of some renown in the crowd who wrote, 'After this what more is possible? After this, do we bow to the Savage God?' The authorities banned the play and Jarry had to flee Paris."

We were descending deeper. "The King in Yellow made Ubo Roi look tame. The authorities, the censors of the Third Republic, banned it before it was ever performed. They ordered all copies of the text destroyed."

"Then these photos were of a production that never happened."

"I wish it were so." There was shame in his voice. "It was a private production, rehearsed and staged in secret. None of our regular performers would participate. We recruited players of ambiguous morals. They were easy to find. Zidler was dead, and his successors at the Moulin Rouge had no use for freaks and deviants. Once Toulouse-Lautrec would have been their voice, but he had gone mad and been confined to a sanitarium, and with him had gone any hope of reason or human compassion. Do you think it odd that I consider that little syphilitic dwarf as the voice of reason, as the voice of morality?"

"There have been stranger sources of laws." I had not missed that he had inserted himself into the story.

"As you say. We were decadents, willing to do whatever in the name of pleasure, in the name of art. It was not the first time such ideas had played out in this theatre. We all knew the stories, the legends; concerning the chandelier, and the Phantom. We wanted to bring some of that madness, some of that grand theater, that gothic majesty back to life; to challenge the Parisian authorities with a morbid spectacle; to show them all what they should truly be fearful of."

"Which was?"

"The Phantom of Truth. The Pallid Mask. The Stranger."

"Death?" I offered.

He laughed. "Bah! Death is just the end of flesh. Men have so many other things to be fearful of. We are cattle being led blindly to slaughter, but that slaughter is not our death. The King and his tattered robe dull our senses, and for that we are eternally grateful."

"I thought The King in Yellow was just a play."

"A sonnet, a play, an opera, these are just manifestations of his divine symphony, vehicles for his infectious melodies. We are his chorus and must learn his book, one way or the other."

"You are mad!" I whispered. I thought perhaps of turning back, of fetching the authorities, but I was driven by some strange force to follow him deeper into that chthonic pit.

"Is it madness to speak the truth? Is it madness that the song remains the same? Our President Felix Faure thought so. He saw our performance, and died that same night. Come with me and I shall show you the truth, and then we shall see who is mad."

Down we went, further and further, and as we did Moncharmin continued to speak, but whether it was to me, or just to hear his voice, I was not sure. "The architect Garnier planned four basements, but the builder did more, many more. There are vast chambers that most never know of. They are used for storage, scene changes, and the like. One entire level houses the machinery that helps move the stage. Most people think there is only the one stage, but beneath that there are innumerable others. An entire separate production could take place in the under theatre, and those above would never know it." His voice had become odd, almost theatrical. "There are so many stages; some of them have been completely forgotten."

We were deep when he finally stopped descending and instead led me down a hall and threw open yet another door. "Behold," he proclaimed, "the 1899 production of The King in Yellow!"

Beyond that door I saw things, things that should not have been possible, not in the Twentieth Century. I stood there entranced as the old man donned that aged costume, as he placed that crown of antlers upon his brow, as he rose into the air, into that darkened space amongst the rafters. He danced there and I recognized him as the character that had been excised from the photographs, and I knew that the actor that had played him had been Moncharmin himself!

Even now, all these years later, I can still hear him reciting his lines with poise and bravado. "The Yellow King is dead," he shouted, "and who shall take his place? Shall it be the White Queen, the Crimson Cardinal, the Black Man, or perhaps the Green? The White Knight still guards the gate, but the scion is already within the walls. The exile returns and he seeks his rightful throne!" He floated down and took his place amongst that horrific tableau. He was a maestro, a master puppeteer; he was the spring amidst clockwork bones and flesh. "Kneel before me," he commanded. "Kneel before the Sepia Prince!"

They say I went mad, that these things did not exist. The Parisian authorities deny all of it. There are no reports concerning what was down there, and the officers I knew to have been involved are now scattered across the country. They claim the fire, the one that three days later consumed that old rehearsal hall, was an accident, bad wiring, but I know better. What they couldn't understand, what they couldn't comprehend, they burned away.

But I know what I saw, and I know what I did

Here is the truth. The old librarian floated there surrounded by his machine, a demonic construct of ropes and wire, of pulleys and desiccated corpses that danced to the sounds of an infernal barrel organ. He floated there, bearing the mantle of the upstart, the exile, the Sepia Prince. He was a terrible thing, the counter to the madness of the Yellow King, but just as mad. He floated there and demanded my allegiance, demanded that I take my place amongst those decayed and corrupted mannequins, demanded that I willingly accept him, and by doing so be corrupted by his dark influence.

I did what I thought was right, what any true man would have done.

I took my pistol from my jacket and I shot him. I shot him once, through his left eye. One shot was all that was needed.

His death is well documented. They could not erase the truth of that. I have seen the report. My name is on it, they acknowledge that I shot the man.

They say that none of this happened, but if that was true tell me why was I not charged?

If I shot that man, and he was just that, a man, and not the Sepia Prince, why was I not charged? If I was mad why was I not hauled away to the asylum?

Sometimes I wish they had taken me to the madhouse. Then, at least, I could have had the illusion that I was mad. I could have let the tattered veil of the King in Yellow fall back across my eyes and be blind once more. Instead I see what others will not.

The worst part is my dreams. Moncharmin lies on the floor dead. The others are there as well, dancing; their arms outstretched begging me to join them, to take Moncharmin's place.

"Have you seen the Sepia Prince?" They cry out.

"Yes," I tell them. "Yes, I have!"

Then I reach out for that pale brown coat, and the crown of horns. I reach for them with intent.

And then I wake screaming.

It is not the screaming which terrifies me. That I still scream at the offer gives me comfort, it tells me I am still a man. The night I no longer scream, when I no longer fear accepting the mantle of the Sepia Prince, that is what I fear the most.

Not my screaming, but when my screaming stops.

NIGREDO

CODY GOODFELLOW

ew cult deprogrammers these days would even try to take someone from Ex Libris. Hardly any even call themselves deprogrammers, anymore. "Exit counselor" is the preferred title, in keeping with the warmer, fuzzier new psychology. A human brain must be more than just Descartes' materialist cognitive model, or its feelings wouldn't get so hurt by the truth.

My methods were not popular, but they worked. Most of my business was by referral. The clients who came to me had exhausted every other hope of recovering their loved ones. When I could not myself convince them to accept that perhaps they were healthier, more enlightened, perhaps even happy, with their new lifestyle, then I had them sign my waiver and went to work.

Ex Libris was a hard target. They didn't greet at airports or convention centers or lurk outside euthanasia booths. They didn't panhandle or turn tricks. Mostly, they meditated to the Master's audiobooks while toiling in digital sweatshops up and down the coast.

Their leader was a creative writing professor. Dr. Preston Marble used the classics—"guided" meditation, hypnosis, sleep deprivation, protein starvation, mild hallucinogens and traumatic writing assignments. Ex Libris grew out of Marble's writing seminars and his "Awakened Editions" series of classic books annotated for neurotics desperately yearning to become psychopaths, harvesting the most hopeless wanna-bes, fans and impressionable victims into a militant bibliomancy cult.

Marble's guide to story structure translated more easily into a practical bible than the Bible, complete with interactive commandments. Every devotee had to compose an "antibiography" of everything they were not and never would be. On average, they ran to five hundred thousand words composed on no sleep and amphetamine-laced oatmeal. When your Editor finally approved your antibiography, you had to burn it and throw the ashes in the ocean or eat it.

If they used Allah, Buddha or Jesus, they'd be on FBI watch-lists, but to the outside world, they're just a fucking book club.

Sometimes, I can dress up as a senior cult official and pull them out with no headaches. This outfit had no slack, so I cut their DSL line, then knocked on their door. Four surfers in each one-bedroom unit at all times. A van came every other day to rotate them out. Eight more places like this, just in this part of town.

Cable guy uniform. Toolbelt. Wig and mustache, cotton plugs in my cheeks, lifts in my shoes. I chloroformed the geek who answered the door, caught him, threw the deadbolt and dragged him into the living room.

No furniture except for four workstations and a couple futons in the corner. Lysol, incense and macrobiotic farts. Two were awake and pecking at their boards. Another lay on a futon with headphones on. The one I wanted.

She wore a biofeedback harness and a Cranio-Electrical Stimulation cap. They listen to his heartbeat and EEG mixed with his audiobook lectures while they work. The more her brain activity conforms to Marble's template, the more mildly pleasurable zaps she gets from the cap.

And all while copy-editing or revising the mass media equivalent of lead-painted, asbestos infant's teething rings. If you've ever watched a slab of direct-to-video dreck or mind-numbing scripted reality show patter and wondered how sane human beings can create such empty noise, well . . . sane people don't.

The system also tracks bodily functions and location for the home office. Anyone unplugging their unit or wandering out of range triggers an alarm and the Editors come running.

I unplugged her and took off her headphones—Marble's sleepy bullroarer voice reading something about an anarchist exploding himself at Greenwich Observatory. She was semi-catatonic, dead on her feet. I didn't even need the chloroform. I stood her up and escorted her to the balcony.

Someone knocked on the front door, then tried the knob.

Out on the balcony overlooking the alley. My assistant waited on the roof of our parked van, ready to catch the product. I bagged her and lowered her over the railing.

Carl caught the bag and gave me a hand down onto the van, then jumped down and caught the product, dropping her in the back. In and out in less than two minutes.

We took her out to Imperial County, to the Olde Desert Inn. It was abandoned long before I set up shop, and no one ever happened by. Two miles off the Interstate, at a dead place that never quite became a town. You can see anyone coming from five minutes away, watch satellites pass overhead at night.

As soon as we got the product strapped down in the honeymoon suite, Carl went home to his family and I got busy. My client had paid a big premium for a rush job. He wanted his wife back. I had to open up the product and find her.

She had the kind of bright, nervous beauty that you feel sparking at you just before you look her way. Smart, fine features; good bones showing too starkly through her pale, jaundiced skin. Avid, hungry eyes.

Real deprogrammers, the old school guys, kept their techniques under wraps like stage magicians, but it's almost always some variation on the old interrogation, aversion therapy model. I didn't have any tricks, training, dirty little secrets.

I didn't interrogate them or break them down the way the burnout FBI agents and MK-ULTRA stooges who started our game did it. I didn't have to. I was more of an assassin. I captured and killed the target with my magic bullet. The product died and the person was reborn, saved by the Elixir.

I liked to measure out dosages not just to body size, age and health, but to degree of indoctrination. I usually interviewed the client before, but this one was unresponsive. Semi-catatonic. She'd get up and go where you pushed her, but there was nobody home.

A quick physical turned up scalp scabs from constant electrical shocks and bruised track marks from recent and intensive IV abuse. Her pupils were responsive and pulse fine, but someone had already worked her.

I wanted to wait, but I gave her the shot. Her pulse spiked, then flattened out. I checked her restraints. If she didn't come around in an hour, I'd give her the second dose I'd prepped.

It wasn't therapy. I studied psychology, but I'm no doctor. Nobody can teach you how to raise the dead. To join any cult, from the Masons to Aum Shinrikyo, you have to die. The old you dies and is buried inside you to fertilize the budding of the new you. To resurrect them, I just had to go digging. The Elixir was a bullet, but it was also my shovel. It's just easy enough, the results miraculous enough, that you'd kid yourself you know what you're doing.

Under the Elixir, you are outwardly conscious. You speak when spoken to. You obey. You don't ask questions. You know nothing but what you are told. You are utterly suggestible. I could make you blow me, hijack a bus and drive it into a nuclear power plant. It's not like hypnosis, where the idiot on stage *wants* to act like a chicken. What the product wanted, who they were, what they would or wouldn't do . . . all of it dies and goes away. In its place . . . whatever I put into them.

But she was doing it wrong.

She took me so completely by surprise that I almost didn't see that I'd found what I'd always been looking for. Someone who could show me what it was like to be nothing.

She babbled in French, faster than I could understand. Then, "*The stars beneath the sea . . .* Do you remember before you were born? You remember what it was like? . . . I'd give anything if you could send me back. . . ."

Usually, the product has to be coaxed out of the clouds. Sometimes it helps to guide them out with imagery; childhood snapshots as stepping stones, recreating the life history with a big red editorial pen.

But this product didn't need me to set the scene. The walls of the motel room turned to stained canvas flats in the wings of a musty black cathedral.

The ceiling vanished in a jumble of scenery dangling from cables. Some I recognized––the apartment, the Ex Libris Chapterhouse, the beach at night, a Hillcrest townhouse—but there were hundreds of others, an armory of scenes. Flakes of corroded varnish fluttered down to settle on her hair like golden snow.

"Before your script was written? Before the Plot had sharpened and bent and broken you to its ends." She winced, trying to smile. "If you're here, you must be an actor. . . ."

"Then you're an actress?"

Her laughter shivered flurries of paintflakes from above. "If you're alive, you must act. Are you so sure you're alive?" She tossed her head and fussed with the ash-roses embroidered in the sleeves of her gray gown. The fabric was dull yet subtly iridescent, like a shed snakeskin. "I like this one ever so much more than the last play. . . ."

"What play was that? What was your role?"

"I was a mirror for a man to admire his own mask. So few real roles for women, now as ever . . . I loved my Lord the King more than my husband. I had forsaken all others to become a thought in my Lord's mind. But then he revealed to me my particular purpose . . ."

"And what purpose is that?"

She knelt before the pool that had been only a square chalk outline on the floor of the stage. "To murder him," she said. The buckled, warped boards were now pitted umber flagstones, the corsages of stained paper extravagantly sexual lilies on still, emerald water.

"Do you want to be free of him? Of . . . all this?"

"Oh, he's no burden. His sinister hand stopped my dagger as if it were a feather. By his fear and by his blood, I knew he was but a pretender. No, the one I want to be free of, no one can escape."

"Who's that?"

She leaned in close and whispered, "The Plot."

Looking up into the gallery, she hunched closer to me. I could feel my warmth leeching away into her. "I like this one ever so much better. So many places to hide . . . Do you not know the French Play?"

I shuddered and told her no.

"No matter, the lines read *you*, as it were. But we must enter! The call! Here, you must don your mask!"

The theater throbbed with the tolling of a vast, leaden bell. She shoved the cold, dry thing into my hands. Before I could look at it, I had pressed it to my face. Shadowy hands came out of the dark to guide us up twisting stairs and through a velvet miasma of rotting curtains into a cold white light. . . .

We lay side by side upon the bed. Her pulse was steady. Her eyes were empty.

I thought better of giving her the second shot, decided instead on a serious sedative. But when I turned around, the syringe was gone.

It was in her hand. Then it was in my neck.

Before 9/11, the airport was much more than a place to wait in line and get searched. It was also really easy to steal people's luggage.

I did it to pick up quick cash after I dropped out of college. It beat waiting to be expelled once my misuse of the clinical psychology department's resources was uncovered, or once the new law requiring piss tests for financial aid went into effect.

At LAX, the passengers would crowd up to the belt even if their luggage was nowhere in sight, so if something went round the loop more than twice, it was probably unclaimed. Missed passenger connection, misrouted baggage, or maybe just a protracted restroom visit. Regardless, within ten seconds of spotting my quarry, I could have it out the turnstile door and into my friend's waiting car.

My friend. Naomi was philosophy on a pre-law track and still doing swimmingly. We had little in common except she enjoyed drugs even more than me, which pretty much guaranteed her at least some sort of regional title. Strikingly homely, smarter than me, and a fry-guide *non pareil.* Any time you wanted to drop acid and go walkabout up the coast, she was down, if she didn't have a paper due. I told myself she hung out with me because she was writing a paper about me.

So this one time, I cased the claim corrals in the international terminal, which was always sketchy and seldom worth it. Flights from Hong Kong, South America or the Middle East, where customs or immigration might hold them up for me, were also searched the most often. Even back then, they had cameras everywhere, and sometimes someone was watching them. I did a paper on recognition cues that guide our treatment of people we see as young/old, rich/poor, ugly/pretty, hostile/friendly, threatening/helpless, etc. The grabs started as part of those experiments. Everyone is a bigot, but a memorable prop or stereotypical mannerisms were cues that one noticed even above gender or race. I got a C+ and a journeyman's degree in spycraft.

We kept a suitcase full of Iranian currency—fifteen hundred dollars after exchange—and two pounds of hash. We pursued the experiments elsewhere—shoplifting, dining and dashing, pharmaceutical burglary, etc. Much was learned.

But this last one . . . it was everything we hoped for and deserved.

I saw this really long, odd-shaped, expensive-looking case on a played-out Cathay Pacific from Bangkok and figured it for something fun. Maybe a musical instrument. I wasn't looking for money, though I was broke and hungry. I wanted secrets.

I was dressed in a distressed linen suit, perfect for humid tropical climes, and a Panama hat with a snakeskin band. The dissolute young sex tourist, bringing back only viral contraband incubating where no customs agent dare search, or the callow expatriate, returning to liquidate a deceased parent's estate before returning to kick the gong around with the ladyboys of Patpong.

Already a scrum of vultures from the next flight were converging on the belt in anticipation of a fresh bag dump, providing plenty of cover from airport security, who had not once asked to see a claim check.

I was on the far side of the belt with a clear shot for the doors. Naomi waited at the curb in her ketchup-red Sentra with a bungee-cord holding the trunk shut. I passed "security" when I noticed I'd grabbed the wrong bag. This one was beat up, dull matte-black brushed steel with three key locks on it. It was too late to turn back, so I ran with it.

Three guesses what was inside.

Naomi and I went to a Shakey's Pizza in Culver City. Her dad was a retired cop upstate, but she learned how to pick locks to steal her classmate's Ritalin and weed in middle school. She got it open before our pie arrived and I lost my last ball on the ancient Zardoz pinball machine.

Neither of us knew French, so we couldn't read the greasy, piss-stinking diary. We got disgusted by the pictures of naked or near-naked Thai boys posed in rice paddies, in muddy alleys, in brothels, coatrooms, and riverbanks. Everywhere this guy went, he must have paid boys to drop trou for a photograph, prologue to fuck knows what. Maybe he paid them in something other than money, for all of them had the same dreamy, vacant expression, eyes drooping shut or fixedly staring up at the contents of their own skulls. I was never so fucking glad I couldn't read French.

I wanted to go back to LAX and play our favorite game, Spot the Pervert, but he wouldn't make it easy by going to security. He'd run straightaway he suspected they were onto him, I reasoned, and anyway, I got to the bottom of the suitcase and found the big bottles of weird yellow-gray powder.

Naomi wanted to snort it. I wanted to consult the diary first. Only the thought that it could be cremains, deadly insecticide or uranium, dissuaded us from a trial bump.

And the rest, as they say, is history. . . . When they don't want to talk anymore about how the chance discovery became destiny, or whom you ran over on the way.

In less than six weeks, I had learned enough French to know what I had, and what kind of monster I took it from. Don't believe that I tried to turn evil to good, to redeem it or myself, by going underground and turning the Elixir to a cult deprogramming tool. I could've become the greatest pornographer in history or a revolutionary therapist, a salesman, anything. . . . But I only wanted to learn what people were made of.

Another experiment.

In the interest of science, Naomi and I tried an intramuscular injection of fifty micrograms in solution of the Elixir. That was his name for it.

I don't remember anything after that. Naomi was gone when I came down. I never saw her again. I freaked out and took off and I hid out here and there and everywhere, shedding myself on the road until I was only the Deprogrammer. I believed that the euphoric migraines that overtook me almost like menstrual clockwork every few months were flashbacks, withdrawal symptoms, but I never tried it again.

Using the powdered Elixir, I delivered fifty-two prisoners of cults and successfully converted all but two of them into reasonable facsimiles of their old selves, minus a traumatic scar or an empty hole that made a cult seem like a good idea. I fixed them.

After four years, my supply of the Elixir was nearly used up. I had a sample tested once and learned it was a fungal derivative, but I'd never successfully cultivated the spores. Nowhere near close to having learned anything real, I was looking at retirement.

Carl came within seconds of my recovering enough to page him. This was because he and his family lived in the motel . . . and also because his "family" didn't really exist, except as an elaborate skein of posthypnotic suggestions. (Carl was my first patient. Mistakes were made.)

Nothing like this, though.

Carl let me get it out of my system. Just apologized and said he didn't see her leave.

Nobody ever escaped from the motel before. An unrehabilitated product would go running back to the cult, which might choose to go to the police. I would have to call the client to let him know his wife was missing with a head full of nameless psychogenic drugs.

Richard Resley, PhD, was a professor of nothing so mundane as one discipline, a postmodern *enfant terrible* who could never be contained by one campus, let alone one bed. The first article pulled up by a Google search called him the Deacon of Deconstruction. I had to get into the double digits to find things I wished I'd known before I agreed to abduct his wife.

I deployed Carl to look for the product and drove into the city to meet with Resley.

He was being interviewed at the local public radio affiliate, but agreed to give me a few minutes between demolishing colonialist patriarchal dialectics and delineating new paradigms for a chubby ash-blond postgrad who looked ready to jump his boring bones.

He took it well.

"So, she is no longer your responsibility then." He nodded to me, turned to go. "She is very headstrong. I trust you did your best."

I took his arm, sure he wouldn't want his pet coed to hear what I had to say. "I won't try to complicate the situation any more than it is, if you'll just tell me why you'd pay good money to have your wife deprogrammed from a cult that *you* still belong to."

His face tightened. "I suppose there's no point equivocating. My interests and Preston's are still deeply entangled, though I was never as devoted to his philosophy as my wife." Air-quoted *philosophy*, the prick.

Resley coauthored three major studies of "psychocultural engineering" with Marble two decades ago, just before he left UCSD and started his sewing circle. Never publicly connected to the cult, but the pattern was there, if you were paranoid enough to see it. "So, you get all the benefits and none of the starvation. . . ."

"My antibiography wasn't all that long. Preston is doing some extraordinary things with expanding human potential, and I've been privileged to witness some of it. Listen, this is beginning to sound an awful lot like some sort of blackmail attempt. . . ."

"It's not. Your wife disappeared in the middle of a session. She's extremely suggestible. . . ."

"I could've told you that," he said. "Listen, if you're so concerned, why not go to the police? I'm sure they'd be very thorough in locating her, once they sorted *you* out." Impatiently, he sped up and crossed the street just ahead of a truck loaded with liquid CO2.

I gave up chasing after him. Just stopped and shouted in the street, "Was it you or Marble who turned her onto the French Play?"

"Jesus fucking *Christ*!" Resley whirled and came back up to me where I waited on the curb.

I couldn't resist. "She dreams she's acting in it. Says she was in another play, too, where somebody tried to get her to kill somebody—"

He hit pretty hard for a middle-aged college professor. The punch folded me into his shoulder, which shoved me back onto the curb.

His face was frozen milk. I smelled urine, and it wasn't mine. "Stay the hell away from me or I'll call *my* police. Would you like that?"

I watched him walk away. The postgrad skipped after him, looking sideways at me as she followed him to his office.

I could've left it alone. Nobody was paying me to press further. I didn't like being used, but if Ex Libris wanted to play games, they would have been subtler about it. The easiest explanation, that Mrs. Resley had been a plant to spy on my methods, would explain it all if anyone had ever gotten up and walked away in the middle of an Elixir session.

One person had, and I never saw her again. And no one under the Elixir had ever successfully dragged me into their head. And I had heard only once before of the French Play, in the journal I found with the Elixir.

"And the games! Such delightful entertainments our pretty toys gave us . . . Never has the French Play been performed with such abandon, as my little troupe put on for the Khmer Jaune Festival. Every performance consumed a raft of Cassildas, a platoon of Thales, and taxed my art to its core. Such ecstasies, such wondrous pitiful pain! My dolls laid so bare the veiled face of power and desire that the Pallid Mask wept tears of priceless ichor and the Hidden City beckoned beyond the rotten red moons . . . We all saw it, and beheld the colorless, cold corona of the Crown of No Nation. . . ."

The King In Yellow was only one more bullet point in an inventory of depravity that yawned at pedophilia and cannibalism. I tracked down and attempted to read it back when I was still trying to find out what I had, but I couldn't tell you what the big deal was. My memory of it was like a hole in a pocket. I ran down a copy at a Xian Science Reading Room where the curator owed me a big favor.

I put out an underground APB on my car with some contacts in the repo and private security industries. I prowled the Ex Libris chapterhouses in Ocean Beach and Encinitas. I got nothing and nowhere, and hoped for better news from Carl when we met at a taco shop on PCH. He had ignored my calls all day, so I assumed he was either busy or had lost it. He was always losing things when I forgot to remind him.

He looked like he'd lost a lot more than his phone. He sat down next to me on a picnic bench out front. The surfers and landscaping grunts had all gone and the shop was deserted. On the wall, they had that mural in every taco shop, of the dead Indian prince on the woman's lap, an Aztec Pieta. . . .

"I found her," he said.

I lit up. I asked her where, how, why didn't he tell me on the phone? . . .

He rubbed his eye, looked absently at the smear of blood on his fingertip. He took out a picture. It was creased and faded. He stared at it, cupped in his big, shaky hands. "Why didn't you tell me? . . ."

Where was she? I asked him.

"She's everywhere," he said, and dropped the picture on the scarred wood table. It wasn't Regina Resley. It was a picture of an emaciated, bald effigy that it took me several seconds to recognize.

It was hard to make out just what he was saying. Words didn't come easy, but he wanted to know what I did to him, to his daughter. Why did he have false memories of another family in the desert, and what was his real fucking name, please?

Before I could think of an answer, he let out a desolate sob and lunged at me, hands around my throat.

Did I leave that part out?

Carl. I didn't let myself think too much about who he was or where he came from. It was so upsetting, I resented him if I even thought about it, because it never bothered him, and if anyone could fix me so I didn't remember about Naomi either, than I would have. I was jealous of Carl, because he had someone to fix him.

Carl came looking for his daughter about a month after the Incident. I had split town and was hiding, but he was a retired cop and a widower with nothing else to do. He wanted to know where his daughter was, and since nobody else knew and I was her good friend and had fled right when she went missing, I had a lot of explaining to do.

Instead, I stabbed him in the neck with a syringe of Elixir. I was still haphazardly translating the journal with a big Larousse French dictionary, and I was seriously considering throwing all of it in the ocean and starting over.

But then I had an ideal subject. It was easy to erase memories, but putting something in its place . . . that took nuance. Starting with Carl, I had gone from something resembling a sleepwalker to someone who believed quite firmly in the fantasy of a normal daily life I had given him, who enjoyed the love of a family in his head every night while he lay alone in a motel room. He was probably happier with my lies than when his wife and daughter were alive.

But try to tell a man that when he's strangling you.

None of my safewords worked. Not even the nuclear one, the name of his daughter. Breathless, I gasped them in his ear, but he was a me-killing machine. More in sorrow than in panic, I took out the injector pen I'd mixed for Mrs. Resley and stuck it in his left armpit.

He went limp, crushing me on the table. I rolled out from under him and sat down, composing my thoughts. The taco shop workers watched me through the window. Cars passed on the street.

All my work ruined. Her name should have shut him down, but he had found it, and come back for me. I couldn't accept that my programming had simply come undone.

To rebuild what he was would be impossible . . . his identity was a patchwork stitched together ad hoc over the last four years. I could leave him blank, but someone would come looking. A man with no memory is interesting, while a man with sad memories can't be buried fast enough. Far easier to restore him to where he was when I found him, with a few hasty updates to account for the missing time.

You've been drinking and drifting ever since you found out your daughter Naomi had died of a drug overdose. But now, it's time to go home, to pick up the pieces and live your life.

I gave him a little more off the top of my head, then put some cash in his wallet. I asked him who did this to him. Who gave him this picture of Naomi, digitally dated four years ago.

Even under the Elixir, he could not, or would not say. The words he seemed to mouth but could not speak aloud, I could only guess that they were, *Your Master.*

I spent the next several hours hiding out from the Plot, trying to figure out what to do next. Waiting to see who tried to fuck me up next.

Reading the French Play.

Like naked celebrity photos or instructions for making a nuclear weapon, you can find no end of fakes and fragments of the French Play on the Internet. But all the versions out there are counterfeits, malware or worse. All the printed English translations, burned and scandalized, omitted much, and if an editor only suffered a stroke or a nervous break-down in the process, he was lucky.

I felt something for Regina Resley that I had not for any of my other products. She was beautiful and smarter than me and she stood at the heart of everything I had thrown away my life to discover. How could I not fall for her?

That's what I told myself, but I loved her as I loved mystery, and because chasing after her lost me in a story less pathetic than my own.

There's just the stories, and people weave them to trap a bit of real-ity and tame it, and people get trapped in the stories and think they're taming the world and playing it like a game to get what they want, like shaking a gourd and doing a dance to make it rain. Sympathetic magic. Spill blood to make it rain, so it'll rain blood.

Stories do all that for us, and what do they ask in return?

I didn't own a copy. But I figured I for sure knew who did. The condo in Hillcrest had three pet grad students in it. None of them were wired Ex Libris drones, just the new crop of coeds from which Resley had once picked Regina. No wonder he didn't miss her.

I didn't have to search Resley's office. It was on the desk in plain sight, nicely annotated with Post-it tongues sticking out of the crumbling, acid-etched pages. He was nowhere to be found, so I sat behind his desk, donned a pair of rubber gloves and started to read. I don't think I got through the dramatis personae before I blacked out again.

I sat upon a threadbare throne hidden behind a moth-eaten screen as the curtain fell. A river of parchment skin and brittle bones rattled applause out of the void beyond the footlights.

"You were marvelous," she said. She took the gold-trimmed tails of my cloak and slit them with a straight razor.

My hands went to my face and touched the mask. It wouldn't come off. Her hand on mine was colder than the razor. "It's a short intermission. Do you want them to see your naked face?"

I had to search for my own voice. The Lines hung in the air like the promise of plague. "In the . . . in the last play . . . your husband hired me to turn you against your master. . . ."

Her hands went to her face. The razor sheared away a wing of her bangs. "Oh, look what you've made me do . . . You're gnawing at my motivation again."

"I'm sorry, Regina. I only wanted to know. . . ."

Her eyes went blank and blind. "We're here now, and that's all that matters. We don't ever have to leave . . . *so long as we play*."

She returned to tattering my wardrobe, hysteria whickering in her throat so I didn't dare press. "All of this to be gotten through . . . all these scenes . . . As if any of it matters . . . But our reward . . ."

"What do we get? What comes at the end?"

She looked up from her work and kissed my frigid mask. "Why . . . you do!"

"In the next act . . . I can't recall the lines . . . but you . . . you're going to murder someone? . . ."

"Imagine that! I couldn't murder my own shadow. . . . Even when She almost . . . No, you won't . . ."

Agitated, she cast about with the razor. "He's not going to find me here. You won't tell, will you? If he doesn't, if we get to the end, then we can go and live where everything has already happened, but we'll remember, won't we? The black starshine won't . . . The sun beneath the sea . . . It won't forget us, because we'll stop it, we'll never have to be born again and we'll stop them, the stopping stoppers . . . stop . . ." The words seemed to come apart in her mind. She looked at me in alarm, the razor clenched in a white, birdlike fist, her soft white wrists cobwebbed with hesitation scars. "Oh my Lord, I'm undone. . . . I have forgotten my lines! He's coming to correct us. . . ."

The screen around us was hoisted into the gallery. The throne withdrew on whimpering casters with me on it, leaving her trembling alone on the boards when the curtain lifted. She threw up her hands and told me to run just before she dissolved in the pale yellow light.

I looked up from the book, my thumb jammed into the last act. He must've come while I was . . . reading? Sleeping? He sat on the leather couch under the picture window overlooking the park. He was wearing the same plum worsted wool suit he had on at school, which was fortunate. It hid the stains.

Resley had no face. Everything from ear to ear, from hairline to chin, was stripped away in a frenzy of slashing, flaying strokes that left only ribbons of gristle dangling from his naked skull. The worst of the mess lay strewn across transcripts of phone conversations with me that lay in his lap.

Two grad students were waiting in the hall. "We've called the police. You really should wait here." They didn't stop me leaving. They shot me with their phones as I fled the scene covering my face with the French Play.

Marble was slated to speak to a few thousand at the Extensions Festival, a massive New Age, human potential snake oil block party on the Prado, by the zoo. I left my car in the zoo lot and cut through eucalyptus groves and twisting canyons to the backside of Balboa Park.

Yellow-gray clouds draped over the park, clammy fever sheets gravid with rain that couldn't fall. Shadows seeped up out of the decaying Spanish colonnades, alcoves choked with morbid satyrs and defaced saints, faces gouged off and bearded in graffiti and guano. Hotter in the shady arcades than under the stricken sun.

I heard the watery echo of amplified voices lapping at the walls everywhere in the park, but it took me a long time to locate it. A cohort of grad students surrounded the Spreckels Organ Pavilion. A screenwriting seminar had bussed their dupes in, so the crowd overflowed the pavilion and swamped the Prado and forked around the goldfish pond to back up against the botanical gardens. And everywhere among them, you could see the earbuds of the ones already listening to his voice, his brainwaves, telling them how to be not just the heroes, but the authors of the story of their lives.

They followed me right into the Model Railroad Museum. One of them shot me in the hand. The projectile was the size of a pub dart. My hand went rubbery and spasmed out from under me as I climbed up onto the tabletop model. I tripped over Cajon Pass, kicked a hole in Mt. Palomar and wrecked the Santa Fe Super Chief. Ancient volunteer engineers in blue caps tried to pull me down, but I staggered towards the HO-scale downtown, intent on stomping Balboa Park, crushing the shoebox-sized replica of the Organ Pavilion and its tiny plastic Preston Marble before Regina could find him. I only made it as far as Fashion Valley. I collapsed on my face and had to be dragged out, numbly clutching two fistfuls of broken boxcars.

Tranquilizer darts. Seriously. It's heartbreaking to devote your life to abducting people efficiently and safely, and then to be taken by sadistic amateurs.

"D'you know how you can tell you're trapped in an inferior writer's universe?" someone said. "Nobody can speak for more than three sentences without sounding exactly like the narrator."

I woke up in a tiny, dusty tea room. The only window was covered up by a faded French, maybe Belgian, flag. I was a prisoner in one of the Houses of Hospitality.

Two big men with thick glasses blocked the door. A thickset man with doleful eyes and no hair of any kind on his head except for a full white handlebar mustache that hid his mouth, so his deep, overly familiar voice could have been coming from anywhere. His left hand rested on his lap like a dead pet, bandaged and splinted as it would be for a deep wound. Say stopping a knife—

"Do you know why cultures die, Mr. —?" He took a cup of tea from a bodyguard with his right hand. Nobody offered me one. "The Native Americans saw their narrative arc demolished by the more dynamic European colonial dialectic. Their myth, their story-way, was gone, and they soon followed it. They were dead inside before we put them on reservations.

"Same with modern America. All our myths gone to rust and reality TV. Fantasies of quick fame and fortune, of being something that everyone else wants to watch, of swift retribution on the lazy, the stupid, the poor. There's no mythic resonance to daily life. That's why everyone dreams of writing a book or a screenplay. Everyone feels one in them, that never gets out. That story they can't tell is *themselves!*"

A bodyguard handed him a napkin to blot the spilled tea. "More powerful than drugs, than God or death or fear itself, are stories. With less instinct than any flatworm, we look for them to tell us what to do, how to behave, how we're going to end up. There're plenty of atheists in foxholes, but none without a personal mythology that gives them meaning. When life seems long and meaningless, stories make it short and exciting, make every accident into a test, into enemy action, into a *Plot*."

My head throbbed from the tranquilizer. I still couldn't feel my hand. Trying not to stare too fixedly at the teacup, I said, "I'm falling asleep again, you dick. Bullet points, please."

He smiled. "Exposition is death," he admitted. He tossed his empty teacup into the cold fireplace.

"Would it kill you to give me something to drink?"

The bodyguards looked at each other. One went to a tea service in the corner and graced me with lukewarm bottled water that wasn't French. It tasted like a kiss from someone with worse breath than mine.

"People call what I do a cult, and that hurts. I help people tell their stories. I teach them to see the magic, the mythic resonance, in their daily lives. I tell them the rest of the world is full of shit, and I'm right. The disciple pays for wisdom with submission. But this isn't a cult. Nobody here worships me. I don't tell anyone what's going to happen to them when they die.

"Everyone who comes to me, I help them articulate their One Story, their narrative arc, and I don't just help them create a marketable masterpiece. I help them tell their story compellingly, because *that* is where they will go when they die."

My sleepy hand wouldn't cooperate with the clapping. "You should say that up front, more people would join up. What's this got to do with the Resleys? You know he hired me to deprogram Regina so he could try to get her to kill you."

He didn't look shocked. He looked delighted. "Of course. He was only following my outline. Do you know the difference between a fringe cult and a legitimate religion?" He anticipated my obligatory smartass answer. "One dead messiah."

"I find it hard to believe you're having a hard time getting someone to kill you."

"With respect, you're not a storyteller. Regina was addicted to escapism and had no real story of her own to tell, so she naturally insinuated herself into mine. Easier to be the villain in your own story than trying to be something you can't imagine. At least you know where the end is."

Pointing at his mangled hand with mine, I asked, "Why didn't you let her finish you off when you had the chance?"

"Timing is everything. Our lives are like coal. Shaped for eons in darkness to be used up in an instant. Stories are the fire in which they burn."

"If we're lucky. So . . . your . . . *arc* comes to a dramatic end, cut down by a traitorous disciple. . . . I think I've seen it before."

"Then you know how it ends. Preston Marble the Man dies, but Marble's Word lives on in *every* man. She'll play her part."

"She's playing it now. She killed her husband, less than an hour's walk from here."

"Nobody seems to have seen her there." He held up his phone to tab through a slew of amateur paparazzi snaps of yours truly fleeing the condo with a gray blur like a struggling dove trapped in my hand. "Just you."

"You don't know where she is."

"We thought you had her, but wherever her body's gone to ground, we're confident she'll rise to the occasion when the curtain goes up."

"Why *The King—*"

Shaking his head vehemently, he hushed me. "Don't." He gathered his thoughts, fetishism warring with fear. He told his bodyguards to wait outside. "Few can bear to read it at all, and most quickly give up or are thwarted, and everyone who claims to have read it has described a different ending, with variations large and small, but no two alike . . . because no one, reader or player, has ever *truly* finished it. . . ."

"But that's not possible. It's just a play, for fuck's sake. How hard can it be to get to the end of a goddamn book? . . ."

"Every reader must enter the text alone. None emerge unchanged. Some never return at all. Regina is that most *rara avis*: a *pure* reader. Only the most extreme spheres of abstraction satisfied her, but once dug in, she was impossible to shake out again.

"To reach her . . . to break her out of her fugue and quicken her to her purpose, we needed some radical outside element to catalyze the last act. You will continue to serve our plot until your arc is complete."

"And your arc will end with her killing you . . . to try to make Ex Libris a mainstream religion? . . ." He shrugged, all false modesty. A bodyguard watched us through the porthole window in the cottage door. I tossed my water at him.

The door flew open and they were on me before it hit him. My head hit the wall, but I saw how he caught it with his bandaged left hand. It seemed to hurt him a lot less than if someone had just stabbed him there.

"You're not Marble," I said, feeling brilliant.

"Well, of course not. . . . But I've played him for many years, and I've only ever quoted the Master. Professor Marble retired from public life three years ago, and communicates only through bibliomancy and doubles."

Quotations selected at random from his own books on writing. "You're willingly going to die just so he can go to his own funeral?"

It was pure hell finding something that didn't make him smile. "He will be alive and yet mythologically dead. He will be, in point of semiotic and phenomenological fact, a living god."

"And did *you* have any say in how this would . . . will . . . happen?"

"*The Secret Agent*, by Joseph Conrad. It's one of my favorites. Have you ever? . . ."

I shook my head. I lie a lot. "You're so tight with the, ah, Master . . . What's he really like?"

"Could you ever hope to attain mastery so complete that when you close your eyes, your disciple opens them, not merely believing in, but *being*, you? That's what he's like. I pray to him: TEACH ME TO BE

YOU. And silently, wisely, he has."

Outside, the pipe organ was crushing the exultant final movement of Saint-Saëns' 3rd symphony. A timid knock at the low, rounded door lifted Marble's double out of his chair. He shuffled through ankle-deep dust, looking over his shoulder at me from the open doorway. "I imagine you're about to be overwhelmed with remorse when you find out what your last patient has done. You're going to become very emotional over the undoing of your perverse amateur brainwashing operation, and with the police at your door and so many ruined lives in your wake, you'll be doing the world a favor. A real one, not like the sick games you played with helpless, vulnerable people's minds."

I couldn't help but nod along. "That does sound like me. Did you write it all out for me?"

Slapping his forehead, he produced his trademark overstuffed spiral-bound journal and shook out a slip of paper from my motel. Someone had surely meditated very deeply upon my choppy block capital handwriting, and nailed it.

"How much do I owe you for this?"

Chuckling, he nodded and walked out into a monsoon of applause. Three bodyguards came into the cottage once he was clear and escorted me to a limousine. The bitter tang of mildewed paper and incense filled the cabin. I got in without making a scene.

The book was gone, but I didn't need it. A bodyguard got in with me as the limo pulled away from the curb. He crushed me against the passenger seat. I hit and kicked to no effect. Try as I might, I couldn't even bruise myself against him. I wasn't there at all by the time he hooded me in a two-ply plastic yard waste bag and wrapped his arm around my neck in a truly professional sleeper hold.

I was back in the gallery. I wore a soldier's uniform. Regina wore a tattered ochre cloak made from a ruined asbestos fire curtain.

She pulled back a drape hiding an alcove and a tarnished brazen bell cover. She lifted the cover and the room was suffused with verdigris-tinted light that seemed to rot all that it illuminated.

Underneath it, her husband's severed, faceless head. Upon his brow, cruelly piercing it, the source of the dismal glow—a plain golden circlet transfixed with barbarous, spiky coronal flares.

"A cabal of Spanish conquistadors who sought the seven cities of gold from California to Patagonia made it with all the gold they found. Cursed by Aztec sorcery and burnt by the Church, in their bitter madness, they dedicated the crown to Cibola, a kingdom that never was.

"A crown must be ritually consecrated by blood and soil to bind the land and the people to the ruler's bloodline. It was drowned in blood, but never has it touched earth. Outside, it's only a curiosity, but because of its potential here, the play has outrun the Plot. Whoever lays claim to it becomes King of Hastur. They shall don it and declare a state of war and lay siege to Carcosa. . . . And bring the curtain down upon us all. If he is not stopped . . . Take it."

I knew it would burn and mutilate my hand. It hurt to touch it, until I realized *I* was hurting me. My fear of it turned to raw, phantom agony, an almost magnetic repulsion.

"Now, I must play my role." The slip of paper clutched in her hand bore a strangely unfinished, yet overripe symbol, a kind of three-headed question mark rendered in saffron ink upon ivory foolscap.

I took her hand. I had no idea of how it ended, but I would do anything to stop it.

I pulled her close and kissed her. Her lips trembled and she clung to me, but her passion dissolved into hysterical laughter. "He's coming! If you don't let me go and perform the scene, then we'll all go into the void. . . ."

"No, let's go." And we ran.

Somewhere, a pipe organ swung deliriously into Saint-Saëns' *Danse*

Macabre, with the slap of whips on flesh for percussion.

I leapt into the nearest canvas flat, but instead of ripping through painted canvas, I pancaked against immovable stone.

The chamber at our backs was crowded with broken statuary, headless kings and armless nymphs, clothed in drifts of crematory dust. The flagstones were gray-veined yellow marble, pitted with tiny marine fossils and worn down with centuries of pacing. Fumbling along the wall in the dark, I clung to her arm. I nearly lost her when a long butcher knife slashed through the *trompe l'oeil* scenery on brittle canvas.

Cassilda cried out and ripped her hand free, so I followed her.

We raced down a flight of stairs and through a courtyard of leafless trees; a cavernous library of books that disintegrated in a whirlwind of debris at our passage; a feasting hall with a bowed table buried to the rafters with uneaten, rotten meals; and a ballroom where the blindfolded organist attacked the crescendo of the delirious, reeling tune in a spastic frenzy. And behind us, just as we escaped each monumental, empty chamber, the butcher knife pierced the canvas and shredded it and our hooded pursuer staggered into fleeting, panicky view.

Breathless, at last we broke through the tall glass doors of the ballroom to end up on a wide balcony overlooking a lake still as stone under two moons. Almost annihilated by the discordant shower of moonlight, on the far shore of the lake and yet somehow further away than the moons, I could see the spires of a city.

Cassilda threw off her robes and cast the Yellow Sign onto the water with a shiver of bravado. "Can you swim, my darling?"

I looked down, shaking my head. "It's not even water. . . ."

She looked at my hand. Only then noticing the crown cutting into my fingers, I threw it after the Yellow Sign.

The jellied ripples from our offerings passed like the quivers of sleeping meat. Deep within it, I could see sepulchral gray lights of unborn ghosts.

The now-familiar purr of steel ripping through fabric and cracking petrified wooden struts echoed through the ballroom. We had been lost, but now were found.

She climbed onto the railing, fingers dug into the eyeless mask of a caryatid. "Come, darling, if we are true, then we shall prevail and gain the far shore. . . ."

She kissed me once and took my hand. "Quickly, before the sun rises beneath. . . ." I climbed up onto the rail alongside her, looking down into the depths of Hali and seeing those imprisoned souls whose dull light bored up through the queasy sheen of doubled moonlight on the skin of the water like the moans of the damned from an orchestra pit.

I kissed her one last time, and pushed her.

She did not grab me, but fell gracefully into the water like a knife.

I watched her dissolve in the darksome gray deeps and heard the chemical scream of her undone body, her defiant soul, a pure peal of doomed beauty like an echo of the emptiness of Heaven. She would have to do it all over again, when next the curtain rose.

I jolted awake to find the trashbag slashed open around my neck, sodden with vomit. The man who'd been killing me only a minute ago now sat with his hands in his lap, looking out the window, pointedly oblivious to our other passengers.

A shrunken, careworn version of the man who'd dictated my suicide note sat across from me. He wore burgundy pajamas and a baggy cardigan with leather elbow patches, stretched out oddly by a bulletproof vest underneath. Resley's copy of *The King In Yellow* lay on his trembling knees, open to the beginning of the last act. His bandaged left hand upon it looked like a swaddled chicken's claw. His eyes were closed, his head bobbing in time with the whispers of the man who sat next to him, who had no face at all.

It wasn't that I can't recall it now, so much as that I simply could not perceive it, except as a colorless glass mask. He talked to Marble, whispering in his ear. Sheepishly, Marble nodded as if grooving on his own thoughts. The bodyguard on his other side looked right through me when I mouthed his name.

The limousine stopped and Carl got out to open the door. Marble shuffled out in corduroy slippers, out of the crosswalk and up the ramp to the Prado.

"It was you," was all I could say, "in the . . . in the play. . . ."

"We've never really been apart," said the faceless man, "from the day you took what was mine."

I stared at him, really *tried* to see him. He smiled. I looked away. For just a moment, he had a face, but it was mine.

"If you knew where I was and what I was doing," I said, "then you could have stopped me. . . . Why didn't you?"

"I could ask you the same question." He turned and rapped on the partition, whispered briefly to Carl. "You could have brought me to the attention of the authorities. We kept each other's secrets admirably. But now . . ."

I was unable to speak. Was there ever a time when I had not been someone's puppet?

He pointed at Carl. The bodyguard slid across the suede acreage of seat to mix a drink.

"When you stole what was mine, I was beside myself, but then it occurred to me that I might learn more from making a gift of it. And how you have taught me."

"I never used it the way you did."

"I know! You attempted to redeem my Elixir! A dismal failure as an alchemist, but what a failure! The raw material, you refined away all the wrong properties. In my own experiments, I called them my angels, because they lacked free will, and were innocent of desire. Your first instinct was to use it to discover, to learn, to interrogate your angels, but you deluded yourself you set them free.

"Your choice of career was, of course, my suggestion. But you deserve the credit for the basic decency that gave me the idea to let you keep it, to let you . . . help people with it."

Help people. Learn things. Lies within lies. He didn't even have to erase my true motivation, I did it myself. I wanted what we all want, love and revenge. A cult orphan, nobody's child in a generic post-acid hippie personality cult where children were assigned to adults as punishments. With a different broken, grudging parent every few months, you get to learn ulterior motives like the Eskimos know snow.

"Well, you're too late," I said. "It's all gone. I couldn't figure out how to make more."

Now, I could see his smile, but without eyes, it wasn't much comfort. "The Elixir's potency comes from the ease with which it penetrates the brain, and that is the secret of its rarity. It only propagates in human cerebrospinal fluid and brain matter, and its progress is exquisitely slow. In my home country, we would keep 'cows,' angels too used up to give pleasure, and milk them, but only a few milligrams can be had every year, unless it is allowed to ripen. This takes—"

About four years, I thought, touching my forehead. The headaches weren't withdrawal. The drug I had come to crave was already in my brain.

"It's not working inside your head, of course; there's a process to catalyze the psychoactive properties, but you've given me a sizable start on a plantation in this country."

Fifty-two clients. Maybe the last few were just starting to have the headaches. Nobody had come to my door to complain yet—

"You know," he said, finishing the drink, "the most remarkable thing about the process . . . is that, as the fungi gradually digests it, the cow experiences some diminished function, to be sure, but remains a dutiful farm animal long after the brain is little more than a stem.

"The Elixir is far more potent, however, from a patient who enjoys at least the illusion of free will. Your associate Carl has no forelobe to speak of at all, and yet . . ." He took his drink from Carl, who'd been waiting to deliver it. "How is the family, Carl?"

"Doing real good, thank you, sir!" Carl replied, smiling.

"So you see, the Elixir makes its own use of the brain, and yet the mind goes on, like a ghost in a haunted house. So long after you have grown weary of your own purpose in life, you may still serve."

He held up a grotesquely long syringe. Carl took hold of my head and pressed it firmly against the opaque black window. "Hold still," he said. I was unable to move it at all even as the needle slid into the soft tissue beside my tear duct, up behind my eyeball and into my skull.

It hurt like being sucked down a black hole, crushed and stretched into a monofilial string. I felt myself surging into the needle's fat reservoir, leaving behind the hapless amateur brainwasher I'd been. I could see the straw-colored fluid dribbling into the syringe, but I was being drained out of myself.

When he let me go, I sagged onto a bus stop bench on Park Avenue, across from the zoo. People were running past me and police cars and fire engines surrounded the park. I lay there for a while until a bus came, and I got on and tried to get on with my life.

I spent two weeks in a motel, hiding out and listening. The news made much of Preston Marble's death at the hands of his fanatical understudy. We all saw the video of the disheveled maniac emerging from the crowd to embrace the terrified, charismatic spiritual leader. The black rubber bulb in one hand looks enough like a grenade that two bodyguards move to pry them apart, but somehow, their actions are confused until both men are engulfed in a blanket of white fire.

The vest stuffed with thermite cremated both men on their feet and badly burned thirteen bystanders. The resulting mess was easily enough spun to hide Marble's conspiracy, but the narcissistic nature of the murder-suicide turned him into another punchline, another hammily-plotted cautionary fable that only proved some people will believe anything.

I never saw Regina again, not even in my dreams of the French Play.

I hope she reached the city on the far side of the lake. Nobody who's been through what she endured should have to come back.

The alchemist was merciful. He told me that he would come to harvest from me only when he had to, and would leave no memory of it. So long as I cooperate, I can go about my business for as long as my brain function holds out. He would leave no memory of his visits, just as he would protect my old patients. He gave me a single dose of the Elixir and told me that if I had remorse about the way things had turned out, I could fix it.

I have recorded a new cover story, a new antibiography, and secured the necessary fake IDs to make it stick.

When I wake up, I will tell myself who I am. But I could not resist giving myself an escape hatch. Next to the tape recorder, Resley's badly annotated copy of *Le Roi En Jaune*.

Whatever the newborn tenant of this motel room chooses, he will deny you the neat, poignant denouement you seek. He will burn this manuscript and go into the world and write his own ending.

MonoChrome

T. E. Grau

heelhouse

The phone rang on the nightstand, sounding like an alarm bell signaling the end of the world. End of a poor night's sleep, at the very least.

It was a rotary phone, robin's-egg blue with proper metal innards and a nest of copper wiring twisted up inside. A solid American-made piece of equipment, 25 years past its prime. The sound it made was horrible, and it kept coming with that relentless 2/4 beat. Two seconds of ring to four seconds of silence.

A groan escaped from somewhere under a twist of quilt and sofa bed. The only thing visible of Henry Ganz was the lower half of a whiskered face peaking through the mass of patchwork fabric. He'd forgotten to pull the phone chord from the wall last night, and the anger at this sloppy oversight fired blood back into his limbs, forcing him to crawl back to the waking world. Worse yet, the phone wouldn't stop ringing on its own. Shards of plastic and wire that had once been a nearly antique answering machine littered the corner of the room, broken under a boot heel three nights ago. So the phone would keep ringing until the caller decided to hang up, or we finally arrived at the heat death of the universe.

Ganz could have ended his suffering and just answered the goddamn thing, but he didn't particularly like phone calls, as they more than likely meant bad news. That or a conversation, which usually proved to be worse. But in his line of work, whatever that exactly was these days, Ganz needed a phone, good news or bad. He'd find an angle for either. That's what he was good at, which made him the cop he once was, the reporter he became, and the high functioning degenerate that he'd always been. Always with the angle. Finding degrees even when everything was bent into a pretzel.

After what was probably its fortieth ring, Ganz snatched the receiver from its cradle and mashed it against the blanket over his ear. The voice on the other end didn't wait for a greeting, as he knew it wouldn't come.

"Secretary quit?" Victor Baumgartner's barrel voice had a sarcastic chuckle to it.

"Ran off and joined the circus," Ganz rasped, unsuccessfully clearing last night from this throat.

"You hear the news?"

"I write the news, motherfucker."

"No, on TV."

"What time is it?" Ganz refused to open his eyes, not that it would have helped. The room was lit by a fat glass lamp with a stained shade resting on the floor next to his pull-out bed. The living room was mostly empty, as were the rooms beyond, aside from the stacks of books and newspapers that rose in dusty columns throughout the house. No natural light filtered through the windows sealed shut with aluminum foil. Like a Vegas casino, never letting in the outside world to remind the poor bastards bleeding their baby's college fund at the craps table that it was time to get the hell out of town.

"2:30."

"AM?"

"What do you think?"

"Then no, I haven't heard the fucking news. Why are you calling me so early?"

"Turn on the TV. KTLA."

"You're an asshole, Bum," Ganz said. He'd long ago broken down "Baumgartner" into simply "Bum," which was far easier to say after a few cocktails. It had predictably stuck. "Goddamn Kraut bastard. . . ." Ganz's head hurt, just like it always did when it was time to get up and sleepwalk through another day, counting his steps to the grave.

"You're just as German as I am," Bum said, feigning insult.

"I'm *Prussian*, you cocksucker," Ganz said. "I got more in common with the Polacks than you lousy fascists. How many times do I have to tell you this?"

"As many times as it takes to make it true."

"I'm going back to sleep."

"Turn on this news first. You still have a TV, right?"

"I'm going to shoot you, Bum. I'm going to find you and I'm going to—"

"Then turn it on. This is a neighborhood matter, and right in your wheelhouse."

"So?"

"*So* . . . the Park Plaza Hotel just ate four people."

. . . "What?"

"KTLA."

Click.

he Hush of Pavement

Ganz stepped out from the porch shade and hit the first cracked step of his compact Queen Anne Victorian, built just a few years on from the turn of the 20th century. Its sash windows, gambrel roof, and offset turret were par for the course for Pico Union at the time, but now stuck out like a gaudy sore thumb, looking as out of place as Ganz. With the passing of years, the erosion of architectural variety led the parade for the general decline of the area, becoming just another one of the many gang-infested urban frontwaters taken over by cheap apartment housing, cheapo strip malls, and cheapjack drug dealers. Pico Union was left to rot by inches through the gutting of post-war factory jobs that drove out the blue collars, filling the gaps with style-blind investors and immigrants from Guatemala and El Salvador, on the run from brutal civil wars and therefore unconcerned with such bourgeois notions as curb appeal. Los Angeles was full of neighborhoods like this, mixed-race middle class bastions gone to shit, with a preponderance of them circling downtown like a rusted halo. Westlake, Crown Hill, Temple Beaudry, and all the Heights (Angelino, Victor, Lincoln, Boyle). South LA, which dropped the "Central" after too many black people made money off of it, and too many white people who wouldn't lower themselves to set foot in the neighborhood thought that rap music gave the place a bad name.

And Pico Union, where a broken-down white guy named Henry Ganz manned the sagging turret of his kitsch relic in a sad, tagged-up barrio hemmed-in by streets and freeways that sounded better on paper, defined as they always were in the hearts and minds of Good America by the ritzier parts of town they bisected. Vermont Ave to the west, the Harbor Freeway to the east. The northern border was marked by Olympic Boulevard, the south ended at the Santa Monica Freeway. No one wrote rap songs about Pico Union, as it was a ghost town in the middle of a teeming city. Not much to rhyme about. People just died here, shot drugs and each other here. Sold ass in alleyways and marked the walls with machoglyphs of indecipherable rage. Very few people truly lived in Pico Union, and that included Ganz. Just ask Bum. That prick thought Ganz sold his TV for Ripple. Bullshit. He only sold his televisions for the good stuff.

Ganz squinted up and down the block as he walked to the gate centering his eight-foot-tall iron security fence, topped by anti-climb spikes the shape and warmth of shark's teeth. The neighborhood was quiet, which seemed odd for three o'clock on a Friday. Or was it Thursday? Whatever day it was, the block never sounded like this aside from that sweet, brief window of time between the downtown bars closing and the dope fiends making their final rounds before dawn. Those were the times when he could really think, and turn those jumbled memories into clay-like images so real he could almost reach out and throttle them.

He unlocked the gate, secured it behind him, and headed north up South Union Ave. He made good time, as the sidewalks were mostly clear. So were the alleyway fences and shop facades, which were normally decorated with colorful murals rendered with various levels of skill, accented by graffiti wars from the overlapping gang sets that crisscrossed the neighborhood, copyediting rival claims with deadly lines of spray paint. But most of the walls were now completely painted over by a color that seemed to be a treacle white from a distance, but upon closer inspection was a pale, industrial yellow. The color of the evaporated milk his mother used to pour out when he was a kid for everything from biscuit frosting to a cure for stomach flu. The city council had been promising to clean up the graffiti problem around the city center since the invention of aerosol cans. Maybe the wrong business finally got tagged by knuckleheads, because the paint-over was extensive, stretching up and down the block, getting into every nook and defaced cranny. The windowless front of the Diamante Mercado, which only days before featured a vibrant Aztec mural depicting brick-skinned Mesoamericans, bundles of maize, and staircase pyramids was now yellowwashed from top to bottom, removing all trace of the cultural tribute. The city council wouldn't fucking dare mess with the Mayans. Too many potential voters were children of *Chichen Itza*. It had to be something else.

Ganz strode on between the sour-milk walls, feeling now slightly detached from the neighborhood that he had loved and hated for the better part of half a century. The street level restoration seemed to drain the life from the block. Not much sound coming from apartment windows and the futbol cantinas that would normally be doing brisk and rowdy business at this hour. Even the impossibly shiny Tacos Tamix truck that posted up on 9th - specializing in such castoff delicacies as *lengua, cabeza, tripa*, and something similarly wretched sounding called *bucha* - was nowhere to be found, taking its reassuring silver gleam with it. The street children who made the pavement their everyday meadowland would have to go hungry today. He couldn't find them, either. Must have chased the truck to more lucrative parts of the city for their fill of grilled organ meat, as everyone loved a food truck in LA. The humble had become hip. Peasants to princelings. God bless us all.

Ganz scratched at the back of his neck, feeling the first uncoiling of The Thirst low in his stomach as he passed the Stuart Hotel and several other shooting galleries where he had rousted skagheads in a different life. He turned down 12th and up Alvarado and on toward MacArthur Park in Westlake, where a classic Neo-Gothic landmark built by the Elks had apparently decided to eat several members of the local population. Ganz walked where he needed to go these days, and caught a bus when necessary, flagging a jitney after hours. He wasn't allowed to drive anymore, which made him even more of an anomaly, not in his own neighborhood, but in Southern California itself. *Nobody walked in LA*, the song said. That bullshit singer never lived where he did. Everyone walked down here, because cars didn't grow on trees. Avocadoes and limes certainly did, but cars sure as fuck didn't. Nor did drivers' licenses for third-strike DUI dopes. But very few people were out walking today, and the ones that were kept their eyes down and hurried, ducking out of sight as soon as they could. The streets were different. Edgy as Ganz's stomach and twice as empty.

He stopped into the Araya Bodega on the corner of 8th and Alvarado for cigarettes and a walking beer, and found it deserted aside from the clerk and his boom box providing ranchero music to all customers at a shockingly high volume. Outside on the sidewalk, Ganz popped his Tecate tallboy, lit a Winston, and pulled out his notepad, an act he had performed a million times before as a homicide cop with the LAPD, then as a street reporter with the LA Times. Now he was neither, but very much both, as those two jobs never completely leave a person. Protector and documentarian come up from the bones of you, and either you have the DNA or you don't. Ganz had both in spades, and pink slips wouldn't change that essential makeup. After two unspectacular falls from grace, he now worked on commission as a freelance writer, sometime PI, and neighborhood fixer for anyone Bum – plugged in as he was to the aristocratic cream – sent his way, which usually meant Hollywood location scouts looking for that "authentic gangsta vibe," or a greenhorn homicide cop working a new lead about MS 13 or 18th Street. Ganz couldn't hold down regular work. His nerves wouldn't allow it, courtesy of the Mix Tape Murders case he worked 25 years ago that cost him his job and then his marriage and then everything else that mattered. This was followed by a brief stint at the Times, where he worked for City Desk Editor Victor Baumgartner, who kept his Pulitzer hidden in his desk where a bottle should have been. Bum was a grinder like Ganz without all the toxins, and Ganz liked him instantly. The feeling turned out to be mutual, but after blowing too many deadlines while holed up in his home with Johnny, Jack, and an array of loaded firearms, Ganz was let go. Now he wrote when he could, selling local interest stories to the Times, LA Weekly, various pay blogs and any other outlet on whatever platform that had the guts to publish unvarnished tales from the seamier side of diamond town. Ganz interviewed hookers, dope fiends, grieving mothers – anyone who fit the story or had a story to tell. Today, he'd be covering a carnivorous boys club turned hotel overlooking the city's first leisure park. Ganz thought he smelled horseshit, as marketing mad men were clever these days, but he also knew that Bum wouldn't yank him from the safety of his reinforced domicile for an unsubstantiated lark. This was one of those Weird Stories, and Bum knew that Ganz was the guy to write it, as much for Ganz's talent as for the fact that the poor schlub needed to eat – or drink – and Bum wanted someone at the scene before the story got stale. Ganz was the obvious choice. Hence, the phone call. And now the walk.

He arrived on the northwestern side of MacArthur Park, the walking beer finished, crushed flat, and stowed inside his jacket like a hidden badge. Police cruisers and fire trucks and news vans and the gathered crowd all stood and looked up like a chorus at the front of the Park Plaza Hotel on the corner of 6th and Park View, facing MacArthur Park. The

Tacos Tamix truck was parked nearby, just outside the media circus. No one waited in line.

lesh and Stone

The carved head stared down from its perch overlooking the bronze front door of the Park Plaza. Above it was block lettering chiseled into the sandstone by the original builders back in the 20's as a calling card for their Lodge:

All things whatsoever ye would
that men should do to you
do ye even so to them

This clumsily constructed proverb was flanked on each side by a pair of war angels spaced twenty feet apart and thirty feet up, hands resting on sword hilts, blades pointed down, ostensibly at the ready for days such as this. Between the angels and the singular head, two drop cloths were slung across the wide matching expanses that made up the outer frame of the front entrance jutting out from the Park Plaza proper. The tarps mostly covered what was underneath, as the LAFD attempted to spare the locals from the latest indignity unleashed upon the populace. Even still, four heavy trails of blood had dripped from whatever was hidden beneath the draping, daring the mind to fill in the gruesome details. Far above this, a phrase was painted across the top floor walls and windows, the blackening blood contrasting sharply with the light yellow stone.

The play's the thing

How did someone reach down that low from the roof? Or how did someone reach up that high from the ground? Firemen's ladders weren't available for loan-out to the local punk ass graff crews. *THE PLAY'S*

THE THING... Shakespeare. Taggers must be getting real uppity these days, or maybe spending more time in JUCO between lowering property values across the city.

The perimeter on Park View in front of the building was cordoned off by yellow police tape, holding back a growing crowd of concerned locals and rubbernecking commuters, cell phones taking it all in for safe keeping. Behind the plastic barrier, gray tarps covered four mounds on the asphalt, two on each side of the front door, shadowed by the building behind them. The size and shape of the shrouded remains seemed too small to be complete bodies, each one measuring what was probably three feet across. The coroner's van pulled up and parked in the middle of Park View. Forensics was already on scene, snapping pictures and bagging up splatter, of which there seemed to be an abundance. A bouquet of lemon yellow roses lay in the gutter next to the van's front tire. Water from a burst pipe up the street streamed down the pavement, stripping off the petals and dragging them into the storm drain at the end of the block.

Ganz sidled up to a beat cop, blond crew cut topping a sunburned cinderblock head that continued unimpeded into his navy blue uniform stretched tight over his juiced up shoulders and arms. He was eyeing the crowd through wraparound Oakleys, the white tan lines on the side of his face wider than the black plastic frames. New shades, purchased from a bygone era ruled by Jeep Renegades and Bon Jovi and wraparound Oakleys.

"How did someone get up that high?" Ganz muttered just loud enough.

The cop didn't take his eyes off the crowd.

Ganz pulled out his pad and jotted down a few notes. "I mean, they'd need some pretty heavy-duty equipment to get all the way up there, with their paints and whatnot ... You think this is some new kind of guerrilla marketing?"

The cop noticed his notepad. "Who are you?"

Ganz shoved a Winston between his teeth and squinted a humorless smile. "You don't know?"

The cop stared at him, his hidden eyes – most likely the empty blue of February sleet – most likely glaring. This wasn't a new thing, his anonymity amongst the LAPD uniforms, but it always surprised him nonetheless. He was all over the news back in '87. This thick-necked fullback in the 80's shades was probably still playing with his Transformers when Ganz was getting interviewed as the hero on the steps of the justice building downtown, just days before a routine investigation turned sideways and everything around him went to shit. Elijah liked Transformers. Ganz hadn't seen Elijah for 25 years. How old would he be now? As old as Ganz was back then . . . Jeep Renegades and Bon Jovi. The smashed can in his jacket itched at his chest.

"Local press," Ganz said, wishing he'd picked up another beer at Araya. He took a drag and pointed his cigarette at the building. "You know who did this? Some new tagger crew?"

"Who're you with? You gotta pass?"

"LA Times. Vic Baumgartner sent me."

The cop puffed out his cheeks and exhaled. "Fucking great . . . Talk to the Lieutenant."

"I have," Ganz said. "He told me to come to you. That you'd have the story."

The cop snorted. "I don't have shit. I'm just crowd control . . . and keeping my eye on those guys."

Ganz followed the sightline of the uniformed fireplug out over all of the black haired heads and baseball caps and Pompano cowboy hats, toward the back of the crowd. There was space between the group of mothers and fathers and grandmothers and children looking up at the building and a half circle of figures standing behind them. All of them wore black canvas shoes, pants and hoodies, topped with featureless white masks covering their faces. Perfectly round black eye holes seemed to suck in everything that stood in front of them, including the middle-aged man with the itchy veins and notebook.

"Who are they?" Ganz asked, this time totally to himself.

"I have no fucking idea," the cop said, clenching his belt with thick hands. Walnut crushers. The leather creaked, and the .45 in his holster rode up higher on his waist. "They look like one of them dance crews my niece watches on TV, but no one is dancing around here today."

"And too early for Halloween," Ganz said, figuring that it was August or thereabouts, based on the heat and the thickness of the smog rimming the San Gabriels to the northeast. September would be worse. The worst month of the year, when the wind stopped and the foothills burned.

"Those ain't Halloween masks." The cop crossed his arms, stress testing the polyester fibers of his shirt.

Ganz left the cop and pushed through the crowd. It wasn't easy going, and as he approached the semi circle of masked figures, he couldn't tell if they were looking at him, as they hadn't changed the angle of their necks, nor their posture. And he couldn't see their eyes inside those weird, contoured masks. Viewing them more closely, it was difficult to tell if they were male or female, as their identical, baggy outfits rendered them thin and sexless underneath. They weren't physically imposing or outwardly dangerous, but somehow seemed threatening by their uniformity, and their stillness. Things on the streets were loud and obvious. Visibly aggro. This group was a mystery. And they didn't move a muscle, even as Ganz approached them and stopped only a few feet away from the group. Just like with the neighborhood walls, what Ganz thought were white masks were actually the same pale yellow as the new coats of paint all over Pico Union, as the stone hotel behind him. The last, tragic shade of yellow before the color fell into an eternal expanse of dead white. And at this close distance, he saw their eyes underneath. They were large and staring, each set of irises populating every shade of the rainbow save red and purple. And none of them blinked. Just stared, with a quivering intensity.

Ganz stepped back, and as he did, the spell seemed to break. The figures turned and walked slowly away from the crowd with hands shoved deep into pockets, scattering a flock of pigeons and stepping over nodded out junkies curled up on the beatdown grass. The birds rose silently into the air, and instead of circling back, took off for another part of the city rather than settling back down on their home base. Ganz had never seen pigeons move with such determined direction, and with such speed. The masked figures continued walking toward the lake at the center of the park, their silhouettes fusing with the palm trees surrounding the alkaline lake that hadn't naturally hatched a live fish since the natives sold the swamp to the broken promise of the 18th century.

f King and Kingpins

Ganz made his way home as the sun set, putting on a private show for him and him alone. He liked this time of day, when the sun gave up and packed it in, giving the night over to the darkness. The dying rays glinted off the skyscrapers to his left, which lorded over downtown like protective pimps minding their stable. He blinked away the flash of dying daylight, and rubbed his eyes with the back of his hand gripped around a fairly fresh beer.

The California sun always hit his eyes strangely, something he first discovered sitting in the back seat of his family's Studebaker all those decades ago, creeping along slowly with Friday afternoon traffic on the 10 Freeway on the outskirts of Los Angeles. While his father chain-smoked his curses at big city traffic, his mother had made a comment about finally being in Hollywood, and Little Henry Ganz sat up straight and pulled himself up to the window, expecting to see movie stars and limousines strobed by machine gun flash bulbs. Silver screen glamour girls like Marilyn Monroe and Jane Russell and Elizabeth Taylor, lounging in deck chairs on the shoulder, winking to all the new arrivals behind giant sunglasses. Frank Sinatra backed by a curtain of diamond palm trees, singing us home. But all he saw was a cloudless pale above him, and the blinding gleam of silver white chrome all around. So little color, and so much bright . . . He never knew he had sensitive eyes until that day, exposed by the endless snake of freeway, scaled with heated steel that singed little Henry's insides. The pallid gleam of those tentacles writhing from the heart of Los Angeles into the ashen desert overwhelmed his sight, accustomed as they were to mud and gray clouds, and his eyes had never gotten used to it, turning one shade of brown lighter that day.

Ganz stopped at an empty bus bench to jot down a few thoughts, leaning back into the jumble of magic marker graffiti scrawled across the backrest. Before he left the park, he'd overheard two detectives talking about the covered remains. What had hit the ground was only half of them. The rest of the four bodies were sunken into the building itself, integrated into the stone of the structure. ID found on the lower half of one of the corpses revealed that he was Hector "Little Death" Alameida, a heavyweight in the Mexican Mafia, presumed murdered eight years ago even though street rumors and *narco corridos* told otherwise. Not only had Little Death been discovered alive, but alive enough to be verifiably murdered in a bizarre and very public way. The other three half bodies didn't have identification, but the extensive Salvadorian prison tattoos on the legs of one of them made it seem real likely that Ernesto Dimas, the head honcho of MS 13 in Los Angeles, had met his end right next to his rival. The third vic was obviously a member of Aryan Nation, based on his own ink of fascist bon mots and Nordic runes, accented by bullet scars and the single shamrock on his backside, which told the cops everything they needed to know. The fourth was a black guy, wearing vintage blue BK "Blood Killer" tennies, and therefore most assuredly someone associated with the Crips. Probably Eight Tray or Rollin' 60's, as they both made runs at this side of downtown on occasion. If his identified cohort was any indication, he and the other unnamed were probably higher up in the ranks than your average drive-by foot soldier, and certainly specifically targeted.

Two, and possibly four, gangland kingpins shoved face-first and torso-deep into the side of a building, everything below the waist severed and left on the ground. Aside from the assault on known physics, this presented a seriously fucked-up metropolitical situation, and could unleash spectacular waves of retaliatory violence and brutal repositioning that Los Angeles hadn't seen since the height of the gang wars in the late 80's, before Rodney King and Chief Gates and the riots that let most of the fizz out of the bottle, paving the way to the color truces and the Big Police Purge of 1993.

It could get ugly around here, Ganz thought, and began a mental checklist of items he'd need to secure for his home, should shit go south in a hurry. At the same time, he thought of the people in the game that he knew – snitches, mostly, but also street-level dealers, couriers, and stick men – who worked in the local gang scene. He smelled a big story brewing, and wanted to be close as it developed, and hopefully be the one to break it. He had so few joys left in life, but uncovering a truth that would eventually fold itself into history was one thing that kept him going. He wasn't paid to take down the bad guys anymore, so he might as well tell their stories, especially when "bad guy" and "good guy" were often only separated by differences in membership cards. Country clubs catered to more killers than any neighborhood gangbanger bar or backyard Inglewood barbeque.

Ganz paused to gather himself, feeling that familiar prickling sensation spidering up his spine that always meant he was on the cusp of a worthwhile new project, when he saw the smoke. It was rising hot and fast in black billowing waves, gathering over downtown like a shroud. Ganz left his beer on the bench and ran across the street, running toward the source of the smoke as the sirens took up their song in hidden fortresses all around the city.

ords to Smoke

He knew what was burning before he even got close. The layout of the downtown map was branded inside his brain from his time at the LAPD Headquarters on 1st and Spring and then the Times Building just across the street on Broadway. He came of age down here, and then slowly began to die, all within the same cement Skinner box.

By the time he got to Figueroa and dashed up to 5th, Flower Street a block over was closed off by the fire department, as the Los Angeles Central Library disintegrated from the inside out and spilled up its dead magic into the darkening sky. A million books and a trillion hard-won thoughts lost to the angry flames. The burn area was so vast that it must have been set in a dozen locations inside by a tanker truck of gasoline sprayed onto the moldering stacks.

Onlookers crowded the sidewalk, traffic froze, and still the library burned. Firemen fanned out and jacked their hoses into rarely used hydrants. It was clear by their positioning that they weren't going to attempt to save the building or its precious contents. They were just going to cut off any spread. Containment.

All around Ganz, amid the jostling mass of bodies both on the sidewalk and in their cars, a single arm of every person was held up in salute, cell phone in hand and pointed at the destruction, to capture a moment for social media and maybe the 11 o'clock news instead of experiencing with their eyes, feeling it inside that part of their being that wasn't connected to the goddamn Internet. These fools saw nothing and felt nothing but recorded everything for some later date that would never come.

Ganz became nauseous. His knees buckled and he collapsed to the curb, covering his face with his hands. He could feel the heat from the flames a hundred feet away and fifty feet up. They started from the top, eating away the roof and announcing themselves to the sky, then chewed their way down.

This was the place that had grown Henry Ganz, drawing him from the dirt and giving fiber and vein to the lost seed blown west, girding in tough bark the man in full who put down roots – thin, thirsty roots, but roots nonetheless. He'd spent rainy days and winter nights wandering the shelves, pulling books at random and forcing himself to read the first ten pages. More often than not, he read the entire book, immersing himself in worlds and subjects he'd never seek out on his own. For a boy who never found anything more substantial than Redbook around his childhood home, this was a revelation. An unlocking of a kennel door, with an unexplored wilderness waiting beyond. Everything Ganz knew – everything he *was* on a cellular level after he evolved from the muck – came from this place that was dying in front of him. The library was more of a father and mother than he'd ever had at home, or ever cared to wish for.

He rubbed his eyes, not sure if the brightness of the flames was making them water or actual tears were leaking out. He'd become a stranger to real feelings two hundred cases of Dickel ago, and they re-emerged from the blur at unexpected times like acid flashbacks.

Ganz staggered to his feet and pushed through the gawkers. Their hunger for the train wreck was palpable, sickening. He had to get away from these goddamn vultures, and get his head around what was happening. He broke from the crowd and made a wide circle around the pyre, ending up on 3rd and Broadway. He stopped, realizing that he was heading for his former places of employment as if on autopilot, as that was exactly how he had arrived on so many occasions toward the end. Intoxicated to the point of blackout, legs moving stiffly, directional compass dug out of his lizard brain and hardwired into the robot.

Today was different. He wasn't drunk. He was in mourning. Ganz felt a presence behind him, high up and looking down. He turned, and while his internal map of the area expected to show him the vibrant Anthony Quinn mural painted on the old Victor building, what greeted him was an upturned rectangle of pale yellow. The mural was gone.

The "Victor Clothing Co" lettering was gone. What replaced it was pure theatre:

TO UNCOVER THE CONSCIENCE OF A KING

Now it was time to get drunk.

Emperor's New Clothes

It wasn't until his third whiskey and water that his brain finally returned to the matter at hand. The work. The story. Had to get back to the story, and kick everything else back down deep into the bucket.

They didn't have Dickel, and even if they did, Ganz couldn't afford it. His disability had been cut in half thanks to the generous nature of the new California taxpayer taking marching order from Orange County, Utah, and a string of glittery megachurches. The writing gigs had slowed, as print media transitioned to digital, and no one wanted to pay for anything they found online. So, he'd suck down whatever they had in the well while he fueled up for the dark walk home. It had been one hell of a shitweird day.

Ganz was drinking in the King Eddy Saloon on East Fifth, another one of his autopilot destinations programmed into his circuitry back in the Clinton Administration. He didn't venture out much these days, and when he did, he never made it this far east, so taking down cheap drinks in dirty glassware felt like a bankers' holiday. The place was mostly empty. The usual cast of vagrants and penny ante hustlers was cut down to a few choice stragglers, flavored by a stereotypical sampling of Silver Lake dropouts and intrepid West Siders who had dared cross the La Cienega Divide. A Latino woman with shock wig hair dyed orange and eyebrows painted up over the center of her forehead stared at the wall covered in old boxing paintings and a framed photograph of FDR. A toothless man with mechanics' hands mumbled over his nearly empty pilsner glass of beer. Two hipsters with newly minted 70's togs, strategically messy hair, and Amish beards strolled through the place, clutching cans of Pabst like they were vessels of holy water and looking at the pictures and faded out signage on the walls, peppering their discussion of a screenplay in progress with cooed exclamations of "gritty ambiance" and something called "gutterpunk."

The bartender walked over and asked if he wanted another. Ganz nodded and looked around the place one more time for the sake of the coming small talk, scratching behind his armpit.

"Kind of dead around here, huh?"

The bartender sighed, pouring another double with a heavy hand. "Everyone's checking out the library fire." Sully used to work the sticks back when Ganz haunted this place. Sully wouldn't be caught dead sighing in front of a customer, or even by himself. Sully killed two-dozen Koreans back in the forgotten 50's.

"You notice the city painting over the murals around town?"

"Nope," the bartender said. "I live in Santa Monica. Don't really see many down there."

Good Christ. A 310 tending bar in an honest to goodness 213 joint. Ganz was appalled, and looked at him more closely. The tailored jeans, the factory-aged t-shirt, the ridiculously expensive shoes made from re-purposed leather stitched with Humboldt County hemp. Who hired this fucking guy? Where the hell *was* he right now, anyway? Ganz glanced around, noticing that the barroom looked like the King Eddy Saloon, but something was definitely different. New ownership. Goddamnit. Some enterprising Millennial had bought the wormy old place, taking everything down, cleaned off the filth and grime and crime and motherfucking *character*, and rebuilt King Eddy to look like the potentate he once was. But these cash maggoting culture pimps never understood that they couldn't put the soul back into the revived body, as it had already fled this mortal coil at the registered time of death. History withers in the face of bleach and paint, even in a place built basement deep by dead bootleggers.

"It ain't the city."

The voice shook Ganz, who looked down the bar. A man he hadn't seen come in was sitting on the corner stool and holding a pilsner glass in front of him like he was waiting to make a toast. He was a Hispanic guy, deeply tanned and even more deeply wrinkled, wearing his slate gray hair long and slicked back, curling up at the nape of his collared white dress shirt. He wore thick tinted glasses, like BB King. There was a distinguished air about him, from the way he held his drink to the golden pinkie ring on his left hand. In another version of Hollywood, he'd be a leading man on the decline, or a producer who owned half of the Hills. The fact that he was down here meant he was neither of those things. Old guys didn't go in for irony. "It's the street painting over them murals," he said. "The new street."

Ganz swiveled in his chair, every cell erect. "How do you know?"

"Because I got eyes under these things, and ears next to 'em."

"Then you've seen it, too."

The man drained his glass of dark beer, foam still rimming the top, and pushed it back away from him.

Ganz finished his own glass and motioned to the bartender for another round for the both of them. "What do you mean by 'street'?"

The man laughed, deep and wet. Smoker. "Come on, man. You know what I mean, right? The *street*. You know the street. You know it just like the rest of us."

Ganz squinted through the low light at the man's face. He looked familiar, but he couldn't place him. Maybe he saw him on TV.

"You're trying to remember, ain't you? You will. I ain't wearing no mask. I ain't seeing that shit."

Ganz's eyebrows shot up. "Seeing what shit?"

The man said nothing, flipping a Zippo between his fingers. A long thin cigarette was stowed behind his ear, poking through the drape of his hair.

"So the masks figure in somehow?"

The round arrived, and the man pulled out a twenty from a large roll of green, pushing it toward the bartender. "For mine." The bartender shrugged, took the bill and rang him up. The man poured the Modelo slowly into his glass.

"Yeah, they figure in." The man didn't elaborate, instead sipped his beer.

"Is this a gang thing? Some bullshit theatrical twist on colors?"

"I guess you could say that."

"Look, friend—" Ganz said, getting up from his stool and moving toward him.

"— I ain't your friend," the man said without turning, stopping Ganz in his tracks by the flat tone of his voice. "And you ain't mine, so why don't you stay where you're at."

Ganz slid back into his chair. He knew this drill and wasn't fazed. No matter how many years he had lived here, he was still the tourist. The interloper. White man on the bus.

"So what's with the masks?"

"You working a case, gringo?"

"No, I—"

The man laughed, cutting him off. "I know. You can't, right? Maybe writing a story for the paper?"

"Wait a minute—"

"Nah, that can't be it either. Maybe you just scared. Scared gringo. Gringos down here always been scared, ever since Avila Adobe. Maybe you got The Fear."

Ganz wanted to say something, but couldn't. The words stuck in his throat. Instead, he watched the man take a luxurious drink of his beer, then dab at his handlebar moustache with a white hankie.

"They don't talk on the street. None of them. They do what they do, quiet, then they put on the play again. Started around Olvera Street, under the church. Lots of things happen under churches. Lots of *things* under churches . . . Our Lady Queen of the Angels." The man chuckled to himself, finished his beer. "Angels." He slowly drained the bottle into his glass, the sediments dropping to the bottom as the foam built carefully on top, rising to the rim and stopping just short of spillage. "More people come, talking about Cassilda. Cassandra . . . One of them white girl names . . ." He sniffed, sitting up straight in his chair, freeing up the war in his lower back. "Everyone gathers round, goes down into the basement. Catacombs where the lizards hide out. See what the play says. Then they go out again. Marching orders. They snatch up the books, anything that ain't the play, and have themselves a barbeque. Fires all around town. Up in them hills around the stadium, north up the Arroyo Seco. Cops blamed the homeless, bored kids, but they know better. Maybe you seen something today, huh? Heard they had a big one."

Ganz wished he had his notepad in his hand, but knew if he reached for it, the story would be over.

"Then all the old *vatos* disappear. All the big boys. OGs. Then the little ones. Then . . ." He blinked under those thick lenses, long eyelashes fluttering. "Then they do another play. Then another. Same show, different showing, see? All over the *barrio*. Boyle Heights. El Sereno. Lincoln Heights. They grow, moving out from the underneath, from the back yards. Bell Gardens, Southgate, up to Highland Park, Eagle Rock. All along the Arroyo Seco. The river walls, that cement, that's their theatre now—" The man snapped his fingers in front of his left ear, then laughed. "After every show, it just gets more quiet. This city wasn't meant to be quiet."

Ganz mulled this over. "Play . . . You mean theatre?"

"A week ago or so, a group of kids was standing on the corner, just down the block from here, over by skid row, all wearing them masks. They wasn't just hangin' out, they were *standing* on the street corner, like at attention. Like military. Just standing there, not doing nothing. Not even moving. Four in the morning. Kids don't hang out down there. Not without baggies in their pockets, and that's a no-no with them guys."

Ganz's mind raced, looking for connections, angles . . . and found none. He'd need more fuel, so he shook his glass. "Weird."

"Fuckin'-a, weird. This shit happens every night, on different corners. Next day, them corners are all clean. Dope dealers gone. Graffiti, colors . . . gone."

He laughed again and motioned for another beer. Ganz tried to intercept the order, but the man shook his head.

"Your buddies roll up on them one night. Two cops, a black guy and some Italian dude. They grab a kid from the group and slam him on the hood of their car, cussing him. Scream at him to 'cooperate'. Kid don't move. They keep screaming, then the Italian pulls off the mask."

"What did the kid do?"

"Nothing."

"What do you mean 'nothing'?"

The man turned to face Ganz for the first time. "I mean nothing, motherfucker. The kid didn't do shit. Didn't do shit or say shit. He just stared at that fucking WOP who cuffed him."

"And then?"

"And then the ambulance comes."

"Why?"

"Cuz someone died."

A new beer arrived and was set in front of the man, who filled his glass, the statement lingering like a serial cliffhanger.

"Who died?"

The man turned to Ganz and held up his full glass. "*Salud*, Detective Ganz, for my 25 years in Pelican Bay."

Ganz nearly choked on one of the slushy ice cubes in his glass. "I . . . I . . ."

The man drained half his beer, and set it down very slowly onto the bar napkin in front of him. "You put me away for what my brother did." The man dabbed his moustache. "You didn't have shit, but you had enough. You had the spic who did it, even when he didn't. Didn't matter which spic it was, as long as you got one, to throw to the wolves riding on the back of a white girl's honor."

Ganz sat back, replaying his three previous lives as if it was a 70's living room slide show, trying to find the right cell with all of the smiling and waving family members. But he couldn't. After a moment or two, he gave up. His brain was tired, and he knew he wouldn't make the connection, recall the damning collar, so he just lowered his head. "I'm sorry," Ganz said, hearing how trivial that sounded, considering. "I don't remember."

The man just nodded very slowly, taking another long drink that finished his beer, still not looking at Ganz. "Yeah, I suppose you're sorry for all of it, ain't you?"

"Yeah, I really am," Ganz said with a long exhale of breath, before draining his new glass in one gulp. He grimaced, sat up straight in his chair, and attempted to commiserate by pulling out a tiny shard from his personal litany. "Police work is a gymnastics routine between heaven and hell. Sometimes we stick the landing, sometimes we don't."

The man turned in his stool and looked straight at Ganz, his dark eyes large and inscrutable behind those thick tinted lenses. After a few moments, he nodded. "Yeah, that landing is a bitch." He got up, headed toward the door. "The play's the thing, holmes."

Ganz shrugged off the specific guilt and overall white man's burden that had poisoned his time at the LAPD long enough to process what he just heard. "What do you mean?"

The man stopped and turned his head slightly. "You done asking questions of me, Detective Ganz." He headed for the door. "See you on the other side. We'll all be waiting."

The door opened, briefly letting in the murmur of the night, and then closed again.

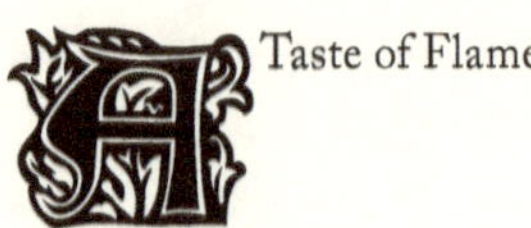 Taste of Flame

Ganz left King Eddy's a few minutes later, his whole body shaking, and dove headlong into those murmuring streets. He could have hopped the last bus, but decided to walk. His legs needed to move under him while his mind worked, processing what he had just heard.

The spider crouching on his spine was now dancing. There was something growing inside the city, moving out from the core to infect the rest of the whole like a cancer. The play. The burning of the library. Olvera Street, the birthplace of Los Angeles. The spread. The rivers. The play. What fucking play? Shakespeare? *The play's the thing, to uncover the consciousness of the king.* Hamlet. College drama class. A poisoned king, a melancholy son. An immoral mother. Patriarchal bullshit. Still, those masks, those slogans . . . What did it all mean?

Following his legs while his head jagged elsewhere, Ganz caught Main and headed straight south until it found Olympic, the one major street cutting downtown that would allow him the best chance of getting home without getting rolled for his shoes. The fire at the library was out, but the smoke from all that smoldering parchment still filled the sky, white and fluffy and lighter than night above it. Ashes of dead books fell like a mockery of snow on a city that would never know it. Didn't deserve it after selling its soul for blue skies and room temp and a citizenry that burned down libraries. Ganz held out his hand and caught a falling bit of ash on his fingertip, raising it on his tongue, like he used to do as a child in Nebraska when the earth froze and turned brown and white and quiet. It tasted like fire. Motherfuckers.

ugs

Downtown seemed to be in mourning with Ganz, or more likely annoyed by the heavy police presence, as it was nearly deserted, the major venues - Staples, LA Live, Nokia Theater, various spike heel clubs - shuttered for the night. The parking lot valets still manned their posts, waving their flags in the dark and ignoring Ganz as he walked past.

Ganz moved quickly away from the electronic circus at Olympic and Fig that advertised everything to no one in the wake of the big downtown revitalization launched a few years back that didn't quite catch on. It was just like Hollywood and Highland to the west, with less TV coverage. Stripping off the grime and crime that made this city the chaotic pheromone that it once was and sterilizing it for minivan tourists and "Vegas baby!" cheeseballs. Ganz passed under the freeway and the cardboard campground that went up there every night, stepping around a few nodded-out sidewalk sleepers, and dove deeper into Pico Union. A fire was burning in a barrel behind an auto shop, like you see in those old movies about New York before Giuliani. Ganz wondered whose books were in that barrel. After several blocks, he noticed how quiet it was. And deserted. Street corners were free of shaved head Latinos, socks pulled up to meet their long blue shorts, waiting for west side party people to drive up and hand them money for a homegrown export shipped north.

Instead of loitering men, Ganz found mattresses. Up and down the block, every fenced-in yard and apartment building driveway featured rectangular slabs of fabric and stuffing propped up on the curb, on light poles, even on parked cars. On each mattress the word *BUGS* was scrawled in black spray paint. Ganz unconsciously itched under his armpit.

Minutes later at his house, Ganz dragged his mattress outside, pushed it through his gate and left it blocking the sidewalk, then headed back inside for a can of spray paint. Before he got to his door, he stopped and cocked his ear to the sky, listening. No revving engines, no shouts, no gunshots. He heard absolutely nothing. Nothing weighs on city ears more than an unexpected silence. Ganz headed back inside, flipping on his TV on his way to his tool closet.

Through his open door behind him, on the street corner opposite his yard, a figure wearing a featureless mask looked on. An identical companion joined him, then another, and another still.

ew Numbers

Victor Baumgartner rolled up Union Ave at 6:00 pm sharp three days later. Ganz was waiting at the curb, peering through pitch black gas station shades up and down the empty streets as if waiting for something. He looked like hell, like he had spent the last 72 hours draining his house of anything remotely fermented and mostly liquid, before finally returning one of Bum's numerous concerned calls about an hour ago.

Bum's Mercedes sedan pulled to a stop. Ganz lurched to his feet and poured himself into the passenger seat, slamming the door behind him.

"Drive."

"Someone after you?"

"They told you?"

Bum laughed. "I was joking. The neighborhood's dead."

"Not dead, sleeping."

Bum chuckled, assuming a joke. "It feels like driving on Christmas morning. Like everyone down here split town. Maybe went back home. Hell, the mayor's already crowing about the new numbers, and they're only a few weeks old."

"What numbers?"

"Hasn't been a shooting or an assault in all the favorite places since that . . . *thing* at the Park Plaza. All the gun boys must be on vacation.

Or maybe they all found Jesus at the same time. East L.A. is like a friggin' sewing circle right now. South Central is just as quiet. Highland Park, Bell, Venice. Ghost towns."

"They're still here, most of them, anyway. They're waiting for something." Ganz pulled down his glasses with a shaky hand and checked to see if they were being followed. DTs, Bum thought, as he could smell three days of whiskey worming its way out of his friend.

"The dealers went with them. The junkies down in tent city are ready to riot, I hear. Climbing the walls, and each other."

"There's a cleansing going on, from the top down."

"A *cleansing*? What the hell's that supposed to mean?"

"Everyone with a rap sheet longer than my pinky has gone missing."

"How do you know?"

"Can't get a hold of any of my snitches, or any of my 'select group of friends'. All MIA. I checked around online, and no one who knows is saying anything, and those wannabes who *are* keep talking about the masks, about there being a new king in town. Big time OG. Outlawing every gang color other than yellow." Ganz spotted something — or someone — out the window, and ducked down in his seat. "They know that I know and now they're watching me. Unblinking eyes burned inside the black. . . ."

Bum glanced over at Ganz. He was talking fast, paranoid, like he hadn't seen for years. Getting poetic in that weird way of his when he had burrowed down too deep. This wasn't good. Ganz was slipping backwards into the tunnel, tumbling toward the bottom of the piss bucket where Bum found him. "You haven't been sleeping."

"Of course not. I got rid of my mattress."

"Why the hell'd you do that?"

Ganz rifled through the glove compartment. "Bugs."

"How long've you been up?"

"A couple days, give or take. Hard to tell, inside the compound . . . But it's good, because I got things to do, people to contact, the ones I can find, anyway. They'll come if I close my eyes. They'll come for my books. I've got thousands of them, Bum. Fucking *thousands*."

"Hank, I don't think anyone—"

"— And you can hear things at night that don't happen while the world's awake. The barks, the whispers. But mostly it's just quiet, which is scaring the proper fuck out of me."

Bum looked closely at him, with that smile he only created for Ganz that was a mixture of genuine affection and a measure of concern bordering on pity.

"How are you, Hank?" Bum handed him a half full Coffee Bean cup. Ganz took it, popped the top and sniffed the contents, scowling.

"Fucking parched. Pull over at the corner so I can heat this bitch up."

"First meatloaf," Bum said, driving past the liquor store, ignoring Ganz's gestures of protest. "Then refreshments. We gotta get some food in you, get you right."

"Fuck food. I'm right right now."

"I know you are, Hank. You're always right. At least watch me eat."

"You take me around food, I'll fucking vomit. I swear to Christ, Bum."

"That's fine. Their meatloaf isn't all that great anyway."

ignet

Bum drove them to Clifton's Cafeteria, finding a parking spot right up front on Broadway. Very few cars were parked anywhere on the block. It was a Saturday, so most of the commuters were far away from downtown. Still, the lack of weekend shopping traffic was odd.

"Check us out," Bum said with a grin. "Rock star parking. Just like the old days." As he pulled up, a dozen people wearing those same light yellow masks and black featureless outfits crossed the street without stopping for Bum's car, or any of the other moving vehicles, causing several of them to slam on their brakes. There were a number of other groups of masked people clustered up and down the block.

"Assholes," Bum grumbled, honking his horn. None of them acknowledged the car. Bum shook his head as he angled his Mercedes to the curb. "One of those nerd conventions in town?"

"No," Ganz said. "These are local. I've seen 'em all over. It's in the notes. Have you read the notes?"

Bum ignored his question. "Is this a gang thing?"

Ganz didn't respond as they both got out of the car and headed toward Clifton's.

"Maybe a bullshit modern art experiment," Bum said. "You ask me, art in this city is on the wane. It's all being painted over."

"You've seen it, too?"

"How can you miss it? Dollars to donuts this is part of the chief's secret gang injunction or something. Part of these new numbers."

"Yeah, maybe," Ganz mused. "All the street art, all the tags, all the gang leaders, all gone."

"The damnest thing."

"That's what I've been saying. Shit ain't right, Bum. Something's happening in this city. Something big and something quiet."

"But then look at that."

Bum pointed across the street to a heavily fenced parking lot, one of hundreds that utilized every square inch of unused downtown real estate. The brick wall behind it that served as a graffiti canvas for decades was now painted that same pale yellow a dozen feet up, wiping clean all those years of expression. In the center of the wall was a single black symbol that looked like a distorted triskelion, topped by a crude question mark, with a pincer jutting down on the lower left and a grasping tendril on the right. Not a drip of paint leaked from the emblem. As if it was stamped, or branded.

"That's new," Bum said.

"Yes it is."

lushing Gators

Bum filled two heavy plastic trays with an assortment of gravy soaked entrées and sugary sides, anything to suck up the toxins swirling in his friend's lower GI tract. He handed a tray to Ganz and they ambled to the back corner of the nearly empty yet still claustrophobic dining hall decorated to look like a forest glade uprooted from the Sierra Madres. They passed under the gaze of a mounted moose head and sat under the shadow of a fake Sequoia that made up the overwrought naturalist décor that was a bizarre cross between a Ranger Rick amusement park ride and a polite 1920's dinner theatre. Bum always brought Ganz to joints like this, that mixed low economy with high camp. He was a specialist in eating cheap, even though he wasn't necessarily a stingy person, and was in fact quite well off. He was just nostalgic, and loved these old school Americana joints like Clifton's, where you could pick up a white bowl of canned corn, tapioca pudding, and grade school green jello with pears embedded inside with your Salisbury steak. In a complicated world, a man tires of caviar and hungers for the simplicity of the grade school cafeteria where everything was still elementary.

"So you read my notes from the Park Plaza?"

"I did, but they didn't make much sense."

"They didn't make much sense when I wrote them, but they're starting to."

"Well, I can't figure any of it out. Lots of gibberish."

"You're not concentrating. It's all in there. It's all taking shape. Order out of chaos."

"You wrote something about organized book burnings, about lizards under the city. Fucking lizards, Hank."

"The Lizard People haven't ever been disproven."

"Neither has the Loch Ness monster."

"Because you can't disprove an avatar, a metaphor that is more real than the truth. You know the Central Library was the tip of the tail, right?"

"What tail?"

"The map of the catacombs crawling under this city. It's shaped like a lizard. They're clever fuckers. Dressing up. Hiding in plain sight. Leaving maps. The head starts in Elysian Park. They're burning away the body in reverse."

"The Lizard People."

"Goddamnit, Bum!" Ganz slammed his fist on the table, spilling his untouched food onto the formica. "The Lizard People are bullshit. Misdirection! A magician's trick! I'm talking about something real. Something OLDER."

"Okay, okay, calm down."

"You think I'm fucking nuts, but I'm not. There's something happening out there. All around us. A *shift*, that's been in the planning stage for years. Hundreds, thousands, maybe. I read reports on the 'net, all of them coming from writers living in neighborhoods orbiting downtown. Reporting the same thing. People disappearing. LOTS of people. They're taking down this city, remaking it. Burning the outposts of the orthodoxy."

"Who's *'they'*?"

Ganz was staring out the plate glass windows, at the trio of masked people taping a flier to a lamppost outside. Dozens of others trailed behind, all holding stacks of fliers. "Them."

Bum decided to humor Ganz, just long enough to get him home, and then call up the best psychiatrist he knew to cash in a favor. "So, Elysian Park . . . The Police Academy's over there. Chinatown."

"Chavez Ravine."

"You think they're targets?"

"I think all of us are . . ." Ganz burrowed down into his thoughts. "The play's the thing," he muttered.

A fire truck escorted by two lit up police cruisers screamed up the street outside. The triad of sound was nearly deafening, even muffled as it was amid all of the tacky woodland trappings. After a few seconds, instead of slowing fading away, the sound ended abruptly.

"The what?" Bum said.

Ganz blinked back to attention, having to remember what he just said. "The play's the thing."

Bum nodded. "To expose the consciousness of the king," he said absently, forking a greasy hillock of meatloaf into his mouth.

Ganz looked at Bum, astonished. "Did you read that on the wall?"

"Hm? . . . What wall?"

"You read any Shakespeare lately?"

Bum snorted. "Yeah right . . . My kid said that to me two nights ago, before he left for his camping trip."

"Joseph?" Ganz asked, assuming the more bookish of Bum's two boys.

"Christian," Bum said. Christian was a wrestler in junior high, leaving behind athletics and authoritarian coaches as he worked his way through several private high schools. Had a few scrapes with the law, all of them smoothed over by daddy. Christian liked to escape Brentwood and slum it with the low rent thugs in Culver City, Echo Park. Downtown.

"He check in since then?"

"Haven't heard a peep. I figured he was just unplugging for a while, but he took his phone."

Ganz's face blanched. "Vic, I think you need to—"

It was then that the power cut, drowning Clifton's in darkness. The fake trees sliced weird shadows in the fading light leaking in from the windows.

"Damn," Bum breathed. "Brown out."

Ganz peered outside. The masked figures were gone, leaving every lamppost on the block decorated with a poster. Bold letters adorned each one, making an identical announcement.

"Let's go outside," Ganz said.

laybill

Outside on the sidewalk, Ganz pulled down one of the fliers, the fading rays of sun peeking over the western horizon, giving last light to those who paid the most for it.

Bum was behind him, looking up and down the street, which was totally deserted. He looked at his watch. It was just a little past 8:00. "Where the fuck is everyone?"

Ganz held up the flier. Hundreds of them in front of and behind him created a repeating pattern of rectangles getting smaller and smaller as they disappeared into the city. The paper was sturdy, like a manila folder. But yellow. The font was fancy, baroque.

The Play
Last L.A. Performance ⁓ Tonight Only
Dodger Stadium
Curtains Up At Sundown
Final Bow TBA
Bring The Family

Bum grabbed it, squinted in the dying light. "A play at Dodger Stadium? During playoffs? Is this some kind of fucking joke?"

"Dodger Stadium is in Chavez Ravine." Ganz started walking.

"Where're you going?"

"Go home, Vic. Get far away from here. Out of the city. Maybe further. I don't know . . ."

"*Vic*? Since when did you start calling me Vic?"

"I wanted you to know that I remember."

Bum looked around at the darkened city. "Something's happening, isn't it?"

"Something's happening," Ganz said.

"A cleansing."

Ganz nodded slowly, half turned. "Vic?"

"Yeah?"

"Christian isn't coming back."

Before Bum could respond, Ganz was already running up the street, heading north, as the last rays of sun snuffed out above, leaving skyscraper-sized shadows as the only remembrance of the day.

he 111 Steps

Ganz ran up Broadway, not recognizing the street. It was dark now in a way that Los Angeles had never been before. The brown out became black. Landmarks blurred, melted together. Only fires – in alleyways, on street corners, the guts of buildings – gave light to a city cloaked in quiet chaos. Yellow light, tinged on the outside with red. Screams and the pop pop of gunshots pierced the hush, but mostly it was quiet in that bloated way that fills up the space right before the perp rushes from the closet, knives out, reaching for your face.

The mask people were everywhere. They stood in groups, lined the sidewalks. They busied themselves pulling people from buildings and stringing up police officers and fire fighters from anything that jutted away from a vertical structure. Ganz gripped the play flier in his useless hands, and it seemed to grant him passage. He soon saw other people like him, faces bared to the world, clamoring up the street as fast as jellied legs would take them, all watched by a thousand sets of eyes hidden under those pallid masks. Some were yanked from the asphalt and dragged away screaming. Some went quietly, as if they knew, or maybe came to an understanding. There were kids amongst them. Little ones. Good Christ . . .

Still Ganz ran, stumbled, crawled on the stained asphalt like a crab. Had to keep moving, sliding through the funnel that was rapidly forming out of the melted plastic of downtown. Move, *MOVE*, you son of a bitch . . . Can't fight them all. Too many. Just too goddamn many, all of them armed to the fucking teeth. Clubs, long knives, SWAT issue assault rifles . . . What *was* this? How did this—? The Thirst was shriveling him underneath his labored breathing. Should have stopped with Bum . . . Baumgartner . . . Wait, who?

Ganz slowed, becoming dizzy. It was too much. He was less than an hour from all of his past lives, an entire world that had slipped into the howling abyss that spiraled down endlessly, sucking up the realness of memories as a black hole inhales physics. An immense blaze burned on the front steps of the justice building as well-dressed bodies were lashed to thick pillars on each side, some without heads or limbs, some with several additional protrusions stuck into their torsos like a child experimenting with Play-Do. A fire engine lay on its side, spinning red lights strobing up the side of a building like a repeating laser site. It was clear what they had done. The masks had moved on the FBI building and police stations, then the fire stations, then the consular offices and the newspaper. Then the Twin Towers Correctional and LA County Jail on the edge of downtown. Any authority figure, anyone associated with the city, state, country, or wider world was taken down, dragged out into the street and hung up on anything high. Ganz faltered, and was shoved out of the way by a woman running past him, howling like a gut-kicked canine. This was the French Revolution on peyote, Bosch painting the apocalypse in smears of human blood. He knew the history. Read about it, dreamed about it. This was the rise of the savage death cults waiting just below the boot print of civilized man. Ganz quickened his pace, determined to finish this marathon of madness. There was no other way.

He descended the hill toward Olvera Street and Avila Adobe. The entire area, boxed up years ago into a tidy historical site and touristy shopping square was teeming with the masked. They climbed on building tops like a hive of angry insects, tossing boxes and furniture and bits of dismembered humanity into their air, stuffing pieces under their masks. Each side of the street was hemmed in by either violence or the complete stoicism of those who wore the masks, with all the side streets blocked by people and things stacked on top of each other. This created a destabilizing effect on the brain, as chaos and rigid order lined up side by side, both serving the same master. Ganz reeled, sweated. He threw up as he moved, spitting slimy foam . . .

Passing under dragons. Chinatown now. The sidewalks were cleared of product bins, and all the trinket shops boarded up, painted over in yellow. Several had been burned down. A few still smoldered. They must have hit Chinatown early in this insane insurrection. How long had this been going on? How many knew it was coming? At every block, a few local residents shuffled from doorways and hiding spots and joined the hunched procession scuttling up Broadway like a parade route of the damned, each holding a flier for the show to come. Tonight only. Bring the family.

The pagoda architecture finally gave way to the open space of Elysian Park. The walkers moved off Broadway and down onto the parade grounds, surrounded by warehouses and the formerly smoking machinery of industrial LA. Then one by one headed down into the basin of the Los Angeles River.

alk the River Dreaming

He walked down the gentle incline to the cemented riverbed, where only a trickle of water flowed, sludged with algae and the sticky sheen of industry. All the trash and discarded appliances had been cleared away and the patchwork graffiti painted over, leaving the LA River clean and uncluttered for the first time since it was paved back in '38. More people were crowded in here, of various ages and races and ease of mobility, joined by others dropping down into the river in every direction. This was the destination chute for all of the living cattle left in the city. Ganz and the rest of the citizens around him were being herded toward the bowl built on top of the hill.

On either side, before him and behind, hundreds of masked figures worked with spray paint on a continuous mural that depicted breathtaking pastoral scenes of 19th century high society and rustic peasant frolicking in bucolic settings. Several crews teamed up on an enormous pronouncement topping the far river wall, painting the letters C-A-R-C-O, continuing on with the rounds and slopes of the next letter. They passed under Suicide Bridge, where strange fruit hung down from the girders and exposed metalwork at the end of thick truck chains, creating a dripping curtain of barely clothed flesh, softening on the outside as the insides stiffened like drying tree branches. They would have rocked in the breeze, but there was none.

Northward the river pointed, and the walkers moved against the rumor of a current, coming to the Arroyo Seco Confluence, where the two enslaved rivers, tamed by cement, crossed paths in shame and continued on their way, dreaming of water and muddy riverbanks tousled with grass. Ganz vaguely remembered an old man with young eyes hiding behind thick glass, who told him about this place. Told him that Ganz had stolen his life, and now he'd see him again in hell. No, not in hell. On the other side. Here. CARCO . . .

On the right, the hills of Cypress Park and Mount Washington leered down at the quivering wretches slogging through the river. On the left, a wooden staircase led out of the cement crevasse. The masked had gathered here, and were ordering the others out of the river with blades and gun barrels, soaked feet squishing up the rough boards of the rickety stairs. Ganz looked up at the sheer hillside. At the very top, what lay on just the other side poured illumination into the dead night sky. The normally bluish white stadium lights were replaced now by a pale yellow glow that pulsed and danced. Writhed. The sky above Los Angeles used to look yellowish at night, with the smog reflecting back the city lights in on itself. A reassuring blanket of human achievement against the dark. Tonight, the sky was black, as all the lights from man were dead.

énouement

Ganz and the others climbed the hill, the interlacing cement tendrils of the 110 and the 5 Freeway growing smaller behind him. The hillside was steep, but Ganz moved steadily, grabbing hunks of stubborn brown weeds, smelling the sharp odor of the dusty soil that for generations had sucked up smog instead of rain while the city grew wild below.

Reaching the crest of the hill, where signal fires burned in six spots around the rim, Ganz stood tall and looked down into the bowl that was once Dodger Stadium. The seats had been ripped out, exposing tight stone steps like those on Mayan pyramids. Temple of Kukulcan. Chichen Itza. The terraced rings were filled to capacity with the masked figures, standing shoulder to shoulder at perfect attention. Sellout crowd. The unmasked citizens milled about on the field, in front of a stage that had been erected over home plate, six feet high and stretching from dugout to dugout on either side. Pale yellow curtains hid the preparations behind. The design of the stagework and draping was ornate to the point of decadence, channeling Louis XIV at his most sodden. The orchestra pit of two-dozen masked musicians wearing flowing robes took up a dissonant tune, heavy on brass and wheedling flute. The prelude.

The push of the crowd moved Ganz through a cut in the perimeter fence and down the stadium steps, loosing him and his companions out onto the grass. He tried to move to the back fence, to put distance between him and the repulsive symphony, but was pushed to the middle of the field, just behind second base, quickly pressed in close on all sides by breathless, moaning bodies that reeked of sweat and shit.

The orchestra swelled with a terrible spike in pitch and volume. Ganz clutched at his ears, gnashed his teeth. He wanted to fall to the ground, to die before his brain popped, but the bodies around him held him up.

A half dozen spotlights shot down from the sky, topped by the whumping sound of heavy helicopter blades. Loudspeakers mounted on the choppers buzzed out words, shouts. *Drop weapons . . . National Guard . . . By order of the President . . . Surrounded . . .* The spots raked the crowd of the masked, who hadn't moved, all focused on the stage. Two beams of light fell onto the front of platform, perfectly illuminating the curtains as they slowly rose.

All around the stadium, those servants of the King removed their masks in one motion. The bellow from the field began at the edge and spread like a wave, wrenching wide every mouth and set of eyes as they saw what lay beneath.

The curtain was now open, exposing the players on stage. The backdrop. The costumes – what at first appeared to be costumes.

To the south, the tops of six downtown skyscrapers exploded with yellow flame, going up like ignited oilrigs. The boom and tremor arrived a second later.

Tongues fell silent. Machines fell from the sky.

The play began.

CONTRIBUTORS

Glynn Owen Barrass lives in the North East of England and has been writing since late 2006. He has written over a hundred short stories, most of which have been published in the UK, USA, France, and Japan. He also edits anthologies for Chaosium's Call of Cthulhu fiction line, also writing material for their flagship roleplaying game. To date he has edited the collections *Eldritch Chrome, Steampunk Cthulhu,* and *Atomic Age Cthulhu,* for Chaosium, and *World War Cthulhu* for Dark Regions Press.

Tim Curran lives in Michigan and is the author of the novels *Skin Medicine, Hive, Dead Sea,* and *Skull Moon.* Upcoming projects include the novels *Resurrection, The Devil Next Door,* and *Hive 2,* as well as *The Corpse King,* a novella from Cemetery Dance, and *Four Rode Out,* a collection of four weird-western novellas by Curran, Tim Lebbon, Brian Keene, and Steve Vernon. His short stories have appeared in such magazines as *City Slab, Flesh & Blood, Book of Dark Wisdom,* and *Inhuman,* as well as anthologies such as *Flesh Feast, Shivers IV, High Seas Cthulhu,* and *Vile Things.* Find him on the web at www.corpseking.com

Cody Goodfellow has written five novels––his latest is *Repo Shark* (Broken River Books)––and co-written three more with New York Times bestselling author John Skipp. He received the Wonderland Book Award twice for his short fiction collections, *Silent Weapons For Quiet Wars* and *All-Monster Action* (both Swallowdown Press). He wrote, co-produced and scored the short Lovecraftian hygiene film *Stay At Home Dad,* which can be viewed on YouTube. He is also a managing director of the H.P. Lovecraft Film Festival–Los Angeles and cofounder and editor at Perilous Press, a micropublisher of modern cosmic horror.

T.E. Grau is an author of dark fiction whose work has been featured in over a dozen anthologies, including *The Children of Old Leech, Tales of Jack the Ripper, The Best of The Horror Society 2013, Dark Fusions: Where Monsters Lurk, Suction Cup Dreams: An Octopus Anthology, Mark of the Beast, World War Cthulhu, The Dark Rites of Cthulhu, Urban Cthulhu: Nightmare Cities, Dead But Dreaming 2, The Aklonomicon,* and *Horror for the Holidays,* among others; and such magazines, literary journals, and audio platforms as *LA Weekly, The Fog Horn, Lore, Tales To Terrify, The Teeming Brain, Eschatology Journal,* and *Lovecraft eZine*. His limited edition novelette *The Mission* from Dynatox Ministries/Dunhams Manor Press was released in August of 2014, with his second Dynatox chapbook, *The Lost Aklo Stories,* released in September of 2014. In the editorial realm, he currently serves as Fiction Editor of *Strange Aeons* magazine. T.E. Grau lives in Los Angeles with his wife and daughter, and can be found in the ether at *The Cosmicomicon* (cosmicomicon.blogspot.com).

Laurel Halbany talked an otherwise sensible college into granting her an undergraduate degree in Mythology, a course of study which was not especially marketable but has proven endlessly useful in her writing. Her work has been published in English and in translation in Japanese, and has appeared in publications including *Night Land* and *Five Million Years to Earth*. She lives in the urban penumbra of San Francisco with her family.

CJ Henderson created both the Jack Hagee hardboiled PI series and the Teddy London supernatural detective series. He also authored *The Encyclopedia of Science Fiction Movies,* several score novels, hundreds of short stories, and thousands of non-fiction pieces. In the wonderful world of comics he wrote everything from Batman and the Punisher to Archie and Cherry Poptart.

CONTRIBUTORS

Gary McMahon is the acclaimed author of seven novels and several short story collections. His award-nominated short fiction has been reprinted in "Year's Best" anthologies. He lives in Yorkshire with his wife, son, and a skittish cat called Moshi, trains in shotokan karate, and likes running in the rain.

William Meikle is a Scottish writer, now living in Canada, with twenty novels published in the genre press and over 300 short story credits in thirteen countries. He has recent novels and novellas published by the likes of Dark Regions Press, DarkFuse and Dark Renaissance. He lives in Newfoundland with whales, bald eagles and icebergs for company. When he's not writing he plays guitar, drinks beer, and dreams of fortune and glory. He can be reached via his website at http://www.williammeikle.com/

Christine Morgan works the overnight shift in a psychiatric facility, which plays havoc with her sleep schedule but allows her a lot of writing time. A lifelong reader, she also reviews, beta-reads, occasionally edits and dabbles in self-publishing. Her other interests include gaming, history, superheroes, crafts, cheesy disaster movies and training to be a crazy cat lady. She can be found online at www.christine-morgan.org

Edward Morris is a 2011 nominee for the Pushcart Prize in Literature, also nominated for the 2009 Rhysling Award and the 2005 British Science Fiction Association Award. He has five collections' worth of published short fiction, most recently in Perihelion SF, *World War Cthulhu*, and issues #11 and #12 of The Magazine of Bizarro Fiction. Edward lives in Portland, Oregon.

Robert M. Price, a fan of H.P. Lovecraft since the Lancer paperback collections of 1967 appeared, began writing scholarly articles and humorous pieces on HPL and the Cthulhu Mythos in 1981. His celebrated semi-pro zine *Crypt of Cthulhu* began as a quarterly fanzine for the Esoteric Order of Dagon Amateur Press Association in 1981 and made it to 109 issues. In 1990 he began editing Mythos anthologies for Fedogan & Bremer and Chaosium, Inc. and still does! His fiction has been collected in *Blasphemies and Revelations*.

W. H. Pugmire has been writing Lovecraftian weird fiction since the early 1970s, beginning with stories published in small press journals. His newest book is *The Revenant of Rebecca Pascal* (in collaboration with David Barker), and he will have stories in *That Is Not Dead*, *Black Wings IV* and *V*, and numerous other professional anthologies. WHP dreams in Seattle.

Stephen Mark Rainey is author of the novels *Balak, The Lebo Coven, Dark Shadows: Dreams of the Dark* (with Elizabeth Massie), *Blue Devil Island, The Nightmare Frontier*, and *The Monarchs*; five short story collections; over 100 published works of short fiction; and several *Dark Shadows* audio productions, which feature members of the original ABC-TV series cast. For ten years, Mark edited the award-winning *Deathrealm* magazine and has edited several anthologies, including *Deathrealms, Son of Cthulhu*, and *Evermore*. He is an avid geocacher, which frequently takes him to fascinating places – many of them quite creepy. Mark lives in Greensboro, NC. Visit him on the web at www.stephenmarkrainey.com

Pete Rawlik has been collecting Lovecraftian fiction for forty years. In 2011 he decided to take his hobby of writing more seriously. He has since published more than twenty-five Lovecraftian stories and the novel *Reanimators*, a labor of love about life, death and the undead in Arkham during the early twentieth century. A sequel, *The Weird Company* was released in the fall of 2014. He lives in Royal

Palm Beach, Florida, with his wife and three children. Despite the rumors he is not now and never has been a resident of Kingsport.

Brian M. Sammons is an author, editor, critic, and Managing Editor of Dark Regions Press' Weird Fiction line. His stories have appeared in the books: *Horrors Beyond, Dead but Dreaming 2*, and *Horror for the Holidays* and in the magazines: *Dark Discoveries, Nightland*, and *Bare Bone*. To date he has edited 10 anthologies including *Undead & Unbound, Dark Rites of Cthulhu, Eldritch Chrome, Edge of Sundown*, and *World War Cthulhu*. He has also written extensively for the Call of Cthulhu role-playing game and has been a reviewer/critic for twenty years. You can follow Brian on Twitter @BrianMSammons

Daniele Serra was born and lives in Italy. He works as an illustrator and comic artist, with work published in Europe, Australia, United States and Japan. He has worked for DC Comics, Image Comics, Cemetery Dance, Weird Tales magazine, PS Publishing and other publications. Winner of the British Fantasy Award. http://www.multigrade.it

Lucy A. Snyder is the Bram Stoker Award-winning author of the novels *Spellbent, Shotgun Sorceress*, and *Switchblade Goddess*, and the collections *Orchid Carousals, Sparks and Shadows, Chimeric Machines*, and *Installing Linux on a Dead Badger*. Her latest two books were released earlier this year: *Shooting Yourself in the Head For Fun and Profit: A Writer's Survival Guide* from Post Mortem Press, and her story collection *Soft Apocalypses* from Raw Dog Screaming Press. Her writing has been translated into French, Russian, and Japanese editions and has appeared in publications such as *Apex Magazine, Nightmare Magazine, Jamais Vu, Pseudopod, Strange Horizons, Weird Tales, Dark Faith, Chiaroscuro, GUD*, and *Best Horror of the Year*, Vol. 5. She lives in Columbus, Ohio with her husband and occasional co-author Gary A. Braunbeck and is a mentor in Seton Hill University's MFA program in Writing Popular Fiction. You can learn more about her at www.lucysnyder.com

Greg Stolze has been paid to give fiction away in a complicated scheme of trust exchange and artistic patronage. Its fruits can be had for free at www.gregstolze.com/fiction_library . Or you can read one of his several horror novels (including *Ashes and Angel Wings* and *Mask of the Other*) or play one of his games like REIGN or A Dirty World. He is tall and thin, with grey hair and a melancholy demeanor.

Jeffrey Thomas has written previously of the city of Punktown, in the short story collections *Punktown, Voices from Punktown, Punktown: Shades of Grey* (with his brother, Scott Thomas), and *Ghosts of Punktown*. His Punktown-based novels are *Deadstock, Blue War, Monstrocity, Health Agent, Everybody Scream!*, and *Red Cells*. Thomas's other collections include *Woship the Night, Thirteen Specimens, Nocturnal Emissions, Unholy Dimensions*, and *Encounters with Enoch Coffin* (with W. H. Pugmire). His other novels include *Letters from Hades, The Fall of Hades, Boneland, Beyond the Door, Subject 11*, and *A Nightmare on Elm Street: The Dream Dealers*. Thomas lives in Massachusetts.

Eric York is an artist who lives in the gloomy forests of northern Arizona where he works as the night manager of an 87 year old haunted hotel. Over the years he's played bass guitar in bands with names like The American Deathtrip, Shrunken Monkey Paw, Super Colossal Beast, Scar Strangled Banger and Evilsaurus Rex, as well as publishing his own zines, comix, coloring books, tarot cards and related effluvia. He has over 1000 pieces of his artwork up on his website: tillinghast23.deviantart.com.

From the publisher who brought you
The Dark Rites of Cthulhu

Future releases from April Moon Books

2014

Short Sharp Shocks Vol. 1: AMOK!
A potpourri of pandemonium; a soupçon of psychosis!

Short Sharp Shocks Vol. 2: Stomping Grounds
Multiple monsters cause mayhem and misery!

2015

Flesh Like Smoke - edited by Brian M. Sammons
Shapechangers galore from today's best authors!

Short Sharp Shocks Vol. 3: Ill-considered Expeditions
Pith helmets at the ready for some unfriendly welcomes!

Short Sharp Shocks Vol. 4: Spawn of the Ripper
Our homage to Hammer, bosoms and blood!

Short Sharp Shocks Vol. 5: The Stars at my Door
Optimistic sci-fi to cleanse the palate!

Questions?
aprilmoonbooks@gmail.com
www.AprilMoonBooks.com